HILLARY

HILLARY

D.W. BUFFA

Copyright © 2016 by D.W. Buffa

Cover and jacket design by 2Faced Design

Interior designed and formatted by E.M. Tippetts Book Designs

ISBN 978-1-943818-28-0

eISBN: ISBN 978-1-943818-42-6

Library of Congress Control Number: 2016942615

First hardcover publication October 2016 by Polis Books, LLC

1201 Hudson Street, #211S

Hoboken, NJ 07030

www.PolisBooks.com

POLIS BOOKS

ALSO BY D.W. BUFFA

CHAPTER 1

RICHARD BAUMAN SAT just inside the doorway to the suite, annoyed that he was reading for the second time that evening the sports section of a day-old paper. He was in the most expensive suite in one of the most expensive hotels in New York, and all he could do was sit there and let his eyes wander down the box score of a game he did not even know had been played. Tossing the paper on the coffee table, he walked over to the window and stared out at the moonlit shadows of Central Park, wondering what it would be like to have the kind of money to be rich enough to come here on his own. The thought vanished as quickly as it had come as he glanced across to the double doors that led into the bedroom.

"Strange business," he muttered, shaking his head.

Three or four times every month they stayed here, in this hotel, and always in this same suite. There was never any reason given; everyone understood. It was a simple matter of logistics, the easy convenience that did not even need the lie. Another room, on the other side of the suite, a door that could be unlocked to add another bedroom, or, which was here the point, kept separate and apart. It was a way to get privacy with discretion, a way to make sure that all the rumors remained only that; rumors that, even if nearly everyone believed them, no one could actually prove.

"Strange business," Bauman repeated under his breath as he checked his watch. Ten minutes past one in the morning, ten minutes past one on a Saturday night. With a gruff sigh, he sat down in the chair and started reading the sports section he had read twice before.

He was just turning the page when he thought he heard something. He put down the paper. He heard it again, louder this time, a brutal, gasping noise. He leaped out of the chair and ran to the bedroom door. It was locked. He could hear someone moving around inside. He pounded on the door.

"Mr. President!" he shouted. "Are you all right?"

No one answered; no one came to the door. Then he heard it again, louder, more insistent, an unmistakable cry for help.

"Mr. President!" screamed Bauman at the top of his lungs, beating on the locked door.

The door flew open. A tall, thin woman in her late twenties or early thirties, with raven hair and frantic dark eyes, stood there, holding a sheet in front of her and pointing toward the bed.

"We were…and then he just stopped, and then he pulled away and he got this strange, crazy look in his eyes, like something had happened and he couldn't figure out what it was, and then he just rolled away and his eyes kind of…kind of went dead."

Bauman pushed past her and ran to the bed. Robert Constable, the president of the United States, was lying on his back, staring at the ceiling with eyes that could no longer see. Bauman checked the president's wrist and then his throat; there was no pulse. Robert Constable was dead.

"He had a bad heart, didn't he?" asked the young woman, clutching the sheet under her chin. Bauman looked at her and told her to get dressed.

"You're in the room next door? Get your stuff and get out of here, get out of here now!" he ordered. His eyes started moving all around the room. "Here," he said with a little more sympathy, "let me help you." He picked up the few of her things still scattered on the floor and handed them to her.

"Now listen to me, listen carefully. You weren't here. You understand me? You were never here. Go back to your room. I'll lock the door behind you. Pack your bag, whatever you brought with you, and leave the hotel. Do it now," he said as he took her by the arm and led her to the door. "Get dressed and leave. You have to be out of here in five minutes, because in five minutes half of New York is going to be here. Now go!"

It had all been instinct, the immediate first reaction: protect the president, even if it was to protect the president against himself. He turned back to the dead body lying on the bed. "What a waste," he told himself. "What a stupid thing to do."

There would be speculation enough, all those hollow-eyed talking heads on television, all those gossip-hungry fools, always full of news, most of which they invented on the spot. Think what they would do with this. Robert Constable, the president of the United States, screws himself to death with a gorgeous young woman less than half his age. Bauman tried to clear his mind. Had he forgotten anything? Had the girl left anything behind? He checked the nightstand next to the bed, and then the bathroom. There was a trace of powder, white powder, next to the sink.

"Crazy bastard," he muttered, as he wiped the counter clean. He caught a glimpse of himself in the shiny silver mirror and for an instant thought he saw his conscience looking out. He looked away, finished what he was doing, and went back to the bedroom.

The girl had not left any jewelry, or anything else that he could see. Then he remembered. He felt a strange sense of impropriety, a violation of privacy, and not just that of the president and the woman he had been with, but of his own, as he searched beneath the pillows and then the corners of the bed, on the chance that the girl had left her underwear behind.

It had been only a few minutes since he first entered the room and found the president dead. He had done everything he thought he needed to, at least everything he could do alone. His eyes darted toward the body. It could not be left like that, stark naked, with…. Why hadn't he noticed it before? Lipstick, and not just on the president's mouth.

"Damn it!" he exclaimed in a whispered, angry shout, as he hurried into the bathroom where he scrubbed soap and hot water into a washcloth.

He almost could not do it, wash away the tell-tale signs of a grown man's infidelity, a womanizer's last-time cheat. He taunted himself with being squeamish and, when that was not quite enough, tried to remember that it was not as if he had to deal with the disappointment he might have felt if this had been a president he revered. When he was finished, he took one last look around and then walked through the sitting room, opened the door to the hallway, and motioned to the agent standing just outside.

"We have a situation."

James Elias, taller than Bauman and ten years younger, had worked with him long enough to know from his tone of voice that this was something serious.

"You want the others?"

"Not yet."

Elias looked down the corridor to where two other agents stood opposite the elevators, and then followed Bauman inside. The doors to the bedroom were open. Though trained to caution, Elias was shocked at what he saw.

"Jesus Christ! Have you called the medics?"

Bauman was all business. "He's dead. Nothing anyone can do. We need to get him dressed, get some pajamas on him."

Elias respected Bauman—more than that, he looked up to him—but while he had been willing to go along with other things to keep the president out of trouble, this was rearranging the scene of a death.

"I've taken care of everything else," explained Bauman, who understood the younger man's dilemma. "You know what will happen if he's found like this."

Elias still did not move. He looked at Bauman, but Bauman suddenly seemed exhausted, too tired to think beyond the immediate present and the thing he had to do next.

"What about the girl?"

"What girl?"

"There was always a girl."

Bauman did not answer; he turned and started toward the bedroom. Elias did not follow.

"Look, what choice do we have?" asked Bauman, his voice betraying some slight irritation. "We were supposed to take a bullet for him, if it came to that. This isn't quite as bad, is it?"

Bauman was not sure himself how he would have answered that question. There was something noble and heroic about putting your life on the line for the president, whom you were sworn to protect; it was hard to find anything to brag about in cleaning up the evidence of this last scene of almost Roman decadence: a sex-crazed politician, dead in the middle of an orgasm, the only witness to his final passing moments, not his family and friends, but some coke-sniffing woman with the face of an angel and a harlot's heart, the kind who only sleeps with men who can sleep with anyone because of who they are.

"Maybe I should have found out who she was, but I didn't," he admitted with a weary, rueful glance.

"The room next door?" asked Elias, as they pulled the pajamas up over the president's dead-weight legs.

"Yeah; we better check it, make sure she didn't leave anything."

"You see her before? She someone he...?"

"No, she was new. Young, gorgeous. A model, maybe—I don't know." He paused, remembering something that made him think. "She wasn't scared. I didn't pick up on it—too many things were going through my mind—but I'm sure of it. She wasn't scared. Her voice trembled a little, like she was—scared, I mean, but her eyes—they didn't move. She looked right at me, almost as if she were trying to measure my reaction."

Elias tied the pajama cord and stepped away to see if everything looked the way it should.

"Wouldn't surprise me, given the kind of woman he seemed to like," he said, tilting his head to the side to look at what he had done from a slightly different angle.

"What wouldn't surprise you?"

"That she didn't look scared." He nodded toward the body of the president, his head propped up on a pillow, now dressed in a pair of dark blue pajamas. "Maybe he's not the first guy who had a heart attack while he was banging her."

An hour later, after the president's personal physician had been summoned, and several other calls had been made, the body of the president was wheeled out the front entrance of the hotel. A crowd had formed, and thousands stood in silence as the body was placed inside a waiting ambulance and, with the siren wailing, driven slowly away. While everyone stood watching, wondering at the shame of such an early death, a young woman on the other side of the street, opposite the hotel, spoke quietly on her cell phone.

"There's a problem. Someone saw me."

CHAPTER 2

Bobby Hart had been at funerals in other places where he had paid his last respects to relatives and friends; he had, years earlier, held his mother's fragile, shaking hand and wiped away a tear of his own, as they stood alone at the graveside as his father was laid to rest. Those funerals had been real, the final, last goodbye, the formal ritual of grief and resignation, in which only those who knew, and even loved, the one who passed away are invited or allowed. This was different; a ritual, yes, but one that instead of serving as a catharsis for the emotions was a playhouse for a fiction, the mourners wearing faces made to reflect a sense of tragedy and loss that most of them did not feel.

Everyone who was anyone in Washington sat crushed together in the pews, come to listen in solemn acquiescence to the eulogy of a man many of them had privately despised. There were those who had hated him because he had taken what they believed belonged to them, the office that, it is fair to say, someone else would have taken from them had Robert Constable never lived. There were others who hated him because he had not given them what he had promised—or seemed to promise, because he had a genius for being vague—when he had asked them to help in what had seemed a long-shot bid for the presidency. And then there were those who thought it still the mark of virtue to keep their vices private and, call it common decency or rank hypocrisy, had nothing but disdain for someone who had let his private life become a scandal that had disgraced the office and disgraced himself. The wonder was that he had always seemed to get away with it. It drove them all a little crazy, that the man they thought one of the world's greatest charlatans, a man without qualities or principles, had somehow managed to break all the rules and laugh at those who thought he might get caught.

Bobby Hart wondered how he would have felt if he had found his own ambitions defeated, his own dreams denied, by someone who, it was said, never remembered the name of anyone he had either hurt or could no longer use. He had barely known Constable. Most of what he knew about him, beyond the things everyone knew from reading the papers, he had learned from some of the other members of the Senate who had their own stories to tell, none of them very flattering, and always accompanied by a request that what they were about to tell him be kept in confidence. For all the president's talk of hope and optimism, the main emotion he inspired among those who knew him best was fear.

The memorial service droned on. Crowded to capacity, with no room to move, the National Cathedral felt almost as breathlessly humid as the August heat outside. Hart tried to listen as one speaker followed another, but the eulogies seemed forced and artificial, what people are supposed to say, rather than what they really think or feel. He was there because, as a member of the Senate, he was expected to be. It was an obligation that went with the office, something you did to keep alive the long traditions of the place.

Hart's gaze drifted away from the secretary of state, recounting the foreign policy achievements of the Constable administration, and began to run along the line of dignitaries in the first few rows. It stopped at the sight of Hillary Constable, the president's widow, sitting in the first row on the aisle. Her face was resigned, respectful, but without any obvious trace of grief. Perhaps it had always been a marriage of convenience; but, he reminded himself, it had lasted nearly thirty years. She must have known what he was like, this need that bordered on compulsion for the company of other women. Or did she? Perhaps she had known at the beginning, one of the first times he was unfaithful, and then, because he would have been forced to admit what he could not deny, taken that confession as a promise that he would never stray again. As Hart looked at her, still attractive with those light blue eyes that seemed to tease you with some secret knowledge, and the ash blonde hair that was always cut so perfectly, he changed his mind; or rather, for the first time glimpsed a different possibility: that she knew, or could have known, everything, and not much cared. Even wearing widow's weeds, Hillary Constable had the look of someone very much her own person. Whatever her husband might have been doing with other women, she could just as easily, and with no doubt greater taste and discretion, have been doing with other men.

The service finally came to an end. The president's widow led the procession back up the aisle, stopping every few steps to touch the hand of someone and thank them for all they had done. Some thought she was quite brave, the way she seemed to be more concerned with the feelings of others than with her own; others had a different impression.

"Still beautiful, and now single and quite rich," a familiar voice whispered just behind him. Hart turned around to find his only close friend in the Senate, Charles Finnegan of Michigan, raising his eyes in a way that suggested, more than irreverence, the knowledge of things best left unsaid.

"You think it's just accidental?"

Finnegan had reddish brown hair and a slightly freckled face, eyes full of laughter, and the quickest smile Hart had ever seen. Always in a state of motion, never quite able to sit still, when Finnegan took a chair it seemed it was just to have a place from which to suddenly jump up. Caught up in an argument, which sometimes seemed the main preoccupation of his life, he spoke in half-sentences, eager to start the next one before he had finished the last; and if he did that to sentences, a paragraph was even worse, collapsing in a rush of incoherence like the drunken revel of a half-mad poet. But now, moving in solemn order in the middle of the crowd, he spoke slowly, quietly, and to the point.

Hart did not respond. There were too many people around, too great a chance to be overheard. With a faint half-smile, he nodded—enough to tell Finnegan that they would talk outside.

As many as had gathered inside the cathedral, a hundred times that number were standing behind the barricades erected on the street, come to pay a final tribute to the president. The air was thick with the humid scent of summer smoke, every movement made uncomfortable, an effort that required strength; things seemed to pass in slow motion, the world become a crawl. Hart blinked into the dusty, reddish sun and felt a sudden disability, a sense of slow paralysis, a loss of all ambition beyond a cool dark place to sit and something cold to press against his lips.

"Remind me to die in winter," he remarked. He stood next to the entrance of the cathedral as the crowd surged past.

Finnegan slipped on dark glasses and loosened his solid gray tie. A slight, caustic grin curled the edges of his mouth.

"What difference the season, if you die in the bought luxury of a Manhattan hotel in the arms of a high-priced hooker?"

"I've heard the rumors," replied Hart, watching the pallbearers load the casket into the waiting hearse. Hillary Constable stood just off to the side, remote, unapproachable, her black gloved hands held neatly in front, her eyes distant and impenetrable. She had not yet shed a tear, neither inside the cathedral, nor here outside, as if she knew better than to overplay her part. It kept the mystery alive, the mystery born of the suspicion that she had never really loved him; or rather, that she had, but had understood that with a man like that she could never count on anything.

"But they're just rumors," continued Hart, looking back at Finnegan. "Everyone thinks he slept with other women all the time. No one wants to believe he could have died alone."

"He has Air Force One at his disposal, but he spends the night in a Manhattan hotel. And he did it all the time. Why do you think he did that, because he thought he could get a better night's sleep there than upstairs in the White House?"

"You've become such a cynic."

Finnegan tilted his head to the side, a sense of doubt in his eyes.

"I didn't want to be, and I wasn't, when I first came to Washington, but then…." Finnegan's voice trailed off, and Hart, who knew exactly what he meant, patted him on the shoulder and they both laughed softly at how much in each of them had changed.

"Did Quentin Burdick get hold of you?" asked Finnegan as they started walking away from the cathedral and the crowd.

"No. Why?"

"He's working on a story, some investigative piece. He told me he had an appointment with Constable, an interview he had finally gotten him to agree to, but it never took place. He was supposed to meet him at the hotel, the one where Constable died, the next morning."

CHAPTER 3

"WHAT'S BURDICK WORKING on?" asked Hart after he put down the cold beer. His eyes moved from one side of the dark, dingy bar to the other. It was a hole in the wall, a place where this time of day, the middle of the afternoon, you half expected to see someone bent over, his head on his arms, snoring in his inebriated sleep. Hart ran his finger around the frosted edge of the glass. A thin smile edged its way across his mouth. "And what the hell are we doing here, anyway? Why did you want to come to a place like this?"

A smile that mirrored Hart's own broke across Finnegan's weathered, freckled face. He leaned against the back of the torn leather booth and tapped two fingers on a scratched up wooden table that, from the look of it, had not been cleaned in years.

"Look around. What do you see?"

"Not a damn thing."

"What else do you want to know?"

Hart rolled his eyes with a weary, almost helpless, disregard at the various obscurities with which Finnegan answered questions. He took another drink. The cold beer felt good against his throat.

"You don't see anything," Finnegan went on, undeterred. "Nobody you know; nobody who knows you. Any more questions?"

Now Hart understood. No one who did business with the Senate, no one who worked on the Hill, certainly no reporter looking for a lead on tomorrow's story, would come looking in a place like this.

"But why did you want to come to a bar, even one as elegant as this?"

"To get drunk—why do you think?" Finnegan threw down what was left in his glass, caught the eye of the bartender, and signaled for another. "We're both Irish," he explained, his eyes alive with the triumph of a well-told tale. "That's what we're supposed to do after we've gone and buried someone: get drunk as hell and tell all the lies we can about what a great good friend he was and how much we're going to miss him." Finnegan hesitated, shook his head in seeming frustration, and looked at Hart with an impish grin. "I forget, you're from California where everyone is all mixed up about what they are. You've probably never been to an Irish wake, have you? Let me explain. If you were really Irish, and didn't just have an Irish name, you'd be depressed at all sorts of things. You wouldn't need anyone to tell you that every so often—at least once a week or so—you needed to get drunk enough to start feeling better about all the unhappiness in the world."

The bartender, stooped and unshaven, with thin gray hair and glasses thick as bottles, shuffled over with Finnegan's second beer. He mumbled something that sounded like a far off greeting, but which only someone who had known him for half a lifetime could possibly have deciphered. Finnegan looked at him as if he had understood

"Thank you, I will," he replied.

The old man's rheumy eyes brightened and for a moment seemed to clear.

He nodded, mumbled something else to himself, and then, sure that he was right, nodded once again, turned toward the bar, and slowly moved away. Hart and Finnegan exchanged a glance, reminded of the frailty of things and how difficult sometimes were the lives of others.

"Quentin Burdick," said Hart, drawing Finnegan back to what they had started to talk about.

"It's something about the money."

"Constable's money? How he got it? Is that what he's working on? You said he was supposed to meet with Constable the next day, but Constable died the night before."

Finnegan shrugged. He was puzzled. Burdick, as he proceeded to explain, had come to see him, asked him a few questions, but had not really told him more than that he was working on something that involved money and the president.

"He asked me if I knew anything about something called 'The Four Sisters.'"

"'The Four Sisters'? What's that?"

"I don't know. I asked Burdick what it meant. He just said it was something he was looking into and that the more he got into it, the more complicated it seemed to be. One thing he said got my attention. The amount of money involved—whatever that means—was 'amazing.' That was his word, 'amazing.'"

Bending forward on his elbows, Hart stared into his glass. The long service, with no room to move around, the oppressive summer heat, and now this dark, lonely place, had left him feeling tired and even a little depressed.

"So now we're going to learn that the 'great man' we just buried was not just a liar but a thief as well? I guess there isn't really a difference, is there? Don't you steal something every time you tell a lie—steal some part of the truth from those who deserve to know it?"

"Careful, don't get philosophic," said Finnegan, his eyes eager and alive. "With that definition, you'll make thieves and liars of us all. But you're right," he added quickly, "I never knew anyone who could lie right to your face and do it with such complete conviction. There was a sense in which, I suppose, it was not really lying at all. He always lied first to himself. He could convince himself of anything, once he decided there was something he had to have, whether it was the presidency or another woman. He was a hustler, knew in an instant what you wanted to hear. His whole identity was in the eyes of others. Women loved him. They could not help themselves. They knew he must have said the same thing he was saying to them a thousand times before; the difference was—and this is the measure of what a great fraud he really was—that this time he meant it, this time he was saying what he really felt."

Shaking his head in reluctant admiration, Charlie Finnegan picked up his glass and took a long, slow drink.

"They weren't alone, those women: the guy was such an engaging fraud, I sort of liked him, too. But he wasn't worth a damn. He wasn't serious about anything. He didn't believe in anything except his own importance. I'm not even sure about that. He had to be the center of attention. He could not stand to be upstaged. There wasn't any central core. He was like a lot of people I meet these days. His idea of hell was to be somewhere all alone."

A broad grin cut sharply across Finnegan's face. He took another long drink, shoved the glass aside, and laughed at himself.

"I can't understand why they didn't ask me to deliver one of the eulogies." He paused, scratched the side of his face, and, growing serious again, furrowed his brow. "There's more to this—Burdick's story—than the money. You know Burdick better than I do. You know what he covers."

Bobby Hart had known Quentin Burdick from his first term in Congress when he felt honored, and a little surprised, when the famous *New York*

Times reporter asked if he might talk to him. Burdick knew a generation's worth of foreign leaders and every president since Richard Nixon.

"You're right," agreed Hart. "There has to be a link to something overseas." He gave Finnegan a searching glance. "You think Constable was doing business, the kind he should not have been doing, with foreign governments?"

"That would be shocking, wouldn't it?" replied Finnegan dryly. "That the Artful Dodger didn't make distinctions among those from whom he was willing to steal? But no, I doubt Burdick has found any direct connection like that. Constable was much too shrewd to be that stupid. He never would have made that kind of mistake."

Suddenly, Hart thought he knew. He remembered wondering about it at the time, when the first reports were published and the scandals started.

"One of the private equity firms, one of those that collapsed—he was involved in that; one of the investors, as I remember. That was before he became president, but maybe something like it happened again, something that no one knew about. Probably something global, if Burdick has been pursuing it."

Hart glanced at his watch. There was a reception for those who had been invited to the service.

"It won't be so bad," he said, as much to encourage himself as anything. "We don't have to stay long."

"Trust me," said Finnegan, as they got up from the table. "Ten minutes after we get there, you'll begin to miss this place." He looked around with a kind of nostalgia at the bare, near empty room, full of the cloying smell of dead air and stale liquor. "You never know how good things are until you have to leave them."

They stood on the sidewalk just outside the bar, blinking like a pair of drunks who have lost all sense of time or place. The sun hung low on the horizon, a pale yellow disk in a sky that was now seven shades of gray. A deep, hard rumble shook somewhere in the distance, threatening a storm. A wind kicked up, stopped, and then, a moment later, hit them from the other side. Hart looked one way up the street, Finnegan looked the other.

"There!" cried Hart, waving wildly for a cab.

They just made it to the taxi before the rain began to fall. By the time they reached the Georgian mansion that, with the generous help of some of their friends, the Constables had purchased to live in after the president left office, the guests had left the spacious rolling lawn in back and hurried inside. They stood in clusters, talking in the solemn tones of men and women afraid of making a mistake. Waiters in tuxedos drifted through the crowd bearing glasses of champagne on shiny, silver platters.

Bobby Hart had at least a nodding acquaintance with most of the people there. Some, like Frederick Gallagher, who had served as secretary of state during the first term of the Constable administration, he had known, if never quite liked or fully trusted, for years. Standing among a half dozen other former officials, Gallagher still had the same, teeming self-assurance in his hooded, half-closed eyes, the same look of forbearance on his slightly smiling mouth, as if he were doing you a favor just to listen to what you had to say. On those few occasions when their paths had crossed—committee hearings at which the secretary testified—nothing had happened to make Hart change his mind that the secretary was full of his own importance and would not give a straight answer if his life depended on it.

But certain things had changed in the years since Frederick Gallagher held office. Bobby Hart had become one of the best-known names in the Senate and a national figure, while Gallagher had become another former office holder, part of the Washington establishment, one of those men who with each passing year become more and more convinced that what they had done in office was not only right, but brilliant and courageous, and that their return to a position of great influence in the government is the best thing that could happen to the country. Bobby Hart, who had meant nothing to him in the past, was now someone he was always delighted to see.

Gallagher caught Hart's eye and insisted the senator join them in a drink.

"It's the end of an era," said Austin Pearce, picking up the thread of what he and the others had been talking about.

Short, with slumping shoulders and slightly overweight, Austin Pearce had the smooth unwrinkled face of a man who had seemed middle-aged when he was young and would seem that way when he was old. After serving as treasury secretary during Constable's first term, he had gone back to Wall Street because, he was reported to have said, he preferred the company of the kind of sharks who did not try to pretend they were doing you a favor while they were eating you alive. He had explained his departure in a somewhat different manner in a private conversation he had later with Bobby Hart. "Greed is a more honest form of corruption than what goes on here, if you get my meaning." Hart liked him enormously. He made the company of Frederick Gallagher almost tolerable.

"Does the era have a name, Austin?" asked one of the others, Eldridge Baker, who had held several different posts in the administration before leaving to get himself elected governor of a small western state. Baker had a talent for teasing others in a way that seemed to bring out something he liked about them. "As I remember, you had a name for just about everything we did, or tried to do—and everyone who tried to do it," he added with a generous twinkle in his large, dark eyes.

Even Frederick Gallagher fell captive to the change of mood. A thin smile stretched tight across his harsh, angular mouth; but then his eyes narrowed and he quickly shook his head as if to remind himself that a smile in the same room as a grieving widow might be misinterpreted.

"Lady McDeath," he whispered, darting a glance beyond their small circle to make sure he would not be overheard. "Isn't that what you once called her, after she kept insisting that we ought to be more aggressive in places like the Middle East?"

"We say a lot of things that only make sense at the moment," said Pearce, looking straight at Gallagher. "Things that sound a lot different now."

He turned to Bobby Hart and with a slight shrug remarked in his pleasant, understated voice that if he had to give a name to the era that had ended with the president's death, it would probably have to be something like "the 'era of great illusions,' the belief that there is no price to be paid for anything, that we can do anything we like, fight any battle, win any war, and do it all without any need to sacrifice; in other words, that America is the exception to all the laws of history and economics."

"That's rather glib, isn't it?" said Frederick Gallagher dismissively. The look in his eyes, however, suggested that fundamentally he did not disagree.

"I was asked what name I would give it," replied Pearce calmly and without irritation. "What would you suggest?"

Gallagher was not interested in taking up the challenge. The conversation started to drift to other things. Gallagher noticed someone else he knew and wanted to know better.

"Let's get together soon," he said to Hart with the quiet urgency of a man of importance. "There are a number of things I think we might discuss."

Hart watched as Gallagher moved across the crowded room, never looking to the side, always straight ahead, certain that he was being noticed by everyone he passed. "Hopeless, isn't he?" asked Austin Pearce, not without a kind of sympathy. "He's one of the smartest people I know," he added when Hart turned to him, "and one of the dumbest. Sort of like poor Robert Constable, when you think about it: afraid that if he ever stopped being the center of attention no one would know who he was."

"I think you just described half of Washington."

"Only half? You seriously underestimate the vanity, and the insecurity, of the American politician."

Pearce reached for a glass from a passing waiter. The rain had stopped, and the sound of thunder had become a distant fading echo in the yellow, sultry sky. Some of the guests started to make their way back outdoors. Searching for a place that would provide more privacy, Pearce took Hart by the arm and led him across the room, next to a white marble pillar. While Pearce sipped from his glass, Hart gazed across at Hillary Constable, watching her repeat with the same look of gratitude and sympathy the words with which she returned each mumbled expression of encouragement and loss. His hand was on the pillar, and he suddenly realized she was just like it: beautiful and cold, as near as anything, and as distant as twenty centuries, a woman who would never break, a woman who would break instead any hammer that tried to break her, unless of course she shattered.

"She is, isn't she?"

Hart turned to find Austin Pearce watching him with friendly interest. Hart waited for Pearce to explain, but instead Pearce shoved his hands deep in his pockets, stared down at the glowing white marble floor, and then, as if giving up the attempt to find an explanation for what he felt, shrugged his shoulders.

"I guess I don't really know—what she is, I mean. I knew her—I knew them both—starting years ago, but even then, she was—they both were—a kind of mystery. Bright, ambitious…." He paused long enough to give Hart a meaningful look. "Everyone in Washington is ambitious, but their ambition—it was of a different kind altogether. I wouldn't tell anyone else this, but it always seemed to me that they weren't constrained by anything; that, to put it bluntly, there wasn't anything they wouldn't have done to get what they wanted." He hesitated, wanting to make sure he got it right, the thing that he had always known and yet had never been able really to explain or even describe. "That makes them sound ruthless, without principles, willing to use any means. They were all of that, all right, but there was something more. There wasn't anything they didn't want. Yes, I think that's it. They didn't stop when they got what they wanted. As soon as they got it, they had to have more."

Bobby Hart tapped his finger against the hard white marble column.

"Like this?"

"Yes, exactly—a house the size of an embassy, as if from being president the next step was to become a country of his own. You think they could at least have waited until his second term was over. That was the reason I left, when I began to understand the outsized needs he had, his gargantuan appetites, this absence of all restraint, and then this thing he did…." His voice trailed off and for a moment he said nothing. "Can you come up to New York?" he asked suddenly.

With anyone else, Hart would have started to make excuses, but this was Austin Pearce and Austin Pearce was different. There were not ten people in the country who knew anything about financial markets and the global economy, maybe not ten people in the world, who would not have dropped everything and flown any distance to spend an hour alone with him.

"You see that man over there?" he asked, nodding toward the head of the receiving line. "Recognize him?"

There was something vaguely familiar about the distinguished-looking stranger who had just taken Hillary Constable's hand and bent close to whisper his own condolences. There was a cultured, foreign aspect to his features, and Hart thought he might be someone with the diplomatic corps, or a member of a European government, there in his official capacity.

"I don't think so. Who is he?"

A strange smile, full of caution, made a furtive appearance on Austin Pearce's fine, intelligent mouth.

"The head of one of the oldest families in France, and what you might call the managing partner of one of the world's most powerful, and most secret, private firms. It is called The Four Sisters."

CHAPTER 4

THE FOUR SISTERS. Charlie Finnegan had mentioned it just a few hours earlier. It was the story Quentin Burdick was working on, the story that involved the president.

"It's a private equity group, an investment house, correct?"

Austin Pearce searched Hart's eyes, looking for reassurance, as it seemed, a sense that he could still trust him and rely on his discretion.

"The Four Sisters an investment house?—I have a feeling it's a good deal more than that."

Hart glanced back to where Hillary Constable had just let go of the hand of the man they had been talking about.

"Who is he?" he asked.

"One of the most fascinating men I've ever met: Jean de la Valette, charming, intelligent, well read—I don't mean the kind of contemporary things we read to stay current, his horizon is rather different than that. I suppose that is inevitable, when your family goes back, not just a few generations, but five hundred years or more." Pearce's gaze became solemn, profound, and full of troubled calculation. "I meant what I said earlier," he said finally. "Come to New York, as soon as possible—this week, if you can. I have to talk to you about something." He made a quick, abrupt movement of his head toward Jean de la Valette, who was just then on his way outside. "It's about The Four Sisters."

He patted Hart on his sleeve and told him he had to go. He had not taken three steps when he turned back.

"I don't trust many people, Bobby; not anymore. What I told you about The Four Sisters—don't tell that to anyone, not even that you know the name."

Hart watched as the former treasury secretary made his way through the crowd. Pearce was a small, average-looking man easily confused for an accountant's assistant, someone brought into a meeting of government officials to take notes or double-check figures, until he began to talk and off the top of his head analyze a budgetary problem or a financial question with the same cogent ease as someone reading from the printed page. Pearce had never been short for an answer, never baffled by a problem, always calm and collected, never irritated or impatient, never for any reason disturbed—until now. He had not admitted it, not in so many words, but he had seemed almost frightened of this thing called The Four Sisters, whatever it really was: an investment house or, as he had put it, something more than that. Who was Jean de la Valette, wondered Bobby Hart, and what was his connection to Robert Constable?

"That looked interesting."

Charlie Finnegan was standing right in front of him, but Hart had been so lost in thought he had not seen him approach.

"You and Austin Pearce seemed to be having quite a conversation. I didn't want to interrupt."

"I'm not sure what it was about. He wants to see me about something. Maybe I'll find out then," replied Hart, glancing at Finnegan in a way that told him that was all he could say. "Have you done the honors?"

"Yeah, I went through, mumbled a few words about what a great man he was. I don't envy her, having to stand there like that, forced to turn private grief into a public ceremony. She called me by my first name. They were always good at that, weren't they?—making you feel you were someone they especially liked."

Finnegan checked his watch. He looked around the room in case he had missed someone he wanted to see or needed to speak to.

"A few more minutes," he said to Hart, "then I've got to go." He nodded toward the receiving line. It was shorter than it had been. "You haven't yet, have you?"

"No, but I guess I better. I'll catch up with you later. We're on for dinner tomorrow, right?"

Hart took another glass from a passing waiter and made his way to the back of the line. He tried to think of what he was going to say, but all he could think about was the great inconsequence, at times like this, of saying anything. He had never yet found words that did not sound empty and false when he tried to express sympathy and support to someone who had lost a husband or a wife, a parent or a child. He was too honest to imagine that anything could make much of a difference to someone who was suffering the unspeakable agonies that come with the knowledge that someone you loved, someone who loved you, was now gone forever. Forever, that was the point. The journey had come to an end and there was no starting over, no chance to make amends for the things you wish you had not said or done, no chance to do what you had always planned to do once you had the time, because time was over, time had died.

The line kept moving forward, and then, suddenly, he was standing in front of her, and he still did not know what to say. The words came automatically.

"I'm very sorry," he heard himself saying as he held her hand for a brief moment in his own. "If there is anything—"

She stopped him with a look, a slight, enigmatic smile that seemed to acknowledge the awkward futility of saying anything with words. She bent toward him.

"Stay. Don't go. I have to see you."

She whispered an instruction to a young man standing just behind her, and looked again at Hart to let him know that, whatever she wanted to see him about, it was important. Then she was taking the hand of someone else, and, in that way she had, making them feel that they were the one she had been waiting all the while to see.

"This way, Senator," said the aide as he led Hart out of the room and down a long corridor.

The house was a labyrinth, hallways that seemed to turn left and turn right, hallways that seemed to turn back on themselves; stairways that spiraled somewhere out of sight and that, from the look of them, had seldom been used in the hundred years since the house was first built. They passed a dozen white varnished doors, all of them shut and probably locked, like the vacant rooms in some grand decayed hotel that were only opened when someone ventured in to clean and air them out. After making at least three different turns, they climbed a narrow back staircase to the second floor. Hart was shown to a suite of rooms where, he was told, Mrs. Constable would join him as soon as she could.

"She asked me to tell you," said her aide, "that it's a matter of some urgency." He paused as if he wanted to be absolutely certain he did not forget even the smallest part of what he was supposed to do. "She wouldn't ask you to wait like this if it wasn't.""

It seemed odd, once he was left alone and had time to think about it, that he had been asked to wait here, this far away from the main part of the house. He was in a sitting room, richly furnished with a sofa and two easy chairs arranged in front of a marble fireplace. Through an open doorway, he could see a large bedroom with heavy drapes drawn across the windows. A second doorway led to a book-lined study. Restless, and with nothing else to do, Hart pulled a leather-bound volume off a shelf. The pages had not been cut. He pulled down another and discovered the same thing. Hundreds of burnished leather–bound books, the pride of any collector, some of the books hundreds of years old, and none of them ever read. They were like the furniture in a roped-off room, there to be seen and never used. Hart wanted to laugh. It was Robert Constable all over again, life as a magician's trick, the illusion of things that never were.

The drapes were closed in this room as well, and Hart, who did not like dark places, pulled them open. To his astonishment, he found himself staring down onto the backyard lawn and the circling crowd that had left the house and gathered outside. For all the twists and turnings that he had been made to follow, Hart was just one floor above where he had started. Whatever Hillary Constable wanted with him, she seemed strangely intent on making certain no one else knew about it.

A few minutes went by, and then a few more. Hart paced back and forth, wondering how much longer he would have to wait. He looked at the long rows of priceless, unread books and the desk on which, instead of pen and paper, were a number of framed photographs, each of them a different size. He walked over to get a closer look. All of the pictures were of Hillary Constable, but never alone, always with someone else: a friend, a relative; photographs taken at ski resorts and tropical islands, photographs taken at different periods of her life; a history, as it were, of life outside of Washington and the usual corridors of power, and not one of the pictures a picture of her with her husband. It was as if Robert Constable had never existed; or, rather, that her time with him had been a public property, an exploitable advantage, something she had not allowed to intrude into what she had had of a private, personal life.

There was a soft whirring sound from the sitting room. A door slid open and closed. It was an elevator, the means by which Hillary Constable could move quickly and easily from whatever commotion was taking place in the first floor public rooms to what, Hart had now determined, was her own private sanctuary. The books that lined the shelves in all their unread splendor, those books belonged to her.

"Damn," she muttered with what seemed like quiet desperation. Holding her arms straight down at her sides, she clenched both fists. "Damn it, damn it, damn it!" she cried. She shook her head, quickly, abruptly, as if to force herself to stop, to get control again. Closing her eyes, she took a deep breath. Then, suddenly, she opened them with a look of consternation. She had forgotten that Bobby Hart was there. She started to pretend that he had not noticed what she had done, and then she gave it up.

"Yes, that's how I feel." Her eyes glistened with defiance. "Do you think I wanted to stand there, spend two hours acting the grieving widow, so that they can all talk about how brave I am, how much I am to be admired for the way I've conducted myself, holding back my emotions, holding back the tears? The truth of it is that the hardest part has been pretending that I care at all that he's dead."

She walked across to the open doorway to the study where Hart stood watching her.

"You always knew he was a fraud, didn't you? Don't bother denying it. If there is anybody in this town who can cut through all the cheap lying, all the stupid hypocrisy, it's you."

She touched him on the arm and then moved past him to an open cubicle in the book-lined shelves where three crystal class decanters sat on a silver tray.

"Scotch?" she asked, as she poured two glasses. She handed him a half-filled glass and then touched hers to his. "Cheers," she said in a voice tinged with weary cynicism. She stood at the window, looking down at the crowd. "You think any of them are talking about what a great president he was?"

She looked away, took a drink as if she were trying to steady her nerves, and then sank into an easy chair. She took another drink, longer, slower this time, and appeared to lose herself in thought. A moment later, she looked up at Hart and gestured toward the chair next to her.

"I'm in some trouble, Bobby, and you're the only one I can think of who might be able to help."

Hart barely knew her. He had never before this had a private conversation with her. He could not think of anything that would have made her think of him. She read his mind.

"You're too modest. Or, perhaps," she added with a shrewd glance that made Hart cautious and a little uncomfortable, "you're not modest enough. You know perfectly well that you can do a good deal more than most people around here. You have great influence; everyone—or nearly everyone, because there are always a certain number of idiots and fools—respects you. The point is you know how to get things done, and, that rarest of qualities, you have a sense of what is important and what is not. Look out that window; look down at that crowd of well-wishers who only wish well for themselves. Think they care anything about the great Robert Constable now? Think they cared anything about him when he was alive, except what he might do for them? They're all free now, whatever they might have owed him. I've got the burden of the great man's reputation, the obligation to make sure that no one ever finds out the truth, the whole truth, of what he really was."

Hart had seen too much of politics and what it did to people to be shocked very easily, but this was stunning, the harsh bitterness with which she described her husband and what his death meant for her. He was almost afraid to ask what she wanted him to do.

"You said you were in some kind of trouble. I'm not sure I understand what you mean."

Hillary Constable stared into the middle distance, her mood changing in the flick of an eyelash from angry defiance into a dark depression. One moment she was all energy, her eyes eager and electric; the next she seemed to have lost the capacity to move, and even the will to live. Suddenly she was on her feet and at the window, shaking her head not just at the vanity of the world but, from the look in her now anguished eyes, something much more personal to herself.

"He died in a hotel, a hotel in Manhattan, of a heart attack," she said, leaning against the window casement. She kept watching the crowd below, fascinated, as it seemed, by the familiar strangers that for so many years had made up the world she had first wanted to conquer and then, having conquered, had begun to despise. "I was in love once, a long time ago, when I was still in college." She turned to face Hart directly. "He was a gorgeous-looking boy. He wanted to be...well, I don't know what he wanted to be, except to be with me. But that wasn't the kind of ambition I thought I needed. I wanted to be something, be someone everyone knew, someone— the someone I became." She tapped her foot, stopped, and then, a moment later, threw her head back and laughed. "I became what I always was—a fool. I married Robert and I got what I deserved, a husband who thought he was being faithful if he went through a weekend without sleeping with another woman. I got what I deserved, Bobby; I got to wear black and sit in the first pew at his funeral, and then stand in that receiving line and listen to everyone tell me how much they sympathized with my loss while they're wondering whether the rumor was true: that he died of a heart attack while he was screwing one of the many other women he often took to bed."

Hart tried to object. "I don't think—"

"It's not a rumor, Bobby: It's true. He was with someone that night. That isn't the problem."

"The problem?"

"The problem: what I meant when I said I'm in some trouble. Robert didn't die of a heart attack, he was murdered."

"Murdered! What makes you think…?"

A dozen different thoughts raced through Hart's brain; or rather, only two: her husband had been murdered and she was in trouble. There seemed to be only one conclusion, but it was impossible, it could not have happened. But he had to ask.

"They think you…?"

"Not that I didn't have good reason, but no, that's not the kind of trouble I meant. It isn't that simple."

She came back to her chair, picked up the half finished glass of scotch, and drank some more.

"Do you know Clarence Atwood, head of the Secret Service?"

"Not very well; we've met."

"I'd like you to see him."

But Hart was still stunned by what she had said.

"He was murdered?"

"He came to see me. Clarence Atwood," she explained. "What I'm going to tell you now, no one else knows. No one else can know. Do you understand what I'm saying? No, of course you don't." Her eyes full of a new vulnerability, she shook her head in frustration. "You have to forgive me. After everything that's happened, things get jumbled up and I'm not always as coherent as I should be."

Hart tried to help.

"Atwood came to see you. He told you that your husband had been murdered?"

"Clarence was the head of the detail when we—I mean when Robert was first elected. We had a certain understanding." She rose from the chair and, as if drawn by the crowd, the need to know that what she had helped accomplish could still dominate the time and attention of other people, went back to the window. "He didn't have to tell me everything—I didn't need to know every time Robert was falling into bed with someone—only when he did something that might become a public embarrassment."

The vulnerability vanished from her eyes, replaced by a cold, and even ruthless, calculation, as she remembered the sacrifices, and the bargains, she had been forced to make.

"I never promised Clarence anything for his help, for his discretion; but when the head of the Secret Service retired, I made sure he got the job. He's remained a loyal friend. He knows how to keep this quiet."

"Keep it quiet?" Hart jumped to his feet. "The president was murdered, and you want to keep it quiet? You can't!"

"Hear me out! Listen before you rush to judgment. It has to be kept quiet. No one can ever know. He was not murdered by some jealous husband; he wasn't killed by someone in a moment of rage! It was an assassination. He was killed by lethal injection, a drug that stopped his heart almost instantly."

Hart stared at her, not certain what to believe.

"I spent most of my time while he was alive doing what I had to do to protect his reputation," she went on. "I have to do the same thing now that he's dead. He was in a hotel room, having sex with a woman who turned out to have been a hired killer. The agent who was with him helped her get away. He didn't know that's what he was doing. The great irony is that he thought he was protecting me. Isn't that just too funny for words? He didn't want anyone to find out that the former leader of the western world was screwing his brains out when he died, so he cleaned up everything and got rid of the girl, told her to get out of the hotel and made sure she was gone before he called for help."

"Then who found out that he'd been murdered?"

"There was an autopsy, private, controlled; the Secret Service arranged it. There was a puncture mark in his armpit. That's what made them think they had better take a closer look at the cause of death. When they discovered the drug, Clarence called in the agent and told him what they had found. Then Clarence came to me."

"What about the FBI? Who's investigating this?"

"There isn't going to be an investigation; not yet, anyway. Not until you find the answer to the only question that matters."

"Me? What question? What matters?"

"You know everything about the intelligence community; you know who you can trust. The question is who was behind his murder and what was the reason they wanted him killed. That's what is important: the reason. Robert had connections all over the world. Everyone wanted something from him, and of course," she added in a curious undertone, "there were people willing to do almost anything for him. But something happened, he got involved in something—I'm not quite sure what—and he started to worry, become even more secretive than usual, and then, for no reason at all, fly into a rage. It was like he found himself inside a circle and the circle was starting to close. I have to know what was going on, what he was afraid of. I have to know why he was killed, if it was because of something he knew, something he was covering up. That's why this has to be kept quiet. Do you have any idea what a scandal like that would do, not just to his reputation, but to the country?—The idea that a president of the United States was murdered to keep him from talking about some criminal enterprise in which he might have been involved. You don't think I'm serious? When did you ever know Robert Constable to think the rules that ordinary people have to live by applied to him?"

The question seemed to answer itself in the silence that followed as Hillary Constable crossed over to the desk and removed a black date book from the middle drawer.

"This is his calendar. I took it from his study downstairs." She opened to a place already marked by a ribbon. "That next week, the week after he was killed, like almost every week, was filled up with appointments, places he had to go, speeches he had to give; but then all of them were crossed out, all except one, an appointment he had for the next morning with Quentin Burdick of the *New York Times*. Why did Burdick want to see him? And why did Robert cancel everything else? Was it because he knew what Burdick was going to ask him, and that it was a story that, once it was published, was going to change everything?"

CHAPTER 5

ROBERT CONSTABLE HAD made a mockery of his marriage by frequent acts of infidelity; Bobby Hart had never once betrayed his wife. He was young and good-looking and, if that were not enough, a United States senator who was not only widely respected but, in the phrase so often used, destined for higher things. In a city in which power, and not money, was the leading aphrodisiac, Bobby Hart did not lack for opportunities, and, except perhaps in the minds of rigid moralists, would not have lacked excuse.

Bobby Hart had been in love with Laura from the first moment he saw her. She had been too shy to trust her instincts and a little too scared of what she felt to come quite as quickly to the same conclusion. It was only later, after they were married, after the collapse, that Bobby fully realized how fragile, how vulnerable, she had always been. Beautiful in a way that at times seemed almost otherworldly, she moved entirely in her own orbit, indifferent to what others might think, or what others might say, interested only in what she knew and loved, which was Bobby Hart and Bobby Hart alone. She would have lived a life of perfect bliss if they could have lived, just the two of them, a life of solitude, but she had tried instead to live the life her husband thought important. She had helped in his first campaign for Congress; appeared smiling at his side in front of crowds that terrified her, and, acting with a bravery that passed unnoticed, even gave short speeches of her own.

Then they moved to Washington and she discovered that she was not just expected to share her husband with the world, but that they were not to have in any real sense any life at all. Other people seemed to thrive on it, the constant movement, the constant rush, the endless gossip, the endless rumors, the belief that Washington was the center of the universe, the only place that mattered, a place where everyone was always busy, where everything, even the smallest detail, was important, a place where everyone was always certain what was going to happen next, and where everyone almost always was wrong. It was a madhouse, a charnel house of incoherent voices, and after a while all she could hear inside her head was the constant, crazy noise, and she knew, deep down inside her, that if she did not leave she would quickly lose her mind. Had she been less unworldly and more experienced she might have decided she was the only sane one there, and become ironic.

No one had seen the inner turmoil beneath the smiling surface of Laura's gentle, lovely face; no one had known how much effort it had taken just to keep herself together, to show the world what the world wanted, and expected, to see. She began to make excuses, invent reasons why Bobby should go to some event alone; and when, rebelling against what she thought her own failings, she forced herself to go, she would sometimes fall into sudden silences or suddenly start chattering aimlessly about something that had nothing to do with the conversation. She was slipping away, but it was gradual, like a slowly changing mood, the way boredom takes the place of excitement when the novelty wears off. Bobby had not understood that the endless whirl of official gatherings and Georgetown parties had lost their freshness and become a tired routine—until the night she told him with a lonely smile that she had to go away.

"I can't live here, I just can't—I've tried. I'd do anything for you, Bobby, but I can't do this. I have to go home, our home, Bobby; the one we bought together, where we said we'd always live. I'm not leaving you; I don't want you to leave me. I'll be there, at home, waiting every night."

It was only then that he realized what he had done to her, and from that day forward his ambition lived, so to speak, on borrowed time. He promised himself, and he promised her, that as soon as he finished the more important things he had started, he would quit the Senate, resign his seat, and come home to Santa Barbara. This was what he thought he owed her, and it was what he wanted for himself. He was still in love with her—he would always be in love with her—and he could not stand the thought that, for however short time, they would live apart.

Laura moved back to Santa Barbara and Bobby started spending weekends there as often as he could, and then, two years later, at almost the same time, Bobby said it was time to quit and Laura told him that instead of that she wanted a second chance. She insisted she was stronger, that she had now quite recovered, and that she loved him too much to let him stop what he was doing because of her. And so she came back to Washington, and Bobby for his part made sure that things were different. They rarely went to Georgetown parties and they seldom saw anyone who was not an old friend. They spent a lot of time with Charlie Finnegan and, when she was not at home in Ann Arbor where she had her medical practice, his wife, Clare.

Bobby did everything he could to protect her. He almost never told her what he learned on the Senate Intelligence Committee, no matter how angry and depressed he might have become listening to more tales of wanton violence and every form of evil. He tried always to be cheerful and eager, as if the only thing he had had on his mind all day was getting home to her. But Laura had acquired an almost mathematically precise ability, a kind of calculus of false exuberance, to measure the degree of his well-intentioned duplicity. She knew what he was doing and loved him even more because of it.

Their life settled into a comfortable routine. And if it was not everything she had wanted, it was good enough. She knew for certain that she would rather live with him in the apartment they had taken in Washington's northwest corner, she would rather live with him anywhere, than live anywhere else, even Santa Barbara, without him. Sometimes, if he was traveling overseas, or had to give a speech somewhere out of town, she would fly back to California where he would join her on the weekend. The week the president died, when all of Washington gathered for the funeral, Bobby told her no one would notice if she was not there.

"I never quite understood what people saw in him," she remarked when Bobby drove her to the airport for the flight home to Santa Barbara. The Potomac glistened in the morning sun as they passed the Jefferson Memorial and started across the bridge. "I'm not sure I liked her any better," she added as she reached in her purse for her dark glasses. "You wonder what goes on in private between people like that." A smile full of puzzled affection broke suddenly across her face. "I suppose there are people who wonder that about us, aren't there? Wonder what we're really like—whether we make love or you just give speeches."

Bobby kept his eyes on the road, but she could see—he wanted her to see—the teasing sparkle in his eyes.

"Did I speak too much last night?"

"I like it when you speak like that," she said in the silky voice that he never tired of hearing. "You can speak like that every night to me."

When they reached the airport, he parked at the curb and got her suitcase out of the car. She put her arms around his neck and laughed softly into his ear.

"Come home, to Santa Barbara; we'll talk some more."

He stood on the sidewalk and watched her walk away, and then, when she was safe inside the terminal and he could not see her anymore, he got back in the car and drove off and felt the sudden aching emptiness and wished she had not gone. It was now, at times like this, that he realized not just how much he loved her but how, through his own unthinking ambition, he had come so close to losing her. The doctors and psychologists might say that she suffered from depression, but, so far as he was concerned, the madness had been his. The choice between spending all his time with the most beautiful woman he had ever seen, holding hands on a beach in Santa Barbara and making love in a moonlit bedroom with a long view of the sea, or wrangling with a pack of penny politicians over cuts in someone's budget was not a choice at all, except to someone quite demented.

The three days away from her seemed like three years, and what he had learned at the president's funeral made the separation even worse. The secret he had been told by Hillary Constable, the secret about the president's death, was something he was going to have to share. This was of a different order, a different magnitude, than the things he had in the past thought best to keep to himself. It was a secret that he had known immediately would change not just his life, but the lives of a great many others. He had to tell her, if not for her, than for himself: he always had a better sense of things after he talked with her.

It was a bright, clear, windless afternoon when he drove home from the airport, the kind of lush summer day that made him wonder, not just what kind of fool would want to fly back and forth to Washington, but what it must have been like, back in the Twenties, when Los Angeles was still new and exotic and Santa Barbara was a long way away from everything and the house that Laura loved was a good half mile from its closest neighbor. Perhaps because his own life, the life he had with Laura, had involved so much heartache and tragedy, he had always had a certain fondness for the past. It was the great secret, the one no one talked about: the great American dream was not about the future, it was about what might have been but wasn't.

He made the last turn on the winding, narrow road. The gleaming white Spanish-style house, buried in the sunburst colors of clinging bougainvillea, was just ahead. He passed through the open gate, parked the car, and went inside.

"Laura," he called, but there was no answer.

He put his suitcase down on the cool tile floor and went into the kitchen. An empty coffee cup with a trace of lipstick had been left on the table next to the morning paper. The paper had been folded back to the third page where the story of the president's funeral had been continued next to a picture of a somber-looking "Senator Robert Hart of California, entering the National Cathedral." Bobby smiled to himself, imagining for a moment the look in Laura's eyes when she turned the page and found the picture of him. He glanced at it again and felt a little the hypocrite for having, like the others, played the mourner for someone he would not miss.

He found Laura in the backyard, the other side of the pool at the far edge of the lawn, cutting roses in her usual methodical way, each one exactly the same length, then laid side by side in the woven wicker basket held on her arm. She treated them like children, speaking soft words of encouragement as she carefully selected the ones she thought were ready. Standing in the shadows of the back patio, Bobby watched with growing amusement as she danced from one rose bush to the next.

"Bobby!" she cried, half-embarrassed when he finally started toward her.

She stamped her foot, pretending petulance that he had not let her know he was home. She put the basket of roses on the ground, unfastened the straw hat she was wearing, and let her hair flow free. Wiping her dusty hands on the sides of her blue summer dress, she laughed self-consciously.

"I didn't expect you until this evening. I thought I'd fill all the vases with flowers and have everything nice."

He was right in front of her. She touched the side of his face and her hand felt warm against his skin. He put his arm around her and kissed her gently on the cheek.

"Let's go inside. I've got a lot to tell you."

They sat in a room just off the kitchen, a small second living room where they often spent their evenings, Laura curled up in a corner of the sofa, Bobby in an easy chair, watching as the sun slipped down the western sky and set fire to the Pacific.

"What is it, Bobby? I read all about the funeral; I watched a little of the television coverage. Why do you seem so worried? Is it whether Russell can do the job?"

"Russell? I'd almost forgotten. Strange. Well, maybe not so strange: if there was ever anyone easy to forget, it's Irwin Russell. And now he's president, though that shouldn't last very long—a year from November to be precise."

"He won't run, he won't try to get elected on his own?"

"That was the reason Constable picked him, the reason he dropped Jamison from the ticket."

"He put Jamison on the Supreme Court. Isn't that what Jamison wanted?"

Bobby arched an eyebrow. He shook his head as if to tell her that nothing that happened in Washington was ever quite what it seemed to be.

"Jamison wouldn't have agreed to become vice president, wouldn't have agreed to be on the same ticket with Constable, someone he didn't think was half as qualified as he was to be president, if he had thought there was any chance he would not be there at the end of eight years, next in line for the office, with a clear path to the nomination. The first time he ever thought of being on the Court was when Constable told him that he was not going to be on the ticket again, when he told him that he could either fill the vacancy that was about to occur on the Court, or go back home and try to run for governor again."

"But why, what did he think Irwin Russell would bring to the ticket that Tom Jamison couldn't?"

"Nothing."

"Nothing?"

"Nothing in the way of any political advantage, but then Constable did not need any help to get reelected. Russell was supposed to be someone who could help him in Congress. He had been there damn near thirty years, was chairman of the Finance Committee, had a solid reputation, members on both sides of the aisle liked him. But he is colorless, dull as dust, slow, plodding, the moment he starts to speak you start checking your watch. In other words, he was the perfect combination: someone who would not cause any trouble and was smart enough to know that the vice presidency was as far as he could go."

Laura folded her arms and frowned. She still did not understand.

"I don't know this for sure," confided Bobby. "No one ever came out and said it, but the rumor was that Constable wanted to stay in office, and that he had a way to do it, or at least that he thought he did. He could not run again, he could not serve more than two terms in office, but what difference did that make, if his wife could take his place."

Laura had never been surprised at anything the Constables had done. She had once remarked that they seemed to think that everything, that all of history, everything that had happened in the past, had been leading up to them.

"I imagine the only real question is which of them thought of it first."

Dazzled by how quickly she could get to the heart of things, Bobby felt the smile fade from his lips.

"There are people who were around them for years, who thought they knew them better than they ever knew anyone, who insist that it was only after a lot of other people started talking about what a great president she would be, and how this was the first real chance to elect a woman, that they began to consider the possibility."

Laura's eyes went wide with wonder. Her mouth began to quiver as if she were about to laugh.

"What was it you told me, not that long ago: the closer some people are to power the more willing they are to believe? But, whichever of them was the first to think of it, that's all gone now, isn't it? Robert Constable is dead. Or do you think she might try anyway?"

"Run for president? I doubt it. She has other things she has to deal with now."

He said this with a worried expression, and then hesitated, not quite sure how to tell her what had happened, and what, because of it, he had to do. He got up from the chair and sat next to her on the sofa.

"Constable didn't die of a heart attack."

Laura guessed at once what it meant.

"Someone…?"

"Murdered him, assassinated him, that night. A woman did it, a woman he was with."

"In the hotel, where he died?" she asked, wanting to be sure.

"He'd picked her up somewhere—which means that she knew where he would be and how she could get his attention, or someone sent her there, someone he knew, someone he trusted. She used a needle, injected him with a drug that stopped his heart, caused cardiac arrest. There's more to it, but that doesn't matter now. No one knows about this. You're the only one I've told. I wish I didn't know, but when she—"

"She?"

"Hillary Constable. At the reception after the funeral, she asked to see me. She wants me to find out what I can about what happened. She thinks that I might be able to do something without anyone finding out. She's worried about what will happen if it becomes known that the president was murdered before we know who did it and the reason why it was done."

Laura jumped to her feet, angry at what he had been asked to do.

"You can't do this, Bobby! She's using you. Don't you see that? The only thing she's worried about is how this might affect her."

Bobby reached for her wrist and tried to give her assurances.

"That's why I didn't promise anything, except to see what I could find out; why I told her that whatever I found out there was going to have to be an investigation, and that the public was going to have to know."

"Why do it at all, Bobby? What good will it do? Why take the risk?"

"Because there's a sense in which I think she's right. Whatever way this affects her—that's not important. What is important is how it affects the country. If I can find out something before it hits the papers we might stop the kind of panic, the kind of wild rumors, that will tear the country apart."

She did not disagree, but neither did she doubt her own belief that he was being drawn into someone else's game.

"There's something she isn't telling you. She's never done anything that wasn't based on a calculation of her own advantage."

Bobby got to his feet and took her by the hand. He smiled in a failed attempt to convince her not to worry, that he could take care of himself.

"Whatever she might be thinking, she can't use me to cover up what happened."

"Because you told her that you wouldn't do that? But maybe all she wants is time."

"If that's what she's after, I'm afraid she doesn't have much left. Constable had a meeting scheduled the next morning with Quentin Burdick of the *Times*. He must have thought Burdick was onto something important, because he cancelled everything else he had scheduled not just that day but the rest of the week. I know Burdick well enough to know that, whatever he was working on, he won't give up."

CHAPTER 6

THE FLIGHT FROM New York arrived in Los Angeles twenty minutes late, but Quentin Burdick had lots of time. He could spend the night in Santa Barbara and not have to leave much before noon. After the dismal, muggy weather in New York, the prospect of an evening walk along the Pacific had the charm of an overdue vacation.

Two hours after he landed, he checked into a motel across from the beach, made a few phone calls, and then, putting on a windbreaker and a pair of sneakers, went for a stroll. Almost painfully thin, with a narrow, angular face and quick-moving, inquisitive eyes, Quentin Burdick looked younger than his age. But today, as he walked beneath the palm trees swaying gently in the late day breeze, he felt older than he was. He had not been able to rid himself of the suspicion that there was more than simple coincidence in the timing of Robert Constable's death. The rumor that he had been in bed with some woman made Burdick wonder whether Constable's heart attack might not have been self-induced, or, if not quite that deliberate, the president had set out to test the limits of his endurance, half-hoping that he would not make it.

He had tried for months to get an interview, but instead of a direct refusal, which might have seemed to confirm the president's involvement, he had been met with ambiguity and evasion, assurances that the president would be only too glad to talk to him once he found the time. There had not been much to work on in the beginning, a few anonymous sources whose information it was impossible to confirm, a few tax returns that raised some questions but scarcely proved anything improper, much less criminal. He had nothing he could use, nothing to write a story that he would want his name on or that the paper would print, and Constable knew it. With each new request for an interview, the excuses became more transparent, until, quite unexpectedly, Burdick got the break he needed. It was just a name, but the name, as he discovered, meant everything. The president now thought he knew a good deal more than he did.

"Tell the president," he had told Constable's chief of staff, "that the story I'm working on is about The Four Sisters, and that I think it's only fair that I get his side of it."

An hour later Burdick got a call back, not from the chief of staff, but the president himself. Cheerful and exuberant, he made it seem that he had been waiting for months to see Burdick, and not the other way round.

"They've got me going from one place to another; no time to do anything I like. Hell, yesterday I was giving a speech in Atlanta, and tomorrow— would you believe it—I'm on my way to Rome for one of those economic summits where all those rich people get together and I try to tell them all the good they should be doing with their money. Now when are we going to get together, Quentin? What's a good time for you?"

Quentin Burdick stopped walking. He sat on a bench and watched the orange red sun grow larger and larger as it settled down on the far horizon and began slowly to dissolve in the sea. Years before, when he lived for a while out on Long Island, reading *The Great Gatsby* and wishing he could write like Fitzgerald, he sometimes stayed up all night just to watch the sun rise from somewhere the other side of the Atlantic and paint the sky a dozen different shades of pink and purple, but this was better, now that he was older, more comforting in a way, a sense of dignity and peace and the permanence of things as the world slipped gently into the night and the dreams you remembered danced once again in your never aging mind.

Burdick sat on the bench, listening in the hush of evening to the vanished voice of Robert Constable, that raucous, roguish voice that had given him a boyish charm well past middle age; the voice that, after the first few times he had had the chance to ask a reporter's question, he had learned it was never safe to trust.

"It's about The Four Sisters, Mr. President," he had replied to Constable's invitation. "I'd like to talk to you about your involvement."

He had tried to make it seem a fair warning, a preview of what the president could expect. It was of course both more, and less, than that. More, because if half of what he had learned was true, the presidency of Robert Constable would be destroyed; less, because in terms of hard evidence, the kind you needed for a story like this, he did not have a thing.

"I'll be glad to talk to you about anything you want, but involvement—that wouldn't be correct. I've heard of them, I'm not denying that. And last year, I think it was, I gave a speech at some conference in Switzerland, and, if I'm not mistaken, they were one of the sponsors. But other than that, I don't know how much I can tell you."

There was a long pause, and Burdick thought the president was waiting for him to say something—anything—that would give him an idea of how much Burdick knew. The silence became strained, uncomfortable, a confession that the president was worried and, more than that, alarmed.

"Why?" he had asked finally. "Have you heard something different?"

The Four Sisters, the name alone, the fact that he knew it, had put the president in a state of something close to panic. The story was bigger, far bigger, than Burdick had thought. If he had been able to talk to him, if Robert Constable had not died, he was almost certain he could have discovered the truth. Constable would have tried to put the best face on things he could, but Constable had been scared—Burdick was certain of that. He might have tried to make a deal, trade what he knew, or some of it, for the chance to minimize his own involvement. But now Constable was dead, and, depending on what happened tomorrow, the story might be dead as well.

Quentin Burdick sat on the beachside bench, listening in the cool night air to voices from the past, the different politicians he had known, some of them decent and honorable, determined to do the right thing, but, especially in recent years, more and more of them driven only by their own ambition, willing to do or say anything to get the next thing they wanted. There were still exceptions: Charlie Finnegan, for one. The junior senator from Michigan was always willing to talk openly and honestly about what was going on, and, if there was something he could not talk about, tell you that as well. Finnegan was as well informed as anyone in Washington. When he said he had not heard of The Four Sisters and did not know what it was, Burdick knew that the story he was after involved a closely guarded secret known only to an unknown few. The president had been one of them, and what Burdick had heard in his voice had told him that none of the others who knew about it were likely to talk, even if he found out who they were. Tomorrow was going to be the last chance he had.

The sun had disappeared. The oil drilling platforms far out at sea became smaller, less obtrusive, in the purple shadowed night. When Burdick got up and started back to the motel, the hillside above the city was alive with a thousand flickering lights. He remembered that somewhere up there, on a winding street with a view that took your breath away, Bobby Hart lived with his wife when the Senate was not in session and he could get away. He had not talked to Hart yet, but he intended to. The senator had sources no one else had: his father had been with the CIA and there were still people in the agency who told him things they told no one else. If anyone could find out about The Four Sisters, Hart could. Burdick shoved his hands into the pockets of his windbreaker and, suddenly hungry, headed down the street to a quiet-looking restaurant where he could get dinner.

A little before noon the next morning, Burdick was back on the road, heading north along the coast, past Santa Barbara, out onto a long flat stretch between the ocean and the empty sun-bleached hills. The road cut inland and a hard wind knocked the car sideways, forcing Burdick, who liked to drive fast when he had the chance, to slow down. A few miles later, he turned off the highway and, resuming speed, followed a county road through the coastal range, where the only signs of life among the spreading wind-bent oaks were a few weathered barns that had stood there for half a century or more. The sense of loneliness, of mystic solitude, made Burdick feel that he was living back before the age of highways and automobiles, when life moved at a slower pace and there was more time to think. He wanted to pull off to the side of the road, get out of the car, and look around at the endless skyline and the rugged terrain, but, glancing at the dashboard clock, he knew he had to hurry or be late.

He drove through a small coastal town, and ten minutes later passed a sign to Vandenberg Air Force Base and was on his way to the Lompoc Federal Penitentiary. It did not look like most prisons. There was none of the stark sense of isolation you felt in a place like Alcatraz, that barren rock in the middle of the San Francisco Bay. There were none of the high fortress walls, none of the glass-enclosed guard towers, of Attica or San Quentin. It had more the aspect of a camp, a series of flat-top single-story wooden buildings that could have been the barracks for an army or the classrooms of a school. Clumps of eucalyptus trees towered along the side of the road, and, stretching out in the distance, large well-tilled fields in which some of the prison's food was grown. Then Burdick saw it, a large blank building with scarcely any windows, surrounded by a cage of metal fencing with double rolls of razor-sharp concertina wire on top.

Burdick signed in at the visitors' entrance. After he was searched and passed through a metal detector, he was taken, not, as he had expected, to a small narrow room where a visitor sat on one side of a plate of thick glass and the prisoner on the other, but to a large, empty cafeteria. The man he was there to see was waiting for him at a round table next to a window that, looking out onto an inner courtyard, let in the outside light.

"Quentin Burdick of the *Times!*" said the prisoner with a huge grin.

He lumbered to his feet, placed one large hand on Burdick's shoulder, and looked him straight in the eye as they shook hands. For a moment, Burdick almost forgot they were in a federal prison and not back in the committee room of the House Ways and Means Committee.

"How are you, Congressman?" he asked with an unexpected catch in his throat.

Frank Morris had been one of his favorites, colorful, profane, with an almost perfect judgment about the strengths and weaknesses of his colleagues, and an equally sharp instinct for just how far he could push them when he was reaching for the kind of compromise by which, as chairman of the committee, he could craft a budget.

"It's maybe not quite what I had in mind for my retirement," replied Morris, as the heavy lines around his aging eyes wrinkled deeper. "But I shouldn't complain. The food isn't too bad and the nights are quiet, although you should have been here last week. Vandenberg is just a mile away. Three o'clock in the morning, they put up a rocket, and not just any rocket, a moon shot. You ever been that close to a launch? The goddamn place starts to rumble, you think you're the one going up. Amazing, how much power those things have. I wonder if they know that the guy that made sure they always had the money they needed is living here, right next store."

Morris had represented the same New York district for nearly forty years, and if he had become a master of Washington and its ways, he had lost none of his native city shrewdness. Heavyset, with broad shoulders and the hands of a mechanic, he had the garrulous manner of a seasoned, back-slapping politician. But even when he was regaling a small crowd of whiskey drinking cronies with some deal-making story, there was always something distant, a little held back, about the way he looked at you. Burdick had noticed it early on, one of the first times he had talked to the chairman in his spacious and ornate committee office, the way that whatever Morris was saying, he was always thinking something else; watching you, sizing you up, putting you in a category that would help him decide how far he could go, whether he could trust you, and, if he could, what use you could be to him.

Morris looked down at his gnarled, spotted hands, folded together on the table. A sly grin inched across his face.

"You didn't come all the way cross country to hear me talk about all the good I tried to do." He raised his eyes to Burdick's waiting gaze. "And I've known you long enough to know that you didn't come to hear me tell you that I'm innocent and should never have been convicted of something I didn't do."

Burdick leaned back in the plastic chair and studied Morris with a sad, friendly smile. He liked him, he always had. Frank Morris had not always told him everything, but he had never lied.

"Were you innocent, Frank? Were you convicted of something you didn't do?"

Morris looked past him, out the window to the courtyard and the shining blue sky above. His mouth twisted down at the corners. He blinked his eyes.

"No, I wasn't innocent. I did what they said I did." His eyes moved back to Burdick, but there was now a sense of urgency in them, as if the question of his own guilt was not the end, but only the beginning, of the story. "The interesting thing isn't that I did it—took money that I shouldn't have taken—the interesting thing is that someone found out. That wasn't an accident, Quentin. I was being taught a lesson, a lesson they wanted others to learn. They wanted me, and certain others, to know that they could destroy anyone who got out of line."

That same shrewd grin, but more serious this time, creased his mouth. He scratched his chin with the tips of two thick fingers and then, as if dismissing what he had started to say, waved his hand to the side.

"But maybe that's the reason you're here. You found out something. What do you want to know?"

Burdick did not change expression. He looked straight at Morris.

"The Four Sisters—is that who we're talking about, the people you say wanted to teach you a lesson?"

"It's the reason for all my trouble, and I'm going to be the reason for theirs."

Burdick took out a notebook. He wrote Morris's name across the top of the page, and then the words "The Four Sisters." While he was doing this, Morris stood up, stretched his arms, and then folded them across his chest. Even dressed in prison garb, blue denim trousers and a blue denim shirt, he looked impressive, someone in charge. When he was younger, the first time he ran for Congress, they said he could mesmerize an audience; that with his curly black hair and piercing blue eyes, once he started talking no one looked away, no one thought about anything except what they heard. From the very beginning, he had been a force to be reckoned with, and now, forty years later, supposedly a broken man, locked away in prison, he still had some of the same electricity, the same ability to make you want to listen, and believe.

"Remember that old line about how all politics is local? It used to be true; it isn't anymore. Politics aren't local; they're global. No one has yet quite figured that out. It's the movement of money. Look, when I was a kid, we understood the way things worked. If you had trouble, if your garbage wasn't being picked up, if you needed some help, if you needed a job, you went to someone, the ward boss, the city councilman—maybe someone in the mayor's office—and they did what they could. And then, at election time, you returned the favor. We knew something else, too. We knew that these guys we elected to office lived a lot better than they could have lived on the salaries they were paid. We knew the way money changed hands, the way that if you were a contractor and wanted to do business with the city—build the new schoolhouse or repair the potholes in the streets—you made sure some of the profit wound up in the pockets of your friends at city hall. All politics was local, because that was where you could make a deal."

Burdick's hand was flying across the page, taking everything down in a shorthand scrawl of his own devising. His hand stopped moving. He looked up at Morris.

"But you never did that, made that kind of deal. What changed? Why did you do what you did?"

Morris shrugged and looked away. He fell into a long silence, as if he was not sure even now what had led him to do the things he had.

"Maybe I was greedier than the others; maybe when there wasn't much money involved I was too afraid of getting caught. It isn't that difficult to turn down a bribe when they're counting in thousands; but millions, and all of it safe, money that will get paid in the form of salaries and stock options after you retire from Congress and become a board member for some international financial consortium? That's something else again. With that kind of money it's easy to convince yourself that you're not doing anything fundamentally wrong, and that, in any case, you deserve it. Not really convince yourself, you understand," added Morris as he sat down again, "but think that a legitimate argument could be made for doing what you might have done anyway, make certain changes that make it easier for certain companies to compete in the new global economy we keep talking about. All that needed to be done was to add certain specific requirements to some major defense procurement contracts, requirements that could only be met by firms owned and controlled by the same investment house."

"The Four Sisters," said Burdick, just to be sure.

"Yes, of course. But you need to understand that the money, the serious money, wasn't in the value of the contract itself. It was in the advance knowledge that the contract was going to them."

Quentin Burdick knew a thing or two about Wall Street and the way serious money was made.

"The jump in the price of the stock, inside information—they could buy before anyone else knew."

"Right. And then with the money they made, they bought other companies; or rather had companies they controlled do it for them, because The Four Sisters does not exist. They moved money all around the world. Some of the money they moved here came from places we supposedly don't do business with. Do you understand what I'm telling you? The Four Sisters is a shell game, a way for companies, and countries, to acquire influence that, if we knew about it, we would never permit. They're into everything: television, movies, the whole entertainment industry; newspapers, magazines, book publishing. That's when I started to question what they were doing, when I threatened to go public and bring it all to a stop. And that's why I'm here— because they would not let that happen."

Burdick pushed aside the notebook and sat back. He did not have a doubt that Morris was telling the truth.

"What about Constable? Was the president involved?"

A look of cynicism and contempt shot across Morris's tired face.

"He was never about anything except himself. I went to him when I found out what I just told you. You know what he told me?—That none of it mattered, that there was nothing to worry about, that we had not done anything wrong, that no one would ever find out." Morris could still not quite believe it. "You imagine? In the same breath: we haven't done anything wrong, and no one will ever find out! Well, someone found out, didn't they? Someone found out because my good friend Robert Constable, the guy I helped elect president, had to tell his friends, and his friends made sure there was enough evidence that when someone tipped off the FBI that I had taken a bribe they could find the money—money, by the way, in an account in the Cayman Islands I didn't know I had."

Instead of cynicism, there was a look of something harsher, and more unforgiving, on Frank Morris's face, a sense of retribution that Burdick did not understand.

"They had to shut me up," Morris continued, the look bitter and aggrieved. "The way to do that was to discredit me, make me out to be a liar and a thief, someone no one could believe. And they succeeded. But they must have had a different problem with our good friend the president, something they could only solve with more drastic measures."

"What are you saying?" cried Burdick, wondering if in his bitterness and rage, Morris had lost his senses. "Constable died of a heart attack the night before I was supposed to see him."

"To talk to him about The Four Sisters?" asked Morris with a quick, eager movement of his eyes that said he was certain he was right.

"That's what I told him, but—"

"Do you really think that was just a coincidence? You don't know what you're dealing with. The Four Sisters isn't just a bank that moves money around in ways it shouldn't. Do you know anything about it? Do you know who the head of it is?"

"I didn't even know what The Four Sisters was until you told me," admitted Burdick.

The door suddenly opened and the guard appeared. Burdick had been there an hour. It was time to leave.

"Come back tomorrow," said Morris with new urgency. "There are things you need to know."

CHAPTER 7

CHECKING INTO THE first motel he found, Burdick went back through his notes, making sure, while everything was fresh in his mind, that it was all there, that he had not forgotten to make a record of the most important parts of what Frank Morris had said. Then, when he was finished, he went back to the beginning and from those fragmentary shorthand notes, wrote out in longhand a full account of what he had been told. He had learned in his years of reporting that even the best memory failed after a fairly short time to recall in all its nuanced specificity the language of a conversation. This was likely to be the biggest story of his career, and he could not afford to make a mistake.

Burdick worked straight through until he had it all down on paper, not just what Frank Morris had said, but how the once all-powerful chairman of the House Ways and Means Committee had looked and sounded, the changes that had made him seem at times a pale imitation of his former self. When he was finally finished, Burdick started to turn on the television to see what news he had missed, but then decided he was too tired to care. He was asleep almost the moment his head hit the pillow.

When he went back to the prison late the next morning, he found Frank Morris more energized, more combative, as if now that he had made his first confession, told Burdick what really had happened, he could not wait to tell him everything. There was something else, another, darker aspect, to the change. Beneath the apparent eagerness to get on with it, to tell Burdick what he knew, there was now a strange, lingering fatalism in his eyes, a belief—no, more than that, a certainty—that what Burdick was going to write would be the last thing that would be written about him, that after this there was nothing.

"Cancer," he explained with a shrug, a show of indifference he expected from himself. "Six months, maybe less." Then, flashing a crooked, modest smile meant to put his visitor at his ease, he added, "Unless that fucking Frenchman gets me first."

"That—?"

"What we talked about yesterday, The Four Sisters. A Frenchman owns it, 'de la' something. I'll remember later. I only met him once, and we didn't exactly have a conversation. There were a dozen of us, members of Congress on a fact-finding trip in Europe, looking at ways to improve trade, that kind of thing—mainly an excuse to travel at taxpayer expense. There was a reception in Paris, hosted by their foreign ministry. The room was full of bankers and industrialists, but it quickly became apparent that they all deferred to him. And I have to tell you, he was one impressive son-of-a-bitch. He spoke perfect English—no accent—like someone who had gone to an Ivy League college, though I don't think he did. I remember someone saying that he was from one of France's oldest families, but I'm not even sure about that. All I know for certain is that he knew more about American history than anyone I've ever met. He told us things about our history I didn't know, and he did it in the course of one of those short welcoming speeches that usually don't say anything. He may have memorized it, it may have been just off the cuff—he didn't have any notes, he didn't read it—but he stood there, and without a false start or a word out of place summarized two hundred years of French-American relations. Maybe that was the reason I didn't like him: it was all too perfect."

Morris looked down at his hands. His eyes seemed to draw back on themselves. A shrewd smile cut across his mouth, a sign that he now understood something he should have known before.

"It's always smart to make a mistake, trip over a word now and then, show the people you're talking to that you're human, just like them. Make a mistake, and then laugh at yourself; no one wants to vote against you if you do that. But this guy, I think he'd kill himself before he'd make a mistake, or admit it if he did. He wasn't arrogant, not the way we usually mean. It went deeper than that. It was almost the opposite of arrogance, someone embarrassed because what he was doing was so easy. Look, I'm no scholar, but I read to all my kids when they were little. That's what it was like, a grown-up talking to a bunch of children. That isn't arrogance; that's someone operating on a different plane, someone who knows how to do something, and someone just starting to learn."

Burdick had stopped making notes. He was too intent on catching the changing expression on Morris's face, the added meaning it gave to what he said. Morris had always had a native shrewdness about the character of other people, a way of gauging what, despite their various levels of self-deceit, they really wanted, but Burdick had never heard him describe anyone quite like this, someone who did not seem to fit any of the normal categories by which vanity and ambition were measured. And there was something more. He was not sure what it was, but he was certain that Morris had left out a crucial part of the equation.

"That isn't the only reason you didn't like him, is it?"

Morris nodded in agreement.

"You don't notice it at first. He smiles when he talks to you—he smiled when he shook my hand—but his eyes… they look right through you in a way that makes you feel invisible. But then, when someone has as much money as he's supposed to have, most people probably are only too glad if he looks at them at all. I noticed, though, which, when you think about it, only makes me worse. I was as eager as anyone else to get what I could from him, or rather from the organization he controls, because, of course, I never did any business directly with him. He left that sort of thing to other people, Americans mainly, who worked for one of his subsidiaries."

Burdick started making notes again.

"Americans. Can you give me names?"

"Sure, but it won't do much good. They didn't do anything criminal, they didn't break any laws. They acted just like any other interest that has business before the Congress. They made their case for legislation, and I listened. They didn't come with envelopes stuffed with cash. It isn't what any one of them did; it's the connections that exist among them all, the way that all these supposedly separate entities are held together at the top: like puppets on a string, and the string held by one man, but the string all tangled up, twisted in a dozen different directions. Here, let me show you what I mean."

Morris took Burdick's notebook and quickly drew a parallel set of boxes connected by two different lines.

"You have a company operating in the United States. It's a subsidiary of another company with headquarters in Great Britain, which in turn is a subsidiary of a company owned, or apparently owned, by a company in Bahrain, a company in which a controlling interest is owned by—you guessed it—a certain French investment firm. Then another American company, controlled by another company based overseas, and that company in turn is…. You get the idea. Add to that the ability to move money from one company to the next, from one country to another, and to do it endlessly, back and forth, move it electronically at the speed of light.—No one can trace it, no one can keep up. No one can measure how much influence it is buying and what the people who control it are going to do next. All you can know is that whoever sits on top of all this, whoever is in control, can do damn near anything he wants—bring an economy to its knees if that serves his purposes."

Morris was breathing hard. Beads of perspiration had started to form on his forehead. He leaned back and shook his head, his eyes full of regret at what he had done.

"Jean de la Valette, that's the Frenchman's name. Maybe the most powerful man in the world and there aren't six people in this country who even know he exists. Even the people who head the companies he controls don't know anything about him. They report to other people, who don't know much more themselves. A European financial consortium, that's the phrase you'll hear; a group of institutions that contribute to the efficiency of the financial markets. What could be less threatening than something that sounds as dull as that? The country is being sold right in front of us, and we're too damn blind to see it. And I get to go to my grave knowing I helped."

Morris scratched the back of his head. A look of discouragement swept over his eyes.

"I'm not sure there's a difference, but I didn't think I was selling out my country. I thought I was doing myself a favor, and while I didn't kid myself and think what I was doing was honest, I didn't think it was going to hurt anyone else. Some people were going to make a lot of money; some people always do. And this time I was going to be one of them. And then, when I found out what they were really up to, it was too late. But Constable—he knew what was going on and it didn't stop him."

Morris rolled his shoulders forward until he was hunched over the table. His jaw moved slowly side to side as he reconsidered the judgment which just the moment before he had uttered with such certainty.

"Maybe he had to do it. Maybe he had to buy her off." Morris leaned back again, stroking his chin. "The one thing you always knew about those two was that whatever kept them together, it wasn't love."

Burdick put down his pen. There was a question he still had to ask, a question he would not have thought of had Morris not already seemed to answer it the day before.

"How serious were you when you suggested that Constable did not die of a heart attack, that he was murdered? All the reports say—"

"Screw the reports. That stuff is all rigged. They'd never let out that he was murdered. That's all the country would be talking about: Who murdered Robert Constable and why? You think the Kennedy assassination led to conspiracy theories? What do you think would happen with something like this? I read the papers, I see what's on television. There are already hints—rumors, according to the cable tabloid networks—that someone might have been there with him the night he died. Died of a heart attack while getting laid, that's what they keep insinuating."

"But you don't know that he didn't die of a heart attack, whether or not he was alone. He had a history."

Morris gave him a caustic, laughing glance.

"He had a history for a lot of things. Did he die of a heart attack, like they say? Yeah, maybe—but did that just happen because his time was up, or he got a little too excited in bed? Or was it caused by something else? You ask me if I know for certain if he was murdered. No, but that's what I believe. He knew too much, and he wasn't someone you could trust. That's what Constable was always too damn stupid to understand. Once he betrayed me, once he told them what I was going to do, they knew what he was like, that he'd sell his mother if he had to, which meant he'd sell them too. You were going to see him; he knew why you were coming. What makes you think that someone who works for them wasn't listening in on your call? What makes you think that one of the people that worked for him, someone who kept track of his schedule, wasn't working for them? Let me tell you something, for all the obvious disadvantages, I have more privacy here in prison than you have out there."

"If you're right," said Burdick, "if he was murdered—how do I find out? Who is going to tell me?"

Morris sunk his chin on his chest. He tapped two fingers on the table and stared straight ahead.

"Start with who feels the worst about what happened," he said after thinking about it. "The agent in charge, the Secret Service agent who was there that night, if you can find him—Ask him about the woman, the one that, according to all the rumors you've heard, was in the room with Constable when he died. Listen, figure it out. The guy is there to protect the president. The president dies. It looks like a heart attack. The girl—if there was a girl, and if there wasn't there had to be someone else—is in the room. The agent had to know she was there. Christ, you couldn't guard Constable for ten minutes and not know what he was like. The girl is there. The first question the agent had to deal with was what to do with her. The president is dead. What is your next obligation—what do you do? If you do things by the book, you hold her there and make a full report, but this is a president we're talking about. What would you do, what would we both do? Protect his reputation, save his family—whatever you might think about his wife—the shame and embarrassment of a useless scandal. That's my guess, anyway, about what he might have done."

Morris moved his head like a boxer, anticipating an opponent's next move. His eyes narrowed into a look of intense concentration.

"He gets rid of her, gets her out of the way, makes sure no one knows she was ever there. But then what happens, if it turns out it wasn't a simple heart attack, if it turns out it was murder? Was the girl involved, the girl he let go? If that's what happened, this guy is now a mess, damned both for what he did and what he did not do."

Morris nodded in agreement with his own conjecture. He looked at Burdick.

"If you can find him, if you can get him to talk to you, he might just spill his guts, tell you what he knows. He's probably dying to clear his conscience, to make things right. Remember, if it was a murder, in addition to everything else, he's now being forced to play a part in a cover-up. Do you think he wants to spend the rest of his life worrying about what's going to happen when someone finds out what he did? Would you?"

Burdick glanced at his watch. If he stayed much longer he would miss his flight and have to stay another day. He folded up the notebook and tucked it back in his pocket. Morris did not want him to go.

"Not yet. There's something you should see."

Burdick watched with a sense of foreboding as Frank Morris stood up and began to unbutton his shirt.

"At the end of my trial, just after the judge sentenced me, when they took me back to jail, I got this."

Pulling his shirt open, he pointed to a three-inch scar on his left side, just below his ribs.

"It was a warning. They were telling me to do my time and not talk to anyone. When I said I was going to die of cancer unless that fucking Frenchman killed me first, I wasn't kidding. But listen to me: write the story, all of it, including what I did. If they come for me, at least I'll die knowing that I got them back."

They shook hands and said goodbye. They both knew they would never see each other again, that within months Morris would be dead and that Burdick was not coming back, but they liked each other too much not to lie. Burdick said he would see him soon, and Morris claimed there was still a chance he might get better. And so they parted, better friends than they had been before.

Burdick thought about that as he drove south along the Pacific shore, back toward Santa Barbara on his way to the airport in Los Angeles and his scheduled flight; he thought about the way that, looking death in the face, Morris had come once again to the knowledge of how he ought to live, how he had thrown away everything for the chance to end his life a wealthy man, and how desperate he now was to change that and make everything right.

It was a long drive, more than three hours, but Burdick made his flight and six hours later was home in New York. He was walking through the airport when he first learned what had happened. Glancing at a television set as he passed by a bar, he stopped when he saw a picture on the screen of Frank Morris. He moved close enough to hear that, according to the reports just coming in, the former chairman of the House Ways and Means Committee had been killed in prison, stabbed to death with a knife.

Burdick's blood ran cold. He looked behind him, and then he began to move quickly, trying to lose himself in the crowd. He did not believe for a minute that Morris's death could have been just another prison stabbing, a mindless act of violence. Someone knew that Frank Morris had talked to a reporter, and they had known it right away. They killed him because the warning they had given him earlier had not worked. Morris had been right: they must have had Constable murdered as well. And if they were willing to do that, murder to keep their secret, there was no reason to think they would not kill him as well.

Burdick began to walk faster, faster with each breath he took, until he was outside on the sidewalk, frantically waving for a cab. He was on the bridge into Manhattan when he remembered who he wanted to call. It was late, but that did not matter. He had his home numbers, both the one on the west coast and the one in Washington, D.C. He felt a sudden surge of relief when Bobby Hart answered on the third ring.

CHAPTER 8

BOBBY HART HAD not been able to stop thinking about what Robert Constable's widow had sworn him not to tell anyone, that instead of dying of a heart attack, the former president had been murdered. That had been shocking enough, but the cold indifference with which she had reported it, her only thought what might have to be done to cover it up, had him shaking his head. At least he had had the presence of mind to insist that while he would find out what he could about who might have had a reason to have her husband killed, there would have to be a full-scale investigation. He had made that quite clear. He was not going to become part of a conspiracy, no matter how noble its intention, to keep the public from learning the truth about how the president of the United States had really died.

Hart stared out the window of the high-speed train he was taking to New York. He felt trapped by a promise that, as Laura had reminded him, he had had no real reason to make. It was almost uncanny, the way he had been maneuvered into it. He did not owe anything to Robert Constable or his memory, and he owed even less to his widow, but she had somehow made it seem that he did. It had been subtle, even oblique. It was nothing that she actually said, but rather the manner of the way she treated him, an equal partner in a shared responsibility. Because he was now in a position to do certain things, to get answers where few others could even ask questions, and she was now suddenly vulnerable and alone, he had an obligation to do something before the story got out and things went insane.

They were twenty minutes from the station, twenty minutes from Manhattan, the end of the short, three-hour trip that Austin Pearce had asked him to make so he could talk to him alone. The secretary of the treasury during the first term of the Constable administration had something important to discuss, something about the same foreign investment firm that Quentin Burdick had apparently been asking questions about.

And now Burdick, for reasons of his own, wanted to see him as well. He had known Burdick for years, but he had never heard him sound the way he had late last night on the telephone. Burdick might look like the proverbial nearsighted bookworm who, with his halting, diffident speech, was afraid of his own shadow, but he had once been a soldier in Vietnam, decorated for his bravery. Quentin Burdick was not afraid of anyone, which made the whole thing even more unaccountable.

Ten minutes from the station. Eager to get a start, some of the passengers began to grab their luggage from the overhead racks. Hart folded his arms and leaned closer to the window, thinking more about the Constables as the skyline of New York drew closer. Presidents were often divided between those, like most of the early ones, who came from the country, and those, like Kennedy and the Roosevelts, Reagan and some of the other, more recent ones, who had their roots in the life of the cities. Constable, on the other hand, seemed to occupy a position that in a way was neither and both. He had come from a small town and become governor of a small state, but there had always been something about him, a grasping ambition that, even when he had the presidency, never seemed to stop. It was an ambition that seemed to embody that same relentless search for fame and fortune that had drawn so many young men and young women from the rural heartland of the nation to the glittering opportunities of New York. Both of them, husband and wife, had acquired by habit and long practice what every native New Yorker had bred in his bones: the ability—what many who lived other places thought the charlatan's ability—to make you think that whatever they wanted was something you really thought they should have.

It explained that cold indifference that Hart had not at first been able to understand. Whether manufactured or authentic, it had been part of the appeal. It allowed Hillary Constable to make it appear that she was only asking him to do what was good for the country, to make the kind of sacrifice she had been making for years: protect, so far as he legitimately could, the president's reputation, find out the reason he had been killed before anyone else knew he had been murdered. Because if the story got out before they knew what had happened, the speculation would not end in their lifetimes. Every rumor, every unfounded allegation, all the sordid details of Robert Constable's storied life, would become the stuff of legend, a tawdry myth that the truth, whatever it was, would never entirely dispel.

The train pulled into the station, and a few minutes later Hart stepped outside into the blistering New York heat. In Washington the heat became thick and oppressive, seeping into your pores, making movement a burden and ambition someone else's mindless dream; here it seemed to make everyone move more quickly, more determined to get to cooler, air-conditioned places where they could get to work. Hart checked his watch as he jumped into a cab. The train had run late, but he still had a few minutes before he was supposed to meet Quentin Burdick.

"I'm in a hurry," he told the driver.

The driver gave him a look in the rearview mirror that made Hart feel a fool. They were in the middle of Manhattan at a time when you were lucky if traffic moved at all. Twenty minutes and two miles later, the cab pulled up in front of a nondescript East Village restaurant with a faded, painted sign, the kind of place no out of town tourist would think to visit, and no one in the city with serious money would think to go. It was the kind of place that the ignorant would have called with a shudder a joint or a dive, but where those who had an ear for serious music would still gather late on a smoke-filled night to listen to some of the best jazz, and drink some of the worst booze, in Manhattan.

There were no jazz musicians now; no one beating out a new cool rhythm on the piano, no one blowing dreamlike on a trumpet's burnished brass. There was hardly anyone here at all, two middle-aged women drinking coffee at a table in front, and Quentin Burdick, sitting quietly in the back. Hart blinked into the darkness, and then, as Burdick rose to greet him, made his way through the scattered empty tables in between.

"It's good to see you, Bobby," said Burdick as they shook hands. "Thanks for doing this on such short notice."

Hart sank onto a hard wooden chair and suddenly noticed the pictures covering the wall, jazz musicians, dozens of them, some of them long forgotten, but some of them still famous. He smiled to himself as his gaze came to rest on one just above Burdick's shoulder. Burdick turned around to look.

"Erroll Garner. Did you ever see him play?" asked Hart, with a distant, wistful look. "In person, I mean. I wish I had. He could not read music, could not read a note, and other than maybe Oscar Peterson, the greatest jazz pianist there ever was."

Burdick's eyes lighted with surprise. He had been tense, nervous, not quite sure why he had asked Bobby Hart if he could see him, not quite sure what he was going to say when he saw him; but now that Hart was here, now that he heard him start to talk about something that none of the other politicians he knew would ever think to talk about, he began to feel a little more comfortable.

"I didn't know you liked jazz that much. I guess I didn't even know you liked music. It's easy to forget sometimes that someone in Washington might actually have a life outside politics."

A young, clean-shaven waiter, an aspiring actor from some Midwestern college, if Hart had had to guess, took their order. Neither of them wanted anything to eat. Burdick, who had already had one cup of coffee while he waited, ordered another. Hart, after a moment's hesitation, asked for a beer.

"You didn't have to come, Bobby. When I asked if I could see you, I meant I'd come there."

The waiter brought Hart a beer and Burdick a second cup of coffee. Hart took a long drink, held the cold bottle in both hands, leaned back, and looked at Burdick.

"You didn't tell me."

"Didn't tell you what?"

"Erroll Garner."

"No, I never saw him play. I saw Oscar Peterson, though." The memory relaxed him, and in some degree diminished the sense of urgency that had not really left him since the night before. "Twice, both times right here, late at night when guys would come in after some other show they had just done, something they had been paid for, and just play for themselves and whoever wanted to listen."

Bobby Hart was watching closely, measuring almost without knowing he was doing it the meaning of each small change of expression on Burdick's narrow, mobile face. It was one of the reasons, the main one perhaps, that so many people felt so comfortable talking to Hart: the way he knew how to listen, to ask the kind of questions that made them want to tell him more.

"There are certain advantages in living in a city like New York, aren't there? I would have given anything to see Oscar Peterson play." Hart paused and took another drink, and then, as if that was all he was going to have, put the bottle on the table and shoved it off to the side. "What is it, Quentin? What's going on? When you called last night…even if I didn't have to be here anyway, I would have come up. You sounded terrible."

"Frank Morris died. He was killed, stabbed to death in prison."

"I know. It was on the news last night; it's in all the papers today. Too bad. I knew him, liked him. He was always straight with me. But what does that have to do with—?"

"I was there, at the prison, just before it happened. That was the reason he was killed, the reason he was murdered—because he talked to me!"

Hart planted both feet on the floor and bent forward on his elbows. He searched Burdick's eyes.

"Because he talked to you? Why? What makes you so sure? Things like that happen, you know. They don't always happen for a reason. People get killed in prison."

"He told me he was dying of cancer, that he had maybe six months, unless 'that fucking Frenchman gets me first.' That's what he said, and he meant it, too. He knew what he was talking about. The Four Sisters—have you heard that name before?"

Hart drew back and tapped his fingers on the table.

"It's the story you've been working on now for months."

A puzzled smile darted along Burdick's thin lips. He began to fidget with the bowtie that had become something of a trademark for him.

"How did you know that I was working on that?" Then he remembered. "Of course! I talked to Senator Finnegan, and he must have…."

"Charlie asked me if I had heard about it. I hadn't; but then, when they buried Constable, after the service, at the reception at his house, I heard the name again. Austin Pearce started talking about it. He said he wanted to see me. That's why I had to be in New York."

"That means Pearce must have known, or must have learned about it. He's certainly smart enough to have figured it out."

"Figured it out? What did Frank Morris tell you? What did he know that would make someone want to murder him?" But before Burdick could respond, a startled expression flashed across Hart's eyes. "Morris said he was going to die of cancer if 'that fucking Frenchman' did not get him first? When I was there, at the Constables' house, talking to Pearce, he gestured toward a Frenchman he said was the head of The Four Sisters. I've forgotten the name. He was just going through the receiving line when Pearce pointed him out."

"Jean de la Valette," said Burdick, with a quick nod. "Morris only met him once, said he was impressive, but that he didn't much like him, and that was before he found out what was going on."

"What was going on, Quentin? What did Morris tell you?"

"You won't believe it. I didn't believe it, not at first anyway. I went out there to see him on nothing more than a hunch, and because, quite frankly, I didn't know what else to do. I had been working on The Four Sisters story for a long time, but I didn't really have anything I could use. I knew—I couldn't prove, but I knew—that a lot of money had changed hands and that Robert Constable had gotten a lot of it, millions of dollars, over a period of several years.

"It was only when I stumbled on the name The Four Sisters that things started to break. I had been trying to get an interview with Constable, but I could not even get close—and then I had the name." Burdick looked at Hart and shook his head at how simple things had then become. "It was like a password. As soon as I said it, things began to happen. Instead of being put off, told by one of his assistants that they would see what they could do, Constable himself called me. You remember how he operated. We were suddenly old friends. He could not wait to see me, could not wait to talk, but I could tell he was worried." Burdick hesitated, reconsidering what he had said. "No, not worried—scared—though I was not sure of what. Exposure, I thought. Fear of what might happen if the truth of what he had been doing, taking millions for things he did while he was in office, should ever come out. But now I think that it might have been more than that; that he wasn't worried about the potential scandal—good God, if there was ever anyone who was not afraid of what a scandal could do, it was Robert Constable—he was worried about what someone might do to him."

Hart was cautious. He had made a promise to Hillary Constable. He looked at Burdick with a blank expression.

"What someone might do to him?"

Burdick shot him a questioning glance. The mask behind which Hart had tried to hide had not worked.

"Is that what Austin Pearce wanted to talk to you about?—What someone might have done, the possibility that Constable did not die of natural causes?"

"He did not say anything like that to me," answered Hart truthfully. "Is that what Frank Morris told you?"

Burdick hesitated, but only for a moment.

"He didn't know that, but that's what he thought: that Constable didn't die of a heart attack, that he was murdered instead. Look, Bobby, I've been doing this a long time. I covered Constable the first time he ran for president. I covered him when he was in the White House. He didn't have a principled bone in his body; there wasn't anything he wouldn't say or do to win. But this!—What Frank Morris told me—I wouldn't have believed it possible for anyone who was president, not even Constable. I would have thought he had, not too much integrity—I knew him too well for that—but too much sense. That was my mistake. I had forgotten that part of his attraction, the reason why people who did not know him, who had never met him, who had never even seen him except on television liked him as much as they did, was this bigger than life quality he had, this feeling that nothing could touch him, that whatever happened, whatever kind of hole he dug for himself, he could always get out of it and end up back in control, stronger, more popular, than ever. The stupid son-of-a-bitch believed it, thought he was too smart, too important, to ever get caught.

"I think maybe that's why Morris did it, took money he knew he shouldn't. It was the whole atmosphere Constable brought with him, the sense that there weren't any limits; that you could do whatever you wanted and take whatever you needed. Morris told me everything. It wasn't bribery."

Narrowing his eyes into a hard, relentless stare, Burdick lapsed into a long silence, as he conjured up the double vision of what Frank Morris had been like when he was one of the most powerful men on the Hill, someone everyone wanted to know, and the last time, barely twenty-four hours ago, when he had become just another numbered inmate in federal prison. Burdick looked up, slightly embarrassed.

"It wasn't bribery," he continued, "the way they said it was at his trial. It was bigger than that, hundreds of millions of dollars were involved, and The Four Sisters was right in the middle of it. In the beginning, Morris thought it was a scheme to get certain government contracts for some of the companies, American companies The Four Sisters controlled. But eventually he discovered that it was more than that."

"More than that?" asked Hart, intensely interested. "The Four Sisters is a private investment firm, though from what I hear, it may be—that phrase you just used—'more than that.'"

Burdick's eyebrows rose up like a pair of open umbrellas. There was a grim, rueful quality in his expression, the look of someone who had been forced to face, if not an awful truth, an awful possibility.

"It may be Murder Incorporated on a global scale."

"You think they killed Constable, and then killed Morris?"

Burdick's bookish mouth twitched nervously at the corner. He blinked several times in rapid, thoughtful succession.

"After what happened to Morris, after what happened to me—yes, I do."

"After what happened to you?" For the first time, Hart felt a sense of alarm. "What happened? When, last night?"

Burdick dismissed, or tried to dismiss, the significance of what he had just said. There was something he wanted to talk about first, something important he thought Hart should know.

"Morris discovered that The Four Sisters had created a kind of parallel financial universe, a system that allowed it to move money from one place to another, one country to another, without anyone knowing anything about it. Think what that means. A company in this country needs capital; a bank in Europe is willing to arrange it. The money comes from another country, a country willing to pay for the chance to obtain some degree of influence over what happens here. Think of what you could do, if you have the billions of dollars necessary to gain a controlling interest in just a handful of the corporations that among them decide what we read and what we watch. Frank Morris knew what it meant. He was willing to take money—he admitted that—but not for something like this.

"Constable was involved. He was the one who first suggested that Morris meet with some people who were interested in making it easier for foreign investors to do business here. Morris went to Constable—the president of the United States, for Christ sake!—and told him what he'd discovered, told him that even though he had taken money he would go to the FBI himself if that was the only way to stop it. Constable told him to forget it, that everything would be all right, that they had not done anything wrong, and that no one would find out. Yes, that's exactly what he said, according to Morris: that they hadn't done anything wrong and that no one would find out!

"When Constable said everything would be all right, he meant all right for him. The next thing Morris knew, he was framed for bribery and sent to prison to make sure he didn't tell anyone besides Constable what he knew. But he told me, and before I get back to New York, he's murdered, and now they may try to murder me. They know I talked to him; they can guess what he told me. Last night, after I called you from the airport, I went home. Someone had broken in, torn the place apart, stolen my computer. They were looking for whatever files I'd been keeping on The Four Sisters, the story I was planning to write. They didn't get much. I keep everything at my office at the paper. I don't think they'll try anything there."

"Where did you stay last night?"

"At a hotel here in the Village, just up the street."

"You better stay there. What Morris told you, that Constable did not die of natural causes, that he was murdered—he was right. I can't tell you how I know Constable was murdered, only that I do. But I don't know why he was killed, whether it had to do with this Four Sisters business, or was for some other reason."

Burdick wanted to be sure.

"You know for certain that he was murdered? You know that as a fact?"

"That's what I was told."

They left the dark seclusion of the bar and restaurant and went outside. The heat was shimmering off the dirty gray sidewalk and the air had the thick dull taste of red brick dust. They lingered for a moment in the choking haze, remembering, each of them, what it had been like when they were young and single and their only thought on a hot sticky summer day had been for the night, and the girl, and the jazz that when you heard it told you that nothing would ever be as good as this again.

"I better go," said Hart, as he started toward the street. "I meant what I said," he shouted over his shoulder. "Don't go back. Stay at the hotel until it's safe."

Burdick, feeling better, laughed as he shouted back, "That might never happen."

CHAPTER 9

STEPPING OUT OF the cab, Hart looked up at the skyscraper towering high above him at the corner of the park. It seemed to him out of place, a strange mismatch in which money, New York money, had won; a losing contest in which taste, and the desire to preserve the old values, had been all but forgotten in the thoughtless desire to find something bigger and more opulent to build. The property that bordered Central Park, the gray stone buildings that ran along Fifth Avenue and Central Park West, most of them built before the war, had always been the most sought after real estate in the city, and among the most expensive in the world. It had all seemed to fit, to be as much a part of the park as the Metropolitan Museum of Art or the zoo, a picture postcard of life, rich and elegant, in the middle of Manhattan. But money formed a democracy of its own, and the majority, those who had the most of it, wanted a view. And so now, a block from the Plaza and the St. Regis, you could buy an apartment, or rent space for an office, in the kind of glass and steel high-rise monstrosity that critics, and not just critics, thought better suited for Singapore or some oil-rich place in the desert.

An unrepentant liberal, Hart was, when it came to places he liked, something of a traditionalist. He often explained to his California friends that the dismal stifling summer weather he had to endure in Washington was a minor price to pay to live and work in a city full of history. His favorite fact, which he thought had saved Washington from going the way of every other American city, was the law passed shortly after the Capitol had been built banning forever the construction of any other building that tall. No one was to be allowed to look down on the Capitol of the United States. In New York, the main thing seemed to be to have enough money to look down on everyone else.

That was a judgment, but it was also an abstraction; a generalization that had nothing to do with individuals, except as it explained, or helped to explain, something about the conditions under which they lived, the set of assumptions, the ingrained and largely unconscious way they expected everyone to behave. Austin Pearce had made the move to an office on the highest floor allowed for commercial use as a matter of convenience, and because, as he explained when Hart commented on the view, they had been in the other place for years.

"This was new, and available, and they said we needed more space. I'm not sure we didn't have too much before, but that's another story." He saw the look of confusion on Hart's face. "Bigger isn't always better; better is knowing what your limits are."

He looked at Hart as if this last remark carried a lesson, the importance of which he was sure both of them understood. He looked away, and then immediately looked back, searching Hart's eyes again.

"I'm sorry," he said, suddenly embarrassed. "Please, sit down."

He gestured toward the chair in front of an antique desk, purchased at a Sotheby's auction some years earlier. The desk was not just his prize possession; he had, as he was quick to admit, an almost sensual attachment to it.

"Touch it," he said, smiling with his eyes like a parent with a child. "Touch it; it's all right. Feel it, how cold it is. Now touch it just a little longer. Feel the warmth? The first owner, so the story goes, the woman it was made for, was an Italian princess who had several husbands and many lovers, some of whom she seduced into helping her get rid of a husband she no longer wanted or needed. Maybe that's what explains it; the way the wood feels when you touch it long enough: the warm blood of a cold-hearted woman. After I left the administration, I took to calling it 'Hillary.'"

There was an impish quality to Austin Pearce's patient smile that Hart found irresistible.

"You like my story—good! I'll tell you something even stranger: It's true. I did exactly that, started talking to the desk, calling it all sorts of names, when I first got back from those four years in Washington." He threw up his small, smooth hands in the nostalgia of a past frustration. "There was no one else I could talk to, no one I could tell the truth! No one would have believed me if I had."

"The truth about what?" asked Hart, more curious now than ever about why Austin Pearce had been so eager to see him.

"About what the president did, the arrangement he entered into with that organization I told you about, The Four Sisters. That was the reason I left at the end of his first term. I would have stayed. I thought I could do some good at Treasury, help put the country's finances on a better footing, bring a little sanity to the way we raise and spend the public's money. Then I discovered that hundreds of millions of dollars, more than a billion by the time I uncovered what was going on, had been moved through various accounts, money appropriated for various foreign aid projects, into a bank in Europe and from there into the hands of certain clandestine organizations in the Middle East. The bank was the French investment firm, The Four Sisters. The money was being used to finance a war, a secret war against some of the governments in the region we did not like. This wasn't using the CIA to work behind the scenes to try to take down a government; this wasn't giving covert assistance to some group within a country trying to overthrow an oppressive regime. This was something different. I did not understand it at first, though I thought I did."

"You thought you did?" asked Hart, following every word.

"Yes. At first I thought—I assumed—that the bank was acting alone, that someone there was diverting the funds for some purpose of his own. I thought the bank might be working with someone in the French government, and that, with or without the knowledge of the government, they were trying to exercise some influence in the Middle East. The French are like that, always willing to cooperate, but jealous of our power. I have friends there, some of whom I trust. I made inquiries, but no one knew a thing. I couldn't do anything more on my own, so I went to the president and told him what I had discovered."

The intensity seemed to fade from Pearce's expression as he remembered back to what had happened. The angry bitterness he had felt at the time was now, when he began to talk about it, more a sense of regret, as of a possibility, a chance to achieve something permanent and important, lost forever.

"We were in the Oval Office, just the two of us. It was eleven o'clock on a Tuesday morning, two weeks after he had won election to a second term. He was always at extremes, and that morning proved it. When I walked in, he looked like he owned the world. He greeted me like I was his best friend and—you know the way he had—for a few moments I felt like I really was. He started telling me about all the great things, now that he had a second term, we were going to do; things he could not do in his first term, when he still had to worry about an election. Then he noticed that I did not seem to share in his excitement, that I had something on my mind. He never liked it when someone did that, held back, even if just a little, from his own enthusiasm. He asked me what the trouble was."

Pearce had a look that seemed to accuse himself of negligence, of failing to grasp what he should have understood, that what he had uncovered was too big, too important, for the president not to have known.

"When I told him what I'd found out, that all the money that was supposed to go for one purpose was being used for another, and that this French investment firm was responsible, he went into a rage. And I mean that literally. He jumped out of his chair, his face all red, started pounding on the desk, swearing at me, telling me I didn't know what I was doing, that I was going to jeopardize everything he had been trying to do. I didn't know what he was talking about. I just sat there, my mouth open, dumbfounded by what was going on. He was so angry, for a moment I thought he might hit me. He told me it was none of my business, that I was supposed to run things at Treasury, that this was State Department business, that how was he supposed to trust me if I was not interested in doing my own job. That's when he did it," said Pearce, shaking his head over what had happened next. "He became quite calm again. The anger was still there—I could see it in his eyes—but now it was something more permanent, something, I swear, close to hatred, the kind that doesn't go away. I had come to save his presidency; I left with instructions to submit my resignation."

Hart could not believe it. Austin Pearce had been the one member of Constable's cabinet that almost everyone thought irreplaceable, a judgment that nothing done by his successor at Treasury had changed.

"He fired you? But wait—he told you that what you discovered about this missing money was something the State Department knew about, that it was something they were doing?"

A look of cold disdain crossed Pearce's face.

"He lied. No one over at State knew anything about it."

"You checked?"

"I made a few discreet inquiries."

Hart remembered what Pearce had said to him at the reception after Constable's funeral.

"What about The Four Sisters? What about your friend...?"

"Jean de la Valette? It would be going a little too far to say we were friends. 'Distant colleagues' might be more accurate. We inhabit different parts of the same world: the international finance system, such as it is."

There was a long, thoughtful silence. Furrowing his brow, Pearce rubbed his hands together, as he struggled to find the best way to explain what he was still not quite sure he understood.

"We've spent time together, attended some of the same conferences; we've even had dinner. But know him, the way I think I know you—have a sense of what he might do in a given circumstance, whether, when the chips were down, he was someone I could trust? No. Though I suppose I could say that—we both could say that, couldn't we?—about a lot of people we've met; maybe even most of the people we know."

He looked at Hart, not with a cynic's grin, but with the gentle smile of a man who had learned to appreciate the few people he knew were his friends.

"It's impossible to get more than a fleeting impression of who he really is," continued Pearce. "He has a different frame of reference, a different sense of proportion about things. We think in terms of how what happened in the last election changed things, and how different things might be after the next one. He thinks in terms of the way things were changed by the French Revolution. I said something about this to you before, how that family of his goes back hundreds, maybe even a thousand years, and the kind of perspective that must give."

Hart studied him closely, searching his eyes for a deeper sense of what he meant.

"But despite that, you liked him? You said he was charming, urbane. You said he was one of the most fascinating men you had met."

Pearce tilted his head, an amused, slightly puzzled expression in his eyes.

"Liked him? Yes, I suppose," he replied, though he sounded none too sure about it. "Fascinated by him?—Who wouldn't be fascinated by someone with a history like that?"

Pearce made an idle, backward movement with his hand. It was a gesture meant to underscore the obvious meaning of his surroundings, the level of success that most other men would have given anything to have achieved.

"I do this for a living—watch and try to calibrate the movements of the financial markets—and I've become reasonably good at it, but I don't find it particularly interesting. What I really love is history, European history mainly, but almost anything about the past. So it isn't too difficult to understand that I would find Jean de la Valette infinitely more fascinating that most of the Wall Street types who can't remember what happened yesterday, much less last year. So, yes, I was fascinated. It was only later, when I discovered what The Four Sisters was doing, that I began to realize it was precisely because of the way Jean de la Valette thought about the past that he was dangerous."

"But what is the connection?" asked Hart, growing more urgent. "The money you talked about, the money that was routed through his bank—you said it was used to finance a private war. What is the reason Jean de la Valette would be willing to do something like that?"

Pearce's thinning eyebrows shot up. He reached for a pencil and tapped it hard against his favored antique desk. His small mouth quivered, his eyes danced with suppressed excitement. He began to laugh, but immediately stopped.

"It's the sort of thing that would get you committed if you told too many people."

Whatever he was about to tell him, Hart was certain that, far from crazy, it was probably the only thing that made sense. Austin Pearce was just about the most rational man he knew.

"Jean de la Valette wants to lead a new Crusade, a war of Christianity against Islam."

"I'll believe that if you say it's true," replied Hart. "But why would he think that was even a possibility? It sounds like he's the one who should be committed."

"But what after all is insanity but intense belief?" asked Pearce with a strange, knowing look in his eyes. "It's what the present usually says about the past. It's what we say today about the Crusades, the ones that started more than nine hundred years ago, the ones that made the name Jean de la Valette not just famous, but for a long time the glory of Christendom and of France.

"You've heard of the Knights Templar? Ever since Sir Walter Scott wrote *Ivanhoe*, the Templars have been used to pack the pages of novelists with tales of secret societies that have kept alive down through the centuries something no one else was supposed to know. It's all nonsense, of course. The Templars weren't formed to keep secret some esoteric knowledge; they were formed to be what someone called 'the sword arm of the Church in defense of the Holy Land.' What we forget, what most of us still don't know, is that the Crusades were at first a great success. Jerusalem was conquered, recaptured from the Muslims who had taken it from the Christians.

"The Templars were motivated by what today we would call religious fanaticism. A Templar was part of a religious order. He took a vow of obedience, which meant that he obeyed without question, and without hesitation, any command he was given. He also took a vow of abstinence and poverty; he gave up both sexual intercourse and all his worldly belongings.

These were men, all of them from the families of the aristocracy, who gave up everything for the chance to die for Christianity. Because they could not marry, could not have children, and could not keep any of their wealth for themselves, the Order of the Templars, like the Church itself, eventually became quite rich. They were formed to defend the Holy Land, but the headquarters of the two thousand Templars in France was a fortress in the middle of Paris, a fortress which at the start of the fourteenth century held the largest treasury in northern Europe. This was the beginning of their undoing, because, you see, the King of France, Philip the Fair, was at that time desperate for money."

Pearce chuckled. His small eyes lit up with mischief. Suddenly, without warning, he slapped the top of his desk with the flat of his hand and sprang to his feet. For a moment he stared out through the glass wall, out beyond the park toward the far horizon and the dark orange sky and the falling red ball sun.

"Philip the Fair," he repeated, the glow of amusement more pronounced on his cheek. "They had such wonderful names." He turned back to Hart, sitting cross-legged in his chair. "My favorite was an English monarch of about that same era: Ethelred the Unready. Madison Avenue could work for years and never come up with something as devastating as that. What if we did that now, gave names like that to politicians?"

"We have," Hart reminded him. "We called Lincoln 'Honest Abe'; Coolidge was 'Silent Cal.'"

With his hands clasped behind his back, Pearce stared down at the floor.

"No, we would have had to come up with things like 'Abraham the Magnanimous,' 'Woodrow the Intransigent.'" He began to warm to the subject. His eyes darted all around. "'Herbert the Helpless,' for Hoover and the Depression. 'Richard the Reckless,' for Nixon and Watergate. And for Constable...?"

"Robert the Dishonest," suggested Hart with a grim, satisfied smile.

"Yes, precisely," agreed Pearce. "And if Constable had read any history—any serious history—if he had known anything about the Knights Templar and the Crusades, he would have secretly envied Philip the Fair and the ruthless way he went about his business. The difference, of course," added Pearce as he came around the desk and settled back in his chair, "is that if he had lived then he would have lacked the courage to do anything that decisive. His wife, on the other hand...."

He let the possibility of what Hillary Constable would have done, how far she would have gone, linger unanswered in a way that left no doubt what the answer would have been. He went back to the story he had started to tell. Like most of the things that get passed down through the generations, most of what history deems it valuable to record, this was all about violence, but violence, that because it happened so long ago, could be viewed with all the detachment of inevitability.

"Philip the Fair needed money. It was as simple as that. His kingdom depended on it. The Templar fortress was seized and, on that same night, every one of the Templars in France, all two thousand of them, were arrested. Nearly all of them were executed. That was in 1307. Four years later, in 1311, Philip reached an agreement with the Church. At the Council of Vienne, the Templar's Order was abolished and its property transferred to the Knights Hospitallers of St. John, an order originally created to provide care and sustenance to those injured in the Crusades but that now took on the same militant function as the Templars. They in turn paid over to Philip the debt he claimed he was owed from the Templars.

"Two hundred fifty years pass, an enormous period of time from our perspective, but only a brief interval in the chronology of a family that traces its origins back to the beginning of France: the Knights of St. John defeat the Muslim leader, Suleiman II, at the siege of Malta. The leader, the Grand

Master of the Knights of St. John that day in 1565, was named Jean de la Valette. Now imagine that instead of an American who—and I think this is true of most of us—can't name all his great-grandparents, you were the direct descendant of a family like that, raised in a country whose history is measured in thousands of years. What do you look up to, what are you taught to remember? What is it you use to measure success? A better job, a better house, a more distinguished career than that of your father and his father before him? Or something that will once again change history and the world?"

By nature shy and retiring, Austin Pearce spent his days poring over statistical charts and graphs, tracking the movements of the world's markets, and his evenings reading the histories that fewer and fewer people seemed to care about. He could act with speed and decision when the occasion required it, and he could deliver a speech that was sharp and incisive, but in private conversation, when he wanted to speak nothing but the truth, he sometimes, like most of us, found it difficult to give adequate expression to what seemed so clear in his mind. He had been trying to explain to Bobby Hart, one of the few men he knew who could look past the usual time-worn categories and grasp the essence of things, why he believed Jean de la Valette was potentially a very dangerous man and all he had managed to do was describe a rich eccentric.

"He's a dangerous man!" he blurted out in frustration, slamming his hands on the arms of his chair, and then laughing in bewilderment at what he had done.

"More dangerous than you know." Hart said this with such a serious expression that Pearce's laughter died in the air.

"What do you mean—more dangerous than I know?"

"You know about Frank Morris? You know what happened?"

"Yes, of course. He was killed yesterday in prison. Terrible thing. But what does that have to do with…?"

"Morris knew about The Four Sisters. He was taking money from them, but he didn't know until much later what they were doing. The strange thing is that it wasn't what you just told me. According to Burdick—"

"Quentin Burdick, the reporter? What did he know about this?"

"Damn near everything, as it turns out. He started working on a story about The Four Sisters months ago."

Astonished, Pearce gave Hart a puzzled look.

"Burdick has a nose for things like this," explained Hart. "He has a sense when something isn't right. There were always rumors about Constable and money, where it came from, what Constable might have done to get it. That was the story, or the start of it, but Burdick didn't have anything, nothing he could use. Then he stumbled on the name The Four Sisters, and as soon as he had that, Constable, who had been dodging him, suddenly wanted to talk. The night before they were supposed to meet was the night the president died. That's why Burdick went to see Frank Morris, on the chance that Morris might know something and, because he had nothing left to lose, might be willing to talk. Morris was willing to talk, all right, but it wasn't quite for the reason Burdick thought."

Hart was still troubled by what he had learned from Burdick just hours earlier; troubled, also, by the new dimension that had now been added by Austin Pearce. The fading sun behind him cast the remnant of his own shadow across the glistening hard surface of the desk that had stories of its own to tell. Hart had the feeling as of time running out, of things happening beyond his grasp, of a danger he could not quite define. He had to tell Pearce about the president.

"Constable did not die of a heart attack, Austin. He was murdered."

Pearce's face turned ash gray.

"Murdered? How? By whom?"

Hart quickly shook his head. His eyes were immediate, determined.

"I need to tell you about Morris first. Burdick went to see him out in California, in prison, and Morris told him everything. He did not know about Constable, he didn't know how he had died, but he was almost certain that he had been killed and that it was because of The Four Sisters. Morris had taken money, not the bribery that got him convicted—that was a set-up, a frame. No, the money Morris took involved a lot more than anything they said he had done. Then Morris found out that The Four Sisters was not just interested in getting rid of obstacles to foreign investment; it was a conduit by which foreign governments could acquire a controlling interest in certain American companies, governments that wanted to influence what, as Morris put it, what we read and what we watch—books, newspapers, television, movies, everything. Morris never said anything about what you just told me: that The Four Sisters was using money from our government to finance a private war."

Pearce grasped immediately what had happened.

"We caught it at different ends, the thread that runs through everything. It makes perfect sense. The Four Sisters uses money from a foreign source, or a set of sources, to do certain things here—buy into a company, get a controlling interest. Then it uses money it gets here—from the government, but also, perhaps, sometimes from those same companies—to do something in the Middle East someone doesn't want the world to know about."

Pearce narrowed his eyes into a look of concentration that with each passing moment became more intense, until his expression had changed entirely, become bitter, bleak, the look of someone close to losing faith in everything.

"He was murdered? The president of the United States? Robert Constable managed to put himself—managed to put the country—into a position where a thing like this could happen? But how did Frank Morris know, how did he find out it was murder?"

"He didn't," replied Hart. "He guessed. It was the only thing that made sense. When Morris found out what The Four Sisters was doing, he went to the president. Constable was the one who had first suggested that he talk to some of their people. He told him that even if it meant the end of his career, he was going to stop it, go public with the story if he had to, but stop it any way he could. Constable told him not to worry, that everything was going to be all right, that—and this drove poor Morris crazy—they hadn't done anything wrong.

"Why Morris trusted Constable, even Morris did not know. Maybe he just wanted to believe—maybe it was the only thing he had left to hang onto—that the president of the United States, even if it was Robert Constable, would not let anyone put the country at risk. But the next thing Morris knows, he's under indictment and on his way to prison. He knew then that if he talked, the chances were that no one would believe him and that he might get killed. He talked to Burdick because he knew it was his last chance to set things straight, and because he knew he was dying of cancer and had only a few months left to live. They killed him just hours after Quentin Burdick's second visit. That's what convinced Burdick that Morris was correct in his suspicion that Constable did not die of a heart attack, that he was murdered instead. I told Burdick he was right."

"You told Burdick that he was right? But how could you…?" There was a new interest and, more than that, a sudden intuition, in the Pearce's eyes. "She told you, didn't she?—Hillary Constable." Pearce caught the slight movement, the subtle change of expression that revealed Hart's dilemma: that he would not lie and could not tell the truth. "It's all right," Pearce assured him. "I understand. But she must have told you for a reason. She obviously doesn't want anyone else to know. The whole country thinks he died of a heart attack; the only question whether he was in bed alone the night he died," he added with a distinct look of disapproval. "The way he lived, a rumor like that had to spread."

He started to say something more along that line: the conduct, notorious, flagrant, that would have barred someone like Constable from office in an earlier time, but which in the age of tabloid television had only added to his celebrity. The fact of what Hart had said suddenly came home to him in all its naked, twisted consequence. Like any second, delayed reaction, it hit with greater force.

"Murdered! My God, someone murdered the president of the United States and no one knows about it? No one is doing anything about it?" Then he realized what he had missed. He looked at Hart in a different light. "You're doing something about it, aren't you? That was the reason she told you. But how did she…? No, never mind. The Four Sisters…Burdick—you both think…?"

Pearce banged his hands down hard on the arms of the chair and leaped to his feet. He began to pace back and forth, three steps in one direction, three steps back, moving quicker with each step he took. He stopped abruptly, swung around, and faced Hart directly.

"It's possible. If Morris was murdered because he talked to Burdick—and Morris was a prison inmate serving a sentence for bribery, someone it wouldn't be too difficult to dismiss as a liar and a thief. But the president! If he talked—and he was scheduled to see Burdick the next day…. But why would he talk? Yes, of course: because he thought Burdick knew more than he did, that he knew all about The Four Sisters and not just the name."

Pearce was still not satisfied. Something did not add up. He stood at the corner of the desk, looking down at the deep shining surface as if the longer he looked the more hidden layers he would discover beneath it, each one changing the meaning of all the others.

"It wasn't the money," said Pearce with a certainty that to Hart was inexplicable. "If The Four Sisters—if Jean de la Valette—is involved in this, if he's responsible for two murders, if he ordered the murder of the president of the United States, it was not because he was trying to keep Constable or Morris from talking about the money they might have been paid. Burdick said he didn't have anything, nothing he could use, until he stumbled on the name—right? But it would have been almost impossible to trace whatever money was given to Constable back to Valette. With all those companies, all the various enterprises, all the ways money can be moved from one account to another—No, it wasn't the money; it was something else, something that The Four Sisters, that Valette, could not afford to have known; something he was planning, and is probably still planning, to do. But kill the president? What could be worth that kind of risk?"

CHAPTER 10

BOBBY HART WAS annoyed and, more than that, perplexed. First he was told that Clarence Atwood was out of town and would not be back until sometime the next week; then, when he made it plain that he would not be put off, that it was a matter of some urgency, he was told that someone would get back to him by the end of the day. No one did. That night Hart called Hillary Constable. An hour after they finished talking, Clarence Atwood finally called.

"Sorry, Senator, this is my fault. With all changes going on—the vice president taking over—my staff has become a little overprotective. I'll be glad to meet with you whenever you like."

He said this in an even tone of voice, calm, unflappable, exactly what one would expect from a man in his position. Hart told him he would like to see him the next morning. At first, Atwood seemed to hesitate, but finally agreed that they would meet at ten o'clock in his office. And then, just before midnight, Atwood called Hart at home and asked if he would be willing to meet the next night instead of the next morning, and at his apartment instead of at his office. He did not offer a reason and, after giving Hart his apartment number at the Watergate, did not wait for a reply. "I'll see you then," was all he said before he ended the call.

Hart got off the elevator, glanced at the piece of paper on which he had jotted down the apartment number, and headed down the hallway. The door opened before he had a chance to knock. Without a word of welcome, Clarence Atwood pulled Hart inside, stuck his head out just far enough to look both ways down the empty corridor, and then quickly shut the door. Hart was wearing a sports jacket and a shirt open at the collar, but Atwood was still dressed in a dark suit and tie, the nondescript clothing of a Secret Service agent trained to blend in with the crowd.

"Anyone follow you?" he asked as he led his guest into the living room. The curtains were drawn. There was nothing, not even a magazine, on the coffee table in front of the sofa that, along with two end tables and a single leather recliner, was the only furniture.

"Did anyone follow me?" asked Hart, more puzzled by the minute. "Why would anyone be following me?" But even as he said it, he knew. "You think whoever did this knows someone is looking into it? But even if they knew that, why would they think I knew anything about it?"

Atwood looked at the sofa, then at the chair, as if he were trying to decide exactly where to sit.

"This isn't your apartment, is it? This isn't where you live?"

Atwood ignored him. He gestured toward the sofa as he sat down on the recliner, but he sat too far back and had to push himself forward to the front edge of the chair. Tall and gangly, nothing seemed to fit him right. His suit pants were just a trifle short, the sleeves on his jacket just a shade too long. Everything about him seemed discordant and uneven; everything except his face, which was for the most part a perfect blank expression, the triumph of either a severe self-discipline or the successful purge of all emotion. He had a way of looking at you that almost made you doubt your own existence.

"What do you know, Senator? What is the reason you wanted to see me?"

"What's the reason…? No, you tell me—why would anyone be following me?"

Atwood shrugged his shoulders. There was no change in his expression.

"No reason."

Hart would have none of it.

"Of course there's a reason. You wouldn't have asked if there wasn't."

There was no response. It was not that Atwood had not heard the question; the question did not count. His gaze remained the same: steady, and if it is not too strange a thing to say, relentless, as if this were some kind of psychological experiment designed to test the reaction of someone systematically ignored. Hart was not in the mood to play.

"You wouldn't have called me last night to ask if I'd meet you here instead of your office if you didn't think—what is this place, anyway?" he asked as he cast a glance of disapproval around the soulless, sparsely furnished room. "A safe location, a place you have meetings you don't want anyone to know about?"

There was nothing, not the slightest movement, in Atwood's immobile face. Hart's voice echoed into a silence that became profound.

"What do you know, Senator?" asked Atwood, and then repeated the second question. "What is the reason you wanted to see me?"

This was maddening. Hart felt the anger rise in his throat. He turned his head, ready to lash out, when he suddenly thought he understood.

"You're afraid of something. What is it?—That someone is going to find out that the president didn't die of a heart attack in that hotel room, find out that he was murdered? Why are you afraid of that? You're the head of the

Secret Service—you don't have any reason to cover this up...."

Finally it was there, the first glimmer of something genuine in that manufactured face, a spark of anger in those deliberately impenetrable eyes.

"It wasn't our fault. We did everything we're supposed to do."

Hart was quick to take advantage. He fixed Atwood with a piercing stare.

"Not your fault? You let a woman into his room, a woman you obviously knew nothing about; a paid assassin, as it turns out, who murdered him. I can understand why you might not want to see that story in the papers, but that doesn't change what happened, or what has to be done about it."

"That was always the hardest part about protecting Robert Constable: protecting him from himself," replied Atwood with a brief nod. "You think we had time to do a background check on every woman he had to have? Do you know how many times he had an agent bring a woman to his room, someone he had just spotted in the crowd? I lost a couple of the best agents I had. I had to transfer them to other duties or they would have quit. President or not, they weren't going to be anybody's pimp. To tell you the truth, they're the ones I most admired. Now, what do you know and why do you want to see me?" He paused, and then relented. "I know what she told me, but I need to hear it from you."

Did that mean that Atwood did not trust the former first lady, wondered Hart, or that he did not trust him? It seemed a point of some importance.

"I understand that you became the head of the Secret Service on her recommendation."

A slight smile flickered briefly on Clarence Atwood's stoic mouth.

"She told you that, did she? It might even be true, for all I know."

"She doesn't always tell the truth?"

"Do you know anyone in this town who does? But don't misunderstand, Senator; I have no complaint of Mrs. Constable. She—and her husband, within his limits—always treated me fairly."

"'Within his limits'? That's an odd way of putting it."

"There were things he did, things that put me in an awkward situation, things I can't talk about."

"I think I understand," replied Hart, trying to feel a little more sympathetic. "You want to know what I know and why I wanted to see you. Because the president's widow asked me to, after she told me what you told her: that the president was murdered. She knows the truth will have to come out, but she first wants to know what happened: who killed him and why. Because otherwise—"

"Everyone will have their own idea, each one more vicious than the last. I can't say I disagree. There are only a handful of people who know about this, and you're the only one I don't quite trust. It's nothing personal, Senator. I don't trust anyone I don't know, and frankly, I don't trust most of those. I've been here too long; I've seen too much. And the others that know about this—it isn't that I trust them any more than I trust you, but they have careers they want to protect. Most of them, anyway," he added in an allusion Hart grasped at once. Hillary Constable had a lot of things, but a career of the sort Atwood could affect wasn't one of them.

"It's true, then?" asked Hart. "There isn't any doubt? A woman he was sleeping with shoved a needle in him and killed him with a drug."

"What have you been able to find out—anything useful, anything at all?"

Hart had agreed to look into things, to see what he could find out; he had not agreed to report to the Secret Service.

"Your job is to protect the president, not conduct an investigation into the cause of his death. This is something for the FBI. The president has been murdered, and you still haven't told them?"

Atwood looked down at his large hands with their three misshapen fingers, broken years earlier in a fight. The lines in his forehead deepened as he pondered over what he was going to say next, and just how far he could go.

"I've had conversations." He said this slowly, as if to impress upon Hart that he knew what he was about; that he knew to protect himself from any later charge that he had withheld information, or delayed revealing what he knew, in a murder investigation of this magnitude.

"You've had a conversation—with the director? You told him that the president was murdered, and the FBI hasn't started an investigation?"

Atwood answered with another silent look.

"They have started an investigation," said Hart, "but quietly, discreetly. Is that what you're telling me?"

"There is some concern about panic, the way the public might react, the kind of rumors that might—"

"Yes, I know all about that," said Hart with a show of irritation.

He got to his feet and walked over to the window. He pulled the drapes open far enough to look out. When he turned around, he did nothing to hide his disgust.

"If it wasn't bad enough that Constable did something that got himself killed, he's managed to involve first his wife, and then the head of the Secret Service, and now the director of the FBI, in a conspiracy to conceal a murder! Don't you see the irony in that? We're doing everything we can to stop speculation about what might have happened in that hotel room when its becoming more and more likely that the truth is far worse than what anyone right now could possibly imagine!"

With a halting, disjointed movement, Atwood got to his feet. He stood there, staring at Hart in a way that, with those who worked under him, was usually all that was necessary to force an explanation. But Hart did not work for him, and the only effect was to make the senator less inclined to tell him anything.

"You know something," said Atwood. "What is it? What have you found out?"

Hart ignored him.

"How long do you think it's going to be before the fact that the president was murdered leaks out?" Before Atwood could respond, Hart shook his head as if to tell him that it did not matter, that the question was irrelevant. "It's already leaked out. There's at least one reporter who is all over this story. This secret you're trying to keep—you're going to be reading it in the papers and there's not a damn thing you or I or anyone else can do about it. So it seems to me that unless you want to find yourself on the wrong end of a congressional investigation, you better start telling me what you know and you better start doing it now."

To Hart's immense surprise, Atwood actually seemed relieved, as if he had been expecting him to put it in precisely these terms.

"Wait here a moment."

He was gone a few moments and when he came back he was not alone.

"This is Dick Bauman, the agent in charge that night."

For the next several hours, until well past midnight, they sat there, the three of them, going over everything that had happened the night Robert Constable died. Atwood became a different man around poor Bauman, who had almost reached the point of blaming himself for the president's murder. Atwood kept telling him that it was not his fault, that his only failure was a failure of decency, trying to protect the president, and the president's family, from Constable's gross misbehavior. Hart agreed, telling him that in the circumstances in which he had found himself, it would have been heartless, almost an act of cruelty, not to keep the tawdry details of Constable's last night private. Bauman's answer stopped them both.

"The fault goes farther back than that. There wouldn't have been any need to do what I did, clean up after him, if we had made it plain in the beginning, when we first started guarding him, that there were some things we wouldn't do."

Atwood could not argue the point; Hart did not try.

"Tell me everything that happened. How did the girl get there?"

"We're not sure. He had this arrangement—whenever he stayed in the city. There was always a second room connected to the suite. He kept the key himself and gave it to whomever he chose. There was always someone."

"But there was Secret Service protection all around him," objected Hart.

Bauman exchanged a glance with Atwood.

"Go ahead. It's all right. You can tell him."

"We learned to look the other way. A woman—a good-looking woman—gets off the elevator. We all understood."

"But this woman—where did she come from? Did Constable meet her somewhere that night? Where was he earlier that evening? What had he been doing?"

"He gave a speech at a fundraising dinner at the Plaza Hotel. It finished up around ten-thirty, but we did not get him out of there for another half hour. He never wanted to leave anywhere if there was someone left to talk to, another hand to shake. It's funny, but now that I think about it, I don't remember him ever saying even once that he wanted to be alone."

"The girl—how old was she, anyway?"

"Late twenties, early thirties, the way most of them were."

"Was she there, at the dinner? Is that where he met her?"

Bauman tried hard to remember. His eyes began to move side to side, seeing in his mind what he had seen before, the tables full of rich contributors and women dressed with money.

"If she was, I don't remember seeing her. She might have been there, but if she was she must have gone somewhere first to change. It was a formal affair, not the kind of clothes she had with her."

"So he must have known her before that night. He must have—"

"Not necessarily," interjected Bauman reluctantly. "There were people, friends of his, who sometimes…."

"Set him up with someone?" asked Hart. Everyone had heard the stories about how helpful certain of the president's friends could be. Hart glanced toward Atwood, sitting back in the recliner, his face again without expression.

"And you kept all this from his wife? Never told her what was going on?"

"It wasn't our place to do that," replied Atwood, looking straight at him.

Was he lying? wondered Hart, searching Atwood's eyes for an answer they would not yield. Or was Atwood telling the truth, and Hillary Constable had been lying when she told Hart that she was kept informed about anything Constable did that might threaten his presidency? He had the feeling that neither one of them had been entirely truthful; that she had been kept informed, but not so often, nor so fully, as she had thought. Whatever deal Atwood had made with Hillary Constable, he would have made another, better one with her husband.

Richard Bauman was a different story. As near as Hart could tell, the agent had only wanted to do the right thing and had not realized that doing that almost always got you in trouble. He liked Bauman, liked him precisely for that reason. Bauman would have done what he was sworn to do: protect the life of the president at the cost of his own, and done it without a moment's hesitation. Atwood, on the other hand, was more likely someone who instead of acting instantly, would think instead of how he could act the hero's part and live to gain the benefit.

"He was lucky to have you," said Hart suddenly, and for no apparent reason. "I know you feel responsible, but you shouldn't. But now, tell me about her, anything you can remember." He turned sharply to Atwood. "I assume that with Agent Bauman's help you worked up a sketch of what she looks like and that you've given it to the FBI. I'd like a copy of it as well, if you wouldn't mind."

Atwood suggested that there was very little chance it would do any good.

"Twenty minutes after she left the hotel, she probably didn't look anything like the way she did. This was not some amateur; she was a professional. Her hair will be different; her eyes won't be the same. She'll look like a thousand other people no one knows anything about. She was probably on a plane out of the country later that same night. There really isn't any chance we'll ever find her."

"The real question," said Hart as he got ready to leave, "is whether we can find the people who hired her."

"Whoever they are, they aren't taking any credit for it. Which means it wasn't some group out there that hates America and wants to show what it can do."

But Hart was not thinking about that. He wanted to know something more about the girl.

"Her manner, the way she talked—anything, the way she moved, anything about her clothes."

Bauman thought about it, or rather tried to think. He was exhausted, wracked with all the psychic pain of endless self-recrimination; haunted by what he thought was his failure to recognize an assassin when she was standing right in front of him.

"Nothing. She was great looking, and she seemed scared, or I thought she was at first, but then—there was something in her eyes—I thought she wasn't. It all happened so fast, and my first thought was—well, you know what I did. I almost pushed her out of there, told her to get her things and get out of the hotel. Unbelievable! But that's what I did."

"Was there anything about her, anything that was different? Her voice— what did she sound like?"

Bauman sat bolt upright. His eyes grew larger and almost frighteningly intense.

"She had an accent! Not much of one, but a little. Why did I forget that? She had an accent, maybe British, or someone who went to school there."

CHAPTER 11

As a member of the Senate Intelligence Committee, Bobby Hart was in a better position than most people to know what was going on in the world. Meeting behind closed doors, he and a handful of senators were given regular briefings by the various intelligence agencies, including the CIA. The committee was not always told everything, however, and there had even been occasions when what they were told was not the truth. When you were trained in the arts of deception, taught how to mislead the enemy, it was not that difficult to convince yourself that lying to Congress about something you wanted to keep secret was not really lying at all. Those who thought like this were mainly the ones who had come later, part of the generation born after the war; the ones who, because they had never been put to the test, never faced an enemy in combat, did not understand what it was they were really there to protect: the country and what it stood for, not the power of some agency that thought it was bigger than the government.

"Some of these guys think they're so tough," his father had said with contempt one day shortly before he died. "They should have been with me at the Battle of the Bulge, freezing their nuts off at Bastogne. That's a little different than plotting the overthrow of some two-bit dictator in the comfort of an air-conditioned room."

Bobby Hart liked to think of that, his father's gruff laughter, the straight, no-nonsense look in his eyes when he talked about the way things had changed in the agency he had once loved. There was always a difference, he had insisted, between those who were there at the beginning of something and those who came later. That was the lesson he had learned, the lesson he wanted to pass on: you had to be there at the beginning to know what it was about and what you were there to do. Things changed, got all mixed up, and before you knew it the thing you created became more important than what it had been created to do.

"I'm not just talking about the agency, you understand. It's true of everything: things are always clearer at the start."

And then he had looked at his son in a way Bobby never forgot, with pride and hope, but more than that, a sense of trust, the certain knowledge that Bobby would not disappoint the high expectations he had for him.

"The first time you ran for office, that first campaign for Congress—you weren't thinking then what you had to do to get reelected; all you thought about were the things you wanted to do, the changes you thought needed to be made. That's why you're different from all the others, the ones who just want to stay in office—you still think like that. The whole point is not to stop."

Though Bobby was certain that his father had given him far too much credit, what his father had said became a kind of second conscience, a constant reminder of the kind of man he was supposed to be. It was surprising how often it had worked in the early years after he was first elected; how often, when he was tempted to go along with a majority opinion with which he disagreed, he heard not just his father's words, but his father's voice. It had become so much a part of him over the years, that second, deeper judgment, that he seldom any longer had occasion to remember where it came from and how it had started, but he remembered it now, as he took his chair in the committee room and looked across at the director of the CIA sitting with his hands folded at the witness table. From somewhere in the shadows of his mind, he heard his father's voice reminding him of his obligation, as clear and distinct as the day he first heard him say it.

The chairman of the committee, Wilson Breyer of New Hampshire, gaveled the session to order. A former state court judge, with a mind narrowed to the strict necessities of the law, Breyer listened to the arguments of others but only seldom expressed an opinion of his own. There were those on the committee who suspected that it was because he did not have an opinion on anything that mattered, and it was a fact that no one could remember when he had voted on anything except with the majority. Hart was more charitable. He was willing to take the chairman at his word when he insisted that it was the business of a chairman to do what he could to get a consensus. Everyone agreed that Wilson Breyer ran things on schedule. The meeting had been scheduled for 4:30, and by 4:32 he had already finished with the opening preliminaries.

The chairman's scholarly face was set in an attitude of interested attention, someone who would never take sides and would make sure that everyone was treated fairly. His hands were a different story. Kept out of sight, lest they betray him, one of them was always moving in a strange, manic dance, the nervous irritation he could never quite control.

"The committee has been called into session to hear from the Director of the CIA, Louis Griswald, what the agency has learned about the reaction to the death of President Constable and his replacement by Vice President

Russell."

Out of the corner of his eye, the chairman noticed that from his place two seats down, Bobby Hart had turned toward him. Breyer's hand stopped moving; a nervous smile flashed briefly across his mouth. Believing that the smile was for him, the CIA director smiled back.

"Thank you, Mr. Chairman. There's really not much to report."

Louis Griswald had never felt the need to hold himself to the tight discipline Wilson Breyer had learned in court. Broad-shouldered and broad across the hip, he did everything with a certain swagger. He did not sit with his feet planted on the floor, looking straight ahead, but sideways in the chair like someone sitting with friends on a Saturday afternoon, lying about his golf game or what he had done on the athletic fields of Princeton thirty years before.

"Not much to report?" inquired the chairman in a quiet, affable tone.

"Nothing that we would regard as serious, radical elements in the Middle East claiming that the death of the president was Allah's act of vengeance for the 'Great Satan,' speculation in various capitals about what, if any, change of policy might be expected from the vice president—I mean from the Russell administration. In other words, nothing you wouldn't expect and nothing that could be construed as a new threat. There's no evidence that anyone views what happened as an opportunity to move against us, either here or abroad."

Shifting his bulky frame around, Griswald placed his thick arms on the table and hunched forward. His eyes, set beneath heavy lids, narrowed into a grim, almost brutal stare.

"That doesn't mean they won't, only that if they're planning something, we don't yet know about it."

Hart knew what was coming next. Anyone who had been on the committee more than a year knew what was coming next.

"As I've told this committee time and time again: we don't have the assets—we don't have the budget, we don't have the legal authority—to gather all the intelligence we need."

The director pushed back from the table, folded his arms across his ample chest, and slowly looked from one member of the committee to the next, daring them, as it seemed, to disagree. Charlie Finnegan laughed.

"Isn't it a simple rule of mathematics, Mr. Griswald," Finnegan said, "that you multiply any number by zero and you still get zero? We could double your budget—we did that, remember, just two years ago—and you would still blame us when you had nothing to report. It's an old game, Mr. Griswald, and I for one am getting a little damn tired of it!"

"We do what we can with what we have," the director shot back. "But you're right: I can't guarantee results, no matter how much money you might give us. All I can tell you is that it would improve our chances. There are no guarantees in this business. We do what we can with what we have," he repeated with all the blind assurance of a catechism.

Finnegan started to say something, but thought better of it, or, rather, just gave up. There was no arguing with this kind of posturing. He glanced across to see if Hart had anything to add.

"Director Griswald, I'm interested in the intelligence you had before the president's death."

The question caught the director off guard. He did not want to admit that he was not sure what the senator meant, and so he did not say anything.

"Before the president's death," repeated Hart.

Griswald bent his head slightly to the side. He still did not answer. The silence began to speak a language of its own. Other members of the committee, reading over a document, conferring quietly with an aide, stopped what they were doing. Hart's gaze stayed fixed on Griswald; the director kept staring back.

"The president's death," said Hart in a voice that took on a new insistence, and a new authority, in the solemn silence of the room.

"I'm not sure I understand the question, Senator," Griswald finally admitted.

"The president died in a hotel room," said Hart, choosing his words carefully. "Died of an apparent heart attack. There have been rumors that he was not alone. If that is true, if he wasn't alone, then…well, you can see where I'm going."

The director was not sure he did. The line across the bridge of his nose deepened and became more pronounced, as his eyes drew close together.

"If he wasn't alone," persisted Hart, "that leads to the possibility that something may have happened, that he didn't…."

"Die of natural causes?" Now Griswald understood. "I suppose it might, but you asked about any intelligence we might have had before the president's death. If you mean, did we hear of a possible attempt on the president's life, then, no, we didn't." With a show of reluctance, Griswald added that, like everyone else, he "had heard those same rumors—about the president not being alone when he died. But for the rest of it, that that had anything to do with his death, I haven't heard anything like it, and have no reason to think it's true."

But that meant, as Hart immediately understood, that if what he had been told by Clarence Atwood was true, that the head of the Secret Service had told the director of the FBI and the FBI had started an investigation, no one had yet told the CIA.

"So then, as far you know, no one in the government, no one in the FBI, is looking into the possibility that President Constable, instead of dying of natural causes, was killed?"

The question, the simple stated possibility, seemed to give the director pause. He stroked his chin for a moment before he replied.

"No. Not that I know of."

Hart pressed the point.

"And if they were, would you expect to be informed?"

Griswald did not hesitate.

"On a matter of that importance: yes, absolutely."

"'Yes, absolutely.' Very good. Thank you."

The chairman started to ask if anyone else had a question, but Hart interrupted.

"There is something else I would like to ask. There have been other rumors—not about the president's death, but about certain dealings he may have had with foreign interests. Have you—has the CIA—any information, any intelligence, on any dealings President Constable may have had in which he received payment from sources overseas?"

The committee, almost equally divided between the two parties, started buzzing. The chairman quickly called them to order.

"Mr. Hart, do you have something specific in mind? That is a fairly broad allegation you're making, and I would think that—"

"I'm not making an allegation, broad or otherwise, Mr. Chairman. I'm simply asking if the director knows of anything that would support the kind of rumors I've been hearing; the questions that I know for certain have become the subject of an investigation."

"An investigation, Mr. Hart? I haven't heard of anything like that."

"Not a criminal investigation, Mr. Chairman. Not an investigation by the Justice Department. An investigation by reporters, one of which, from what I understand, might be published in the papers any time now."

The chairman pressed his hands against his head. There was a bleak expression on his face.

"Even in death…," he muttered, a reference to the character of the late Robert Constable that did not need to be explained. "Yes, yes, all right," he added quickly, anxious to move on. "Go ahead. Ask the director what you were going to ask."

"Have you, Mr. Griswald, learned of any improper dealings with foreign interests, whether these were foreign governments or foreign nationals?"

The director had begun to sense that there was more going on than a routine attempt to run down a rumor. Hart knew something, and that meant it was not safe to answer until he had a better idea exactly what it was. He took refuge in a bureaucratic excuse.

"I'm not prepared to answer that at the moment."

"You're not prepared to…?" Hart warned him with a look. "Are you sure that's the answer you want to leave with this committee?"

"I can't answer the question, Senator," he replied, turning up the palms of his hands to show that it was out of his control. "What I'm trying to say is that I don't have any personal knowledge of what you're asking about, but the agency keeps track of a fairly large volume of financial transactions, so it's possible that someone—"

"I didn't say anything about financial transactions, the kind the agency tries to follow. I asked whether you had any intelligence about the possibility that the President of the United States had been bribed, bribed to do certain things that benefited certain foreign interests. I'll ask you again, Mr. Griswald: Do you know anything about this?"

"As I said, I have no personal knowledge—"

"Does the agency have any intelligence on a French investment firm, The Four Sisters?"

"The Four Sisters? No, I don't recall that name."

"Would you mind checking into it and getting back to us?"

"Yes, of course, as soon as I can."

"Immediately, if you don't mind," said Hart with an icy stare.

"Yes, Senator; right away."

When the session ended, Charlie Finnegan caught up with Hart in the hallway outside.

"What's going on, Bobby?"

Hart kept walking. He did not look at Finnegan. Their footsteps echoed in the empty marble corridor. Finnegan did not press the issue until they were outside the Capitol and starting down the steps.

"Something happened in that hotel room. You said 'died of an apparent heart attack.' Apparent? You think he was murdered, don't you?"

Hart stopped on the first landing. The summer heat was still intolerable. Dark clouds marched in a long unbroken line across a broken, yellow sky. His mood, prisoner to the weather, became somber and almost fatalistic, a sense that things, however bad, would soon get worse. He turned to Finnegan, the closest friend he had, and with a rueful expression in his deep-set eyes confessed that it was not a question of suspicion.

"This is between us: the president was murdered. The woman who was with him was a hired killer, an assassin. The Secret Service thought she was just another one of the women he took to bed. The agent actually helped her get away. The poor bastard thought he was doing the right thing, what he had to do to protect the president's reputation."

Finnegan whistled between his teeth. Shoving his hands deep in his pockets, he kicked at the stone step. The questions Hart asked Griswald, the answers Griswald gave, took on a new and different meaning, a meaning Finnegan was not slow to grasp.

"Constable was murdered, but if Griswald was telling the truth, the CIA doesn't know anything about it. And from what he said, neither does the FBI?"

"I was led to believe they did," replied Hart. "Which means that, if Griswald is telling the truth, either the FBI has lied to him, or someone has lied to me."

"Someone?"

Hart did not hesitate. He trusted Finnegan and he was getting nowhere on his own. He needed help.

"The Secret Service. Clarence Atwood told me two nights ago that he had kept the FBI informed and that the bureau had begun its own investigation."

"An investigation?—Constable was murdered, and no one is talking about it? What in the world…?"

A group of schoolchildren, taken on a tour of the Capitol, were coming down the steps. Eager to get away from their dull history lesson and out into the open air, they drowned out everything with their cheerful, triumphant voices. Finnegan waited until they passed.

"Someone has put you in a box, haven't they?" He searched Hart's eyes, certain he was right. "Constable was murdered. You know it, but you can't talk about it—can't even ask about it except in this oblique way, raising every question with Griswald except the one that counts. But who, why would anyone…? She told you, didn't she? She asked you to find out what you could."

It was a point of some interest, how quickly those who knew something about her thought that whatever was going on Hillary Constable must be at the center of it. Hart, as he had gradually come to recognize, had been like everyone else in this regard. He had not been at all surprised, the day she had asked him for his help, to learn that the Secret Service had reported to her what had happened and then, for all intents and purposes, left it to her to decide what to do next.

"When did she do it—last week, after the funeral?"

"I said I would see what I could find out: if there were any rumors, any intelligence, about who might have wanted to do it. The concern is what happens when this goes public, when everyone finds out that it wasn't a heart attack, it was murder."

"It's been a week," objected Finnegan. "How long do you think you can keep something like this secret? And, for God's sake, how long do you think you should? It's going to come out, you know."

Finnegan kicked at the step again, harder this time, more emphatically. He swung his head up, not all the way, just far enough to search Hart's waiting eyes.

"It's coming out soon, isn't it? Quentin Burdick is on it, isn't he? You asked Griswald about The Four Sisters; what Burdick was asking me. That's the connection, isn't it? What are they—The Four Sisters? What have you found out?"

Hart glanced back up the steps. More schoolchildren were coming, and groups of sweaty, red-faced tourists dressed in shirts and shorts, cameras slung over their shoulders, heading for the relief of air-conditioned buses that would take them to other famous landmarks or back to their hotels. A few of them, catching sight of Bobby Hart, began to wave.

"Let's get out of here," said Hart under his breath as he smiled and waved back.

They moved in the lazy rhythm of a burning southern summer, a slow, unhurried procession, through the leafy park-like grounds of the Capitol. The heat was all around them, each step a dim reminder of something distant, far away, as if instead of moving forward they were destined never to move at all, held in one place by the thick molasses air. They walked in silence until they crossed the street and passed through the side entrance of the Russell Senate Office Building. Speech required effort.

Hart's office, or rather his suite of offices, was on the second floor. His staff, overworked and underpaid and all of them glad for the opportunity, were crammed into cubicles so small that if one of them stretched her arms there was the danger she might hit both her neighbors at once. They worked from early in the morning until late at night, and weekends they worked just as hard at home. It was not a job; it was a calling, and they thought themselves far more fortunate than friends of theirs who had gone to work in hot pursuit of money and the things it could buy. Most of them were in their thirties, still too young for disillusionment. Some were younger, just out of law school, with long-distance dreams of one day winning a Senate seat of their own. A few, like Hart's administrative assistant, David Allen, a rumpled veteran of the political wars both at home in California and here on Capitol Hill, were older than the relatively young senator and more devoted to him than anyone other than his wife.

Allen did his best to conceal it. He seldom praised anything Hart had done and did not hesitate to let him know in no uncertain terms when he thought the senator had made a mistake. They both understood what Allen was there to do. Practically everyone in Washington, from the most senior member of the Senate to a first term congressman elected in a fluke, was so often called great that in no time at all they came to believe it, and, believing it, to need it, the constant echo of their own achievement. It made every small thing they did major; every routine vote they cast an act of unexampled courage. Hart hated the self-importance of it, the sense of entitlement, the emptiness of a life bound up in other people's adjectives. Part of David Allen's job was to make sure he remembered that and did not become what he despised. It was one of the things Allen liked best.

The door to Allen's small cubbyhole office was open as Hart passed down the narrow windowless hallway. Sitting at his cluttered desk, poring over the latest budget numbers, Allen did not look up.

"Nice of you to drop by," he remarked in a dry, caustic voice. "I'd get up, but I've aged a lot since the last time we saw you and...." He had just caught a glimpse of Charlie Finnegan. He sprang to his feet and started to straighten his sleeves. "Sorry, Senator, I didn't realize..." he sputtered.

Finnegan came into his office and with a huge grin shook his hand.

"It's me, David—Charlie. I wouldn't want you to treat me any different than this fraud you work for." He looked over his shoulder at Hart, standing in the doorway laughing, and then looked back. "Why don't you come and work for me. I lead a pretty dull life compared to Bobby here. I'm always in the office."

Allen liked Charlie Finnegan, liked him a lot. There was not any false posturing with him; you always knew where you stood.

"Would I have to become a Republican?"

"What the hell for? Most people don't think I'm one." He turned to Hart. "Though it's hard to see why I'd still claim to be one if I wasn't. Not much advantage in it these days, is there?"

They left David Allen to get back to his numbers and went into Hart's private office, a large, well-appointed room, with two tall windows and a gray marble fireplace. Oriental carpets were scattered over the floor. A white sofa and two easy chairs were arranged below the windows, while, at the other end of the room, in the corner opposite the fireplace, sat Hart's desk, with a gray leather chair, worn to his dimensions, and two straight back chairs in front of it. This was where he met with anyone who had come to make a formal case for something they wanted from the senator; it was not where he had a conversation with a friend like Charlie Finnegan. Hart dropped into one of the easy chairs near the windows, while Finnegan settled onto the sofa. Finnegan nodded toward the door they had just closed behind them.

"Does David know?"

"No one knows, except Laura, and now you."

Hart's gaze rolled from one window toward the other one. He waved his hand in a listless gesture and then shook his head and, after that, scratched his chin.

"That's not true," he said finally. "Everyone knows. That's not true, either," he added quickly. "Quentin Burdick knows. He knew already; I confirmed it. I didn't tell him how I knew, only that I did. Austin Pearce knows, too. I didn't tell him how I knew, but like you, he guessed." Still curious how quickly they had both jumped to that particular conclusion, Hart looked at Finnegan. "Not really a guess, though, was it? As soon as you heard it, you knew—both of you. She always had a reputation for having the real power in that marriage, even in that presidency."

For the next half hour, Hart described everything that had happened, everything he had learned, from the day Hillary Constable asked him to find out what he could to the night, just the day before yesterday, when he met with Clarence Atwood of the Secret Service.

"How long is Burdick going to sit on the story?" asked Finnegan when Hart was finished.

"I talked to him yesterday on the phone. He's got an interview with Austin Pearce tomorrow. Assuming Austin tells him what he told me, not long at all. He knows Constable was murdered. He was convinced of it after what Morris told him out in Lompoc, after what happened to Morris. I confirmed it, but I wouldn't tell him how I knew it. He won't use that; he won't attribute it to me—not yet, anyway. After he talks to Austin, my guess is that he'll want to find out more about this Jean de la Valette and The Four Sisters, but you're right, we're looking at most at a few days, maybe a week, before this thing breaks wide open. Which means I don't have any time at all. I have to go to France."

"To France? To see Valette? Are you sure that's wise?"

"I'm not sure of anything. But after all I've heard I'd like to see for myself what he's really like, whether it's even possible he could have arranged to have Constable murdered."

"When are you leaving?"

"As soon as I can; a day or two at the latest."

Finnegan got to his feet, ready to leave, but then he thought of something, and wondered why he had not thought of it before.

"What about the president?"

"Constable?"

"No, our new one: Irwin Russell. How do you think he's going to react when he finds out Constable was murdered and that the Secret Service knew it and did not bother to tell him? Or do you think they did?" That thought led to another. "And what do you think the real reason was that Hillary Constable asked you to look into this? If she's as ambitious as we all think she is—everyone knows she thought she was going to be her husband's successor—doesn't she want this kept quiet long enough to figure out how to handle it with the least cost to herself?"

"I know the rumors," replied Hart, "the deal that was supposedly made. Russell goes on the ticket, but with the understanding that he wouldn't try for the nomination—he didn't have the kind of support on his own that would let him try for the nomination—at the end of Constable's second term."

"But now things have changed," said Finnegan. "Dull and uninspiring as he may be, Irwin Russell is president, with every right, if he wants to, to run on his own." Finnegan began to pace, his eyes moving quickly from one thing to another. "Everything has changed." He stopped abruptly, wheeled around, and looked straight at Bobby Hart, who had turned at an angle in his chair as Finnegan had moved away. "Think about the difference it makes whether you've become president because your predecessor died of something as common as a heart attack, or your predecessor was killed in office, struck down by an assassin. It's the difference between, in the one case, filling in the time, and, in the other, having the chance to pull the country together, take charge, and unleash the full power of the government in the hunt for whoever had the temerity to murder an American president. If he does that, he becomes unbeatable. If he doesn't do that, if something happens and he does not have the chance, then, assuming she is still interested, Hillary

Constable can claim that she should be allowed to continue the work her husband was not allowed to finish."

There was a brief knock on the door and then David Allen stuck his head in.

"Sorry to interrupt, but there's a call I thought you'd want to take. Hillary Constable is on the line."

CHAPTER 12

THE HOUSE WAS all lit up, that was the first thing that struck Bobby Hart when he got out of his car. It seemed oddly out of place, jarring in a way, that the house where little more than a week ago Hillary Constable had stood in a receiving line to accept condolences on the death of her husband should now look so alive. When he knocked on the white lacquered door he half expected to be welcomed into another crowded reception, not to mourn a death, but to celebrate a completely different kind of occasion: a birthday, an anniversary, or, because this was Washington after all, the election returns in a race the outcome of which had been decided long before the polls had closed.

He was not far wrong. The house was full of people, dozens of them, some busy arranging stacks of files, organizing them into the right categories, others busy on the telephones that had been set up on two long tables in the same living room where Hart had watched Hillary Constable go through her widow's ritual. At yet another table, six young women sorted through the contents of several canvas mail bags, cards sent by people from across the country and around the world expressing their sorrow on the death of the president. There were thousands of them and every one of them was going to be answered with a short note, a few words, and then signed by a machine, but no one who received them would ever know they had been signed that way. They would have instead the double pleasure of believing that the president's widow had not only read what they had sent, but had been so moved—that was the phrase that had been chosen after consultation with several of her advisors—that though she could not answer all of the wonderful cards and letters she had received, she had to answer theirs. It was what in an older political tradition might have been called a boiler room for grief.

Watching it, Hart marveled at the slow precision of the work, the methodical organization, the way each name to whom a response was addressed was made part of a list, a list that, from what Hart had been told, the Constables had started back when they were still in college, a list that had expanded with the years, people whom if they had only met them once, or even if they had never met them in person at all, would receive a card every Christmas and a request for money at the start of every campaign. By the time Robert Constable ran for a second term there were literally millions of people to whom he could write that one of his greatest satisfactions was knowing that he had such a good friend on whom he could always count when things were difficult and he needed help. And they believed it, the grateful eager recipients of those yearly smiling photographs of "Bob and Hillary" standing in front of another White House Christmas tree. Robert Constable might be dead, but the list that he and his wife had built up with such enterprise and effort was still growing, part of the inheritance, if you will, left to his wife.

"Hello Bobby, thank you for coming."

Hillary Constable was suddenly standing right next to him. She was dressed casually in a blouse and skirt. A soft blue cashmere cardigan that brought out the color of her eyes was thrown over her shoulders. Her ash blonde hair was pulled back and she had on her reading glasses. It might have given her a shy, reserved, and bookish look, a woman who taught literature in the shade tree environment of a small liberal arts college, but her eyes were too immediate, too much in the present, the eyes of a woman on the verge of impatience, a woman who was used to being the standard, the only standard, for what was important.

"Don't mind all this," she remarked, nodding toward the organized chaos. "We always had a rule that anyone who wrote to us got answered."

She said this without nostalgia, as if she were simply reporting a principle of modern management, one of those learned from a book of sound practices, a proven method of achieving success. Her eyes made a quick circuit of the room. It would have been easy to miss the brief, decisive nod, the closed judgment on what she observed. Hart had the feeling that she did this fairly often, come to see whether in her absence everyone was still hard at work. She started to turn her attention back to him when she noticed something that was not quite right. A stack of envelopes, addressed and ready to be mailed, was too tall and had begun to lean. Dividing it in half, she carefully set the two shorter stacks next to one another. Without a word, just a look, but a look that behind its apparent kindness suggested consequences for failure, she let the young woman sitting at the table know that even the smallest things had to be done right.

"It's amazing how much time I've had to waste teaching people the obvious," she remarked as she took Hart by the arm. She looked back over her shoulder and flashed a smile of encouragement at the young woman she had just corrected. "Everything is important," she explained to Hart. "That's what no one seems to understand: everything. Now, let's go somewhere where we can talk."

She led him through the living room, past the marble pillar where he had stood talking to Austin Pearce, the marble pillar that curiously had reminded him of her, across the hallway toward a door that, as he now realized, was the entrance to the elevator that went to the private suite of rooms directly overhead.

"Scotch all right?" she asked, as she walked over to the mahogany shelves crowded with books seldom opened and never read.

Handing Hart a glass, she took a drink, seemed to enjoy it, and took another. She invited Hart to sit down, but she continued to stand next to the desk and the photographs of what had been her private life. There was an odd, pensive expression on her face as if she were in some doubt about how to begin.

"You said it was important," Hart reminded her. "You said you had to see me right away."

It was almost indistinguishable, the way the muscles around her jaw tightened, and then swallowed without taking a drink. She seemed to have to force herself to look right at him and not to look away.

"What have you found out?" she asked finally.

Hart had the feeling that she did not really want to know, that for some reason she was almost afraid of the answer. But then why, suddenly, had she wanted to see him, insisted that it had to be right now, tonight? Or did that explain it: the fear that had been building up inside her had become intolerable and she could not wait to hear what she was not sure she wanted to learn? Or was it something else, something that Hart had not quite been able to put his finger on, but that was palpable, real, somewhere below the surface that he had not yet been able to penetrate?

"Have you found out anything—what we talked about before?" she repeated when he did not answer.

Hart sat on the edge of the chair, trying to read the meaning in her nervous eyes. His relentless gaze seemed to make her uncomfortable. She took another drink and then, biting her lip, stared down at the floor. A moment later she looked up.

"You have, haven't you?—learned something, I mean."

"What can you tell me about The Four Sisters?"

She seemed puzzled, then annoyed.

"The Four...? What does that have to do with—?"

"The Four Sisters, the investment firm your husband was taking money from; the firm that was helping foreign interests buy control of certain American companies; the firm that was using government money—our government's money—to finance a war we didn't know anything about. Are you going to tell me that you didn't know anything about it, that you never heard of The Four Sisters, that you never met Jean de la Valette, that—"

"Of course I've met Jean de la Valette! He's a very prominent man in financial circles. And the—what is it again?—The Four Sisters. Yes, that's the name of the firm he runs. But what about it? Those other things you said—I wouldn't know anything about what he does with his money. And as for Robert taking money from…. That's a fairly serious accusation. Are you suggesting he was being paid to do something, that he was taking bribes?" Her eyes became distant, remote. "What proof do you have of that?"

"It's what Quentin Burdick was working on, what he was scheduled to see the president about the morning after the night the president was killed."

Hillary Constable walked across to the window and stared into the enveloping night. When she spoke her voice was dry, flat, the rich emotion gone.

"You talked to Burdick?"

"Yes."

"And he told you that?" she asked, her gaze still fixed on the black, starless sky.

"He had been trying to get an interview for months. When the president found out that he knew about The Four Sisters, he called Burdick and set up the appointment himself."

"And cancelled everything else he had that week," said Hillary Constable as if she were reminding herself of what had happened, the sequence of events that starting with this had led to his death.

She turned and faced Hart, but did not move away from the window. She had reacquired something of her old composure. The slight smile was there again, as well as the look of self-assurance in her eyes.

"Burdick thought something was going on, that The Four Sisters was involved in something, and that Robert was involved as well?"

Hart tried to be diplomatic. "There were certain questions...." He gestured toward the rich interior of the room and by implication to all the other things that the two of them, the president and his wife, had acquired. "...about the sources of the president's wealth."

She shook her head, disparaging the kind of rumors that had always followed them, rumors she had so often been forced to deny; rumors, as she had never tired of repeating, that their political enemies tried to use against them because they could never win an argument, or an election, on the merits.

"We have a lot of friends," she said, lifting her eyebrows just a shade to convey the deeper meaning. "People who understood that there were certain things we needed—yes, including this house—things we would have ample means to pay for as soon as we left office."

It was curious how easy it was for her, even now, after her husband's death, to step into the first-person plural when she talked about the presidency of Robert Constable. She had done it to what some thought an embarrassing degree when he was alive, an assumption of an influence that was unsettling to those who liked to think of their presidents as men of independent judgment, and an erroneous suggestion of equality to those who were in a position to know how often Robert Constable had been forced to yield to what she wanted.

"And we will—I mean pay back the loans that were made, the personal loans made by friends of ours."

Hart remembered now why he had not liked the Constables, why he had never trusted them: this sense of entitlement, this belief that whatever they wanted, they should have; this grating certainty that whatever they needed to do to get it, whatever means they had to employ, was justified because they knew what was best for everyone.

"And was one of those friends Jean de la Valette?"

Her eyes flashed with a moment's heated anger; and then, as quick as that, they changed, became reasonable, willing to forgive an easily understood mistake.

"He might have been, had we asked. But no, the friends I'm talking about are people we had known for a long time, before we ever ran for the presidency. We understood what it would look like if…." She smiled in a way that suggested that what she had been about to say was not important, and then quickly changed the subject. "But you were telling me about Quentin Burdick and the story he was working on. He thought Robert was involved in something that would have gotten him in trouble?"

She asked this in what seemed to Hart a strangely neutral tone, as if she were doing it purely for the sake of form rather than out of any concern with whether it was true or not. He got up and stood next to her desk. Drumming his fingers on the edge of it, he glimpsed a picture hidden behind the others, a photograph of Hillary Constable, taken when she was years younger, splashing in the surf of some South Seas island. She was still a good-looking woman, but at the time that picture was taken she had been nothing short of gorgeous.

A thin, furtive smile, the smile of a woman who, understanding the source of the power she has over men, has come to despise them because of it, was there waiting when Hart looked back. It told him something that before that moment he had not really known for sure. He had been given a hint of it that first time they had been in this room, when she had suddenly and quite without warning confided that she had once been in love, not with the man she had married, but with a boy—some "gorgeous boy" was how she had put it—that she had known in college. That was what the look of disdain had meant: the knowledge when she was young that she could have any man she wanted had been, as it were, her fatal flaw. The power to attract, to make men submit, could never last, and she had been a fool to ever think it could.

"Quentin Burdick," she reminded him. "What is it he thinks he knows?"

"That millions of dollars ended up in your husband's pockets; that it was routed through a number of different sources, but that all of it originated with The Four Sisters. This isn't based on some vague suspicion he has; Frank Morris confirmed it."

"Frank Morris, the congressman who was killed in prison? What does he have to do with any of this? Wasn't he convicted of bribery?—He doesn't sound like a very credible source."

"Burdick thinks so. He went out to California, talked to him in prison. Morris was murdered right after that, the same day."

"And Morris said...?"

"That he had been taking money from The Four Sisters, helping get defense contracts for some of the companies The Four Sisters controlled, but when he discovered what they were really up to—helping foreign interests acquire some of the major media companies in this country—he decided he had to stop it. He went to see the president and the next thing he knew he was on trial for bribery and sent to prison."

"You're suggesting the president had something to do with that?"

"Morris told Burdick that the president had been the one who first encouraged him to talk to the people connected with The Four Sisters, and that—"

"That doesn't prove anything!" cried Hillary Constable, throwing up her hands. "Suggesting that someone talks to someone hardly constitutes a crime!"

"He knew all about it!" Hart shouted back. They glared at each other across the room. "He knew everything. He told Morris there was nothing to worry about. He told him that they—'they!'—hadn't done anything wrong. He—"

"They hadn't done anything wrong—that's what he said? You see, he hadn't. Isn't that what—?"

Hart looked straight at her, his eyes cold, immediate.

"He said no one would ever find out!"

Hillary Constable turned on her heel. Folding her arms in front of her, she stared out the window, too angry to say another word. She began to tap her foot.

"What have you found out about his…death?" she asked finally.

She would not turn around, would not look at him. Hart's eyes were drawn back to the photograph of her on the beach. The thought flashed through his mind that she must have had a temper then as well, but had always gotten away with it: No one who wanted her would have risked telling her that she had misbehaved. How many times has the beauty of a woman taught cowardice to men?

"Your husband was involved with The Four Sisters. He was taking money, vast sums of it, in return for doing things he shouldn't have done. He told someone what Morris told him. Morris was convinced that by doing that the president signed his own death warrant, that—"

Hillary Constable wheeled around. She seemed puzzled and confused.

"Signed his own death warrant? Even if all this is true, why would the fact he told someone that Morris had changed his mind about what he was doing mean that?"

"Because if the president was willing to betray Morris, there was no reason to think he would not betray the people he was doing business with."

"That doesn't make any sense. If you and I are in a conspiracy with someone else and you tell me that the other person is thinking about telling the police, I can understand getting rid of him, but why get rid of you?"

She said this as if instead of conspiracy and murder, she was discussing a problem in formal logic. If A equals B, and B equals C, then A…whatever follows, follows; there is nothing moral or immoral about it. Hart had a different understanding of things.

"Because it's the only way to be absolutely safe, the only way to make sure, now that everything is starting to fall apart, that there isn't anyone left who knows what you've done."

"Yes, I suppose you have a point."

Pursing her lips, she seemed to think about it. She went over to the bookshelves where she kept the liquor and poured herself another glass. She closed the bottle and then remembered.

"Would you like…?"

"No, I'm fine," replied Hart, glancing at the drink he had barely touched. Instead of going back to the window, Hillary Constable took the easy chair next to his.

"What do you think of our new president?"

Though he tried not to show it, Hart was stunned. They were talking about the death of her husband, talking about who might be responsible for his murder, and all of sudden she wants to know his opinion of Irwin Russell?

He searched her eyes, but he could see nothing beyond what appeared to be a genuine interest. That in itself revealed more about who she was than anything he might have discovered had he been able to penetrate the veneer of near perfect self-possession.

"What do I think of…? I'm afraid I've been a little too busy trying to find out who might have murdered your husband to have given much thought to his successor."

"Interim successor might be the better description. Irwin was the perfect vice president: quiet, inoffensive, someone everyone liked because he was not a threat to what anyone wanted for themselves." She gave Hart the knowing look of the consummate insider, someone who can size up a situation, take the measure of everyone involved, judge the play of forces with a physicist's precision, and do it all in the blink of an eye. "That was the reason we chose him," she added. "Unlike most of the people in Washington, he didn't wake up every morning full of resentment because someone else was president."

"And now he is," said Hart in a way that suggested something more than the obvious fact. "I'm sure you're right. I doubt he ever felt any resentment that someone else was sitting in the Oval Office, but are you sure he never thought about it, never wondered what it might be like, especially after he was put on the ticket and became vice president?"

That same knowing look was in her eyes.

"Oh, he thought about it, all right; rather I should say, worried about it; worried whether he could hold up under the strain, the pressure, the requirements of the office—if something ever happened. Do you know the first thing he wanted to know when Robert asked him to be his running mate?—Was his health as good as the published reports said it was. Was his heart condition really just a minor matter? Does that sound like someone who spends his time dreaming about what a great president he would be?"

The irony of course, as Hart quickly noted, was that was exactly the kind of question someone desperate for the office might ask; and exactly the way someone would have to ask it, as if his only concern was that nothing was likely to happen and that he would not have to serve. But she was right about Irwin Russell: he was that creature almost extinct in Washington, a politician without ambition for what he did not have.

"As I say, I really haven't had any time, and it hasn't yet been two weeks. But everyone seems to think he's doing as well as could be expected under the circumstances. Why do you ask?"

She stood up and, holding her drink in her hand, crossed over to her desk. She seemed distracted, uncertain what to do next. Her eyes darted from one thing to another, until, finally, they came to rest on the same photograph that had caught Hart's attention. For a moment it seemed to take her back, not just to the past, but to a different remembered future, to a time when she had lived her life in the expectation of things that had not happened. Her blue eyes brightened and the rigid discipline of her mouth gave way to something softer and more sincere.

"Have they always called you 'Bobby'? They never called him that. It was always 'Robert' or 'Bob.' 'Bobby' is more endearing, isn't it? There is a kind of intimacy in it—you know, the easy familiarity you have with someone you grew up with, someone who knows all the innocent secrets you had when you were kids. That's the way people feel about you. But you know that, don't you? You're too smart not to know that. No one ever called him that," she went on, caught in a recollection that was new to her. "He wouldn't have let them; he wasn't strong enough for that. He thought it sounded weak. 'Bobby.' I asked him once about it. I mentioned Bobby Kennedy; he started talking about Jack, and how it sounded better, more in charge, than 'Johnny.' He thought about things like that. Names—they don't mean anything, really, do they? And then, again, they mean everything, don't they? There are people who want me to run; people who think I should be the nominee. What do you think I should do?"

There was not so much as a pause between the one thing and the other; not so much as a second's delay before she went from what seemed an idle reminiscence about her husband's name and the announcement that she was thinking about running for president herself. Hart was beyond the point of being shocked, much less surprised, by anything she said. He was watching what he knew was a performance, but he still was not clear why she was giving it. He was sure she wanted something; he just was not sure what it was.

"You asked me to see what I could find out about your husband's death. You told me that he had not died of a heart attack, that he had been murdered," he reminded her in a firm tone of voice. "I've talked to Clarence Atwood, and I've talked to the agent who was in charge of the detail that night. They confirmed what you said. How could you even be thinking about running for president, how could you be thinking about anything, before we get to the bottom of this? And remember something else: I told you at the beginning that this couldn't be kept secret for more than a very short time, that it was going to have to come out, that there would have to be an investigation."

He was becoming angry as he spoke, angry with her, angry with himself. He should never have agreed to any of this. He should have turned her down and insisted that an investigation begin at once. He had made a mistake; he was not going to make another.

"The president was murdered! That's the only thing you should be thinking about, the only thing that matters. I said I'd see what I could find out and I have. He was murdered because someone wanted to keep him quiet; murdered so he couldn't tell anything to Quentin Burdick. And it seems pretty damn obvious that The Four Sisters—someone involved with The Four Sisters—is behind it. The president was murdered. And if you don't tell what you know to the authorities, I will!"

"But he wasn't murdered! That's what I had to see you about, what I said was so urgent."

Hart was on his feet, staring hard at her.

"What are you saying? You told me he was given a drug that caused his heart to stop. They found evidence of it at the autopsy. Atwood confirmed it."

Hillary Constable stepped closer. She seemed almost contrite, as if she had bungled things and made his life difficult because of it.

"I was distraught, out of my mind with grief; and yes, I admit it, with anger, too. He dies in bed with some whore, one of those women he always had to have; and worse than that, everyone knows it, everyone is talking about it! The pressure I was under, all the things I had to do—I overreacted, misinterpreted what I was told. Clarence Atwood didn't tell me that—"

"You're going to tell me that Atwood didn't tell you your husband was murdered? Atwood told me that himself. And you can trust me: I didn't misinterpret what he said!"

Her chin came up a defiant half inch.

"You may find he's changed his mind."

Her eyes were hot and full of warning, but then, an instant later, they changed, became, if not quite friendly, accommodating, willing to discuss their differences.

"It doesn't really matter how he died, does it? He's dead. Why tarnish his reputation with more allegations, more rumors about things he might have done that he should not have done? He did some good things, some great things, as president. It seems to me we have some duty to protect that, the legacy, the public record, of what he did."

"Protect it with a lie?" cried Hart, as angry as he had ever been. "Lie about the fact that he didn't die of natural causes, that he was assassinated? Lie about the fact that in the years he held office he was part of a criminal conspiracy? Lie, so you can run to take his place, the widow of our beloved president, and not the widow of a charlatan, a fraud?"

"I'm going to run, and I'm going to win! I need your help, Bobby," she said with a savage look. "Don't let me down. There's more at issue here than you think."

Hart did not answer. He turned on his heel and started out of the room.

"Think about it, Bobby!" she shouted after him. "I'll deny I ever said anything about the way my husband died. And don't think that Clarence Atwood will back you up. He'll say whatever I tell him to say."

Hart wheeled back around.

"Don't you care anything about the fact that your husband was murdered, that someone assassinated the President of the United States?"

"Of course I care about that. But there's nothing can be done about it that won't make things worse."

"That's the difference between the truth and the lie: whether it makes things better or worse for you?"

"Not for me," she insisted. "For the country."

"What kind of country do you think this is: a country too stupid to deal with the truth?"

CHAPTER 13

TEN MINUTES AFTER Bobby Hart left Hillary Constable, ten minutes after he stalked out of her lit up house, he was not quite sure what had happened, why she had changed her mind. She had told him that contrary to all the published reports her husband had been murdered and asked him to find out what he could, impressed upon him the urgency and the need for discretion, the concern that they find out who was behind it before it became public knowledge that the president had been murdered and all the rumors started. And now for some reason she had changed her mind, decided that it had not been murder after all; or rather that it was simply better, more advantageous, to ignore what had happened, ignore the fact that her husband had been murdered, because she had political ambitions of her own. Austin Pearce thought Hart had missed the point.

"She always means what she says, when she says it."

He clasped his hands behind his neck and leaned back. They were sitting in the living room of Pearce's townhouse on Washington Square. Austin Pearce was in his favorite chair, next to the open French doors where almost every evening and nearly every Sunday afternoon, he could, depending on his mood, look up from the book he was reading and gaze across the street at the moving crowd in the tree-lined park, the young women who brought their children to play, the old men who sat in silence on the benches reading the newspapers, or glance instead at the bookshelves that towered fifteen feet up to the gold inlaid ceiling of a building that, he was almost certain, had been the one Henry James had in mind when he wrote his story about a long vanished family that had lived here more than a hundred years ago. Even if it was not true, Austin Pearce liked the thought of it, the way it seemed, like his own attachment to the past, to give a greater sense of permanence to things.

"I don't think she changed her mind at all," he said. Sitting up, he looked at Hart, slouching in another easy chair on the other side of the French doors. "She asked you to find out what you could about who might have murdered the president, and you did, didn't you?"

Hart heard what Austin Pearce said, but he did not quite understand it. He was still angry about what had happened the night before, frustrated by his inability to see what he suspected must be right in front of him, something that he thought might be obvious to Austin Pearce, who not only had the most penetrating intelligence of anyone he knew but had known both of the Constables for years. It was the reason he had flown up to New York.

"Consider what you've done for her, what she knows now that she didn't know before, and probably wouldn't have known, if you had not helped."

"The Four Sisters?"

"Yes, of course. She knows that was the story Burdick was working on; she knows that was the reason that the president was meeting with him." Pearce spread his fingers and tapped them together. He seemed to concentrate on a thought, a question that was taking shape in his mind. "Did she seem surprised?"

"She didn't deny that she knew Jean de la Valette, and she knew the name of the firm. She resented the suggestion that any money might have changed hands; insisted that the money they had came from friends of theirs who would have been paid back from what they expected to make after Constable left office. But, no, now that you ask, she didn't seem surprised. She never does, though, does she? Seem surprised, I mean."

"She's hard to read, I'll give you that. But the point is that, thanks to you, she knows the story is out there, that Burdick is onto it. She knows about Frank Morris, that Morris implicated the president and that Morris believed that The Four Sisters had the president killed. She knows something else, too: she knows that there isn't any way to prove any of this without her or the Secret Service." The brown eyes of Austin Pearce seemed to take on a deeper shade as he tried to grasp her intentions. "Has it occurred to you that maybe Robert Constable wasn't murdered after all?"

"What are you talking about? She told me he was murdered, and Atwood confirmed it."

"Would you have gone looking for his killer, would you have discovered anything about The Four Sisters—would you have been all that interested in what Burdick told you—if she hadn't told you that? Don't misunderstand, I think she told you the truth when she told you he had been murdered, but I don't think that's the reason she wanted you to find out what you could. I think she wanted to know what was out there, what someone with your connections could discover. She wanted to know what she had to worry about. She was lying when she told you that a few close friends gave them the money they needed. That was a cover story they fabricated together. What was it she said to you?—that Jean de la Valette is someone they could have asked if they had wanted to; could have asked, but didn't, because they knew what it would look like. You see, she understood exactly what the position was, what they had to do to protect themselves against too close an inquiry. They had friends who would help them, and a lot of them did, but not the kind of money—tens of millions, if not more—that The Four Sisters moved into various accounts for them."

This was news to Hart. Pearce explained.

"I've made some inquires," he said with a cryptic glance. "What Morris told Burdick is true, although Morris didn't know the full extent of it. The scheme is complicated in the details, but extremely simple in principle. Several foundations were established, charitable enterprises to do various good works; but, and this is the key to everything, none of them do the work themselves. They give out grants to applicants who want to start a literacy program in the inner city, or a public health program in a third world country—that kind of thing. Each of the foundations has a paid staff, overhead, buildings in Manhattan and in several capitals overseas, buildings that were rented, and buildings that were bought and paid for. The house in Washington is owned by one of them. Everything gets paid for by the foundation: the people who work for you, the planes you lease, the cars you drive, the hotels you stay in, the expensive restaurants you go to eat— everything! It was all there, waiting for the president, the day he left office."

Austin Pearce rose from his comfortable chair and stood in front of the open French doors, listening to the soft muted sounds of Manhattan that, for someone who lived there, had a music of its own. The rhythm of it, the way it had for so much of his life been a part of who he was, the raucous, endless beat that faded in and out, the sense of romance that came every night in Manhattan, especially when you were alone, made the past, his past, what he had lived through, what he had seen, what he remembered about what had happened, as real as anything that was happening now.

"I saw the Kennedys, Jack when he was president, and then Bobby, later than that; saw them here in New York, heard both of them speak. I didn't know them of course," he added, still staring into the square. "I was too young for that. They were heroes to me, people you could look up to, people you could respect. They were both of course quite ruthless when it came to getting what they wanted, but not in the way we mean it now." He turned a knowing eye on Hart, who was leaning forward in his chair. "There were things they wouldn't do; things—and this, it seems to me, makes all the difference—they wouldn't think of doing. They didn't think they were more important than the country. The other difference," he remarked with a quick, dismissive laugh, "is that they both had read something; serious things, I mean. Bobby used to quote Aeschylus, and no one thought it strange that he did."

With a wistful smile, Pearce shook his head at how much had changed. He fell silent for a moment, concentrating, as it seemed, on the long vanished voices that at times still echoed briefly in his mind.

"By the way, have you talked to Burdick?" he asked, engaged again with the present.

"We've traded phone calls. I tried him again, just before I got here—but we haven't talked. But you talked to him, didn't you? He has the story."

"I wonder if he does," said Pearce with a distant, slightly abstracted gaze. "I wonder if anyone ever will. All of it, I mean: the whole story of what really happened. But yes, Quentin Burdick came to see me. I told him what I knew. He's quite persuasive. There is something about that manner of his that makes you want to talk, the way he makes you feel that he's grateful just to have a few minutes of your time, and then, before you know it, you're telling him things you thought you would never tell anyone." Pearce shrugged his shoulders and laughed. "Damned if I didn't tell him about that day in the Oval Office when I confronted Constable with what I knew, the day he went off into that obscenity-laced tirade and told me I was fired."

Austin Pearce clasped his hands behind his back and with his head bowed thought hard for a moment.

"We're in a fairly difficult position. If Hillary Constable insists on lying about the murder, if Atwood goes along with her, there isn't any way to confirm any of this. The president died of a heart attack and that's all there is to it. The Four Sisters is just a story about a complicated financial arrangement that can easily be denied and that, in any case, won't make sense to anyone."

"But Quentin Burdick has the story," objected Hart. "He has what Morris told him, and—"

"Frank Morris, disgraced member of Congress, convicted of bribery, a liar, a thief, and now dead, murdered in prison."

"Murdered after he talked to Burdick!"

"Murdered in prison, no provable link to anything, much less that he happened to talk to a reporter." Pearce waved his hand, dismissing in advance, as it were, the next objection. "And as for what Morris said about the president's death—the bitter speculation of a convicted felon."

Pearce paced back and forth, like a lawyer in the middle of his summation, except that the audience he was playing to, the jury he was trying to persuade, was a jury of only one.

"Burdick can write all he wants about the financial dealings that went on between the companies controlled by The Four Sisters and the late, lamented Robert Constable, but he can't say anything about a murder. The only people who know about it have, for reasons of their own, decided not to talk about it."

"But they did talk," said Hart. "They talked to me. I told Burdick that Constable had been killed. I confirmed what Morris had suspected. I told him I couldn't tell him how I knew, but I can tell him now," continued Hart with some heat. "I told Hillary Constable that this couldn't be kept secret, that I wouldn't be part of some cover-up. I told her that I'd look into it, see what I could find out, but only for a few days, and that after that there was going to have to be an investigation."

Pearce seemed worried, concerned about the implications, about what might happen.

"Are you sure you want to do that? If you become the source, if you're the one who claims that the president was murdered and that his wife knew it and has been covering it up—what do you think happens to you? Remember who you're dealing with. The basic rule of the Constables has always been to attack."

Pearce's visage darkened. His eyes seemed to register astonishment at the catalogue of cruelties that marched through his mind, the parade of half-truths and lies that had become the regular, and expected, method of political warfare practiced by the Constables against not just their opponents, but anyone who got in their way.

"And the second rule has always been to make it appear that they're only defending themselves against an attack, an outrageously unfair attack, by the other side. Are you sure you want to expose yourself to that?"

A shrewd grin full of false confidence flashed across Bobby Hart's fine, straight mouth.

"At least I won't be alone."

Pearce had anticipated the point.

"Because of course I can confirm that you told me almost immediately what you had learned, and that this isn't some recent fabrication on your part. All right: I agree we can't afford to wait. This has to come out; the country has to know. The president was murdered and we damn well have to go after the people who did it."

"She must have suspected what had happened, that it had something to do with The Four Sisters," said Hart with all the force of a sudden realization. "If she knew what was going on, if she knew about the money, if she knew—

or even if she only suspected—what her husband was going to talk to Burdick about—that's why she wanted it kept secret, why she wanted me to find out what I could: so she could know for certain if The Four Sisters—if Jean de la Valette—was behind it. She's afraid of the scandal, for what it would do to his reputation—with all that means for her own ambition. The president is on the take and gets killed when he's about to talk! It's the end of everything for her if that comes out."

Austin Pearce sat down. He beat two fingers hard against the arms of the chair, and then leaned back and, as if he were seeing it for the first time, a visitor in someone else's home, made an idle inspection of the room. He seemed to approve of what he saw, the rows of well-read books all neatly arranged, the pair of portraits of men he had never known, Italian noblemen from three centuries ago, painted by an artist whose name was now, like theirs, buried in the vast obscurity of time.

"She's going to run," he said presently. "I'm almost certain of it. Russell as president!—It's a caretaker government. That's certainly the way she sees it, at least. This isn't just the best chance she'll ever have; it's better than the chance she had before, when Robert was alive. There would have been resistance then, serious resistance to what everyone would have seen as a third term for the Constables. But now that he's dead, now that she is the brave and grieving widow, no one looks at it like that. She can run to finish what he started, what he would have done himself if he had not died. The sympathy for her in the country right now is overwhelming. Even if Irwin Russell wanted to run, get elected in his own right, I'm afraid he wouldn't have much chance. Strange the way things change. She used to be seen as someone trying to take advantage of what her husband had achieved; now she is seen as the only one who can complete his work." Pearce slapped his hands on his knees and stood up. "You're going to tell Burdick everything?"

"What choice is there—help cover up a murder?"

"He'll have to contact her to ask her response, ask whether she can confirm that her husband was killed."

"Maybe that will force her to tell the truth," replied Hart, unconvinced. "Maybe when she knows he's going with the story, that there isn't anything she can do to stop it, she'll decide she can't afford to lie."

"I wouldn't bet too much on it. She has another problem to worry about," said Pearce. His eyes darted all around before settling on a point just beyond where Hart sat waiting. "If they killed her husband because of what he knew, why couldn't the same thing happen to her? It may not just be the scandal she's worried about—what would happen if the world learns about her husband's involvement with The Four Sisters—she may be worried about her life."

Hart did not feel sympathetic.

"Even if she won't talk about what she knows, there are other people, people who don't have the same fear, or the same ambition. Clarence Atwood—"

"Will do exactly what she wants him to do, just like she said," interjected Pearce. "As long as he thinks she might become president. Look what kind of leverage this gives him, knowing what he knows, if she pulls it off. She'll have to give him anything he wants."

"There's the agent," insisted Hart, "the one who was there that night. I gave his name to Burdick. He didn't strike me as the type that could be convinced to cover up something like this, not the way he feels about what he did with the woman, the hired assassin he helped get away."

"If they haven't already shipped him out to some place in South America," said Pearce with a skeptical glance. "The important thing is that we tell Burdick what we know. Once he has the story, once that happens, everything changes." Pearce suddenly remembered. "Jean de la Valette. There's still no proof he was involved. We don't have what the lawyers call circumstantial evidence. Well, after Burdick runs his story, no one will be able to stop an investigation getting started."

Pearce was thinking fast, trying to put everything together.

"I have to make a call." He started toward his study, thought of something else, and turned around. "Why don't you call Burdick? Try to see him right away; tonight, if possible." He smiled apologetically. "I'm sorry, I shouldn't be telling you what to do. Actually, don't call Burdick just yet. Let me make this call first." He glanced at the antique clock on the mantel. "It's only five in the morning in Paris, but he's always bragging about how early he gets up."

When Austin Pearce came back ten minutes later he was shaking his head.

"He was up, all right—in the middle of his French lesson, he had to tell me right away." Pearce dropped into his favorite chair, spread his legs out in front of him, and with a look of helpless astonishment shook his head again. "Five years he's been there, the American ambassador to France, and almost every time I talk to him he has to tell me how his stupid French lessons are coming!"

Hart began to share in the astonishment.

"He doesn't speak French?"

"No, even after five years—well, that's not fair: it overstates the effort. He is a man of frequent enthusiasms, always eager to start something new, never quite able to finish anything he's started. He starts French lessons every year." Pearce folded his arms across his chest. He seemed to ponder the point, search for some deeper significance, and then gave up on it. "He has the short attention span of the rich. That's how he became ambassador, of course: raised a lot of money for Constable in his first campaign and then, after Constable won, thought he would like to live in Paris. Nothing complicated about it. When I asked him if he spoke French, he assured me that it didn't matter because every Frenchman he had ever known spoke English. And we wonder why the French don't like us!"

Hart had been trying to remember the name. Pearce reminded him.

"Andrew Malreaux."

"At least the name is French."

"That's the reason he thought he was qualified," replied Pearce, rolling his eyes. "But I shouldn't be so hard on him. He's always been helpful." There was a glint of mischief in his eyes, and more than a little irony as well. "We used to be enemies, when we both were here in New York, but then, after I was in Washington he didn't remember that anymore, and by the time he became ambassador and I told him what a good job he was doing, he was quite certain that we had always been friends. It's good when someone doesn't hold a grudge; in his case it's because he can't remember it."

Austin Pearce spent so much time reading histories that he sometime started composing them himself when he talked about other people. Hart, as politely as he could, steered him back to what was immediately important.

"There was a reason you called the ambassador."

Pearce looked at him as if he did not understand. Then, an instant later, realizing that he had gone off on a long digression, he denied it.

"You need to know that about Malreaux; you need to know his limitations. He'll get us what we need, put us in touch with the right people, but he's not someone you want to talk to about something as sensitive as this. I asked him to have someone in the embassy's political section prepare a dossier on Jean de la Valette. Malreaux did not ask why. It was enough that I said that a member of the Senate Intelligence Committee would be there tomorrow."

"Tomorrow? I'll need to make a reservation, I'll need...."

Pearce slowly got to his feet.

"No, we'll take a private plane. It's better that no one knows we're going."

"You're coming, too?"

"Of course! Don't you remember?—I know Jean de la Valette; you've never met him. It won't seem unusual if the two of us happen to be in Paris, consulting about the mutual interests of France and the United States."

"But tomorrow—?"

"I don't see how we can wait—do you? We don't know what he's planning, and this business about the president's death...."

That reminded Hart that he had to talk to Burdick. It was late, but Burdick answered on the first ring.

"What did he say?" asked Pearce after Hart ended the call.

"He was down in Washington. He's just gotten back. He asked me if I could meet him right away. He said he discovered something. He wouldn't tell me what it was, only that—and he sounded worried when he said it—it 'changed everything.'"

CHAPTER 14

QUENTIN BURDICK WAS not sure what to do. He felt a little like a fool, waiting for someone who was already half an hour late, someone who had probably changed his mind and was not coming at all. It would have been bad enough if he was meeting him in New York, but he had come all the way to Washington to talk to the agent who had been in charge the night Robert Constable died. Richard Bauman had been reluctant even to talk to him on the phone and was on the verge of hanging up when Burdick told him that Senator Hart—"Bobby Hart"—had given him his name and suggested he ought to give him the chance to tell his side of the story before he published his account of what had happened that night in the hotel. There had been a long pause, and Burdick had the sense that Bauman wanted to talk, but that something, or someone, was holding him back.

"I trusted him," said Bauman finally. There was another, shorter, pause, tentative and full of meaning. "Do you?"

Burdick immediately understood that something had happened, and that it was not what had taken place in that hotel room; it was something that had happened after that. Burdick told him the truth: that the senator had never lied to him and that he would trust Bobby Hart with his life.

"Talk to me," Burdick urged him. "I'll come to D.C.; we can talk there, wherever you like. I won't use your name, I'll protect your identity. But we both know what happened, and we both know that it's going to come out."

Bauman then said something that made Burdick sit up and take notice, something that made him wonder if somewhere along the line he had made a mistake, failed to understand the story he thought he knew inside and out.

"Are you sure you know what happened?" There was a bitter, cynical edge to Bauman's voice, as if he knew something that Burdick did not, something that would change everything if only Burdick knew it too.

"What is it?" he asked. There was another long silence and Burdick was afraid he was going to lose him. "I'll be in Washington tomorrow. Just tell me where you want to meet."

And so here he was, sitting in the middle of Union Station, waiting for someone he would not have recognized if he were standing right in front of him. It struck him funny now, that he did not know what Bauman looked like. Bobby Hart had mentioned something about his age, but all he had said about his appearance was an offhand remark about the way that, like other agents of the Secret Service, Bauman was someone who could easily pass unnoticed in a crowd.

Burdick checked his watch. Bauman had said to meet him in the station lobby at two-thirty in the afternoon, and it was now ten minutes after three. He was not coming; he had changed his mind. It was just a short walk to the Capitol. The Senate was still in session. Instead of calling Bobby Hart later that night to tell him that he had reached Richard Bauman and that, after some initial reluctance, the agent had agreed to meet him but then had not shown up, he would try to see him now.

He checked his watch again. It was quarter after. Bauman was not going to come. A train had just arrived and the lobby was full of noise. Burdick got up and started toward the doors and the street outside. Just as he got there, someone took hold of his arm.

"You forgot this." Burdick stopped and turned around. A stranger, a middle-aged man, was holding a thick manila envelope. "You left it on the bench next to you when you left. I'm sure it's something important."

Burdick started to explain that the package was not his, that someone else must have left it on the station bench. Then he saw his own name written across the front of it.

"As I say, I'm sure it's something you wouldn't want to lose."

They exchanged a glance. The station was crowded, people coming in and out, people all around them. Richard Bauman pushed open the door and, with Burdick right behind him, headed toward a long line of taxicabs waiting at the curb.

"You were late; I didn't think you were coming," remarked Burdick as the cab they had climbed into pulled away. "I waited forty-five minutes."

"Yes, I know," said Bauman without apology. "I was there when you arrived."

"You were there when…? Then why did you wait until I was ready to give up?"

Bauman was bending forward, watching out the window as if he were looking for an address. He did not reply.

"Turn right at the next street," he told the driver. "You can drop us halfway down the block."

As the taxi driver made the turn, Bauman looked back over his shoulder. There was nothing casual in the way he did it. His gaze was too intense for someone who was just trying to get his bearings, remember where he was going from the familiar surroundings of where he had been.

"You think you're being followed?" asked Burdick. "Or do you think I was? Is that the reason you let me sit there like that—to see if someone was following me?"

They had turned onto a busy commercial street filled with small shops and restaurants, the kind frequented mainly by people who lived in the neighborhood and did not want to spend much money.

"Any place here," said Bauman as he took out his wallet and handed the driver twice what he was owed. He grasped the door handle, ready to get out. "Someone knows what you've been doing. Frank Morris was murdered just after you saw him; your apartment was broken into just before you got back to New York."

"How did you know that?" asked Burdick. But it was too late. Bauman had opened the door and was getting out of the cab.

Burdick caught up with him on the sidewalk. Bauman's eyes were moving quickly side to side, searching, as it seemed, for anything that was unusual, anything out of place, the way, as Burdick imagined, he must have done every time he was at work, guarding the president from the threat of assassination. Burdick clutched under his arm the package he had been given, wondering at the thick bulk of it and what it must contain. They walked to the corner, crossed the street, and then started down the other side. They stopped in front of a dismal-looking café with a dust-covered window and a neon sign that barely flickered. Bauman held the door open, and, as Burdick passed in front of him, darted a glance first in one direction, then the other, before he followed him inside.

"I don't live far from here," explained Bauman as they took a table in back.

The place was quite empty, all the other tables not only deserted but without any sign that they had recently been used. The soft hum of the air conditioning underscored the dull oppressive silence. It was dark, the only light what came through the grimy front window from the street outside. The waitress, who doubled as the short-order cook, flashed a girlish smile, all that was left of her long-vanished youth, and started to recite the specials of the day. Bauman nodded gently and told her they just wanted coffee.

Burdick reached for the package that he had set next to him on the table. Bauman reached across and held him by the wrist.

"No, not yet; tell me about Hart. I know what you said on the phone—that you'd trust him with your life. That isn't what I want to know."

The waitress brought their coffee. Burdick stirred in milk and sugar, tasted it, and then added a little more milk. There were some things about which he was always precise.

"What is it you want to know?"

Bauman did not even look at his coffee. He shoved the cup to the side and hunched forward on his elbows. It was insufferably hot outside, but he had worn a coat and tie, a habit that not even this vile weather could break.

"Is he as good as they say he is?"

It seemed a strange question to ask; one, moreover, Quentin Burdick was not certain how to answer. With a reporter's instinct, he grinned and answered with a question of his own.

"How good do they say he is?"

Bauman looked at him with grudging admiration. Burdick was smart and, better than that, because there were a lot of smart people, knew how to get to the heart of things.

"I was seven years with Constable, from when he ran the first time to the night he died. I never once heard him say anything good about him—Hart, I mean."

"And that led you to think that...?"

"That he was someone he couldn't handle, someone he couldn't bullshit," said Bauman, his wispy brown eyebrows inching upward with each new phrase. "Someone he couldn't con into doing what he wanted."

"All that may be true, but it doesn't explain why Constable would have been afraid of him."

With a pensive expression, Bauman stared down at the floor. He began to swing his foot, slowly, methodically, like someone keeping time.

"We're like potted plants, or wallpaper, part of the room itself. We stand there, silent, barely moving. After a while, the people you're guarding forget you're even there; not forget, really—it's more like they forget you're human, with a mind of your own, remembering what they say, making the same kind of judgments anyone would who heard the kind of things that were said."

Bauman stopped swinging his foot. He raised his eyes, not all the way, but far enough that Burdick could see the rueful expression, the almost savage mockery, that danced inside them.

"Seven years! Can you imagine all the things I heard, all the things I saw?" His eyes met Burdick's waiting gaze with a candid, harsh appraisal that, more than words could have done, told the contempt he felt. "He was afraid of Hart—they both were: he and that wife of his. I'm not sure why. Maybe because of what I said before: that they couldn't get to him, couldn't force him to fall in line. Constable was always making some disparaging remark about him. Maybe he was just afraid of the comparisons people made. You know, how Hart never cheated on anything, and that's all Constable ever did. That's why I asked if Hart was really as good as they say he is."

"Yes, he's that good; better than that, really. There are a lot of people who think he should have been president, a lot of people who think he still might be."

"You know him pretty well, then?" asked Bauman with more than idle curiosity. He seemed to Burdick intensely interested in the answer.

"Yes, I'd say so. I've known him since he first came to Congress."

"You know him well enough to warn him? Would he believe you if you told him something, even if it seemed not just unbelievable, but impossible?"

"Impossible? What are you talking about?"

Richard Bauman put his left elbow on the shabby faded tablecloth, opened the fingers of his hand, and then closed them into a fist, and then did it again, and again after that, a steady drum-like repetition. His gaze became distant, remote. He turned his hand, made a fist again, sideways this time, and tapped the hollow end softly, patiently against his chin.

"I would have taken a bullet for him," he said in the way of someone coming to terms with himself. "He may not have deserved it, but he was the President of the United States and I'll be goddamned if I would have let someone kill him. That's what we sign up for, what we swear to do: save the president, no matter what the cost, take the bullet, because if someone has to die it's better that it's you."

"I know you were there; I know you were in the room," said Burdick, certain he understood what the agent was trying to say.

"No, I was in the other room, the way I always was, sitting there without a damn thing to do, just outside the bedroom. I didn't know he had someone in there. Don't misunderstand, I was not surprised he had a woman with him—I would have been surprised if he hadn't—but I tried not to think about it. I tried to tell myself that it was none of my business. It was, of course, and that was my—that was our—mistake. But that's the way he wanted it, what we had to let him do."

Burdick sipped on his coffee. He wanted Bauman to take it slow, to tell him everything that had happened that night, and after that night.

"Then you heard something, knew the president was in trouble, and that's when you went in, that's when you found her?"

To Burdick's astonishment, Bauman vigorously shook his head.

"The door was locked! I should have known right away that something was wrong, that he had not just had a heart attack. Look," he went on, angry with himself, "we let him get away with it, let him give a key to any woman he wanted, but we never let him lock a door. That was one rule we would not let him break. He understood that. He knew it had to be that way, and that we'd never just walk in on him. And I forgot that—forgot to even think what it meant—when I heard him cry for help and I started pounding on the door. It was locked. She opened it."

"The woman, the one he was with, the one who—?"

"Opened it like she was scared to death, half out of her mind with fear and no idea what to do! One minute she's in bed with the president, the next minute the president is dead. Why wouldn't she be scared?"

"This woman, the one you saw that night, the one who killed him—what did she look like? Can you describe her for me?"

Bauman's mouth pulled back into a tight, corrosive look. His eyes flashed with what seemed to Burdick bitter, angry disillusionment. He nodded toward the package that lay unopened on the table. Burdick picked it up, eager to see what was inside. He remembered that Hart had told him that Bauman had worked with a sketch artist to get the girl's likeness, but instead of a drawing, a second-hand rendering of what she looked like, Burdick pulled out a black and white photograph, and not just one, but half a dozen of them. He did not even try to hide his surprise.

"But how? When?"

Bauman was still sitting there, he had not moved, but part of him seemed to disappear, vanish into the darkened corner of the vacant café, as if the answer, or rather what lay behind the answer, had come at a cost greater than he could bear.

"I'm no longer with the Secret Service. Two days ago, the director told me that because of what had happened it was decided that I should take early retirement. I wasn't given a choice. He wanted me out. He tried to tell me he was doing it for me, that it was the only way to prevent a serious sanction, a black mark on my record, for what I had done, letting that woman, that assassin, go. I believed him; I thought he was telling me the truth. I mean, what I did—deciding that it was more important to protect the president's reputation, save his family from the embarrassment, instead of just doing my job—there should have been sanctions for that. But then I remembered something. It did not mean much at the time. I thought he was just trying to cover his ass a little, that he didn't want Hart to think he wasn't on top of things."

With a quick, puzzled smile, Burdick twisted his narrow head slightly to the side.

"Hart?—You're talking about when he met with Clarence Atwood? What happened?"

"I told Hart everything I knew; I answered every question. I told him the truth, and then Atwood lied. It did not seem that important. What difference did it make that he had not done it yet; I was sure he would have me do it right away. It's like I said, Clarence was just trying to protect himself." Bauman's eyes became hard, resentful, and full of disappointment, though, it seemed to Burdick, mainly with himself. "Clarence was always good at that," he muttered, staring off into the distance.

"What did he lie to Hart about? What was it you thought he was going to have you do?" asked Burdick with an insistence that brought Bauman back to himself.

"The drawing, the one you thought was there," he replied, gesturing toward the manila envelope that lay open on the table. "There never was a drawing, an artist's sketch of what the girl looked like, never. I was never asked to do it. I wasn't asked to describe to anyone—anyone except Atwood— what she looked like. Atwood lied about it to Hart, and he lied when he told him that he had given copies of it to the FBI. I was still so shaken by what had happened, by what I had done—that instead of protecting the president I had helped his murderer get away—that I didn't understand how that lie meant that he had lied about that other thing as well."

Bauman's eyes, trained to search a crowd for the least little thing unusual, to move in a constant, relentless circuit, watching, waiting for something to happen, did not move at all. They stared straight ahead, empty, bleak, disconsolate, two hollow orbs sunk in a black depression. Burdick coaxed him out of it.

"That other thing?" he asked in a friendly, sympathetic voice. "Tell me what it was. It's important, isn't it?"

"What?" Bauman blinked his eyes. "Yes, it's important. I don't know why it didn't seem that important when I heard him say it to Hart. It wasn't just lying about a picture, a drawing of what the girl looked like, something we could have done the next day or even that night. He told Hart that copies of the drawing had been given to the FBI, and that the bureau had started an investigation. That's what I remembered when Atwood told me I was finished, that I had to leave, that it was the only way I had to protect myself from public embarrassment when the truth came out that the president had been murdered and that I had helped the killer get away. There was no picture; nothing had been given to the FBI. Do you understand: Nothing had been given to the FBI—Atwood had never talked to them!"

"But he's the one who told you that the president had not died of a heart attack, that he had been murdered. Why wouldn't he tell the FBI? Why wouldn't he want them to start an investigation right away?"

Bauman turned to make sure they were still alone, and then bent forward.

"When he told me, when he called me into his office the day after the president died and said there had been an autopsy and that some drug had been used, I thought the investigation had already started. I asked him who I was supposed to talk to, who was in charge. He said he'd let me know, that there were some other things that had to be worked out first. He didn't tell me what they were, and I was so distracted, so upset, I didn't think to ask. It was only later, after he talked to Hart, after I began to realize what he had lied about, after he told me I was finished, after more than a week had gone by and everyone was still talking as if the president had died of natural causes, it was only after all that, that I decided to find out. I broke into his office." He nodded toward the package and what it held inside. "It's Atwood's file."

"You took the file; you didn't—?"

"No, I made copies of everything; he doesn't know I have it. His office is just down the hallway from mine. I was there late at night, cleaning out my things."

Burdick tapped his finger on the cover.

"Is this the only copy?"

"No. There's someone else I thought might need it."

Burdick glanced at the black-and-white photograph. She was more than good-looking, she was extraordinary, with large, bold eyes and a mouth that seemed somehow both vulnerable and defiant at the same time. He wondered why Bauman had thought to include several copies of the photograph instead of just one. Then, when he put down the first and picked up the second, he realized that they weren't the same photograph at all; that they, and the four others as well, showed her not just in different outfits and different poses, but with such completely different looks that she could have passed for six different women. He put them down and searched Bauman's eyes

"This is the girl, the woman you saw that night, the one who murdered the president?"

"That's not a face I'll ever forget."

"But how—how did Clarence Atwood get a photograph, six photographs, of her? How did he even know what she looked like, if you didn't work with a sketch artist?"

"Don't you get it? She was working for us. Clarence Atwood hired her. The head of the Secret Service hired the woman who murdered the President of the United States!"

CHAPTER 15

THEY SAT IN a kind of stunned silence, neither of them wanting to believe what they both knew was true. Bauman had been right: It was more than unbelievable, it was impossible; impossible that anything like this could have happened, impossible that the president of the United States had been murdered on the order of the head of the very agency sworn to protect the president's life. It was more than betrayal, it was treason.

The more Bauman thought about it, the angrier he became. This awful secret had been locked up inside him for days, with no one he could talk to, no one he could trust. For more than twenty years, he had done what he had been told. Like a soldier in a war, he had understood that his job was to react, not think for himself. And now, suddenly, he had to decide on his own what he was supposed to do. He knew he had to do something; he could not just forget what he had discovered. He had helped a murderer, an assassin, get away. He was not about to let the man who hired her go free.

But who should he tell? This was not something that Clarence Atwood had done alone. If he hired someone to kill the president, it was because someone told him to. He could take what he had to the FBI. He had friends there, people he had worked with in the past. But what if he made a mistake, told the wrong person what he knew? The risk was too high, the danger too great. He was not just thinking about himself, though he knew how easy it would be to put him out of the way; the real danger, the one he worried about, was what might happen if these people, whoever they were, got away with it, murdered the president and no one ever found out what they had done. The more he thought about it, the less certain he was about how to proceed. Each alternative seemed less promising than the last. And then he thought of it, and wondered why he had not thought of it before.

"Hart," he mumbled to himself.

"Hart? What about him?" asked Burdick.

Lost in his own reverie, Bauman had not realized he had spoken out loud. He looked up from the table, blinked his eyes, and then remembered.

"I was going to tell him, but then you called. I thought I could trust him. Atwood lied to him, which meant that Hart could not have known, could not have been a part of it."

But the question about whom he could trust, whom he could safely tell, was secondary to a deeper concern, one that had troubled him from the time he first read what was in the file he had stolen from Atwood's office, troubled him so much that he had scarcely slept at night. It was still there, gnawing at him, driving him a little more crazy each time he went back through what had happened and how he had been made a part of it, an unwilling accomplice in a conspiracy to murder. Suddenly, all that pent up emotion exploded, and he hit the table with the flat of his hand so hard that the waitress, sitting on a stool next to the cash register in front, jolted sideways with the noise. When she saw it was nothing, the startled glance vanished and she turned back to the newspaper that lay spread out on the counter in front of her.

"That explains it, doesn't it?" insisted Bauman, his eyes aflame. "Why Atwood didn't have me work with a sketch artist, why he didn't want an investigation. He arranged it, he organized the whole thing: the murder, the cover-up—everything!"

Burdick smiled patiently. He understood the pressure Bauman was under, the guilt he must feel, but still he had to wonder why, despite all that, he had not seen the flaw; why, despite his emotions, he had not realized his mistake.

"But Atwood is the one who told you that Constable had been murdered," he reminded him in a quiet, sympathetic voice free from any hint of criticism. "If he hadn't told you that, you wouldn't have known there was anything to investigate."

Burdick thought this would cause Bauman to hesitate, to reconsider what he had said, but instead Bauman dismissed the objection out of hand.

"He didn't have any choice; not after I had seen the girl." Bauman's eyes were eager, alive, filled with a certainty so complete that it was impossible to doubt that he had thought it all through and was utterly convinced he was right. "It didn't go the way they thought it would: Constable didn't die quietly, he didn't just pass out from that injection. He cried out for help. Maybe he saw the needle, maybe he saw what she was going to do; maybe when he first felt it he struggled to get away. Whatever happened, he made enough noise that I went running for the door. She had to open it; she could not just hide behind that locked door. Everyone on the floor would have been alerted and she never would have gotten away. She knew that, she had to know that. She had to open the door; she had to go into that act of hers: pretend she was scared, panic-stricken, that in the middle of having sex with the president he had had a heart attack and died!"

Burdick waited, expecting more. Bauman seemed momentarily transfixed by the certainty of his own account; sufficient, it seemed to him, to remove every question, every doubt. Burdick gave him a puzzled glance.

"But that still doesn't explain why he told you that Constable had been murdered. You saw the girl, but you didn't know then that she was pretending anything. You believed her when she told you what happened. That was the reason you…the reason you did what you did."

With a brief nod, Bauman acknowledged the truth of what Burdick said. Then he gestured toward the package.

"It's all in there: the autopsy, the report. There had to be one, but Atwood made sure it was carried out in private, as few people as possible involved. It probably never occurred to him that anyone would notice a small puncture wound, and if that hadn't been discovered there wouldn't have been any reason to look for evidence of a drug. It would have been a simple case of heart failure, exactly what you would expect to find, given his age and his history."

But even as he said it, Bauman now seemed uncertain. Despite his seeming confidence, he was bothered by a latent suspicion that would not go away.

"Or maybe it did occur to him," he ventured after a pause. "Maybe that's what he was counting on; maybe that's what he wanted: a way to prove that it was not a heart attack, that it was murder."

"What do you mean? If he hired her, if Atwood hired someone to kill the president, what reason could he have to want anyone to know that the president had been murdered?"

A look of contempt shot across Bauman's troubled mouth.

"Why would he want it known that the president had been murdered?—I guess that would depend on who he wanted to blame."

Leaning on his elbow, Burdick rubbed his chin as he seized on that fugitive thought and tried to follow it through to all its awful consequences. If Bauman was right, if Atwood had hired someone to kill the president, the obvious question was why. It was more than doubtful—it seemed to him an absurdity—to think that Atwood could have had any reason of his own to want the president dead. Robert Constable had made him head of the Secret Service: that seemed to rule out the possibility of some deep sense of disappointment, the kind that required revenge. But if it was not personal, then Atwood had to have been acting at the direction of someone else, someone who had something to gain from the death of Robert Constable, something they could not have so long as Constable was still alive. And not just that, it had to be someone who could convince Clarence Atwood that it was worth his while to betray his office—betray his country, if you will—and risk his own life, to say nothing of his reputation, on a charge of conspiracy to murder the President of the United States. Burdick was almost afraid to ask.

"Who put Atwood up to this? Who is he working for? Do you know?"

Bauman began to scratch the back of his heavily veined hand. Staring blindly into the distance, he kept scratching at it, scratching it as if it were the only way to erase from his memory what he wished he had not learned.

"It's all in there," he said finally, though even now he refused to shift his gaze, to look back at the package that now belonged to Burdick. "Every rotten, dirty part of it." Slowly, and as if with a conscious effort, his eyes came back round. He looked straight at Burdick. "You won't believe it, the first time you go through it. You'll think it's all a pack of lies. You'll want to destroy it, throw it in the fire and burn it, hope that once you've done that it will leave you alone and you won't remember it," he remarked in a strained, hopeless voice. "It's sort of like being told that someone you love is dead. I lost my wife a couple of years ago; she died in an accident. There's a moment when you think that if you can just go back a few minutes, even just a few seconds, you can start all over and that what you've just been told won't happen. But you can't, can you?—And then you know with that awful, perfect certainty that nothing is ever going to be the same again."

Looking somehow much older than he had just an hour earlier, when Burdick had first seen him, Richard Bauman stepped out from behind the table with the threadbare tablecloth and the tarnished silverware and stood for what seemed a long time in the darkened silence of the deserted café. Finally, he put his hand on Burdick's shoulder and told him that whatever the consequences, no matter who it might hurt, it all had to come out, and that he trusted Burdick to make sure that it did.

"The country deserves the truth."

"Where are you going to be?" asked Burdick. "How do I get in touch with you?"

"I'll try to reach you, but right now, I've got to disappear." He glanced one last time at the package, the tale of horrors he had found in Clarence Atwood's private office. "Read that; you'll see what I mean. And be careful. No one is safe." And then he turned and headed out the door, into the streets of Washington and the hoped for anonymity of the city.

Burdick watched him go, struck by the cautious efficiency of the way he moved, the pigeon-toed gait that former fighters and former football linemen had, the clean discipline of the athlete, trained to strength and quickness, who knows as little about hesitation as he does about fear. If he was not certain of it before, he was certain of it now: Bauman was not bragging when he said he would have taken a bullet for Robert Constable. It was who he was.

After the door swung shut and Bauman was somewhere safe outside, Burdick asked the waitress for another cup of coffee and, measuring in the right amount of milk and sugar, began to examine the contents of the stolen file. He started with the photographs. The longer he looked at them, the more unlikely the young woman seemed for the part of a killer. She looked too young, too alive, too innocent, really, to have anything to do with death. But then perhaps that was why she was so good at what she did, why she found it so easy to get close to the men she killed. That was one point on which Burdick was quite clear: this woman who appeared to be still in her twenties had done this kind of thing, not just once or twice before, but probably dozens of times. You did not hire an amateur to murder the president of the United States.

He put the six photographs to the side and discovered a kind of ledger listing a series of payments made into a Swiss account, four separate transactions spread over six months, each one in the amount of one million two hundred fifty thousand dollars, for a total of five million. The last payment, he noted, had been made the day after Constable died. It listed the payments and the dates on which they had been made, but there was nothing to indicate where they had come from, or who, if it had not been Atwood, had made the arrangement to hire her in the first place. The next several documents had to do with the president's itinerary, every place he had been scheduled to be, starting the month before the assassination. That seemed to mean that the time and place of the assassination had been left up to the killer. The woman hired to do it had first to get close to him, meet him somehow, let him know she might be available, that she understood the game and knew how to be discreet, that he could take her to bed and trust that she would not talk about it.

Burdick riffled through the next several pages, but there was nothing about when she finally met Constable or what happened between them when she did. If the evidence, or the lack of evidence, was any indication, she did not make reports. It occurred to him that perhaps she did not have any contact at all with those who hired her, that she simply did what she was paid for and then vanished out of sight. But that, he realized immediately, would not explain the photographs and the fact that they were in Atwood's possession. She could not have been a hired assassin in the sense in which that was usually meant: someone who worked for anyone, someone who would kill anyone for a price. Someone like that would never allow anyone to know what she looked like, much less let them have half a dozen photographs of her.

She was a hired killer—there was no question about that—but a hired killer who worked for only one kind of employer, the kind that had a regular need for the service she performed. That meant the government, and perhaps other governments as well; intelligence agencies that shared with each other not just information but the means by which to eliminate someone seen as a threat. Whatever laws were on the books against political assassination, everyone understood that it was sometimes necessary to choose the lesser of two evils.

Burdick turned the page, and then he turned another, and each time he did it, turned to the next page in Atwood's secret file, he did it with reluctance, worried what he was going to find, a feeling followed almost immediately by a strange sense of relief when, instead of a shattering revelation of the sort Bauman had talked about, it was another fairly pedestrian report, an account of expenditures, a reckoning of costs. Then he found it, a chronology of what had happened, a list of everyone involved, a detailed account of the first, and every subsequent, meeting where the matter had been discussed, debated, and decided.

He had not finished the first paragraph when his mouth went dry and his stomach started to churn. For a moment he thought he was going to be sick. Bauman's words echoed in his brain, not just about not wanting to believe it, but what he had said about Bobby Hart, when he asked if he trusted the senator enough to tell him something that was not just unbelievable, but impossible. Because that was what this was: impossible. It could not have happened, not here, not in our lifetime; but it had. The impossible had happened, and with what he had in this file he could now prove it.

Quentin Burdick had read enough. He pulled out his cell phone and called Bobby Hart. There was no answer and all he could do was leave a message that he had to see him right away. He was not sure what to do next. Then he remembered what he had been going to do earlier, when he was sitting at the station and thought Bauman was not going to show up. The Senate was in session. He could talk to Hart when he finished on the floor. He left the waitress a sizeable tip and caught a cab.

Clutching the package in his arms, Burdick found himself watching the passing sights of Washington with new eyes. All the old, familiar landmarks had taken on a strange and different meaning, almost as if the country had been taken over by a foreign power. The buildings, the monuments, the vast open avenues—none of that had changed, but instead of a tribute to the nation's greatness, it now seemed to represent something important that was in imminent danger of being lost.

Burdick got out in front of the Russell Senate Office Building and hurried inside. The receptionist told him that the senator was not available; David Allen told him the senator was in New York.

"She's new," explained Allen as he led Burdick through the narrow passageway to his small backroom office. He removed a pile of documents from the only other chair and then went round to his desk. "Is that for him?" he asked, nodding toward the package Burdick held in his lap.

"No. I mean yes…well, sort of. It's something I wanted to talk to him about. But you say he's in New York. I just came down this morning."

He looked around the cluttered room, books and papers everywhere; the plain wooden desk behind which David Allen somehow functioned, a mountain of what looked like debris, but which Burdick knew from experience was actually organized in a scheme that only Allen could understand, a method that allowed him, and no one else, to find anything he needed. It gave a certain antic, almost magical quality to the otherwise humdrum exercise of filing papers, the ability to find a needle in a haystack without so much as the bother of a search. Despite everything he had been through that day, despite everything he had learned, Burdick could not quite suppress a smile.

"When do you expect him back?"

"I thought tonight, maybe tomorrow; but now—he just called a few minutes ago—I don't really know."

"Can you find out? I have to see him; it's very important."

Allen had known Burdick a long time; not well, it is true, but in the way someone who worked on the Hill, someone who dealt with the press on a daily basis, would know a reporter. He knew him well enough, or at least he thought he did, to detect a nervous anxiety he had not seen before. Quentin Burdick was smart, insightful, with a judgment about people and events that went as deep as anyone and deeper than most. He had covered politics and government since the year before Richard Nixon was elected and he could still rattle off the names of those who had served in the cabinet of Lyndon Johnson as easily as he could give you the name of the present secretary of state. Burdick had seen everything, from Watergate to war, enough to know that most of what the current crop of politicians thought new and innovative was little more than a pale imitation of things that had been tried before. Nothing surprised him; nothing made him lose the calm, unflappable demeanor that Allen had often marveled at and sometimes envied; nothing, that is, until now.

"What is it?" asked Allen. "You look like you're ready to come apart."

Pressing his lips, Burdick spread his long tapered fingers and began to tap them together. Then he locked his fingers and tapped his thumbs, and then, shaking his head, he threw up his hands in frustration. With a quick glance, and a brief, apologetic smile, he let Allen know that it was not something he could talk about.

"Not yet, anyway; there are some things I still need to do."

"Like talk to Bobby?"

"Yes, as soon as possible. He knows what it's about." Burdick looked away, struck by how incongruous that now sounded. "No, he doesn't know what it's about. He'll think he does, but he doesn't."

He realized that it made no sense, that Allen could not possibly know what he meant. He felt a strange giddiness, a compulsion to laugh out loud; what he might have felt listening to an argument about who was going to win the World Series, or the next election, after just learning that the world was going to end the day after tomorrow. He did not laugh—he had not lost quite that much control—but a stupid grin hung for what seemed forever on the ruined simplicity of his mouth.

"No, he doesn't know what it's about," he said, pulling himself together. "If you talk to him, tell him it's about what we talked about before—The Four Sisters—only that there's more, a great deal more, to it than what I had thought then."

Allen knew that, whatever it was, it was serious. He picked up the telephone and called Hart's private number.

"He has it turned off. He'll call me back as soon as he is finished with whatever he is doing. I'll ask him to call you right away."

Burdick thanked him and started to leave, but Allen did not want him to go.

"Let's talk a little—not about what you're working on, what you want to talk to Bobby about—about what's going on this week."

Burdick sank back in this chair, glad for the chance to think about something else, to have a reprieve, as it were, from what had been weighing so heavily on his mind.

"There are a lot of rumors," continued Allen, as he put his feet up on the corner of his cluttered desk.

His shirtsleeves were rolled up almost to the elbow and the striped tie he wore almost every day was pulled down from an open collar. The lamplight glistened on his round, balding head. As he started to talk, his eyes took on the manic quality of the player who loves the game, the political insider who can never stop talking about things that have not happened and might never come about, a future formed by speculation that changes with the hour. Who was in, who was out; who was up, who was down; and all of it conditioned by the certain knowledge, which made a principle of uncertainty, that if the future was like the past, nothing would turn out even close to the way everyone was convinced it would. Where else but politics could you gain a reputation for wisdom by talking about things that did not yet exist?

"Rumors that Russell is going to try to get the nomination; rumors that he is going to step aside; rumors that Hillary Constable is going to run and no one, least of all Irwin Russell, can beat her; rumors that even if she doesn't run there are others he couldn't beat either."

He started to list them, the other potential candidates to succeed Irwin Russell in the office to which no one had ever seriously thought him qualified. Burdick stopped him.

"Have you talked to anyone in the White House? What are they saying? Do they think Russell is going to run?"

Burdick's expression had changed. In place of the nervous anxiety, the palpable sense as of something gone terribly wrong, there was now an intense interest, a single-minded concentration on the issue at hand. Noticing the difference, Allen wondered at the cause.

"I've had a few conversations," he replied, guardedly. "But those were all with Constable's people. Whatever they really think about her, and some of them—this is off the record, right?—have, to put it charitably, never liked her; but they're all part of the Constable machine. They worked in that first campaign; that's how they got their jobs in the White House. Everything they have, everything they want, has always depended on the Constables staying on top. They have no loyalty to Irwin Russell. Hell, most of them thought it was a mistake to put him on the ticket. They thought—"

"Why was he put on the ticket?" interjected Burdick, sliding forward until he was close enough to put his forearm on the desk. "I know the reason that was given: that Russell brought Ohio into play; I know that the real reason was that they wanted someone who didn't have ambition, someone who wouldn't challenge Hillary for the nomination when Constable finished out his term. But there were others who could have served the same purpose—why Russell in particular?"

Allen pulled his legs off the desk and sat up. Pondering the question, he thought back four years to when it happened, remembering what he could about the backstairs intrigue that had had everyone in Washington talking. It had proven, as if any more proof had been needed, that Robert Constable had a genius for the game, the way he had replaced one vice president with another and made it seem, publicly at least, that he was doing both of them a favor. Anyone could be ruthless with their enemies, once they had them in their power; Robert Constable could be ruthless with his friends.

"He knew Russell better than he knew the others. Remember, Russell was chairman of the Senate Finance Committee. He always did what the president wanted him to do. And that's what he wanted on the ticket: someone he could trust."

Burdick nodded thoughtfully.

"That's always been Russell's strength: he knows as much about the federal budget—about money—as anyone in Washington."

"Sure. The only person who might have known as much was Frank Morris, who chaired Ways and Means."

Burdick crossed one leg over the other and sat sideways in the chair. A look of puzzlement and doubt spread slowly across his long, angular face.

"So you take someone who as chairman of the Finance Committee can do more than anyone else to help you get through Congress what you need and make him vice president because he doesn't have any ambition for higher office? Why would Constable have done that? And why did Russell go along with it? It seems to me that, on the surface anyway, both of them gave up something they wouldn't have wanted to lose: the president, automatic support on the committee; Russell, control of one of the two or three most important committees in the Senate."

Allen was surprised. No one in the press had written more thoughtfully about what made Robert Constable different from most of the other men who had had become president. How could he have forgotten this? He felt almost a fool, quoting back to the man who first wrote the sentence that had become the conventional wisdom about the failure of the administration to measure up to what had seemed its promise.

"Constable was always more concerned with politics than with legislation."

Allen paused, expecting some reaction, but Burdick was too impatient, too caught up in the conversation, to notice, or, if he noticed, to care, about the origin of words. He was only interested in what Allen thought. ·

"He wanted someone on the ticket he knew would not try to challenge his wife, and in Russell, he got it."

"Even granting that," remarked Burdick, "it doesn't explain why Russell did it, gave up all that power and prestige to hold an office that if you don't want to be president, doesn't mean a thing. The only one who stood to gain from that arrangement was the president's wife. Or so she must have thought."

"Must have thought?" asked Allen as Burdick got to his feet. "What do you mean?"

Burdick tapped his fingers on the package he held in his other arm.

"There is a reason why Russell ran for vice president, and it isn't what anyone thinks. Russell did not have a choice. I'm afraid I can't tell you any more than that; not yet, before I check a few things first. Would you tell the senator when he calls that I'll be back in New York sometime late tonight and that I need to see him right away?"

All the way to the airport, all the way on the flight to New York, Quentin Burdick kept hold of the package. The only time he let go of it was when he passed through security at the airport, and then he held his breath, afraid that if he took his eyes off it even for a moment it might disappear. He was still holding onto it on the cab ride into Manhattan when Bobby Hart finally called.

"We keep missing each other," said Hart. "Where are you? David said you were coming back to New York tonight."

"I just got in. I'm in a cab, just a few blocks from the apartment."

"You're not going back there, are you?" asked Hart, worried. "After your place was broken into, I thought you were staying in a hotel."

"I did, for a couple of days, but I couldn't stay there forever. I have to see you. I know it's late, but is it possible tonight? I've just gotten something—I was in D.C. and…well, never mind, I'll explain later. But it changes everything, all of it, The Four Sisters—the whole story about what happened that night. Look, can you come now, right away—my place on Sixty-third? You've been there before. Half an hour? Perfect. I'll see you then."

Burdick began to relax. He had his story, the story of a lifetime, and as for the rest of it, Bobby Hart would know what to do, how to stop what had started from going any further. He paid the cab driver and got out in front of the pre-war building on East Sixty-third where he had lived for the better part of the last twenty years. He was home, and even if, unlike California, the heat was almost as bad late at night as it was during the day, he could not imagine living anywhere other than Manhattan. Though he could not sing a note, the words "I like New York in June," ran through his eager mind as if he were sitting somewhere in a jazz joint listening to some kid, some bright new talent, play a riff of it on the piano.

"Hello, Mr. Burdick," said a woman with a soft, breathless voice.

He was just at the entrance, on the first of the three short steps that led to the door. He turned and saw a late-night apparition, a gorgeous young woman in a blue silk dress. She had that expensive New York look, a woman who was used to money.

"Good evening," said Burdick, smiling to himself at how much she reminded him of the endless, priceless vanity of things, the way the city drew everyone to it, the promise of what was just waiting for you to take it, if you were young and ambitious and beautiful and rich.

"I love reading the things you write," she said, sliding closer.

She had the brightest, most entrancing smile Burdick thought he had ever seen. She was still smiling at him, looking right in his eyes, when he realized that he had seen her before, seen her in photographs, six of them.

"You—!" he cried out, and then he felt it, the gun pressed hard against his stomach, and then, an instant later, everything went black and he did not feel anything.

Several people passed by on the sidewalk while Quentin Burdick's dead body lay on the landing, three steps up, but if any of them noticed, none of them stopped. He lay there in a pool of blood, his eyes frozen in a vacant stare, until a cab pulled up and Bobby Hart arrived. Before Hart was halfway across the sidewalk, he knew that Burdick was dead. He bent down beside him to make sure, and then called 911. He did not think that it was a robbery, but he checked for Burdick's wallet just to make sure. It was still in his jacket pocket and Burdick's watch was still on his wrist. David Allen had told him something about a package that Burdick had treated as if it were the most valuable thing he owned. Hart glanced around, but there was nothing there; if Burdick had had it with him, it was gone.

He wanted to close Quentin Burdick's eyes, to give him that much peace, but he reminded himself that this was now a murder scene and he had better not do anything more than he already had. So he sat down on the step and in the humid summer heat waited for the police, promising himself, and promising his friend Quentin Burdick, that this was going to be one New York murder that did not go unsolved. Then he pulled out his cell phone and called Austin Pearce.

"Quentin Burdick has been murdered. We better leave tonight."

CHAPTER 16

LAURA TRIED TO make a joke of it, teasing him about flying off to Paris with Austin Pearce instead of her, when he called from the airport to tell her where he was going, but he did not laugh, and she knew that something serious had happened.

"What is it, Bobby?—Tell me."

"Quentin Burdick—he's been murdered."

"Murdered, like the others, like the president, like…?"

"I found him on the steps to his building." He did not add any of the details. He did not want to tell her, and she did not want to know. "It's all connected somehow: what happened to Constable, what happened to Frank Morris…and now Quentin Burdick. I have to find out. Whatever is going on, someone has to stop it."

She wanted to tell him that someone else could do it, she wanted to tell him to come home, tell him that she could not survive if anything happened to him, but she knew that if stayed home safe he would think himself a coward, and so she did not tell him anything except that she loved him and wished he did not have to go.

"Go home tomorrow," he told her; "go home to Santa Barbara. I'll fly out as soon as I get back."

There was a long pause. There was something he did not want to tell her, something that she had already heard in his voice.

"You don't think it's safe here; you think that the same people who murdered Quentin Burdick might be coming after you! That's why you don't want me to stay, why you want me to leave."

"Promise me—you'll go tomorrow, first thing."

"I'll need to phone the airline, I'll need—"

"It's been taken care of. You're on a ten o'clock flight. Now try to get some sleep. I'll be back before you know it."

Laura slept, but only for a few minutes at a time, and even then she might as well have been awake, the only difference whether what she feared the most darkened her imagination or came to her in dreams. Bobby slept, but only for the last two hours of the flight, and only then because he knew he needed it to get through what he knew was waiting for him in Paris. After five minutes with the American ambassador he began to wonder if any amount of rest would have helped him keep his eyes open. Andrew Malreaux was among the most profoundly dull-witted men he had ever met.

"France is a really interesting country," remarked the ambassador as if he were sharing a fact that not many people knew or could be expected to know. "Interesting people, interesting buildings, interesting food— interesting language, too, once you get the hang of it." He said this with a bright, confidential look, as of one who has, after some effort, achieved the competence required to make a considered judgment.

In response, Austin Pearce spoke to him in near perfect French. The ambassador squinted and nervously scratched his chin.

"I got some of that," he said, confirming with a silent nod of his head that he had indeed understood at least a few of the words.

Pearce beamed approval.

"Your French lessons are coming along, then? You've certainly improved."

"Yes, well, I work hard at it. One of these days, I might even catch up with you, Austin. You never know."

"That's true, Andrew: You never do. We don't want to take up any more of your time. Did you have a chance to arrange to have…?"

The ambassador stared at him, waiting to be reminded what it was he was supposed to have done.

"You were going to have someone brief us on someone. I'm sure you didn't forget."

"No, of course not. That was…?"

"Jean de la Valette, the head of a banking firm that the senator wants to know more about."

"Valette! Yes, of course. Follow me." He turned and led his two visitors down a long hallway. "The head of our political section—Aaron Wolfe, very intelligent fellow: Yale, Yale Law—has put something together." He stopped in front of the second door from the end. "Poor Robert Constable! He had it all, and then, just like that, he's gone. Tell me, are the rumors true: Was there a woman with him that night—is that how he died? I imagine that's the way he would have wanted to go. He always did like a good piece of ass." Malreaux started to smile at the thought of it, but the smile died on his lips. "I have to admit, though, I didn't much like it when he made a pass at my wife."

"Angelique?" asked Pearce, rather surprised. Malreaux had only married her the year before.

"No, the one before—Alexis. Remember her? Not sure that was the only pass he ever made at her, either. Not sure, to tell the plain truth about it, that the son-of-a-bitch wasn't successful."

The memory of a former wife's possible deceit was now just that—a memory—and if Malreaux knew how to do anything, it was how to forget. His former wife was gone, and now so was the president who might have taken more than just his money.

"What's going to happen now, with Russell, I mean? Do you think he'll run, or will she?"

Pearce seemed to ponder the question, to take seriously what the ambassador wanted to know. He put his hand on his shoulder and looked him straight in the eye.

"Chances are that one of them will."

"Yes, I think you're probably right," said the ambassador, after thinking about it a moment. "In fact, I'm almost sure of it."

Suddenly, he remembered who he was with. His face reddened slightly as he turned to Hart.

"I'm not sure I should tell you this, but I suppose it can't do any harm now. The Constables thought you might run when his second term was over. They were worried about it. Those of us who had raised money for him were being asked to get ready to do the same thing for her. They thought that if she had all the money locked up, you'd have to think twice about getting into it."

He said this with a look that suggested he did not think it would have worked, and that he would not have minded if it had not; a look that said his relationship with the Constables was as transitory, as dependent on immediate need, as any other type of investment. Malreaux may not have known anything of history or culture, or anything else of lasting importance, but he had, like other men of business, an instinct for his own advantage.

"Any chance you might do it, run this time?" he asked point blank.

"She'll beat Russell, if he tries to run, but you can beat her. You're the only one who can."

"I didn't have any plans to run before," replied Hart, an oblique reference to the calculation, bordering on paranoia, with which the Constables had planned their campaigns. "I certainly don't have any now."

It was exactly what someone who was planning to run would say. No one shut the door on the chance to be president.

"If things change," said Malreaux with a knowing smile, "there may be some things I can do."

Nodding his satisfaction at the prospect, he opened the door to the conference room and introduced his two guests to the head of the embassy's political section. Then, begging other pressing commitments, he left them alone and, full of news, hurried off to his next appointment.

Aaron Wolfe was all business. The head of the embassy's political section through several changes of administration, he had seen ambassadors come and go. A career foreign service officer, he kept his opinions to himself and offered advice only when he was asked to do so. Though it might seem a paradox to others, he preferred serving under an ambassador like Andrew Malreaux to one who came to the position thinking that he knew something about the French. Malreaux had no choice but to depend upon him; certain others, like Malreaux's immediate predecessor, thought that because they had lived in Paris for a few months in their twenties, or read a few French novels in their forties, knew everything there was to know and could decide things on their own. Wolfe was only thirty-eight, but intellectually, especially compared to the ambassador, he felt ancient.

"The ambassador asked me to tell you what we know about The Four Sisters," he said, folding his hands in front of him.

He was sitting at the head of an oblong conference table, a map of France on the wall behind him. Hart and Austin Pearce had been directed to chairs on opposite sides. The windows behind Hart looked out on the interior courtyard of the embassy.

"This isn't usually the sort of thing we share," continued Wolfe. "Senator Hart, of course, as a member of the Senate Intelligence Committee would have access to everything we have—through the normal State Department channels; and as secretary of treasury, you, Mr. Pearce, would have been entitled to the same information, and by means of the same process. I mention this only because—"

"Because you're not sure the ambassador hasn't made a mistake, and you don't want to find yourself being hung out to dry," said Hart, with a friendly, earnest look that took Wolfe off guard. Hart bent forward on his elbows. "I can't tell you why we're here, I can't...."

He seemed to change his mind, to wonder why he was continuing the pretense, why he did not just tell him the truth and impress upon him the urgency of what they needed to know. He glanced across at Austin Pearce to make certain Pearce would not object.

"We're here because the president of the United States didn't die of a heart attack, the way it has been reported. The president was murdered, and there have been two murders since, and both of the men who were killed knew something about it. There are only a few people who know about this, Mr. Wolfe, and if you so much as mention it to anyone—if you breathe a word of this to the ambassador—I'll make sure that instead of Paris, your next assignment will be somewhere in the sub-Sahara in the middle of a civil war. Now, what can you tell us about The Four Sisters and Jean de la Valette?"

Aaron Wolfe no longer felt ancient, but suddenly young and out of his depth. He fumbled with the papers stacked in front of him, the copious notes he had prepared, no longer certain quite what to say or what to do.

"But what does The Four Sisters...what does Jean Valette have to do with that?" he asked without thinking. The only response was a blank stare. He started to mumble an apology.

"Just tell us what you know. Then we can figure out what it means."

Removing his glasses, Wolfe pushed the notes he had written off to the side. He did not need them to remind him of the facts.

"The Four Sisters—the name itself tells you something about the French and their history, the price they sometimes had to pay for survival. The grandfather of Jean Valette was the only son of a banker. He was only twenty-five when he died, a soldier killed at the famous Battle of the Marne, when the German army was stopped just outside Paris in the first great battle of the First World War, the battle in which Marshal Petain saved France. He had a son, just a boy at the time of his death, a boy, moreover, who had lost his mother in childbirth, but he had four sisters. They took on the management of the bank and, in addition, the education of their nephew. By any measure, they did a remarkable job of both."

Aaron Wolfe drank from a glass of water. There was a troubled expression in his dark blue eyes. As much as he tried to concentrate on the task at hand— the brief chronology, the history of the last hundred years, of the family of Jean Valette—he kept coming back to the awful secret he had just learned.

"It's true," said Hart, not without sympathy for the shock he knew the other man must have felt. "Hard to believe, I know, but it's true. There's reason to believe that The Four Sisters is involved."

Wolfe thought for a moment, trying to gauge the possibilities.

"Valette is a very strange man in some ways, remarkable—more remarkable than perhaps anyone in France; more remarkable, perhaps, than anyone anywhere, so far as that goes—but involved in something like that? It doesn't seem possible."

Austin Pearce brought him back to the point where he had broken off his narrative.

"You were about to tell us something more about the sisters and what they did with the bank."

"Yes, sorry. Where was I?—The Depression. Half the banks in Paris, half the banks in France, suffered losses or went under, but the four sisters not only kept their bank afloat, but, bankers to the core, had the foresight, and the nerve, to buy up everything they could get—other businesses, other banks,—at fire sale prices. They were able to do this, not just because they were smart and, to call things by their names, utterly ruthless in their dealings, but because they were extremely well-connected, as connected as you could get. The Valettes had for generations been one of the leading families of France. It isn't widely understood, other than by the French themselves, that there are two hundred families in this country that through every change of government—and there isn't any place you can think of that has gone through more changes of government than France—make sure nothing really changes, that they continue to have all the wealth and all the power. The Valettes have always been one of them, and at times one of the two or three most important of them. One of the sisters—the youngest one, if I remember right—was married to a Rothschild."

Austin Pearce was not as interested in what the four sisters had done to improve the position of the bank as he was in their dead brother's son.

"Jean Valette's father, the boy the sisters raised—what can you tell us about him?"

Aaron Wolfe had sharp, quick-moving eyes, but at the mention of Valette's father he stared straight ahead in an attitude of puzzled respect. It reminded Austin Pearce of the way he felt when he came upon some surprising fact in a history he was reading, a fact that made him see a famous figure in a new and surprising light, better and more complicated than he had thought before.

"You're fascinated by him, I take it; there's something about him that astonishes you, correct?"

Wolfe turned and looked at Pearce with that same look, admiration for the older man's insight and intelligence.

"He did something that took more than just courage, something extraordinary. You wouldn't have thought that about him early on, when he became one of the most prominent bankers in Europe. France, in the 1930s, was rotten to the core, determined not to fight another war with Germany, more afraid of Communism at home than of any threat beyond its borders. You know all that, I'm sure. Like a great many others in financial circles, Paul Valette was convinced that democracy, and particularly French democracy with all its different parties, none of them willing to compromise long enough to fashion a working majority capable of governing for more than a few months at a time, was doomed. A lot of people thought that then. What set him apart was his belief that what Hitler was doing in Germany was the wave of the future; that if France was to survive, it had to follow his example: find someone strong enough to impose a discipline, a unity on the country; someone who could keep France from destroying itself."

Wolfe raised his eyebrows, a silent commentary on the inadequacy of words, the way he had, quite without meaning to, misled them at the beginning.

"The wave of the future—I should have said that he saw in Germany a way to restore something of what he thought the glory of the past. That was really what fascism was about: a rejection of the modern world, democracy, and a market economy, the whole concern with the rights of the individual, as opposed to the supposed greatness of the nation. This had a powerful appeal for someone like Paul Valette, who came from a family that could trace its origins in the origins of France. He became one of the leading figures in Action Francaise, a fascist organization headed by Charles Maurras, a classicist who, it was said, loathed the modern world and everything it stood for. It is important to know this about Paul Valette, but what makes him interesting is that once the war began, once the German occupation started, he did not support the collaborationist government of Marshal Petain and Pierre Laval. No, that same Paul Valette who thought France should follow Germany's example, joined the French resistance."

Wolfe fell into a long silence as he considered the strange futility of even trying to guess what might have driven Paul Valette, or anyone, to do something not just brave, but completely unexpected. History was full of examples, but while history could remind you that the exceptional case was possible, it could only tell you what had happened, not that it would happen again. Psychology sought to paint a broader picture, to find a pattern in human behavior, but psychology looked at things in terms of averages, and if there was anything that characterized every, even the most disparate, form of courage, it was that none of them were average.

"He was incredibly effective, the work he did in the French resistance. He was, in the eyes of the world, a notorious collaborator. The bank, his bank, the bank that had been in his family for years, handled most of the financial transactions the Third Reich made in occupied France. He was, to all appearances, as much a friend to the Nazis as they could want; and the whole time he was giving the information he gathered about what the Germans were doing to his contacts in the resistance and, through them, to the allies. Someone betrayed him, one of the people he worked with, probably forced to betray him under torture—everyone has a breaking point. Valette was arrested by the Gestapo in the last days of the war and put in front of a firing squad. It was one of the last executions the Germans did in Paris."

Watching Aaron Wolfe, Hart was struck by the way he made it seem that he was talking about someone he had known—a friend or a relative he had respected and admired—rather than telling a story torn from a long forgotten page of history. It was unusual to come across anyone, especially someone still relatively young, who had the capacity to grasp in all its anguished uncertainty the moral dilemmas of the past.

"No one knew that he had been a hero of the war, a hero of the French resistance; no one except a few men in the French underground, not all of whom survived. All that the public knew was that this rich banker from one of France's oldest families had been only too eager to take German money and, while others suffered, live as well, or even better, during the occupation than he had before the war began. When he was shot, lined up against a wall and executed, most people thought it was just another act of German barbarism and that, unlike most other German executions, Paul Valette had gotten exactly what he deserved."

The head of the political section tapped his fingers together. A smile of something close to vindication, a shared sense of triumph, the decent human feeling for the kind of bravery we all wish we had, ran clean and straight across his mouth.

"It was only several years later, several years after the war ended, that the truth finally came out: that far from being the traitor everyone had imagined, Paul Valette had been one of the great French patriots. The effect was to cast his heroism, his sacrifice, in tragic colors. More than honored, the Valette name was almost worshipped in France."

Austin Pearce was sitting on the edge of his seat, his hands clasped together on the gleaming hard finished table.

"He must have known, during the years he acted the part of a collaborator," he said in a quiet, solemn voice, "that the truth might never be known, that he might be killed, taken out somewhere and shot in the back of the head, and that his family would go down in history tainted with what everyone would believe had been a crime." Glancing across at Hart, he added: "Everyone likes to think they would be a hero, willing to die for what they believe. The world will know, and honor, what we did. But this?—" he asked, looking back at Wolfe as if to draw him into the conversation, "—Give your life for your country, knowing that there is every chance that you will be known forever as a traitor? How many of us would be willing to do that, I wonder? It is heroism of a different order than what we are used to."

"What about his son, Jean Valette—the one we need to know about?" asked Hart.

"If you're asking what effect this had on him, what his father did, the way he died—I can only speculate, but it must have taken on an aura of epic proportions. Jean Valette was a small boy when his father was murdered by the Germans. Curious, isn't it?—That both of them, father and son, lost their fathers in a world war; but then, millions died in those wars and millions of children were lucky to still have a mother. Jean Valette did not have a father, but he had the lesson of his father's example that the only life worth living is to believe in something for which you would gladly die. Jean Valette became what by even French standards is eccentric, not to say extreme."

Austin Pearce thought he knew what Wolfe was referring to.

"You mean the way he talks about the need for a new Crusade, a war between Islam and the West?"

Wolfe nodded vigorously. Then, abruptly, he changed his mind.

"He doesn't mean it quite in the literal sense. When he talks about a crusade, he means it more by way of analogy, reminding people of what, historically, the Crusades were—what they were meant to be and what they actually achieved, or failed to achieve. I don't think he means—I certainly haven't found anything in his writings to suggest that he means—an armed invasion of the Middle East by the Western powers. He isn't talking about that 'war of civilizations' that people who know nothing about history sometimes talk about. He has something else in mind, but I'm not sure I could tell you exactly what it is."

"But he has written about this kind of thing—politics, history? He isn't just a banker, the head of an investment house?" asked Hart.

"Given his father's example, I should think that for him the two things are intertwined."

Wolfe's gaze became more intense, more determined. There was something he wanted Hart to understand.

"The Four Sisters, ever since Jean Valette took control of it, seems less interested in making money—though it's made a great deal of it—than in broadening its influence. Have you read anything about Florence in the time of the Medici? The Medici made a fortune in banking, but the money was a means, a means to power, and a means, also, to start the Renaissance. Whatever Valette wants—whether it is to do something like the Medici and change the way Europe thinks, or gain power for himself—The Four Sisters has gone from a bank that only did business in Paris to a financial institution that is active all around the world. One thing has not changed, however: Almost everything it does is cloaked in secrecy. The joke in Paris is that when a Swiss banker has money he wants to hide, he opens an account with The Four Sisters."

"What about Valette himself?" asked Hart, anxious to learn more about the man. "Apart from what he believes, apart from the long historical view he takes of things—what is he like? You know the reason we're here." He bent toward Wolfe. "When I told you that the president had been murdered, and that we had reason to believe that The Four Sisters is involved, what was your honest reaction? Were you surprised? Was your first thought that it was impossible, that we must be making a mistake?"

"Honest reaction? I didn't have time to have a reaction. I've been too damn numb—sorry, forgive me for that," he said, embarrassed by his candor in front of two men he respected but did not know. "The president was murdered? I still can't believe it. And no one knows? Why is it being kept a secret? I don't understand. It's almost two weeks since he died." Despite his confusion, Wolfe was too quick, and too experienced, not to see the implications. "Someone doesn't want...?"

"It's complicated," replied Hart. "I can't tell you everything, but if we're right The Four Sisters is the key to everything: the murder of the president and the reason why certain people don't seem to want there to be an investigation. Now, whatever you can tell us about Jean Valette, anything that would have given him a motive, a reason, to want the president dead."

Wolfe scratched his head as he tried to think. His eyes lit up; he sat forward in the chair with an air of certainty that vanished as suddenly as it had come.

"No, that's absurd. It makes no sense," he said, lecturing himself.

"What makes no sense?" asked Austin Pearce, who did not think anything at this point beyond the realm of possibility.

"The Knights of St. John," explained Wolfe with a dismissive glance. "There's a connection, but it doesn't mean anything."

"A connection—how?" asked Pearce, intrigued.

"Valette's ancestor was—"

"Also named Jean de la Valette, the Grand Master of the Knights of St. John," interjected Pearce. "He fought, and won, the battle of Malta in the year fifteen—"

"You know about that? Yes, exactly. The Knights of St. John, or as they are sometimes called, the Knights of Malta, still exist. Irwin Russell, our new president, is a member. And of course Jean Valette is—"

Astonished, Hart bolted forward.

"You're suggesting that the president of the United States is a member of some bizarre ancient order, some secret society, and that Robert Constable was murdered so that someone who owes his loyalty to this organization that Valette controls could become president?"

"No, absolutely not! I said it was absurd. In the first place, the Knights of St. John are not—"

The door to the hallway suddenly swung open and the ambassador, nervous, agitated, and obviously alarmed, motioned for Wolfe to join him outside. He stood there, shifting his weight from one foot to the other, glancing first in one direction then the other, almost as if he were trying to avoid looking at anyone. Then, just as Wolfe got there, just before he closed the door, he shot a brief, frantic look at Austin Pearce.

"There must be a crisis somewhere," said Pearce, when the door swung shut and he and Hart were alone. "Given his absence of any sense of proportion, it could be anything from an impending nuclear attack to someone having forgotten to bring him the right brand of coffee. Still, that look he gave me…. It may be serious."

A moment later, the door opened again and Aaron Wolfe came back into the room with a solemn, pensive expression. He sat down, but instead of turning to either Hart or Pearce, he stared for the longest time down at his hands. Finally, he looked at Hart.

"The ambassador just told me something that I'm not sure I believe, and he has asked me—I should say instructed me—to do something I'm not sure I should. You took a chance when you told me that the president had been murdered. Why did you do that, take a chance like that with someone you didn't know?"

There was a palpable sense of danger, and while Hart did not know what the danger was, he knew—he could feel—that it had something to do with him. He told Wolfe the truth.

"Instinct. We had to trust someone; I had a sense we could trust you."

"Instinct? I suppose, when you get right down to it, that's the best reason there is."

"Why?" asked Hart with a growing sense of urgency. "What's happened? What's going on?"

"You're staying at a hotel? Don't go back there. Don't go anywhere.

Disappear." He reached in his pocket and pulled out a card. "No, go to this address. It's my apartment. No one will think to look for you there." He nodded toward another door, one at the far corner of the room. "Go out that way. It leads to the backstairs. But be quick—there isn't much time. They're waiting for you downstairs, at the front entrance."

"What are you talking about?" cried Austin Pearce, rising from his chair. "Why should the senator have to do anything of the sort?"

"The ambassador has just been informed—it's in all the morning papers at home—that the president didn't die of a heart attack, that he was murdered instead."

"Which is exactly what we were telling you, the reason we're here, that the president was…!" Something in Wolfe's expression made him stop. "The president was murdered, but…?"

"The president was murdered by a conspiracy, a conspiracy led by Senator Robert Hart."

CHAPTER 17

Austin Pearce was angry, as angry as he had ever been in his life. This was worse than a mistake, this was an outrage: this was insane. He was on his feet, glaring at Aaron Wolfe.

"Who is the idiot responsible for this? What fool decided that Bobby—that Senator Hart—could have had anything to do with this? He's the one who has been trying to find out what really happened, for Christ sake!"

"I don't know," insisted Wolfe, who then turned immediately to Hart. "All I know, Senator, is that if you don't leave right now, you won't get out of here at all."

Hart sat staring straight ahead, frozen to the spot, a dozen different thoughts racing through his mind. If he ran, tried to get away, everyone would think he was guilty, that he had done what they said he did: took part in a criminal conspiracy to murder the president. If he was charged with a crime—any normal crime—a crime for which he could be certain of having a chance to prove his innocence, have a trial with all the protections given a citizen, there would not be any doubt what he would do. His brain was spinning, pictures of courtrooms, of judges and juries, flashed in front of him, but they did so at a distance, pictures of a place he knew he could not go.

He was being accused of something he did not do, and the only people who would do that were the people who were trying to protect themselves; powerful people who could manufacture the evidence they needed to place the blame for what they had done on someone else, and do it so effectively that agents of the government, the government of which he was an important part, were about to place him under arrest and take him, bound and shackled, back to the United States. But not to stand trial. Whoever was doing this, whoever was involved in the murder of Robert Constable, could not afford to let him tell anyone, much less a crowded public courtroom, what he had learned. An hour after they had him, he would be shot while trying to escape.

"Call Laura for me," he said to Austin Pearce as he started toward the door. "Tell her I'll be all right."

"Where are you going? What will you do?" asked Pearce in a plaintive voice.

Hart looked back at Aaron Wolfe.

"I'm going to trust you. I'll be at your place this evening. I need you to find out something for me."

Wolfe did not hesitate.

"Yes, of course—anything."

"Jean Valette. Where does he live—how can I get to him?" Hart thought for a moment. "How are you going to explain this? What are you going to say about why I didn't come with you? You could lose your career—and maybe more than that."

Wolfe was so certain of Hart's innocence, so certain that he was doing the right thing, that the thought that he might be about to destroy his career made him only more eager to take the risk. The sense of liberation was intoxicating, and for once in his careful life he felt the thrill of flamboyance.

"Maybe I'll just tell them the truth: they'll never believe that."

And he almost did. He and Austin Pearce waited until Hart was safely gone down the backstairs, and then, as if they had nothing on their minds more pressing than the weather, came down the main staircase speaking French to one another. The ambassador was waiting just inside the front entrance, along with three of the embassy guards—marines in their dress blues—and two men in dark suits. Pearce guessed they were CIA. The ambassador's mouth was rigid, and his face had turned to chalk. His eyes darted past Pearce to the stairs.

"The senator will be coming down in a minute?"

The head of the political section looked at the ambassador first with surprise, then with a deeper sense of puzzlement.

"He didn't come down this way? As soon as I went back in the room— just after we talked," he said in a way that suggested that the nature of their brief conversation was still secret, "—the senator said he was running late and had to leave. But you didn't see him?"

The veins on Malreaux's temples began to throb violently. His eyes became intense. He could barely control himself.

"You just let him go!—After what I told you? Don't you know—?"

"You really didn't see him?" interjected Wolfe, with a brazen smile that registered astonishment at the incompetence of the ambassador. "And you just waited down here, didn't send anyone to make sure that he didn't get away?"

"Get away?" asked Austin Pearce, with a look of incredulity that, under the circumstances, was not hard to produce. "What are you talking about?

What's going on, Andrew?" he demanded. "Why do you have these guards here? Are you going to have me locked up?—Because if you are, I'd damn well like to know the reason!"

Malreaux was almost too flustered to talk.

"No, of course not," he replied, angry with Pearce for even asking.

"Then maybe you'll be good enough to tell me why you're taking that tone with me!" insisted Pearce, showing some anger of his own.

"What? Why I've taken…? Sorry, it isn't you that's in trouble." He was trying to figure out what to do next, but he was not someone who could easily deal with two things at once, and Austin Pearce kept demanding that he deal with him. "It's not you that's in trouble," he repeated as if he needed to give assurances.

"That's nice to know," said Pearce in a harsh, caustic voice. He locked his eyes on Malreaux to keep his attention. "I come all the way from New York, bring with me one of the most distinguished members of the United States Senate, come to you because, as I explained earlier, there was something extremely important we had to do; and now, instead of having a few minutes to say goodbye, you stand here with an armed guard and tell me that I'm not in trouble. That's a fairly strange way to treat someone who has always regarded you as a friend!"

The three marines, trained to a rigorous discipline, stood still as statues, but the two others—the ones Pearce thought were CIA—were screwed as tight as drums, up on the balls of their feet, leaning forward, working their jaws, desperate to stop talking and act.

"I told you, this has nothing to do with you. This—"

But nothing could stop Austin Pearce from dragging things out. It was the only way he had to help Bobby Hart get away.

"We came here to follow a lead." He stepped closer until he and the ambassador were not six inches apart. "The president did not die of a heart attack, Andrew—he was murdered. That's why we're here. Hart is on the Senate Intelligence Committee. He thinks he knows who is behind this, so whatever you think you're doing, think twice about it."

The ambassador's eyes went blank. Now he did not know what to believe. One of the CIA agents put his hand on Pearce's arm.

"Do you know who I am?" demanded Pearce, as he jerked it free.

But the agents were not listening anymore. They barreled past, and with the marine guards right behind, ran up the stairs, shouting directions to each other as they started a search.

"Hart is the one they're looking for," said the ambassador. His eyes were blinking rapidly. He bit hard on his lip. "Hart's the one that had the president killed. I just found out. They call came in just a few minutes ago. I was supposed to hold him, I was supposed to—"

"Who called? Who told you this, who told you that Hart was involved? He wasn't—but who said he was?"

"The secretary called; he—"

"The secretary of state?"

"Yes, the secretary—he said it was in the papers."

"What was in the papers? That Hart was involved—I know that—but what else? Who said that he was involved?"

The ambassador stopped blinking. In the midst of his confusion, he became for a moment quite lucid.

"The head of the Secret Service. He said they had known within days of the president's death that he had been murdered, but that they kept it quiet while they launched a full-scale investigation."

Pearce did nothing to hide his astonishment.

"That's what the head of the Secret Service said: that they launched a full-scale investigation?"

Malreaux had never seen Austin Pearce this upset. He was not sure how to reply.

"Look, Austin—all I know is what I was told: that there is evidence Hart was involved and that they want him back in Washington for questioning."

They were standing there, the three of them alone—Austin Pearce, the ambassador, and Aaron Wolfe. The marine guard, the plainclothes CIA, could be heard scrambling through the rooms on the floor above. Pearce exchanged a glance with Wolfe before turning to the ambassador.

"It appears that you'll have to inform the secretary that the senator got away."

What neither Austin Pearce nor Aaron Wolfe could know was how close Bobby Hart had come to being caught. Less than a minute after he made his way out of the building and walked through the back gate of the embassy, less than a minute after Pearce's stalling tactic finally failed, the alarm had been sounded and no one was allowed in or out. Hart was in the streets of Paris, safe for the moment, but with no clear idea what he should do next.

The streets were full of traffic, and full of noise; the sidewalks packed with smart-looking women and well-dressed men. Hart moved quickly, trying to put the embassy as far behind him as he could, but not so quickly as to draw attention. It was a windless, sultry summer day, the sun a tattered reddish disk fastened to the thick fabric of a gray oppressive sky. There was perspiration on his face and dampness on his palms and he laughed a little at his own sudden doubt how much was because of the weather and how much his own fear. He stopped and looked around, and wondered what he was looking for. Unless someone was running after him, shouting his name, how would he know which face in the thousand faces he saw on the street belonged to someone trying to find him? No one was after him, he told himself, not now, after he was out of the embassy. The only place anyone would know where to look for him was the hotel where he and Austin Pearce had checked in that morning; and that was the one place he was not going to go. He was safe so long as he clung to the anonymity of the crowd; safe until evening came and he could go to Aaron Wolfe's apartment and, if Wolfe had done what he had asked, begin to track down Jean Valette and get to the truth.

He walked slower, more under control. He had to think, to try to understand what had happened, why from being asked to find out what he could about the murder of Robert Constable, he was now thought to be the person responsible, the head of some fictitious conspiracy. Start at the beginning, he told himself; remember how you first got involved, what you were asked to do. Go back to the beginning and start from there.

"Hillary Constable!" he muttered between his teeth. Shoving his hands in his pockets, he shook his head at how easily he had been used. Laura had been right about her; Laura was always right when it came to the motivations of ambitious people. And Austin Pearce had been right as well. Hillary Constable's husband had been murdered, but all she was worried about was whether anyone could trace back to her The Four Sisters and Jean Valette. But why was she worried about that?—Because of the damage it would do to her husband's reputation and, more importantly, her own chance at the presidency? That's what Pearce had thought, or rather had suspected as a possibility. And he may have been right, especially after what she had said that last time they met, upstairs, in her study at home: that flagrant lie she was willing to tell, that ruthless determination to keep the secret of the president's murder from coming out, the contempt with which she had announced that she was going to run for the presidency and that nothing could stop her from getting what she wanted. That seemed to be at the core of it, the devil's bargain she had made to protect The Four Sisters, to cover up a murder in order to hide the truth of what her husband had done.

It all made sense, and, as Hart realized immediately, it did not make any sense at all. Everyone now knew that the president had been murdered. The cover-up had failed. Or had it? Was it possible that it had been part of the plan from the beginning, to let the truth come out about the murder, because whoever was involved understood that it could never have been kept secret for very long? Had he not told her himself that he would not let it stay secret, that there would have to be an investigation? Was it part of the plan from the beginning to get him involved, and then blame the murder on him? Hillary Constable had brought him into it, but had she done that on her own, or had she been acting at the direction of someone else, someone like Jean Valette, desperate to cover all traces of what The Four Sisters had done?

Hart walked for blocks in the sizzling Paris heat, oblivious of everything except the logic of his own entrapment. He felt like a character in a novel by Kafka, damned by an accusation he did not understand. There could be no evidence against him: he had not done anything. Or had he? Was there some link he did not know about between him and the woman who had been with Constable that night? Could someone have been that clever, that diabolical, planned the crime so far in advance, and in such precise detail, that there would exist some documentation—a photograph perhaps—that would make it seem that he had known her and… He remembered something Quentin Burdick had told him, how part of the evidence used against Frank Morris had been an account in the Caymans Morris did not know he had. A shiver ran up his spine.

He checked his watch. He still had hours to wait before he could go to the address Aaron Wolfe had given him. Across the street was a sidewalk café. He could sit somewhere out of the way, have something cold to drink in the shadows and try to think. Moving slowly in the enveloping heat, he stepped off the curb. He did not notice the black Mercedes that turned past him until he heard the ragged noise of screeching brakes and squealing tires.

"There he is!" shouted one of the men who jumped out to the two others who quickly followed.

Hart wheeled around and bolted, an adrenaline rush giving him more speed than he knew he had. Weaving in and out of startled pedestrians, banging into several he could not avoid, he ran as hard as he could. He looked back over his shoulder and for a moment thought he had lost them, and then, suddenly, the same car shot past him in the street, slammed on the brakes, and started backing up. Hart sprinted forward, moving close to the buildings until he reached the next corner, where he turned and headed down a narrow street jammed with cars. With no room to pass and the traffic stalled, drivers cursed at each other as they leaned on their horns.

The car following him could not follow him here. There was a cross street just ahead. Once he turned the corner his pursuers would not know where he had gone. He jumped across the front hood of a tan Peugeot and started running up the sidewalk on the other side. He felt a surge of confidence, a sense that he could not be caught; the feeling, brought by danger, that he was indestructible. He wanted to turn around and make some last gesture of defiance—give them the finger—before he hit the corner and disappeared. It was arrogance, pure and simple, and he reveled in it—until he felt something whiz past his ear and, an instant later, heard the shot. Then he forgot all about defiance, all about everything, except an instinct for survival.

He darted into the first doorway he found, hit the door full speed with his shoulder, and forced his way inside. He was in the back of a restaurant, in the middle of the kitchen, and then he was shoving past an outraged waiter though a maze of tables crowded with eager diners, out through the front door onto the sidewalk on the other side. A middle-aged couple was just getting into a taxi. Smiling an apology, he got in with them, and when they started screaming at him in French, said in English that he was a United States senator and that he was very sorry for the inconvenience but that someone was trying to kill him. The couple looked at each other, knew he was an American, decided he was crazy, and asked him where he would like to go.

"Not far," replied Hart. "I'll just ride along for a few blocks, if you don't mind."

The woman, Parisian down to her shoes, seemed amused.

"Are you really a United States senator?" she asked quite calmly.

Hart was looking out the window, his eyes darting all around, searching for anyone that might still be trying to follow him. His heart was racing, every muscle in his body tense. The strange, the unexpected thing, was that he was enjoying it: not just the sense of danger, but his own reaction, the speed with which he had made his decision, the absence of any real panic. There was nothing like a bullet whizzing past you, nothing like the threat of violent death, to make you feel alive.

"Reagan said that," he remarked, turning to the woman as if, instead of perfect strangers, she had been privy to his thoughts. "When he was shot," he explained. "He said there was nothing more exhilarating. Reagan could always deliver a line, especially when it belonged to someone else. Churchill said it first, in something he wrote, about the last cavalry battle ever fought. He was in it."

He saw the mild astonishment on the woman's face. His eyes were full of mischief at what he had done.

"Yes, I am a member of the United States Senate; and yes, to that other question you are too polite to ask—I probably have lost my mind."

The taxi was just passing the Eiffel Tower on its way toward a bridge that crossed the Seine. Hart had the driver pull off to the side. He started to get out, remembered he had been an uninvited guest on someone else's ride, and paid enough to cover the fare for wherever the couple wanted to go. He watched them travel on across the bridge on their way to the Left Bank, and wondered what they would think when they learned later that the crazy American they had just ridden with was wanted for murder, and not just any murder, but the murder of the president. It might have been only vanity, or more likely self-respect, but he wanted to believe that no one who had spent time with him, even two French strangers in a Paris taxi, would believe he could have had anything to do with something as unthinkable as that. Though he did not know their names, and would never see them again, he felt almost as if they were friends. It was absurd, of course, but only, he realized, if you were not facing the prospect of your own imminent death. Then the last face you saw, the last voice you heard, the last momentary connection with another human being, had more meaning than what you had known of someone with whom you might have had a brief conversation, exchanged a few, meaningless words, every day for years. He watched the cab recede into the distance and with a wistful glance wished the two strangers well.

"Now let's get the hell out of here," he mumbled to himself as he started walking. "And for God's sake—try to think!"

He had gone perhaps a quarter of a mile, collecting his thoughts, trying to make sense of things, when he remembered that he had not done the one thing he should have done as soon as he was out of the embassy and free on the streets. It was one thing to ask Austin Pearce, but this was something he had to do himself. He might be in danger, but Laura was in trouble. Even safe in Santa Barbara, reporters would be all over this, camped out in the street, badgering her with questions she could not answer about her husband's involvement in the assassination of the president. He pulled out his cell phone and started to call, but then he remembered that it was only late morning on the East Coast and Laura was booked on a ten o'clock flight.

"If she ever got to the airport," he said out loud. He stopped walking and looked around. He had changed directions and come back along the river until he was only a stone's throw from the Eiffel Tower. He dialed the number, but Laura did not answer. Perhaps she had gotten away before the story broke, but that did not seem possible, if it was in all the morning papers.

Maybe she saw it, the headlines in an airport newsstand, and remembered what he had told her, how important it was that he know she was safe, and had gotten on the flight instead of turning back to find out what was going on in Washington. He called Santa Barbara. At least there would be a message waiting for her when she arrived.

"I'm all right," he told her as calmly as he could. "Stay there, wait for me. I know who is behind this, and it won't take long to prove it."

It was one of the few lies he had ever told her.

Turning away from the Eiffel Tower and the long lines of tourists, he walked toward a landing on the river where he bought a ticket for an open boat ride under the bridges of Paris. Just as he was about to board, he heard someone speak his name. Several women, Americans from the sound of their voices, who had already taken their seats, where pointing at him as they whispered among themselves. Pretending that he had misplaced something, Hart left his place in line and began to walk away.

"That's him!" yelled one of the women, jumping to her feet. "That's Bobby Hart—the one who killed the president!"

Hart kept moving, walking at the same, measured pace, trying to lose himself in the crowd. The other women started shouting as well, a strident chorus of accusation, shouting until they were red in the face, but to their astonishment, and Hart's relief, no one seemed to pay attention, dismissing with French indifference the shouted demands of the Americans.

Even in Paris he could not pass unnoticed. Anywhere on the street he might pass an American, a tourist out for a stroll, and be recognized, and, recognized, accused. He was a fugitive who, even in a foreign capital, could not count on anonymity. There was no time to alter his appearance, no time to change the color of his hair, but he could at least change his clothes, get out of his suit and tie and dress more like a man who lived there. He found a small men's store where he bought a pair of black pants, a short, two-button brown jacket, a pair of walking shoes, and a green shirt. The proprietor bundled up his suit and dress shoes in a brown paper package.

He felt safer now, free from his own identity and less noticeable in a crowd. It was nearly six, and with gray skies pregnant with a summer storm, almost as dark as winter. The cars on the streets had their lights on and all the shop windows were lit up, but Hart wore dark glasses and stayed off the main avenues. He was not sure what time he should go to Aaron Wolfe's apartment. If he got there too early, before Wolfe came home, someone might notice him, someone might recognize him, someone might call the police. He decided to wait until eight. Wolfe was sure to be there by then, and if by chance he was not, it would be dark enough, whatever the weather decided to do, to stay out of sight.

He fell into a small café, took a table in the back corner, and picked at dinner. He had a glass of wine, and then had another, and he tried not to think too much about what had happened or what he was going to do. To get his mind off the immediate danger, he calculated the time difference between Paris and California, and then what time, his time, Paris time, Laura would make the long drive from the airport in Los Angeles to their home in the hills of Santa Barbara.

Even before the second glass of wine, he had begun to feel tired, very tired, as tired as he thought he had ever felt; weary with fear and frustration, fear of what he could not control and frustration over what he did not yet know: who was doing this and why they had decided that the best way to protect themselves was to make him a scapegoat, a fall guy, an assassin. His eyes felt heavy, his legs thick with fatigue. The only sleep he had gotten was the two fretful hours on the plane, a flight that now seemed like it must have happened weeks ago.

He started to order another glass, but glanced at his watch and thought better of it. He could not afford to be tired: there was too much to do to think about sleep. He caught a taxi outside the café and gave the driver Aaron Wolfe's address in the 18th arrondissement.

The head of the American embassy's political section lived three blocks from the Seine at the end of a short narrow street in a four-story building that had been there from sometime in the eighteenth century. Wolfe had one of the two apartments on the third floor. Hart pushed the button next to Wolfe's name. When there was no response, he stepped back onto the sidewalk and looked up. The lights from Wolfe's apartment were on. Hart tried the buzzer again, but again there was no answer. A woman carrying a bag of groceries was just coming home.

"Mr. Wolfe?" asked Hart. "Do you know if he's home? He's expecting me, and I saw the lights on from the street."

She was a middle-aged woman who walked slowly and with a limp. A single bag of groceries seemed the limit of her strength. But she had a pleasant face and kind, if rather tired, eyes. She started to open the door with her key and found that it was not locked. She turned to Hart as if she was sure he would be as surprised at this as was she.

"It's always locked, you know. Well, perhaps he left it that way so that you—"

There was a sudden violent noise: a burst of gunfire, two shots—or was it three?—in rapid succession, and behind it, shouted cries for help. Hart dashed past the woman, who was staring helpless at the landing overhead, and took the stairs three at a time.

"Call the police!" he screamed down at the woman.

The door to Wolfe's apartment was wide open. Wolfe was lying on the living room floor, his eyes gaping in now dead wonder at what had happened, a hole in his forehead where the bullet that killed him had flown to his brain. Someone, a man Hart did not recognize but who looked like one of the men who had been chasing him earlier, was lying face down on the floor, his arms spread apart, a gun—the gun he must have used to murder Aaron Wolfe—lying just beyond his outstretched hand. Hart picked it up, and then he heard a voice, a voice he did not want to hear. It was Austin Pearce, sunk back in an overstuffed chair, his shirt front oozing blood. With the last strength he had, Pearce raised his hand and pointed. On his knees next to the body of the unknown intruder, Hart wheeled around and, without even a moment's hesitation, fired the gun he had just picked up. Crying out in pain, a second assailant, a second killer, dropped his gun and clutched his right shoulder. He started to go for the gun again, but he knew, he could see it in Hart's eyes, that he would be dead if he tried. But he also seemed to know that he could still get away, that Hart would not shoot him in the back. He turned on his heel and vanished down the hallway.

"Austin," said Hart, rushing over to him, "what happened?"

"We had only just got here. There was a knock on the door. Wolfe kept a gun. He managed to shoot the first one, but the other one was right behind him, and...."

"Save your strength. An ambulance will be here any minute."

Pearce grasped Hart's hand and held it tight.

"In my pocket—an address...a time...."

His grip grew tighter, and then, slowly, Austin Pearce let go.

CHAPTER 18

HART COULD HEAR the wail of sirens in the distance. The French police were on their way. The man he had shot—the one he had let get away—was probably already calling for help, telling his confederates that he had just missed killing Bobby Hart and that if they hurried they could still find him there. Perhaps the wounded assassin did not have to call them; perhaps they were waiting just outside in a car. Hart could not stay there another second.

He was halfway to the door when he remembered. With his last breath, Austin Pearce had told him that there was something in his pocket: a time, a place, something Hart had to know. He bent down and began to search, the second time in two days that he had to look in the lifeless eyes of someone he had liked and respected, both of them, Quentin Burdick, and now Austin Pearce, willing to risk everything to get at the truth. And both of them murdered because they knew him, knew what he had been asked to do, knew enough about what had happened to cut to pieces any claim that Hart had been part of a conspiracy to murder Robert Constable.

Hart thought he was going to be sick, watching, and not wanting to watch, the glass-eyed stare that each time he forced himself to look away seemed to force him back, to make him look again at death's final work. There was nothing in the outside pockets; he slipped his hand inside the blood-soaked jacket, and there, next to Pearce's black leather wallet, he found a single half-sheet of blue paper, folded twice. Despite the blood, it was still possible to make out the words.

"Tomorrow. Mont Saint-Michel. Four p.m. Jean Valette."

What did it mean? Had Austin Pearce arranged a meeting, made an appointment, with the head of The Four Sisters, the man behind everything that had happened? The police sirens were louder, closer, almost here. Hart stuffed the half sheet of paper in his pocket and stood up. Then he saw it, on the table next to the chair where he had placed it, the gun, the gun he had picked up from just beyond the outstretched hand of the first assailant, the gun that, with Austin Pearce's warning, had saved his life. He hesitated, not sure whether to leave it behind or take it with him. He looked one last time at Austin Pearce, lying dead in the chair, and then grabbed the gun and headed down the stairs.

The woman he had left at the front entrance, just inside, the woman he had told to call the police, was cowering in fear. The grocery bag lay on the floor, a mess of broken eggs and coffee. She looked up at Hart with a sigh of relief.

"Mon Dieu! You're safe! When I heard the other shot, when I heard someone running away, down the hallway and out the back, I thought you must be killed." She opened her hands as if to pray forgiveness. "I should have come up, seen if you needed help, but I couldn't—I couldn't make myself move. I called the police, but after that, I couldn't...."

Hart touched her shoulder and told her that he understood. The sirens were deafening, the street outside echoing with their noise. He had no time left.

"You did fine, better than I could have done. Tell the police the truth: that I was here, with you, when we heard the shots. My name is Robert Hart," he said. "Robert Hart. Can you remember that? Tell the police that the men who came here were looking for me, that they came to kill me; they did not come to take me back."

Hart was on the street, walking fast. The police raced past him. They did not see him, or if they did, paid no attention. He thought about turning back, going to the French police, to show them that instead of a fugitive trying to get away, he was the victim of a conspiracy meant to have him murdered. But they might simply hand him over to the Americans, the same ones who wanted him dead. He hurried on, wondering how he was going to get to Mont Saint-Michel and what he was going to do when he got there and was finally face to face with the infamous Jean Valette.

He had been there, to Mont Saint-Michel, on the border of Normandy and Brittany, once, years ago, when he and Laura had spent a long, blissful month traveling through France. It was one of the best times he had ever had, moving from one place to the next, never in a hurry because there was never any place they had to go. They had wandered through and around Notre Dame, taking note of what it looked like inside, what it must have felt like to a Christian of the Middle Ages, listening to Mass, and then, after Mass, what it looked like from the different vantage points from which it could be seen on a bright, sunlit afternoon. From Paris, they had gone, not immediately, and not by the direct routes followed by tourists grimly determined to see as many things as possible, to the cathedral at Chartres; and, as if they knew that the best would be last, only after that to Mont Saint-Michel and the cathedral that had stood for a thousand years, as close to heaven as anything human hands could build.

They had rented a car and driven all over France. If he tried to rent one now, he would have to provide identification, information that would almost surely be traced. His own government was after him, and the French had no reason not to help. He took a taxi to the train station and tried to buy a ticket. The clerk only shrugged.

"There is no train to Mont Saint-Michel."

"No train tonight, or no train?" asked Hart patiently.

"No train, tonight, tomorrow, anytime, monsieur. Perhaps you would prefer to go somewhere else?" he asked with a look of bored indifference.

"All right," agreed Hart without hesitation. "I'll go there instead."

With a balding head and a small, hawk-like nose, the clerk's round face seemed in danger of slipping past his chin. Despite himself, he was starting to like the manner of this American who seemed inclined to let the conversation, such as it was, go where it would.

"I'm not sure how much that particular ticket would cost, monsieur. As you might imagine, 'somewhere else' is not one of our most requested destinations."

"Perhaps if you had a special train…?"

The clerk's eyebrows shot halfway up his vacant skull.

"Then you could of course go anywhere—wherever there were tracks—but the cost!—Nothing short of astronomical." His eyes tightened, became confidential. "But perhaps that is something you can afford. Still, it would take time to arrange, and, if I am not mistaken, you are in something of a hurry. A special train is out, and we have no train to Mont Saint-Michel. How do we solve this dilemma? Ah, perhaps I have the solution. We have a train—it leaves in an hour—to a station ten kilometers away from where you want to go. From there, you can take a taxi, or even walk, if you prefer."

Hart appeared to think about it.

"Well, if that's the closest you can get."

Though recently refurbished, and spotlessly clean, the train station had the gaslight atmosphere of the late nineteenth century, dimly lit, with intricate, iron latticework columns and shiny marble floors. The only thing missing was the rush of steam from a heaving locomotive. The new high-speed trains that shot across the country, and the continent, in less than half the time it had taken before, ran quieter and cleaner than that. Hart tried to imagine what Laura would say, the quick, easy commentary on the things she saw, the sudden insights that made so much sense to him perhaps precisely because he had never had the same thought himself. Laura always looked at things through different eyes. She was never much impressed with the urgent demands of the present. Others thought her odd, eccentric, for that, and even a symptom of the instability that had brought her close to a breakdown; Bobby was convinced that it was the source of the strength that had saved her sanity. He was desperate to talk to her, to hear her voice, but afraid that after he had called her once, left that message for her to hear when she got home, the next attempt would be traced.

Staying in the shadows, he wandered around the train station, passing the time. With trains coming and going, departures and arrivals every few minutes, the crowd was always changing, no one there long enough to notice anyone twice. Even if someone thought for a moment that his was a face they recognized, they were in too much of a hurry to remember where they might have seen him before. He felt safe enough to buy a paper.

As soon as he saw the front page, he wished he had not. His picture was plastered all over it; his picture, and that of Robert Constable, the president that, according to the lurid headline, had been murdered at the direction of a conspiracy led by Robert Hart. Alone on a bench next to the track on which his train was scheduled to arrive, Hart read with growing anger a blatant fiction in which he had been cast, not as the victim of a colossal ambition, a senator who wanted to be president, but as a husband driven to murder by his wife's infidelity. This was evil multiplied by itself: blame the murder on a man who did not do it, and pin the motive on his wife. His stomach twisted into a knot, tearing at him until he did not know if he could breathe. He crumpled the paper in his hand and spread his feet apart, bent forward over his knees, and threw up.

Wiping the vomit from his mouth, he straightened out the paper. Whatever they were saying, no matter how distorted, he had to know what he was up against. A photograph of Robert Constable beaming at the beautiful wife of the senator, taken at a fund-raising dinner during Bobby Hart's last campaign, was enough to establish an interest, which, given the president's reputation with women, meant something close to confirmation for whatever prurient-minded people were willing to imagine. There was a genius in simplicity. Robert Constable never looked at a beautiful woman without wanting her. Laura Hart was as beautiful as any woman anyone had ever seen. Did the president have an affair with the wife of a senator of his own party—what other reason would Bobby Hart have had to hire someone to murder him?

That at least was the venomous logic of the unnamed source, identified only as someone close to the investigation: Hart was guilty, and this is the reason he did it. Infidelity, betrayal, and anger—more than justified at what Robert Constable had done—would have been decent motives for revenge; but, more importantly, what evidence had been fabricated to convince people that he was guilty of the crime? His eyes moved swiftly down the endless column inches. He read to the end of the page and then followed the story to the next page after that.

He stopped at another photograph, halfway down the page: a woman, young and attractive, lay sprawled on the pavement outside her tenth-floor apartment on Manhattan's West Side. Her name was Sophie Jardin, a French citizen, and the hired assassin who had killed the president. According to the report, she had fallen from her balcony while trying to get away a little past midnight—an hour, as Hart calculated, after Quentin Burdick had been murdered. The evidence against Robert Hart had been found in her apartment: records of a series of payments made to a bank in Switzerland. Richard Bauman, the Secret Service agent who had been with the president the night he died, had given the FBI a description of what she looked like; an anonymous source had told them where she lived.

"An anonymous source!" muttered Hart in frustration.

The woman, the assassin they had hired, had been dead from the moment she agreed to take the job. She had always been the one essential, and completely expendable, part of the real conspiracy, the one that had gotten rid of the president and wanted to get rid of him. Killing her removed a potential threat, someone who could lead an investigation back to them; but more than that, it made her a witness against Hart, an accomplice, if you will, in the very conspiracy that had resulted in her death: There was no one left to question whether the records found in her apartment were really hers.

A noose was closing around his neck, and he had the awful, empty feeling that there was nothing he could do to stop it. He had the strange, dark sensation of falling through a trap door, knowing he had only a second left to live. He got up from the bench and started pacing back and forth, growing more determined, and more desperate, to get to Mont Saint-Michel and, if he had to, force Jean Valette to tell the truth.

The train seemed to stop every few minutes as it wound its way through the rolling Norman countryside. Hart sank low in a seat next to the window, grateful that the car was nearly empty and no one had to sit beside him; grateful, also, that the few passengers who got on and off were too busy with their own affairs to pay him any notice. The train rolled on through the endless night, lost in the darkness until, finally, three hours later, it arrived at the village where, sometime the next afternoon, Hart could take a taxi the rest of the way. He woke the porter at the only hotel, paid cash in advance for a room with a window in the back, and collapsed on the soft, down-filled mattress like a soldier just come back from the front.

He did not wake up until almost noon, and when he did, was not sure where he was. Nothing seemed real, nothing seemed quite right. People had been murdered! He had tried to do something about it, and now he was the one being blamed. People had been murdered, including anyone who could have helped prove that he had not been involved. His teeth ached, his head hurt, his eyes felt like the ashen embers of last night's fire. The only clothes he had were the ones he had been wearing. In a cloudy mirror over a scratched up wooden dresser, he saw a face older than the one he remembered, a face lined with fatigue and worry, and with eyes uncertain and confused. Splashing water on his face, he looked again, but the only change was that he now felt somewhat more awake.

He wanted to go outside and get some air, forget for a while what had happened and what he had to do, lose himself in whatever caught his eye. He wanted to remember, to feel again, what it was like to have a life that was not under constant threat of death and scandal. A few more hours, he told himself, that was all he had to wait. Better not to take a chance that he might be seen by someone who remembered who he was. He lay on the narrow bed with four iron posts, listening in the silence to the dresser clock bring the past closer to the future. Ten minutes, fifteen, then twenty; he could not stand it any longer. He threw on his clothes and stumbled down the stairs and out the door into the bright sunshine of a windless summer afternoon.

He fairly sprinted down the empty street, swinging his arms to match his stride, filling his lungs with air, forcing himself to feel alive. Passing a bakery, he turned back, bought a coffee and a roll, enough to keep him going, and began to look for a taxi, a car and driver, to take him the last few miles to Mont Saint-Michel and his meeting with Jean Valette. He was not sure that he had a meeting. He did not know what Austin Pearce had arranged, or if he had arranged anything. All he had was that fragmentary and enigmatic note: a name, a place, a time.

Mont Saint-Michel at four o'clock and it was now past two. Plenty of time, but Mont Saint-Michel was not a small place, and it was not even clear whether Valette would be inside the cathedral or somewhere in the near vicinity. A million people visited every year, and today, in the middle of summer, tourists from all over would be tramping through it. How would he find him, how would he find anyone, among all those people? Would Valette be looking for him? If there was a meeting, if Austin Pearce had set up an appointment, what was the reason Valette had agreed to it? Why would Valette, who had organized everything, murders without number, want to meet him, unless it was to have him killed, to hand him over to the same people who had just the night before arranged to have Austin Pearce and Aaron Wolfe both murdered?

It did not matter what Jean Valette wanted, Hart reminded himself. What mattered was that this was his chance, his only chance, to get to Jean Valette; the only chance to save himself, and stop whoever was involved in this from getting away with murder.

He found a driver sitting idly in his cab, studying with nostalgia the smoke from what was left of his cigarette. With a flick of two tobacco-stained fingers, he sent the stub flying into the cobblestone street.

"Mont Saint-Michel," said Hart as he climbed into the dust-covered back seat.

The driver gave him a blank look in the rearview mirror. Hart started to repeat it, to give it more of a French accent. The driver winced in apprehension.

"I understood; but it wasn't necessary." Starting the engine, he threw the car into gear and pulled away from the curb. "From here, no one goes anywhere else. From here," he added with a shrug, "there is no other place to go, unless you live here, of course. But then, if you live here, you don't need a taxi, do you?"

A few minutes later, with the village already out of sight, he asked, with the same casual interest he inquired of most of his fares, "Have you been to Mont Saint-Michel before?"

Hart sat forward on the cracked leather seat, suddenly eager for the opportunity to talk to someone who did not know who he was.

"Yes, some years ago. I was here with my wife. We spent a month in France, and—"

"It hasn't changed."

"France hasn't—?"

"Mont Saint-Michel," corrected the driver. His eyes sparkled with pleasure, the way they did every time he had the chance to make this remark to some returning tourist, someone coming back for a subsequent visit; usually, if not always, many years after the first, the ones who had come as students and then come back again at that point in middle age when they wanted as much to remember how things had been with them than for what they wanted to see of the ancient cathedral. "Mont Saint-Michel hasn't changed," he continued with greater interest. "That is not to say that it has not changed since it was built a thousand years ago, in the eleventh century, but it has not changed since you were here. The changes that have happened take much longer than something so short as a lifetime."

The road banked to the right and then ran slightly uphill for perhaps half a mile, and then, at the crest, it was there, Mont Saint-Michel, towering high above the sea.

"Extraordinary, isn't it?" said the driver. "Imagine doing something like today, and on a rock that sticks two hundred forty feet up in the air: build a cathedral, a monument to God hundreds of feet high on top of it, and know, when you start, that it is going to take a hundred years. I said a monument to God, but more than that, it is a tribute to the Archangel, Michael, who conquered Satan. When they became Christians, the Normans put themselves under his protection. He was, for a while, the patron saint of France." The driver glanced in the mirror. "You're an American—yes? I read something written by an American—though I have forgotten who it was—someone who wrote a long time ago. He said—and I liked it so much I've never forgotten it—that 'the Archangel loved heights. Standing on the summit of the tower that crowned his church, wings upspread, sword uplifted, the devil crawling beneath, and the cock, symbol of eternal vigilance, perched on his mailed foot, Saint Michael held a place of his own in heaven and on earth.... The Archangel stands for Church and State, and both militant.'"

The driver's eyes brightened with the knowledge that he could still recall the passage, remember every word, and then, content with what he had done, lapsed into a silence.

"You don't remember who wrote that?"

"No, I'm sorry, I don't, but he wrote a whole book about our cathedrals. If I remember right, he came from a famous family."

They were almost there. The mouth of the Couesnon River could be seen in the distance, along with the causeway that leads across it to the entrance, fortified against English attacks in the Hundred Years' War by a series of heavy stone towers and heavy thick walls.

"You've been here before, you know how to get to the top: follow the old pilgrim's route, past all the shops that sell souvenirs, past the Eglise Saint-Pierre, all the way up to the abbey gates."

Pulling the car off to the side, he got out to open the door for his passenger. He had developed a temporary fondness for him because of the way he had listened so attentively. He looked at him with the sympathy of a well-meaning stranger.

"You said you came here before with your wife. But this time you come alone?"

"I hadn't really planned this trip. I only just found out I'm supposed to meet someone here, and I'm not even quite sure where." He made it sound as if his confusion were a simple mistake, a misunderstanding that would not have any serious result. "Perhaps you know the man I'm here to see—Jean Valette?"

The driver looked at him as if he must be kidding, as if it were some kind of American prank, like saying, in an earlier time, that he was there to meet Charles de Gaulle. Then he seemed to reconsider. With his feet on the sidewalk, he sat down on the front seat of the taxi and glanced up at Hart, standing in front of him. He seemed particularly intrigued by the way Hart was dressed.

"Are you sure you want to go like that?"

Hart turned up the palms of his hands, and with a puzzled glance asked him what he meant.

"The way you're dressed—I would have thought…I mean everyone else is—how shall I say?—More formal: suits and ties, and the women, of course, also quite properly."

"What are you talking about?" asked Hart, growing more perplexed.

"You said you were meeting Jean Valette. I assume you mean Jean Valette, the famous financier."

"Yes, now if you know where I can find him, I'll—"

"Doesn't it say, on your invitation?"

"I don't have that kind of invitation. The meeting was arranged by someone else, and, as I said, I was just informed of it late yesterday. I barely had time to get here."

"Four o'clock," said the driver, to Hart's astonishment.

"Yes, but how did you know…?"

The driver got out of the car. There were people passing by, and he did not want to be overheard. Placing his hands on the small of his back, he stretched up on the balls of his feet and then took a deep breath. He would try again.

"It always starts at four o'clock; every year as far back as I can remember. I drive a number of them over myself, usually the night before, sometimes in the morning. Some of them, of course, stay here, in the abbey; some of them for as much as a week. They like to get the feel of what it was like a thousand years ago, when it first happened."

Despite his attempt at resistance, Hart was running out of patience. As politely as he could, he asked, "When what first happened?"

"The Crusade, of course. They come here, the same time every year, to commemorate the first one to happen, sometimes a hundred people, sometimes more; and every year, late in the afternoon, the head of it gives a speech. That's the reason you're here, isn't it, to hear Jean Valette?"

"At four o'clock," said Hart, just to be sure. "But where?"

"In the Refectory, of course. Where else would they gather for a meal?"

"The Refectory, at four o'clock," said Hart, as he began to move away.

That was what Austin Pearce had learned: that Jean Valette was here, that he came here every year. There was not any meeting, there was no appointment. Neither Jean Valette, nor anyone else, knew Hart was coming. The advantage was all his.

"You won't have any trouble finding it," the driver called after him. "There should be signs all around."

Hart stopped and turned back.

"Signs? About what?"

The driver threw up his hands.

"The annual meeting of the Knights of St. John—what else?"

CHAPTER 19

THE CRUSADES, THE eleventh century, the Knights of St. John, what did this ancient history have to do with anything that mattered? Hart was wanted for a murder he did not commit, and the only way he could think to prove his innocence was to climb up the well-worn stone steps of a thousand-year-old cathedral perched high above the raging waters of the Atlantic and listen to a man he had never met give a speech about something no one in his right mind would care about! It was ludicrous, he told himself as he pushed through the crowd; worse than ludicrous, stupid, because what could he do when he got there?—Put a gun to Jean Valette's head in front of the audience that had come to hear him speak, force him to confess the intricate and deadly conspiracy he had set into motion for reasons that Hart could even now not begin to guess?

Slowly, and with a kind of fatal inevitability, the thought came to him that if he had to, he would. If it were the only way to stop this thing from going any further, the only way to end the this vicious string of murders, he would use the gun, not just to bluff Jean Valette into a confession, but kill him. The thought grew on him, became clearer and more certain of itself, the closer he got to the cathedral. The spire was now directly overhead, Michael the Archangel, sword lifted up to heaven, symbol of the eternal vigilance of God.

He was inside the cathedral, searching through the crowds for the way to the Refectory and Jean Valette. Twice he went off in the wrong direction before a friendly tour guide pointed him toward what appeared to be a passage between one set of buildings and another, but was instead the place where the monks had lived and the visiting nobility had taken their meals. Passing the entrance to the dormitory, Hart found the staircase that led down to the Refectory below. The doors were shut and, as a woman at a table just to the side made clear, would not be opened. Even someone with an invitation would not now be admitted.

Hart started for the door anyway, but a guard in plainclothes quickly stepped in front. The woman reached for the telephone to call more security.

"I was asked to be here at four o'clock!" insisted Hart. "Told to be here by one of Mr. Valette's closest friends, and you say I can't go in because I'm late by two minutes?"

The woman was a study in precision. Her only response was to raise an eyebrow and look down her nose. Four o'clock was four o'clock, she seemed to say with that glance of silent disapproval; nothing could be simpler, more self-explanatory, than that. She had no sympathy for those who had yet to learn the lessons of punctuality. From behind the closed doors came the muted sound of applause. They were just getting started.

"Here," said Hart, as he quickly pulled out his wallet and removed his card. "Take this in there, give it to Jean Valette." Bending slightly forward, he pulled his jacket open so she could see the gun. "And tell him," he shouted as she got up and hurried toward the door, "that Austin Pearce told me to come here, last night, just before he died!"

The guard took a step forward; the woman stopped him with a look. She slipped inside, and they stood there, Hart and the burly, square-shouldered guard, eyeing each other with suspicion, until, a few moments later, the door swung open and the woman motioned for Hart to enter.

He was at the back of a long, narrow room, lit almost as bright as day by the light that streamed through the windows high above in the walls. Two hundred people could dine together in the Refectory, and there were nearly that many here now. Almost as if he had been expected to arrive late and somehow force himself in, there was an empty chair just inside the door. At the opposite end of the hall, perhaps a hundred feet away, an elderly gentleman with stooped shoulders and a substantial nose, wearing around his neck a three-colored ribbon with a large gold medal in the shape of a five-pointed star, was nearing the end of what even to Hart's somewhat limited ear for French seemed a dazzling display of wit and good humor.

The audience was clearly captivated by the old man who was obviously well-known and used to their praises. With the impeccable timing of a paid performer—which in some sense he must have been—an actor, a lawyer, or perhaps a retired politician, someone who had lived a long life on one sort of stage or another—he brought each well-turned phrase to a dramatic stop, pausing to let the audience share in common delight what, with just those few words, he had been able to achieve. Hart began to lose all sense of himself as he listened, fascinated, to a talent that, for all the speeches he had heard in Washington, he could only envy. Though his French, once again, was far from perfect, he could follow well enough, once he caught the flow. He understood, almost word for word, the few sentences in which, flushed with triumph, the old man moved from his own brief remarks to the introduction of Jean Valette.

"The head of one of the nation's most important institutions, head of one of the most illustrious families in France, a family that at every stage in our history has played a leading, and sometimes a decisive, part." With a dramatic flourish, he stretched out his arm to the man sitting in the chair on the left side of the podium. "The head—the honorary head—of the Order of St. John, the order through which, and by which, his namesake, his ancestor, five hundreds years ago at the Battle of Malta saved Christendom and, saving Christendom, saved France!"

Everyone, men and women alike, were on their feet, applauding with an intensity that if Hart had just wandered in, without any knowledge of the reason they were there, he would have thought that Jean Valette had either just won an election, or just won a war. Then, as he stood there clapping with the others, he realized that these people were really applauding themselves, their history, and, more than what they had become as a people and a nation, what they had been. That was the key to it: what they remembered, or wanted to remember, about what they, or really, their distant relations, the men and women whose own lives had been, in every sense, the necessary precursors of their own, had done in that time made even more glorious by everything that had been forgotten.

Jean Valette said nothing about what had been said about him, and apart from a bare nod of his head, did not acknowledge the audience. He stood at the podium, waiting, while the applause of the crowd gradually played itself out. Though of only medium height, if that, he seemed, with his shoulders held straight and his head erect, much taller. His eye was bold, unflinching. It was impossible to think of him ever looking away; it was impossible to think of him, even as a child, trying to avoid the gaze of someone, even a father, who had doubts about something he had done. He would not have allowed anyone, except perhaps a father—and later in life, perhaps not even him—to be so familiar as to even think to do that. And yet, at the same time, despite what could easily have seemed an astonishing conceit, there was nothing that made you feel irritated, much less angry, at the way he looked at you with those dark, penetrating eyes of his. The slight smile that danced along his lip told you in the politest way possible that he frankly did not care enough about your opinion to have any great interest in hearing you express it. Even if you agreed with him, you would have been wrong, because, in the nature of things, what you thought you knew had really been nothing more than a lucky guess. He was that arrogant, if you call arrogance what someone of unusual ability considers his own worth.

Then he began to speak, and the sense of distance began to disappear. His face became alive with expression as he described what he called the dilemma in which they lived, divided between two traditions in conflict with one another.

"We are on the one hand, as witnessed by our presence here today, the inheritors of the ancient glories of Europe and of France. While other, smaller, peoples were still forming nations, we led a cause; while they formed petty states and principalities with all their endless bickering, we marshaled the forces of Christendom and protected civilization, defeated Islam, and saved the West. But then, barely two hundred years ago—the blink of an eye in the long history of humanity—we gave birth, through the greed and ambition of a corrupt and frivolous aristocracy, to the French Revolution, and produced the modern world of democracy and mass movements. This ended all established order, destroyed even the notion of a hierarchy of values, and began the abolition of the fundamental difference between better and worse. We produced, in other words, the modern belief in equality and the diminishment of man."

This would have been unsettling, a remark like this—there is, after all, nothing quite so insulting in the age of equality as to be told that you are only average—but with a near perfect grasp of just how far he could challenge convention, Valette flashed a smile and quickly added:

"We wish we could have done what our ancestors did who went off on the great adventure to save Jerusalem from the infidels; and we would have, too, if only we had lived back then, when such things were still possible."

Hart could almost feel the collective sigh of approval and relief, and, more than that, could almost see in their eyes the past recaptured in the safe privacy of a dream. They would have been warriors—they did not have any doubt of that—but now they wanted to hear something more about their former greatness as a nation, and then they wanted dinner.

"The things that were possible then do not seem possible now. But is that because we no longer face that kind of danger, or because, if I can be so bold, we no longer take things as seriously as we once did? Let me tell you a story of how the world used to be, when men believed in God and never thought to doubt either hell or heaven. You all know how the Order of St. John was changed from an order that took care of the sick and wounded into an order trained to fight and die; how the Knights Templar were first destroyed by the King of France, Philip the Fair, and how the Pope, Clement I, gave the king permission to dissolve the order. How many of us know what happened to them because of it?"

The eyes of Jean Valette glittered with the remembered malice of a strange, and to an audience trained in the secular disciplines of modern science, unbelievable, act of revenge.

"The head of the order, the Grand Master, had been tortured into a confession of blasphemy and lies. Burned with hot irons, his skin torn from his body, his bones broken on the rack, he admitted that he had given up Christ to worship the devil, that he had engaged in every imaginable sin and, worse yet, had not regretted any of them. But then, a few months later, in March of 1314, brought forward for his trial, the Grand Master, Jacques de Molay, who had been not only the king's close friend, but godfather to his daughter, recanted his confession, an act of courage and honesty that led almost immediately to his being burned at the stake."

There appeared at the edges of Jean Valette's mouth the first hint of a secret, one he was about to share, that made of the prospect of this scene of awful terror and burning flesh, a triumphant reversal of all normal expectation. For a moment, but just for a moment, he let that unknown possibility, that promise of something without parallel, hang heavy in the air.

"The fire had been started, the flames leaped from the faggots piled around his legs, the smoke was rising up to his rope-bound chest, when Jacques de Molay called to the crowd to witness his word that God Himself would soon begin to exact a price for the sacrilege committed by Pope Clement and Philip the Fair, that God in his greatness would carry out the curse that with his dying breath he was calling down upon the king and his descendants through the thirteenth generation. He died insisting that before the year was out, both the king and the pope would be summoned to meet him before the judgment seat of God."

There was another pause, as Jean Valette, contemplating the mysterious workings of providence, invited his audience to wonder at the power of an age in which such things had been possible.

"Pope Clement died within a month; Philip the Fair died seven months later. The king was only forty-six, and if you are wondering at the cause of his death, the only thing we know with any certainty is that he was not ill and that he did not die in an accident. He just died."

Valette raised his hand, dismissing the matter as one better left to others to solve. He had another, more important, point to make.

"That happened again in 1324, more than two hundred years after the First Crusade, and more than two hundred years before the Battle of Malta, almost five hundred years between the recapture of Jerusalem and the fight on an island to save the West from the resurgent Muslim invader. We need to understand that, to remember that; to remember that Europe, the West, once understood the threat it faced and was willing to do whatever was necessary, and for however long it took, to save itself.

"Now we face that same threat again, a new war of religion, a war between Islam and the West. Only this time, while Islam still believes in its own importance, the West no longer believes in anything, except the equal right of everyone to believe anything they like. We cannot win that fight. The question is: what should we do? What can we do?"

Valette had been speaking without a text, without notes of any kind. His eyes never strayed from his audience and, more than that, never felt the need. Hart had the feeling that he could go on like this for hours, never repeating the same thought twice, speaking solely from memory and the stunning clarity of his mind, as much at home in the history of things dead and buried for a thousand years as in the events of his own, contemporary, world. But, for the first time, Valette reached inside his suit coat pocket and pulled out what looked like a standard three-by-five card.

"Some of you may have heard of Jacob Burckhardt, the great historian who died early in the last century. He wrote something about the Jesuits, how they were able to acquire so much influence in the world, which seems to me to suggest what we need to do now. Let me read it to you. I've written it down so I won't make a mistake."

He glanced at the card, too quickly to have read anything on it, and then looked back at his audience and did not look at it again.

"'It is not so hard for firmly united, clever and courageous men to do great things in the world.'—Remember that. 'Ten such men affect a hundred thousand, because the great mass of the people have only acquisition, enjoyment, vanity, and the like in their heads, while those ten men always work together.'"

Valette put the card back in his pocket, the card he had not needed, and began a long disquisition on the truth of Burckhardt's observation. He recalled, one after another, examples, almost all of them from French history, of the way a few men, or even, in the case of Napoleon, a single individual had done things no one had thought possible. There was no doubt that his intention was to show that things that had been done in the past could be done again, that anything was possible with the proper will; and yet, unless Hart was deceiving himself, there was a tone of the deepest irony in what he said, as if he did not believe it, or, and the possibility was fascinating to Hart, he wanted you to think that he did not believe it. That was inescapable, the thought that he could so easily have a double meaning, and maybe more than that; that everything he said, no matter how straightforward he made it seem, was really an enigma wrapped inside a doubt. He seemed proof of the ancient dictum, if anyone was proof of it, that only someone who knows how to lie has any knowledge of the truth.

What was he really trying to do, wondered Hart, as he sat there in the back, watching the performance of a man who seemed capable of anything except, strangely enough, the very thing that had caused Hart to seek him out. There seemed to be too much intelligence, too much—call it arrogance, call it pride—to demean himself with something as sordid, as commonplace, as murder. But all the evidence, everything Hart had learned, had pointed him to Valette and brought him here to Mont Saint-Michel. The Four Sisters had been involved in everything. He was not wrong about that. He warned himself against the easy seduction of intelligence and charm; warned himself against mistaking talk of ancient history and the grand sweep of time with the absence of all ambition. No one became one of the richest men in the world without some degree of self-absorption. And what was his concern with history and the origins of France if not an expanded, not to say delusional, sense of self-importance, a way to make himself the embodiment of far more than the experience of his own generation? Still, for all that his conscious mind could tell him, he could not rid himself of the feeling that with Jean Valette something else was at work, something deeper and more profound than the kind of motive that would result in simple murder. But what? That, he did not know.

"The difficulty, of course," Valette was saying, "is to know how to find men like those, how to establish in advance the conditions which make such men possible, the 'ten men who can do great things in the world,' a task especially difficult in this barbarous age in which we live, when we have forgotten the past and what it means, and, as someone once remarked, unable to think back any further than our grandfathers we 'drown all time in shallow waters.' This is the challenge of our generation: to think back to what we might again become, and raise the next generation to understand the crisis of the West and what can be done about it.

"That is the reason for the school we founded five years ago, the academy that, with your continuing support, has already begun to broaden the horizons and deepen the understanding of the young men and women that each year are sent to us. The Academy of St. John is, I believe, unique among contemporary educational institutions in that we think it more important that our students learn how to live, rather than how to work; to learn about the world, rather than how to make a living. As you can imagine," he remarked to general laughter, "we are the best kept secret in France. But then, we don't need a hundred thousand; we need only ten."

Jean Valette looked out over his audience one last time. Then, with a silent bow, he lifted his arm in the air and quickly sat down. The applause was immediate, sustained, but more an acknowledgment of respect for the man than any great enthusiasm for anything he had said. That, at least, was Hart's impression. Though he did not know any of them, they seemed for the most part serious, sober-minded people, too prosperous to be anything but conventional in their thinking. They were the kind willing to listen to new ideas, especially those firmly rooted in the past, so long as there was not any real chance anyone would try to put them into practice. This business about a school, whatever innovations might be involved, could not possibly be a threat to anything; it was too small to do anything except give a few perhaps gifted students an education in the useless curriculum of another age. If some of them, most of them perhaps, were willing to give financial assistance to this new academy, it was because they had always given money to museums and other places connected with the arts when they were asked to do so by people to whom they could not afford to say no.

The applause faded into silence and the audience took their seats again. It must have been announced at the beginning that after Valette spoke he would take questions. As soon as everyone was settled, a man sitting not far from Hart was back on his feet and Valette was again at the podium.

The questions came one after another, and with each one Valette seemed more eager to take the next. Hart could not count the times he had had the same experience, taking questions from an audience, reluctantly at first, but then becoming more comfortable, grasping by some instinct how to meet the inquiry on its own terms, respond directly but always within the limits of the questioner's knowledge and experience. But, as he understood at once, there was something more than that, a completely different dimension, with Jean Valette.

As soon as someone asked a question—sometimes even before they finished asking it—Valette's eyes would flash with the answer. Not just the answer, but the precise way he wanted to phrase it, the exact wording, came immediately to his mind. He thrived on it, questions from people who, as was sometimes plain, had barely understood anything he had said and had perhaps agreed with even less than that; thrived on it—and this was what Hart finally understood—not because he learned anything from what they said, from the questions they asked, but because he learned so much listening to what those questions forced him to say. He knew the answer; it had been there, buried in his subconscious mind, but he did not know he knew it until someone asked a question and he took possession, conscious possession, of it for himself. At the end, when the last question had been asked, he seemed genuinely grateful for the chance he had been given to learn from the best, the only, teacher he had.

There were no more questions and no more speeches. The invited guests began to talk among themselves as they waited for the chairs to be rearranged and food brought to their tables. Hart watched as Jean Valette stood at his place next to the podium exchanging brief greetings with the men and women who came up to express their appreciation for his remarks, or to ask a question they had not wanted to ask in front of an audience. Valette had just finished talking to someone and was about to turn to another when, suddenly, he looked the length of the room straight at Hart. He nodded, and then broke into a smile, as if he were greeting an old friend, or someone who might become a new one.

Hart had come to Mont Saint-Michel believing Jean Valette to be the head, the Grand Master, of a world-wide organization for which murder and political assassination were just other ways of doing business, only to discover that, if he was telling the truth in the speech he had just given, the main, the only, ambition he had was to be the master of a school that would teach a handful of students to see the future through the eyes of a very distant past. Hart felt helpless and confused, without any idea what he should do next, whether he should confront Jean Valette or just get away. Nothing made sense, and the more he tried to understand, the less he understood.

Still, he was there, and given what would happen if he did not find some answers, there was nothing to lose. He started toward the front of the Refectory and Jean Valette. Someone took him by the arm and held him back. The heavy-set, plainclothes security guard who had tried to stop him from getting in was insisting that he leave. Hart tried to free his arm, but the guard's grip only grew tighter.

"Jean Valette wishes to see you," said the guard as he turned Hart around and marched him toward the door. "He's not someone you want to keep waiting."

As soon as they were out into the hall, he reached inside Hart's jacket and removed the gun that Hart had forgotten he had. A smile full of cruelty and knowledge curled over his large, misshapen mouth, and then, as if at some private joke, he began to laugh, and he kept laughing as he dragged Hart down the hall and out the back to an open courtyard and a waiting car, a black limousine with dark tinted windows. He let go of Hart's arm, and to Hart's astonishment, gave him back the gun.

"No one goes armed to a cathedral, Mr. Hart. Even an American should know that."

The back door of the limousine swung open and in the shadows on the other side sat Jean Valette.

"Please get in, Mr. Hart. Bring the gun, if you think you need it, but I can promise that, while you might kill yourself with it accidentally, no harm will come to you from me. I have been waiting too long to talk to you to let anyone hurt you."

CHAPTER 20

HART WAS NOT sure whether to take Jean Valette at his word or err on the side of caution. Valette caught the look of indecision.

"Perhaps it would be better if you kept it. After everything that has happened, I can understand why you might feel reluctant to trust me." He turned to the plainclothes guard, waiting with his hand on the door as Hart got in. "Come with us, Marcel. We'll give you a lift to your car. It's too far to walk, and besides, there are a few things we need to discuss."

The limousine started down a winding, narrow street, around the back of the cathedral to the village in front and, beyond it, to the causeway across the river. There were tourists everywhere, crowding onto the steps up to the famous place where kings and queens had come to worship, pushing into the shops that sold souvenirs to remind them later of where they had been. For a few brief moments, Jean Valette viewed the scene with grim amusement, as if, like someone come to honor a long dead relative, he had discovered the cemetery taken over by a visiting troupe of puppeteers, come to give a children's show. With a distant smile, he turned to his guest.

"If I had known for certain you were going to be here, Mr. Hart, I would have tried to speak with more intelligence. As it was, with this audience...." The thought finished itself. Then he tried to explain. "And I only do it, you understand, because of this strange obligation I feel to try to keep certain things alive. But enough of that! I'm very glad you came and we finally have the chance to— But you must be exhausted, and—how thoughtless of me— terrified, after what happened last night. No, that is the wrong word, the wrong emotion. You don't strike me, Mr. Hart, as someone who would ever be terrified of anything. Still, after what you've been through.... Poor Austin Pearce! He was remarkable, as I'm sure I don't need to tell you; one of the most—one of the few really intelligent men I've met. I can't believe he's gone, and murdered like that! Incredible!"

Valette shook his head in disgust. He leaned back in the corner of the seat and lit a cigarette and for a short while watched the thin trail of smoke spiral into the air. And then, cracking open the window to let the smoke out, shook his head again, but this time with an air of resolution.

"What do we know so far, Marcel?" With a sudden, helpless shrug, he looked at Hart. "Where are my manners? This is Marcel Dumont, Mr. Hart: Inspector Dumont, chief detective of the Surete Generale." He had anticipated Hart's surprise. "You thought he was there to provide security, a private guard? You could probably do that, couldn't you, Marcel?" He turned back to Hart. "Marcel was on our Olympic boxing team."

Marcel Dumont grinned modestly.

"Nearly thirty years ago, and I did not make it past the quarterfinals."

"He lost to the one who went on to win the gold medal."

"As I say," insisted the inspector, "thirty years, and about fifty pounds, ago. But about last night," he went on, becoming serious. "You're lucky you're still alive, Mr. Hart."

Valette lifted his chin and tapped his fingers together. His mouth was shut tight and his eyes half-closed in the way of someone used to calculating probabilities.

"I doubt Mr. Hart feels very lucky, do you, Mr. Hart? The whole world thinks you're a murderer. No, I don't imagine Mr. Hart right now thinks he's been very lucky at all. But go on, Marcel—what do we know about this? Austin Pearce and the head of the embassy's political section—he was a kind of spy, wasn't he?—were murdered. One of the gunmen was killed, and the other one wounded, but got away. You did that, didn't you, Mr. Hart? Go ahead, Marcel: What else do we know? That woman—the landlady—she told the police that Mr. Hart here was downstairs with her when the shooting began. It's a good thing she was there; otherwise, everyone would think you killed both of them. Although I'm not sure that would have made things any worse for you than what's happened instead. I'm sorry. I'm getting ahead of myself. Go ahead, Marcel."

The driver turned into an alleyway on the other side of the river and pulled up next to where the chief of detectives had left his car.

"Monsieur Valette is correct. The landlady gave us a very precise account of what happened. You came there looking for Mr. Wolfe— Aaron Wolfe. You told her you were expected. Is that true, Mr. Hart— did Mr. Wolfe expect you?" he asked, exchanging a glance with Valette.

Hart noticed the glance. They knew something he did not. He began to worry that he had stepped into a trap.

"I went there to see Wolfe. That's true."

"But did he expect you? We know that you were about to be arrested at the embassy, and that you got away. Did Mr. Wolfe warn you, did he tell you that was about to happen, or did Mr. Pearce do that? You came over on a private plane, and Mr. Pearce and the ambassador were old friends, were they not?"

Hart looked to Valette for an explanation, but Valette lit another cigarette and said nothing.

"What difference does it make if I was expected? I went to see him; that fact has been established. I went to see him, heard the shots, told that woman—the landlady—to call the police, ran upstairs and found Wolfe dead and Austin Pearce dying. Wolfe had shot the first one, and I picked up the gun, and Austin warned me, and I looked behind me and saw the second one and I fired and hit him in the shoulder."

"Did the man you shot say anything? Could you tell where he was from? Was he an American?"

"No, he didn't say anything. So if you're asking whether he spoke French or English, I don't know. But I was chased in the streets after I left the embassy, and I can't be sure, but I think he was one of them."

The inspector raised his eyebrows and nodded as if that fit with what he knew.

"The dead one, the first one through the door, the one Wolfe managed to shoot, was an American, but we couldn't be absolutely sure about the other one."

"He had identification? You found something that told you who he was?"

"They were in a hurry. They probably started chasing you as soon as they discovered you had left the embassy. They didn't have time to plan anything. So, yes, we found identification on the body. He worked at the embassy, a 'cultural attaché,' which means in his case someone with one of your intelligence agencies. That's why I'm asking whether Mr. Wolfe expected you. How did they know to go there? They could not have been following you; they were already there when you arrived."

"Well, Wolfe wouldn't have told them, would he?"

"Then he did expect you? Before you left the embassy, you had made some arrangement." With a knowing look, the inspector turned to Jean Valette. "Which means that Wolfe had some reason to believe that the charges against Mr. Hart weren't true, and that Mr. Hart was somehow being used. Is that what happened, Mr. Hart? You have some evidence that you weren't involved in the murder of the president, Robert Constable?"

Hart's first reaction was to ignore the question, but then he changed his mind. He was tired, confused, and fast losing patience.

"Maybe he just believed me. Maybe because I had come all the way to find out who was behind the murder of the president, and whether or not The Four Sisters might be involved," he added with a quick, questioning glance at Jean Valette that stopped just short of being an accusation, "he realized that the suggestion that I might have wanted the president dead did not make any sense."

Inspector Dumont did not show any surprise. He turned to Jean Valette. "The Four Sisters?"

Valette stoked his chin as if he were considering the possibility.

"Everything you've learned leads back to us, doesn't it, Mr. Hart? The Four Sisters, I admit it, reaches almost everywhere. There would be no reason not to think that we might be involved in something like this. We wouldn't be the first financial institution to help get rid of someone or bring down a government we didn't like. But the question, Mr. Hart—the immediate question—is what Marcel has just now asked: How did anyone know that after you left the embassy you would be at that apartment?"

"It's what I said before," said Dumont, referring to an earlier, private, conversation.

"Yes, I think you must be right," agreed Valette.

"Right? About what?" asked Hart.

"They didn't go there for you," replied the inspector. "You had gotten away, lost them in the streets of Paris. That's when they decided they had to clean up the loose ends. It would not have been difficult to figure out that you had been warned—told you were about to be arrested—when you were at the embassy. They had to believe that Wolfe knew something, and that Pearce, who was in the room, had to have known the same thing: the name of the person you thought was really behind the murder of the president. They could not afford to let them talk to anyone. That was the reason they went to Mr. Wolfe's apartment: to kill them both. If they had gone there to kill you, they would have waited for you, but they didn't do that, did they? Not only did they not expect to find you there, you ruined their plan when you showed up."

"Ruined their plan? They did what you said they had gone there to do. Both Aaron Wolfe and Austin Pearce are dead!"

"Yes, unfortunately, that fact is true. But, you see, I'm almost certain that they planned to blame both murders on you."

"Me? But why would I kill Austin Pearce? Why would I kill Aaron Wolfe?"

"You?—A fugitive from justice, someone who arranged the murder of a president? What would stop a man like that from killing two people who might have known where he was heading, or who might have refused to help him get away? The question of a motive would never have entered into it."

Something had been bothering Hart since he first found out that Marcel Dumont was the chief detective of the Surete Generale.

"Why were you here today? Why were you waiting outside the door? Of all the different places I could have gone, how did you know I would be coming here?"

The inspector exchanged a glance with Jean Valette and then opened the door.

"Do you think anyone recognized him?" asked Valette.

"He was sitting in the back, and we got him out before anyone had a chance to really notice. So, no, I don't think so. Still, there is a risk…."

The inspector got out of the car. Valette followed him and closed the door behind him. They stood together, talking earnestly, and while Hart could not hear what they were saying, he could tell from the way they were gesturing that it was about him. After a few minutes, Valette got back in the car and told the driver to start.

"You'll come home with me," he explained to Hart. "You'll be safe there." He paused, and then added with a serious expression, "At least for a while. Marcel wanted to arrest you, take you into custody. He is an old friend, but he's a policeman, and you, I'm afraid, are the most wanted man in the world. Every police organization in Europe has been told to look for you."

"I didn't do a damn thing!" protested Hart, letting all his pent-up frustrations burst forth.

Jean Valette had a way of tilting his head back at an angle that made his gaze seem distant, remote, detached from any feeling of common sympathy or understanding. It was the look of someone completely analytical.

"That, of course, is not, strictly speaking, true."

"You think I had something to do with—?"

Valette stopped him a quick movement of his head, a look of disapproval for an obvious mistake.

"What you did was to let yourself be used. You came here to discover who, or what, was behind the murder of Robert Constable. You, a single individual—an important one, it is true—but not part of some investigative unit of your government! And you did this before there was any investigation, any official investigation; before there was so much as a public announcement that the president had not died, as first reported, of natural causes. That means, does it not, that someone knew, or had reason to know, that the president had been murdered and had some reason to ask you to look into it?" A shrewd, knowing smile crossed his lips. "I can understand why Hillary

Constable would want someone to do that; the more interesting question is why she chose you. Do you think it was because someone intended to blame you from the beginning?"

"I didn't tell you that Hillary Constable asked me to look into it."

"No, you didn't."

"And you still haven't told me—your friend, the chief inspector, didn't tell me—why he was here."

"He came because I asked him to come. I knew you would come, Mr. Hart. You had to come; there was not anything else for you to do. There isn't anything mysterious about it. Austin Pearce called me yesterday, just after you left the embassy, just after you made your escape. He was very agitated. That is a serious understatement: He was angry. He accused me of all sorts of things. I had a very difficult time getting him to calm down. He told me why you had come, what you thought I had done."

In the failing light of late afternoon, the limousine raced down a tree-lined country road. Sunlit shadows cast a dappled pale glow on Jean Valette's finely formed auburn-colored face. He had to be over sixty, but he looked almost as young as Hart, even though Hart, still in his forties, also looked younger than his age. There were differences, of course. Hart did not yet have any of the gray hair that, in the right proportion, added a certain distinction, and none of the web-like lines around the eyes that made Jean Valette's face, even in repose, look so serious.

"He told me why you had come," he repeated in a way that suggested not so much astonishment as a deep curiosity. He seemed intrigued by what Austin Pearce had told him. "He demanded—there is no other word for it—demanded that I tell him if it was true; demanded to know if I had had anything to do with this plot to murder Robert Constable."

Valette seemed almost to enjoy it, the memory of that accusation. If Austin Pearce had not been murdered, if he were still alive, it is quite possible that Valette would have laughed out loud as he recounted their strange conversation. Hart, on the other hand, did see anything even the slightest bit amusing in any of it.

"And did you?—Did you have anything to do with this, the murder of the president, the murder of Frank Morris, the murder of Quentin Burdick, the murder of—?"

"Mr. Hart! I promise you, I'm not what you seem to think." Valette's eyes flashed with contempt. "What did I care whether Robert Constable lived or died? What did I care about any of this? I'm not interested in what happens to this person or that person; I'm not interested in individuals. I'm not interested in what happens today or tomorrow; I'm interested in what is going to happen fifty years from now, a hundred years from now."

The look in his eyes changed. Contempt vanished; something more hidden, more enigmatic, took its place.

"Though I could have told you that what happened to Constable, and what is happening now, was all but inevitable; perhaps not in that form— murder—but in some other. We can discuss that later. Let me finish what I was telling you about what Austin said to me, let me—"

"You're not concerned with individuals—you're only interested in what might happen a hundred years from now!" exclaimed Hart as he leaned forward and jabbed his finger in the air. "Austin Pearce was murdered! He died looking into my eyes, and you don't care what happened to him? I'm supposed to believe you—Austin was supposed to believe you—when you insist you weren't involved in any of this?" His gaze sharpened and became more intense. "Did Austin tell you where he was going? Did he tell you he was going to be at Wolfe's apartment?"

"You think I sent those people—? If I had done that, why would you be riding in my car? Why wouldn't I have just let Marcel take you away, turn you over to the Americans and let them dispose of you? By this time tomorrow, I can almost guarantee that you would be dead."

"Why didn't you—let your friend, the chief inspector, arrest me?"

"Austin Pearce, of course."

"What did Austin do that made you—?"

"He asked me—after I gave him my word that I didn't know anything about what had happened, that I did not even know Constable had been murdered until he accused me of being involved—he asked me, or rather he insisted, that I do whatever I could to help you get to the bottom of this."

Jean Valette looked out the window at the rolling hills in their patchwork colors and the river that ran not far from the road, out to the dark green forest that marked the beginning of where he lived; the forest that, if he could not yet see it with his naked eye, would be there, in full view, in just another few minutes. There was a certain satisfaction, a sense of possession, in seeing things that others could not yet see.

"You knew Robert Constable, of course," he remarked after a long silence. "But how well did you know him?"

Hart thought about it, wondering how to answer the question that, in the last few weeks, he had often asked himself. He gave the one answer he was sure about.

"My wife did not know him at all."

Valette's head snapped up. His eyes brightened with approval.

"That's exactly what Austin told me. He had seen the papers, read the story, said that no one who knew you both would believe a word of it. Good for you, Mr. Hart; good for you. A man who doesn't doubt his wife! I once had that privilege. But never mind. How well did you know him, Robert Constable?"

"I never thought I really knew him," confided Hart. "He was too elusive, always calculating what he wanted and how he was going to get it—and how you were going to help him—to be someone you could really get to know. And now, after what I've learned—after what I've learned about his connection with you, with The Four Sisters—I'm not sure I knew him at all."

The line across the bridge of Valette's prominent nose deepened and became more pronounced as he drew his eyes together into an attitude of the utmost concentration. He scratched the side of his face with the back of three fingers. A smile that barely broke the line of his full mouth seemed to reflect a considered judgment that nothing could now change.

"Then you knew him as well as anyone did; better, really, because you knew him for what he really was: a man who, when dealing with others, thinks only of himself; a man who, when he tries to understand himself— if he ever does that—thinks only of what others believe. He was an actor, someone who always played a role—the only thing important that everyone else believe he was important, so that they would always want to see and hear him. That's why he wanted money: so he could continue to occupy center stage. And that, of course, is why he came to me."

"He came to you? You—The Four Sisters, the companies you control— didn't go to him, didn't offer him millions in exchange for making it easier for you to do business in the United States?"

"When you want money, Mr. Hart—when you ran for reelection the last time—did you wait for people to come to you, or did you ask them for their support? Yes, I understand there is a difference: that you weren't offering to do anything specific in exchange. I understand the difference, Mr. Hart; we both do. But Robert Constable did not. The truth is that Robert Constable did not really understand much of anything."

Valette stared down at his manicured hands, folded neatly in his lap, troubled, as it seemed, by this last remark, not so much for what had been said as by what had been left out. He closed his eyes and shook his head as if there were no point going on with it: that nothing he could say would explain what he meant. But then, because he thought it important, he turned and searched Hart's waiting eyes.

"Though obviously from a distance, I have watched your career with some interest. You seem—how shall I say this?—more grounded than the rest of them, the ones like Constable who only run for office because they would not know what to do with themselves without the attention of the crowd. You were going to quit a few years ago, I understand; go back to California and live a private life—something having to do with your wife, if I am not mistaken. I understand you have even been known to read a serious book. It's no wonder you don't seem to have many friends. We have at least that much in common."

It seemed at first a strange remark, but then, a moment later, Hart thought he knew exactly what he had meant: reading anything, but especially about the past, took you away from what people in the present thought important. He tried to use that thought to penetrate deeper into what for him was still the mystery of Jean Valette.

"You must have read a great deal to be able to do what you did back there, at Mont Saint-Michel: speak without notes for nearly an hour and then answer questions."

Valette's eyes filled with irony.

"The best thing that happened to me as a boy was to have a tutor who would scarcely let me read anything until I was nearly sixteen. Among the other interesting results, my memory was much improved."

Hart did not try to hide his astonishment.

"You didn't read anything until…?"

"One book: *Robinson Crusoe*. My tutor was very strange. He had read Rousseau's *Emile*—and believed it! Rousseau said *Robinson Crusoe* was the only book a boy should read because it teaches the lessons of necessity and the advantages of freedom; teaches you to see things with your own eyes and not the eyes of others. Perhaps that is the reason that I have always liked it here so much," he added with a look of mischief, "cut off from the outside world like Crusoe's island, and yet less than half an hour from all the luxury and madness of Paris."

They had come out of the forest and were approaching a massive iron gate. Behind it, stretching through a double row of poplars, was a driveway, a two-lane road that went on as far as the eye could see.

"It's only a few miles to the house," said Valette, explaining a fact without importance. He pointed to a rock outcropping on the right. "There is a path that leads to a small lake on the other side. I used to swim there as a boy. They say that buried somewhere at the bottom is a chest full of gold and silver, precious jewels, brought back from the Crusades. But I searched all over one summer and never found it. 'St. John's Treasure,' is what they called it, whoever started the legend after that other Jean Valette, my long dead ancestor, came back from Malta."

Folding his arms across his chest, he smiled to himself, and then looked closely at Hart.

"The Order of St. John. Some of what I told that audience today is actually true."

"But not all of it?"

This produced a look of vast amusement in Jean Valette.

"That's one sin of which I think I can claim never to have been guilty. Although I'm not sure it really makes any difference," he said as the smile on his face faded into obscurity and his gaze became more thoughtful. "I try to be careful, not go too far, in what I say, but I sometimes wonder why I bother. Those people I just spoke to—members of the Order of St. John—I could tell them exactly what I thought and they still would not understand it, and even if they did, they would think I was being ironic. They think I'm too intelligent not to believe exactly what they believe."

Hart remembered his own reaction, his sense that Valette kept his real meaning hidden, sometimes by putting it out in plain view.

"The suggestion that great things can be done again, that what was done in the past can be repeated, that there could even be another Napoleon? You don't think anyone believes you really mean it, and that is the reason you can say it? Everyone thinks you're only talking about some remote possibility, something that, if it were ever to happen, is not going to happen any time soon: this war between Islam and the West, to take another example."

Valette nodded in agreement with what Hart was saying, but stopped abruptly at this last remark.

"That war never stopped! If Robert Constable had only understood that, he'd probably still be alive!" he exclaimed in apparent frustration.

Hart stared at him in disbelief.

"What do you mean—he'd still be alive? What does this war you keep talking about have to do with his murder?"

"Nothing," he said with a shrug. "And everything. If he had understood what was at stake, the whole future of the West, he might have decided to do something important, something that history would remember, instead of just trying to become what he thought other people—the great, anonymous crowd—wanted him to be."

Hart wanted to laugh out loud. It was crazy, insane; he was trying to find out who was behind the murder of the president, trying now to clear his own name, and he was being told that Constable had brought it on himself by not being sufficiently serious. He did not laugh out loud, but he might as well have done. Valette had understood at once Hart's reaction.

"You think I don't know what I'm talking about. Well, consider this: All this money he got from The Four Sisters, all those millions—do you think that would have happened if I had not thought that it would, one way or the other, bring about his destruction?"

Hart did not know what to think. He was about to demand that Valette explain what he meant when the driver suddenly hit the brakes and Hart was thrown forward onto the floor. Valette helped him back onto the seat.

"There," he said, pointing to an enormous stag standing in the middle of the drive. "Isn't he magnificent?" With proud indifference the stag stood there, daring anyone to try to move him, and then bounded off the road and into the dense forest. "The park is full of animals now, wild boar and deer that used to be hunted. I put a stop to it. I never understood this desire some people have to kill things that cannot fight back."

He leaned forward and rapped gently on the glass, a signal to the driver to move forward again. The road, this endless driveway from the iron gates miles behind them, began a steep ascent, winding through one hairpin turn after another, climbing high above the valley floor and the river that in the distance glowed blood red and orange under the soft, dying light of the twilight sun. They reached a clearing several miles square, bordered on the other side by another forest and another, taller range of hills, and passed through yet another iron gate, smaller and more ornate than the first. They were now on a great stone paved circle that led past a series of spouting fountains and close-cropped lawns and hedges to what Hart could only think was a much older, if slightly smaller, Versailles.

"It was built about the same time as Mont Saint-Michel, a thousand years ago," explained Jean Valette. "Like the cathedral, it has been rebuilt and restored who knows how many times. They burned it to the ground, or tried to, those great believers in equality, in the early days of the Revolution, and murdered—cut the living hearts out of some of them—the people who lived here. The wonder, I suppose, is that we ever got it back. We wouldn't have, if we had not learned the secret of this new world of ours."

"The secret?" asked Hart as they got out of the car.

Jean Valette stood in front of the ancient stone chateau that seemed to stretch endlessly in every direction, inhaling the sweet, clean air. His eyes glittered with the remembered knowledge of something perhaps taught to him as a child, or learned later, somehow on his own.

"The secret of the age of equality: the more equality there is, the more desperate people are for something that seems to set them apart, makes them different, better, than the rest. That's why money has become the only thing anyone believes in anymore. It isn't because of what it can buy; it's because of what it tells everyone about you. Want to see a completely miserable human being? Introduce someone worth a hundred million to someone worth twice that amount. Every age has its own form of insanity, Mr. Hart. Money is ours. That's what got Robert Constable killed, and, directly or indirectly, it's what is likely to get you killed as well. But let's go inside now. You must be famished."

CHAPTER 21

UNABLE TO SLEEP, Hart lay awake, seeing ghosts, fleeting fragments of faces he had known, murdered, every one of them, by some lethal, hidden hand. If Jean Valette had not ordered the assassination of Robert Constable—if this strange, erratic, and ultimately enigmatic character was telling the truth—then he was back at the beginning, knowing less than he had known before about who was behind a conspiracy that had thus far been so successful that the only one under suspicion was him. Who had reason to want Robert Constable dead, and, more importantly, was in a position to arrange the murder of a president and then eliminate anyone who might learn what they had done?

Jean Valette may not have been involved, but everything still led back to him. He was the one who had known the secrets that, had they been discovered, would have destroyed Constable and his presidency. Was that what Valette had meant by that astonishing remark: that he had given

Constable all those millions precisely to help bring about his destruction? But why, what motive could he have had, to do something as Machiavellian as that? Hart had hoped to sound him out that evening, to see if any of it made sense, or was only the fantasy of a disordered mind. But Jean Valette had disappeared.

As soon as they arrived, Hart had been taken upstairs to his room, or rather a suite of rooms as large as any apartment. The chateau, a castle by any other name, might be as old as the Crusades, but in this part of it at least there was nothing missing to provide for the comfort of a guest. Soft, oriental carpets were scattered over stone floors polished so smooth that when the light was just right you could see your own reflection; and instead of the dancing shadows of ancient chandeliers with tiered layers of wax-dripping candles, modern, recessed lighting cast a steady, even brightness in the room. The furniture was modern, comfortable, with well-upholstered chairs and a bed stacked waist high with mattresses. Exhausted, frustrated, and confused, Hart had taken a long, hot shower only to discover that someone had taken his clothes. He slipped on a robe that he did not remember seeing on the hook behind the door and, when he went back into the bedroom, found a liveried servant waiting to show him his new wardrobe: slacks, two sport jackets, a dark suit, a half dozen shirts and several ties, socks, clean underwear, and three pairs of shoes.

"If these aren't suitable, if you would prefer to see some other things…?"

"No, I'm sure these will be fine. But how did you know that I'd be here, or that I would need something to wear?"

"Things are always kept on hand for unexpected guests," explained the servant with a cursory nod.

He left the room while Hart got dressed and then, the very moment Hart finished tying his shoes, there was a brief knock on the door and he reappeared. Dinner would be served in half an hour, and, to his regret, Jean

Valette would not be able to join him. He had pressing business, work that would occupy him until very late. They would meet again in the morning and, until then, if there was anything Mr. Hart wanted, all he had to do was make his wishes known.

Hart dined alone at a table with nineteen vacant places, and ate next to nothing. His mind was too entangled in the labyrinth of trickery and deceit in which he found himself to think about food. Back in his room, he kicked off his shoes, propped his head on two enormous pillows, and tried to find answers to the questions that would not stop screaming in his brain, taunting him with his own incompetence. He needed to get home, back to the United States, back to Washington. There was one person left alive who had to know something: Clarence Atwood, the head of the Secret Service. He could see him, sitting awkwardly in the chair in that Watergate apartment that was not his, explaining that the president had been murdered and that the investigation had already begun, but only after he had first tried to question Hart about how much he knew. Atwood had been close to everyone: Constable, Constable's wife, and now, still head of the Secret Service, close to Irwin Russell, the new president he was sworn to protect. Who was he really protecting? What did he really know?

Every question had a dozen different possible answers, and every answer raised a dozen new questions. The only thing that seemed certain in Hart's angry and bewildered state was that he had to do something, anything, whatever the risk might be. He could not wait for someone else to solve the mystery of what had happened; he could not just stay here and do nothing. He had to act.

"Do something, damn it!" he cried in the silence of the room as he sprang from the bed and started pacing back and forth. "Do something, for God's sake—anything!" He stopped dead in his tracks, wheeled around as if he were facing an accuser, beat his fists against his head, and swore out loud in desperation. Then, suddenly, his shoulders slumped and all the fire and defiance left his eyes. He was tired, used up, and not just discouraged, depressed. What he had felt before, false bravado, an embarrassment to his now empty, sober mind. He had no chance of winning, no chance at all; probably no chance of coming out of this alive. He knew that now, but he knew something else as well, that he could not give up—that if he was going to die, he had to die trying. He owed that much to Laura.

He tried to sleep, but the faces of those he had known, ghosts of those who had died, kept marching through his mind. If he did not die, if he lived a hundred years, he would never forget the look in Austin Pearce's eyes, the sad certainty with which Austin had in those last few moments faced his death, the absence of all complaint, the last thing he did, the last thing he tried to do, telling Hart that there was something for him in his pocket. And that, after he had with that warning gesture saved his life. Austin had warned him once before, about what Hillary Constable was after when she asked him to find out what he could, whether what her husband had done with The Four Sisters could be traced, whether there was anything that could threaten her own ambition. There was something else Austin had said, a small thing, it had seemed at the time, but that now, when Hart remembered it, took on a larger significance. The Order of St. John, the order that Jean Valette had spoken to that day—Austin had said that Irwin Russell, the president, was a member. What did that mean? Did all of them—Constable, his wife, Irwin Russell—have some connection with Jean Valette, with The Four Sisters? Hart had never thought about Russell.

Finally, fitfully, Hart drifted off to sleep, but then, a little after three in the morning, he was awakened by the sound of a plane passing low overhead. He went to the window and in the distance saw the parallel lights of a landing strip and the fast descent of a private jet. It was too far away to see who got off or got on, or what might be happening. Hart wondered if it had anything to do with him, or whether this was part of the pressing business that had forced Jean Valette to miss dinner.

Ten minutes after the plane landed, it took off, and the headlights of a single car wove through the darkness toward the chateau. It was the same limousine in which Hart had ridden on the journey from Mont Saint-Michel, but this time Jean Valette was not in it. He was waiting at the steps, tapping his foot, as the driver and another man helped out of the back seat a man wearing a blindfold with his hands tied behind his back. Valette stood there, watching, as his newest guest was helped up the steps, and did not say a word when he passed in front of him and was led inside.

Someone had been brought a prisoner to the chateau. What did that mean for him? For all Jean Valette's protestations of sympathy and good will, what did he really have in mind to do? Hart threw on his clothes, determined to find out. But the door was locked, he could not get out! He pounded on the thick wooden door, shouting for help, demanding that someone come at once. But nothing happened, no one came. He was a prisoner, and there was nothing he could do except wait to see the next move in a game he did not understand and did not want to play. He went back to bed and, staring at the ceiling, wondered how much longer he would be alive.

When he woke up, a little after dawn, he found the door again unlocked. He looked outside, but there was no one there, no one standing guard, no one to stop him going where he would. He dressed quickly and started down the long corridor and down a flight of stairs. He stopped at an open doorway, the entrance to a gallery he estimated to be at least two hundred feet in length, a room with a high, arched ceiling and, at discreet intervals, tall peaked windows to let in the light. Along the entire length of both facing walls were painted portraits, most, though not all of them, life size or even larger. Hart stepped inside to look closer at the first one in the series, a knight in full armor, a white tunic emblazoned with a red cross, holding a shiny plumed helmet in his hand, standing next to a white charger. In the background, at the crest of a shadowed hill, lay the smoking ruins of a tan-colored stone fortress.

"The First Crusade," said a voice just behind him.

Hart turned around to find Jean Valette sitting on a backless wooden bench. Instead of a business suit of the sort he had worn yesterday, he was dressed in a fashion that, if not nearly as old as the chateau, was still years out of date. He looked like something painted by one of the Impressionists, or one of the painters themselves, in flowing green corduroy trousers and a loose-fitting yellow linen jacket, a lavender shirt, brown calf-leather shoes, and blue socks. He was lounging on the bench, half-reclining on his elbow. There was a drowsy, languid expression in his eyes, and, as if to serve as a counterpoint, a mocking smile on his lips. With an idle gesture of his hand, he motioned toward a portrait that, from the long angle of his perspective, looked like a single portrait, a single person, seen in the infinitely receding image of a double set of mirrors.

"Doesn't everyone greet their family at the beginning of a new day?" he asked with a slight tip of his head that signaled the double meaning of a private joke. With surprising agility, he sprang to his feet. "Come, I'll introduce you."

Hart did not move.

"Someone locked me in last night. Am I being kept a prisoner?"

"No, of course not. The door wasn't locked this morning, was it? You're free to go wherever you like, to do whatever you please. Yes, it was locked last night, but there was a reason. Had you come downstairs in the middle of the night, it might have been—what shall I say?—awkward."

"Because I might have tried to do something about what was going on: that man you brought here, blindfolded and tied up. I may not be a prisoner, but he certainly is!"

Jean Valette seemed faintly amused at the suggestion. Placing his hands in the oversize pockets of his jacket, he lowered his eyes. His head moved side to side in the rhythm of someone used to being misunderstood. He looked up and shrugged.

"He would have come if we had invited him, but, as I think you'll agree after you meet him, it's better all around if his coming here is a surprise."

Apparently, it was to be as much a surprise for Hart as for this mysterious, unwilling guest. Valette pointed to the portrait that had first caught Hart's attention, and began a long disquisition on his ancestor and the founder of his house.

"We don't know these things for sure, but it would be reasonable to suppose that he must have been one of the close confederates of William the Conqueror. He was certainly one of the leaders of the Normans when William conquered England, a man who would have been where we were yesterday, Mont Saint-Michel, when it was first constructed and all the Norman nobility would gather there to make their plans and say their prayers before embarking on that first crusade to return to Christendom the birthplace of Christ."

Moving slowly from portrait to portrait, Jean Valette offered a few insightful remarks about each of his once famous ancestors, but none of that was as interesting to Hart as the way he described each life, each heroic achievement, as links in a chain that bound them all together, points on a line drawn by a hand none of them could see.

"Step back," he advised Hart. "Let your eye run down the wall, then turn around and do the same thing the other way. Don't study their faces, don't look at them as individuals; look instead at the changes in the long sweep of time. What do you notice?" he asked as Hart turned and looked. "What is the first thing you see?"

Jean Valette led him down the gallery, moving past each portrait, but not stopping in front of any of them.

"Notice the way the armor changes. It starts with a whole suit of it, every part of the body covered in steel; then, gradually, there is less of it, until, finally, when we reach the seventeenth century and the reign of Louis XIV, there isn't any armor at all. We are no longer warriors, ready to die for our religion; we are courtiers—Look there! See how that one is dressed—velvet, silk, and satin; his fingers full of rings. Look at the difference! In those earlier portraits you could almost feel the sense of adventure, the strength, the courage, the lack of any hesitation. They knew what they believed in— they did not have any doubt about it. They were willing, eager, to die for it. When they listened to the Song of Roland, they were listening to a story about themselves: men for whom the only real sin was not to fight when war was needed. And this courtier, this preening favorite of the court? Do those look like the eyes of someone you would follow into battle? They are too full of cunning, too full of contempt for all the people he looks down on. He never rides a horse; he sits in a carriage. He doesn't fight with a sword; he uses words to wound. Still," added Jean Valette with a wry glance, "though only with words, he at least sometimes fought face to face. When we get to the nineteenth century, he does not fight at all; he only makes money. Look over there," he said, turning toward the wall behind them and a long line of portraits of men dressed in black. "We became bankers, financiers. We didn't believe in anything enough to go to war about it. We only believed in profit."

Jean Valette had begun to get nervous, agitated, as he spoke. He held his hands behind his back as if it were the only way to keep them under control. He became conscious of what he was doing and began to laugh without embarrassment at what he seemed prepared to concede were his own peculiarities. One hand on his hip, he scratched his head with the other.

"I'm being very unfair, of course. Many of them were men of decency and courage, generous and kind: my father, for example."

"I've heard what he did in the war."

Jean Valette seemed surprised. He looked at Hart with gratitude.

"Later, perhaps, I'll tell you something about him."

He was silent for a moment, pondering, as it seemed, what his father had done. Then his eyes brightened and he motioned Hart to follow him back to the other side and the portrait of that other Jean Valette.

"Painted, as you might expect, to show him at the forefront in the Battle of Malta. Look at the way he stands there, the flag with the cross in one hand, the sword held high in the other. He looks like Saint Michael himself, Jean Valette, Grand Master of the Order of St. John!"

"Five hundred years ago," said Hart, turning away from the portrait to Jean Valette, "and the order still exists. You spoke to them yesterday, at Mont Saint-Michel. You do every year, I gather. But the people who were there— they aren't the only members of the Order, are they?"

Jean Valette was at first confused, but then he understood that the confusion was not his.

"Five hundred years ago, yes, but even more than that, back to the early part of the fourteenth century, when the Templars were all executed and their order dissolved. But you think...? Yes, I see: an ancient order, full of mystic secrets—always existing, never gone away; kept alive through passwords and special codes, down through the generations, waiting for the day when it can spring back to life and take its proper, leading part and save the world!" exclaimed Jean Valette, his eyes now bold, cheerful, and defiant. "I wish it were so. I wish the Order of St. John was what it was at the beginning, when it replaced the Templars as the militant arm of the church, when the church still believed there were things worth fighting for. I wish it were almost anything but what it has actually become: a church auxiliary for the idle rich, people who give money so they can call each other knights and think they can buy a place in heaven!"

He cast another long look at the portrait of his same named ancestor, and laughed at the thought that there could be any comparison between the Grand Master and what the Order he had led in battle had become.

"Names stay the same; their meaning changes. It was always a struggle between Christianity and the truth, the need to take care of things here on earth. The Order of St. John, the Knights of Malta, did not take an oath to turn the other cheek, to forswear violence; they swore to conquer for the church or die. But then, later, the church went through another one of its frequent periods of insanity and became Christian again. Instead of fighting for what it believed, it taught, as someone once put it, that it was 'evil to speak evil of evil.' Those people yesterday, part of some secret society? Impossible!"

"Then why do you go there every year, why go speak about the past? Is it just to raise money for that school of you mentioned, the one named after the Order?"

A shrewd smile stole across Jean Valette's face.

"You don't have to ask me that question. You already know the answer."

"You don't need their money; you need their approval, their consent. Some of them send their children there," said Hart, certain he was right.

"As I say, the names of things stay the same, and sometimes—not often, but once in a while—the meaning that has changed can change again. Perhaps one day there will be a new Order of St. John like the old one, and another Grand Master. To most of us, the future remains impenetrable."

They continued their brief journey through the portrait gallery and the chronology of Jean Valette, the time it had taken to pass through all the generations that had ended, finally, with him. When they reached the end of the facing wall, they were back to where they had begun.

"There," he said, "one last, vacant place; room, should anyone ever want it, for a portrait of me." He stared at that blank space on the wall like someone staring into a grave. "There won't be anyone after me. I am the last."

Immediately, a look of contempt shot through his eyes. He disliked pity in any form; he hated it for himself.

"There is another picture, or rather I should say, pictures, that I think you might want to see," his eyes again bright and eager. "You may have noticed—you did notice—that all those portraits are of the male descendants in my line. There are no women, and women in my family have been very important."

"You mean the four sisters who raised your father and ran the bank?"

"You are very well informed, Mr. Hart. Though I must say, I am not surprised. Yes, they raised my father and made us rich, turned a small banking establishment into a center of international commerce. They started with certain advantages. They were all four of them quite brilliant, but two of them were quite beautiful and became the willing mistresses of more than a few wealthy men and their money. Come with me and judge for yourself."

Hart was led down a wide marble floored corridor, past several large rooms, to a pair of double doors at the end. They opened onto a room with windows facing west. Hart looked around, but there were no pictures on the walls. Jean Valette said nothing for a moment, and then raised his eyes to a domed ceiling where, from each of four quadrants, the faces of his father's four aunts looked down with painted elegance and grace. They must have been in middle age, or even older, when the decision was made to make this, as Jean Valette explained, the Hall of the Four Sisters, but the artist had captured them forever in the bloom of youth. Far from exaggerating, it had been something of an understatement to say that two of them had been quite beautiful. One of them seemed to Hart to bear an uncanny resemblance to his own wife, Laura. His host noticed how it had drawn Hart's particular attention.

"I was not sure until I saw your reaction, but I was struck by that, too: the resemblance to your wife. I'm certain, however," he said quietly, "that the resemblance ends there. My great aunt, as I suggested, was not the kind of woman any husband could trust." He checked his watch and frowned. "It's later than I thought. But I wanted you to see this room. We'll meet here again this afternoon, shortly after lunch, you and I and our other guest."

"What does this have to do with me? Who is this person and why have you brought him here? I can't sit around waiting for something to happen. I've lost enough time as it is."

"Patience, Mr. Hart. You'll understand everything soon. I agree with you, by the way, that there isn't any time to lose, but I'm afraid we don't for the moment have much choice. We can't do anything without the inspector."

"Dumont, the chief inspector, is coming here? But why? I told him everything I know. You said yesterday he wanted to arrest me. Is that why he's coming—to take me back to Paris and turn me over to the people who want to kill me?"

Jean Valette had already started walking to the door.

"As I said, we'll meet here again this afternoon. In the meantime, I'm afraid you'll have to excuse me. There are a thousand things I need to do."

CHAPTER 22

WHEN HART WAS summoned back to the Hall of the Four Sisters that afternoon, Jean Valette was sitting at a long table, directly across from Marcel Dumont. Valette had changed out of the flamboyant costume he had been wearing earlier in the day into a dark business suit. Like his clothing, his mood was decidedly more subdued.

"This goes too far," protested the inspector, shaking his head in disagreement. "If I had known you were going to do this...."

Seeing Hart in the doorway, he stopped in mid-sentence, got up, and walked to the window. He stood there, deciding what to do about a situation that was getting out of hand. Tall and overweight, on the downside of middle age, and with all the cautious instincts of the policeman, he had still the confidence of the boxer he had been in his youth. He might get beaten, but he would never be intimidated, not even by the famous and formidable Jean Valette.

"First you make me an accomplice in hiding an international fugitive! Now you want to make me party to a kidnapping! Incredible!" Holding his hands behind his back, he began to pace, and with each step his face became more animated until, finally, a broad smile broke hard and clean across his face. "Yes, well, why not? I've gone this far against my better judgment; might as well see just how big a fool I really am!" Waving his hand in the air, a signal that he had given up, he came back to the table and took his chair. "Let's meet this other American of yours."

Jean Valette picked up a telephone and issued instructions. A few minutes later, two men brought in the person Hart had seen from his window. His hands were now free, but his eyes were still covered. He was put in a chair across from the inspector and then the two men left.

"Can I take this off?" he asked, running his right hand along the blindfold.

"Yes, of course," replied Jean Valette. "And I am sorry that you were subjected to this indignity. It was necessary to take certain precautions, Mr. Carlyle."

"Like grabbing me off the street in Manhattan?" he said with rising anger as he removed the blindfold. He looked at Jean Valette, sitting next to him, and then shot a glance at Marcel Dumont. "Who the hell—?" But then he saw Hart, and his mouth dropped open. "Jesus Christ!" he exclaimed. "What are you—? Where are we, anyway?"

"My name is Marcel Dumont, Mr. Carlyle: chief inspector of the Surete Generale. The gentleman on your left is—"

"My name does not matter," interjected Jean Valette. "But I'm the one responsible for bringing you here. And again, I apologize for the way it was done. My only excuse is that I thought you would probably want to come and it was the only safe way to get you here."

Jean Valette turned to Hart, who still did not know who this Mr. Carlyle was, except that he was an American in his early thirties who kept staring at him as if he had just discovered gold.

"Philip Carlyle, Mr. Hart, is a reporter: a colleague of your friend Quentin Burdick, if I am not mistaken."

Carlyle looked across at Dumont.

"Chief inspector? The Surete? I'm in France, somewhere in Paris?"

"In France, but not in Paris," replied Jean Valette. "You'll go there next, with the inspector, if, after hearing what we have to say, you decide that is what you want to do."

Carlyle was confused. He glanced at Hart, and then again at Dumont.

"The senator is wanted for murder, conspiracy to murder the president, but instead of placing him under arrest, you have me kidnapped and flown across the ocean?"

However much he might disagree with what Jean Valette had done, dealing with the accusations of this American was a different matter. Folding his arms across his chest, Dumont fixed him with a look of studied indifference.

"Would you like to leave now, flown back home? It can certainly be arranged."

The young reporter could not keep his eyes off Hart who was sitting there, just a few feet away, the story that would make his career.

"Really," persisted Dumont, rather enjoying it. "We can have you on a plane in an hour. And perhaps, after all, it's for the best that you go." He glanced at Jean Valette. "I told you this was not a good idea, forcing someone to come here against their will, just to give Mr. Hart, who despite the fact that we have reason to believe he is just a pawn in someone else's game, is still wanted by the American authorities, a chance to tell his side of the story. You had no business doing this. It could put the French government in a very difficult position should Mr. Carlyle here decide to make a formal complaint."

"Me? No, I'm not complaining about anything!"

"But you were kidnapped, 'grabbed off the street in Manhattan,' is the way I think you put it," said Dumont, shaking his head in evident disapproval of the way the young man had been treated. "And tied up and blindfolded, besides. This is a very serious matter, Mr. Carlyle."

Carlyle could not take his eyes off Hart.

"No, really, I'm sure there were good reasons," he insisted.

Jean Valette took his cue.

"If anyone had known where he was going," he explained to the inspector, "if anyone had known whom he was going to see, I doubt very much that Mr. Carlyle would still be alive."

Dumont stroked his chin as he appeared to take this possibility under advisement.

"Yes, perhaps. But tell me, Mr. Carlyle: Other than the fact you were taken against your will, have you been otherwise ill-treated? Have you been fed properly?"

Carlyle's blue eyes lit up at the memory of what he had been given, better than any restaurant, at least of the kind he could afford.

"And the room was terrific," he added, eager to start asking questions of his own. "Everything has been great. And if I had been allowed to see anything except the room I was staying in, and now this one, I'd probably never want to leave." His eyes shot back to Hart. "You didn't do it—you weren't involved? Then how in the hell did all this happen?"

"Did you really think I was?" Hart asked with a stern, caustic glance. "How well did you know Quentin Burdick? Did you know what he was working on when he was killed?"

"Not exactly."

"What do you mean, 'not exactly'?"

"I knew he was supposed to see Constable, but then Constable died—

murdered, as it turns out—and I knew he went out to California to talk to Frank Morris and that Morris was killed. He told me that someone had broken into his apartment the night he got back. He told me he thought everything was connected to something called The Four Sisters."

"And your Mr. Burdick was right," said Jean Valette, exchanging a glance with Hart. "But put that aside for the moment. There was another murder, here, in Paris—"

"Austin Pearce," said Carlyle, with a quick nod. "And the head of the political section of the embassy." He reached inside his jacket for his notebook and then looked from face to face. "You don't mind if I start making notes?"

"So long as you don't use my name," continued Jean Valette.

"I don't know your name."

"I insist on anonymity, and not just my identity, but where we are. No one can know where this conversation took place. Do you understand that?"

"But I don't know where I am, except that it is somewhere in France."

"Do you agree?" asked Jean Valette.

"Yes, I agree."

"Then, my name is Jean Valette, and I am the head of investment house known as The Four Sisters."

"The Four Sisters? Burdick said everything led back to—"

"And it does, as I just told you. But first, the murder of Austin Pearce. Marcel, perhaps you could explain."

Placing both arms on the table, the inspector hunched forward and began to describe what had happened the night before last in the apartment of Aaron Wolfe in the 18th arrondissement.

"And so you see," he said when he was finished, "Mr. Hart arrived only after the two killers were already there. He was downstairs talking to the landlady when the shooting stared. That means, as you can see, that they were sent there, the two Americans from the embassy—both of them with one of your intelligence agencies, unless I miss my guess—to kill Pearce and Wolfe. There could be only one reason for this: to keep them from telling what they knew about who killed your president."

Carlyle scribbled furiously a moment longer and then looked at Hart.

"You didn't have anything to do with this—I don't mean the murder of Austin Pearce—the murder of the president?"

"Because he slept with my wife? It never happened. This whole thing is a set-up, a way for the real murderers—the real conspirators—to get away with what they did. I didn't hire that woman, the one who supposedly died trying to get away. And all that evidence they found—bank transactions, money I paid into her account—do you really think a paid assassin would keep records like that, and keep them in a place where they could so easily be found?"

As Hart watched Carlyle, measuring his reaction, he was reminded of Quentin Burdick. There was the same focused attention on the matter immediately at hand, the same concentration on getting the basic structure of the story right. Carlyle did not yet have Burdick's years of experience, but he had that deep curiosity about things that experience, by itself, could not teach.

"I told Quentin almost everything I knew. I'm the one who confirmed that the president had not died of a heart attack, that he had been murdered instead."

The next question was out of Carlyle's mouth before he even thought about it.

"And who told you, how did you know Constable had been murdered?"

"Constable's widow, Hillary, the day her husband was buried."

Carlyle did a double-take.

"She knew it then, that soon?"

"She wanted me to find out what I could about who might have done it, what reason they might have had. She thought—or at least she said—that if we didn't know something before the story became public the rumors would never end. She may have had another reason."

"Another reason?"

Hart hesitated, wondering how far he should go. Then he started to laugh, which produced a puzzled reaction, which made him explain.

"Half the country—more than that, for all I know—probably thinks I should be lynched, and I'm worried whether something I say might get someone else in trouble!" A grim, determined expression twisted slowly across his mouth. "I'm going to tell you everything I know, Philip Carlyle, but Quentin knew something and I still don't know what it is. The night he died, we talked on the phone. It was late, but he wanted me to meet him at his place right away. He said he had discovered something—he had just gotten back from Washington, so it must have been there—and that it 'changed everything.' I don't know what he meant."

For the next hour, Hart described in detail everything that had happened, from that first conversation with Hillary Constable in her study at home, to the meeting in the embassy with Aaron Wolfe.

"It was probably a mistake, that I agreed to find out what I could, but then, when she told me that I should forget everything, that it was better if everyone was left to believe that her husband had died of a heart attack, I knew something dangerous was going on. I just was not smart enough to know what it was. But Austin was. He thought I had been sent to find out what could be discovered about the president's death so that it could not be discovered again."

Jean Valette had sat in silence listening intently to everything Hart said, but now he had a question.

"But why were you chosen, Mr. Hart? The head of the Secret Service, this Clarence Atwood, should have been able to conduct that kind of investigation. Instead of starting at the beginning, start at the end: start with what you know now. You're being blamed for the murder. Isn't it just possible that this was always the intention?"

"But why?" asked Carlyle, riveted by the possibility that Hart was the subject of an elaborate conspiracy, a plan that had been in place from the beginning. "What would be the point of doing this to you?"

Before Hart could answer, Jean Valette offered a suggestion.

"What other reason than to get rid of a competitor, someone who might take away the thing you most wanted in your life? The presidency, Mr. Carlyle. The White House. Isn't that what it was about from the beginning?"

Jean Valette leaned back and with a pensive expression tapped his thin, tapered fingers together. His eyes grew hard and distant. A shrewd, death-like smile made a fugitive appearance at the corners of his mouth. He had no illusions about the dark side of human nature.

"The president is dead, and someone else takes his place. Fate, chance, the inscrutable workings of providence, God's will? Is that what we believe, that someone murdered, someone planned the death, of Robert Constable, and it had nothing to do with—as you Americans would put it—the biggest prize of all?" Gesturing toward Hart, he challenged the reporter. "Don't you think it more than strange—is it not a new record in mass stupidity—that an enormously popular United States senator—a man, from what I'm told, a great many people hoped would run for the presidency himself—is accused of murder because the man he murdered supposedly slept with his wife? These things happen. I don't need to be told that. A crime of passion has a certain appeal. But hire a professional assassin? Where is the passion—where is the honor—in that? You feel so strongly about a wife's infidelity that you want the man she slept with dead, but you don't want to do anything about it yourself? Where is the passion in that, Mr. Carlyle? There isn't any. This was no crime of passion; this was passion of a different kind: the passion for power, the desire to take control, to seize an office, in perhaps the only way you could ever have it."

Jean Valette tapped his fingers together once more, and then dropped his hands onto the table and sat straight up.

"Tell me, Mr. Carlyle, you cover American politics—that is the reason we invited you—what were the chances, if Robert Constable was still alive, that Irwin Russell would ever become president?"

Carlyle's eyes almost popped out of his head. He looked immediately at Hart, but Hart was still staring at Jean Valette, wondering what he was going to say next. Inspector Dumont, for his part, sat with folded arms, gently rocking back and forth, listening with the slightly bored expression of a man who had heard and seen too much to ever be very much surprised at anything.

"Everything leads to The Four Sisters," said Carlyle. His eyes were cold, immediate. "You confirmed what Quentin Burdick said. How does this tie into that? What is the connection between The Four Sisters and the possibility that the president had something to do with Constable's murder?"

His elbow on the arm of his chair, Jean Valette stretched two fingers along the side of his face and placed his thumb against his chin. He sat there, in that attitude of repose, moving his head side to side, keeping rhythm with his thoughts; debating, as it seemed, how best to answer.

"When you leave here today, Mr. Carlyle," he said finally, "you will take with you a collection of documents assembled from some of the companies in which The Four Sisters has an interest. Copies of checks, bank transfers, financial transactions—some of them quite complex—that in some cases go back more than ten years."

"What do they explain about the murder?" demanded Carlyle, who wanted a more immediate answer than a series of old bank statements. "Our president was murdered and you're telling me that another president killed him?"

To Hart's astonishment, Jean Valette denied it.

"That's not what I said, Mr. Carlyle. I did not accuse Russell, or anyone else, of anything."

He said this with a calm, almost playful gaze. He was enjoying it, this game of words; enjoying it as if the question who murdered the president, a political assassination, was nothing more than an intellectual exercise, a method by which to sharpen one's wits.

"I only raised the question whether Irwin Russell could have become president in any other way. The same question could be asked about the president's widow, couldn't it? Would she have had any chance to become president if her husband had lived?"

"Good God!" cried Carlyle. "Now you're suggesting…. You really think she could have done it: arranged to have her husband murdered?"

He seemed more interested in this possibility than in the other, perhaps because it seemed to fit better the known facts of the former first lady's ambition, not to mention the known facts of her husband's rampant infidelity.

"The answer to your question," said Hart, turning to Jean Valette, "is that you made a mistake in your assumption."

Jean Valette cocked his head. A thin, knowing smile threaded its way across his mouth.

"A mistake?"

"Irwin Russell probably could not have become president if Constable had lived, but Hillary Constable could have. She would have run as her husband's successor; the nomination would have been hers. It's doubtful anyone could have beaten her; it's doubtful anyone would have tried. That was one of the reasons he was picked to run with Constable in the last election: so there would not be a vice president who would try to run against her."

The smile on the face of Jean Valette deepened and became more profound.

"Are you sure that was the reason they wanted Irwin Russell on the ticket, Mr. Hart? Are you sure it was really their decision?"

"Russell helped him carry Ohio," insisted Carlyle. "With Constable, everything was a political calculation."

But Hart and Jean Valette were still looking at each other, measuring, or trying to measure, what the other one knew, or thought he knew.

"It doesn't really matter why he was chosen," observed Hart. "It doesn't affect the fact that Russell could not have won the presidency on his own and that Hillary Constable could have, and still might. What motive could she have had to want her husband dead? You seem to think she had one. Why don't you just tell us what you think it was?"

Jean Valette looked across at Carlyle as if he were seeing for the first time how young he was, and how eager to get this story right, the story that any reporter would have killed to get. That was what struck Hart as he watched: how conscious Jean Valette was of the effect the story was going to have on everyone, not only those directly involved in the events, but those who were going to tell the story, and who would, immediately upon the telling, become the new subject of other people's stories, the center of attention for everyone who wanted to know more about the secret interview with Bobby Hart and the anonymous and enigmatic source that somewhere in France had first revealed the involvement of The Four Sisters and provided the documentary evidence necessary to prove it. Hart could not quite rid himself of the feeling that everything that was happening, everything that had been said in that room, was exactly what Jean Valette had expected. It was a feeling that immediately became more pronounced.

"Mr. Hart already knows what it is," said Jean Valette with perfect confidence. "And so, Mr. Carlyle, do you. You said it at the beginning, what your friend Quentin Burdick first told you: everything leads to The Four Sisters. That's the secret they shared, the secret none of them could afford to have anyone learn: that millions, tens of millions of dollars, had passed into their hands, money provided through one means and another by companies in which my firm had an interest."

Inspector Dumont got to his feet.

"Perhaps this would be a good time for me to leave. I don't think I should—"

"No, it's all right, Marcel. We weren't involved in any criminal wrongdoing; certainly nothing that broke the laws of France. There is a difference, after all, between bribery and extortion. I didn't—The Four Sisters didn't—offer to give Constable or any of his friends and associates money in exchange for any help we needed. He came to us, explained that he wanted better trade relations, and that the only way to do that was to help elect people who wanted the same thing. He was really quite ingenious, when it came to working out a scheme for his own advantage, ingenious and quite corrupt. Everything with him was a maneuver, a way to get around whatever obstacles stood in his path. Foreigners could not contribute to American political campaigns? Give money for other things—a foundation, a library—or move money into an American company, a subsidiary, and get the money into the right hands that way."

"Some of that money came from foreign interests that weren't supposed to be doing any business in the United States," added Hart with a sharp, accusatory glance. "And in exchange, because of what you did, some of those same interests were able to get control of companies that have a direct effect on what Americans think."

"It's a global economy, Mr. Hart. The point is that Robert Constable had taken millions—forced us to give him that money—and so had several others."

"Frank Morris, who changed his mind and got sent to prison because of it, and then, after he talked to Quentin Burdick and told him what he knew, got killed," said Hart, growing more agitated by the minute.

"Yes, I've heard this," said Jean Valette, who seemed almost amused. "That would have been something Constable would have arranged."

"Constable was already dead!" Hart reminded him forcefully.

"Exactly."

"Exactly?"

"It makes sense, doesn't it? Who other than Constable could have set the wheels in motion? Who else could have had the congressman charged with a crime, turned out of office, and sent to prison? Do you think he wouldn't have given orders that if it became necessary, if Morris started talking about what he knew, he should be eliminated? But if Morris was killed to protect the secret, why wouldn't Constable have been killed for the same reason? This gets us back to the same two people, doesn't it?"

Carlyle slammed the ballpoint pen on the notebook and let out an expletive.

"Russell was one of those taking money?" His eyes brightened with a new intensity. "Morris, chairman of the House Ways and Means Committee; Russell, chairman of the Senate Finance Committee. Constable had to be able to use them both." He looked sharply at Jean Valette. "You—The Four Sisters—would have needed the help of both, if—"

"If we had played an active part in this. But we only did what Constable said we should, what, as he explained, was the only reasonable way to obtain the changes that would be good for everyone."

"Changes that made you a great deal of money!"

Jean Valette almost laughed.

"It depends, doesn't it, on what you consider a great deal of money?"

Hart bent forward, following intently everything that was said, and, in the case of Jean Valette, the meaning of every look and every gesture. A picture was beginning to form, but there were still a few blank spaces that needed to be filled in.

"Russell was taking money, too. He shared the secret; he knew what Constable was doing. But he didn't change his mind, like Frank Morris. He was not concerned with what any of this might do to the country. He became vice president, instead. Is that what you were trying to say, that it was not what Constable wanted; it's what Russell decided was the price of his silence?"

With slow precision, Jean Valette lifted an eyebrow, his face fixed again in the attitude of someone playing at a game, or rather, watching one, measuring with an expert's practiced judgment the feeble attempt of amateurs.

"Perhaps that is to give your new president too much credit. It may be that it was Constable's idea instead, a way to ensure himself that Russell would not be tempted by a suddenly resurrected conscience into such an inconvenient confession."

"And Hillary Constable—what motive...? Oh, I see," said Carlyle, nodding his head. He picked up his pen and scrawled a few short, abbreviated sentences. "Quentin Burdick. He was onto the story. He had an appointment with.... She would not be able to run for anything, much less the presidency, if all of this came out." With a puzzled glance, he turned quickly to Hart. "She asked you to look into it, see what you could find out about—?"

"The murder, and The Four Sisters," said Inspector Dumont, who had been sitting, almost forgotten, for the last half hour. "That way she finds out what someone might find out about the secret they share, and because, by putting you, Mr. Hart, in direct connection with everything that has happened, the accusation against you acquires the credibility of proximity. Why else would you be so close to all of this, if it weren't because you were trying to cover your own tracks? And then, whatever you may have uncovered about the murder and The Four Sisters, no one will believe it. Especially," he added with a humorous glint in his eye, "if you were to wind up dead."

Hart did not entirely agree.

"I don't believe she's behind this. I wouldn't have believed it about Irwin Russell, either; but I didn't know he was a crook, as big a crook as Constable. So they both had a motive, but he's the one who ends up being president, at least for a while. She can still beat him, and the election is only a year away." Suddenly, he remembered. He looked at Carlyle. "Neither one of them will be running for anything, will they?"

Carlyle folded his notebook.

"If those documents prove that Constable and Russell were taking money, tens of millions, then I imagine the only thing either one of them will be thinking about is how to stay out of prison. It does explain what just happened, though. Everyone thought what you thought, Senator: that Hillary Constable would run against Russell for the nomination."

"It seems like I've been gone for years, even though it's only been a couple of days. What happened? Did she announce that she was not going to run after all?"

"No. Russell announced that she had agreed to become vice president. He's sending her nomination to the Hill this week. They're going to run for reelection as a team."

CHAPTER 23

THAT EVENING AT dinner, alone, just the two of them, at the table with eighteen vacant places, Hart expressed his gratitude for what Jean Valette had done.

"I was certain you were behind everything: that you had Constable killed to protect the secret of what The Four Sisters had done. I thought you had hired the assassin, and instead you've done everything you can to help prove my innocence."

Jean Valette had changed again from a business suit to a radically different kind of costume. With Hart on his left, he sat at the head of the dining room table wearing a long flowing white silk robe over a loose-fitting white silk shirt. Had he worn a beard and had darker skin, had he seemed less ascetic, he might have passed for a wealthy Arab dining in the luxury of his palace.

"It's perhaps not quite as simple as that," he replied. A slight, thoughtful smile crossed his mouth. "It would not be true to say that I bear no responsibility for what happened, that I was not, in some way, involved in what Robert Constable did to others, and what others did to him."

Shoving his plate aside, Hart pushed back from the table. With folded arms, he studied Jean Valette, wondering what he meant.

"I don't mean that I knew that Constable would do what he did—have Congressman Morris locked up somewhere with orders to have him killed if he talked—or that I knew that someone would have him killed," said Jean Valette who seemed to consider quite carefully what he wanted to say. "That isn't the same thing as saying that I didn't know it would happen, or, rather, that something like that might happen. Only a fool could have failed to foresee it. Once you let people like those become involved in something illicit, something they could not resist—and, if you will forgive me, how many Americans could resist tens of millions of dollars with the promise of tens of millions more, money that could never be traced back to its real source, money that did not require you to do anything except what you wanted to do anyway—As I say, only a fool could fail to see that evil only follows evil. Once someone commits a crime, he will do anything, even murder, to keep the truth from coming out."

Hart had seen enough of Jean Valette to know something of his intellect and the subtlety of his judgment. Only a fool—he had used that word several times—would have failed to foresee what might happen next, and whatever else he might be, Jean Valette was certainly not that.

"So you knew—at the time you were first approached by Constable, when he told you in so many words that if your companies were going to do business in the United States, you were going to have to pay millions for the privilege—you knew how this all might end? Then why didn't you—?"

"Stop him from destroying himself?" laughed Jean Valette. "It would seem to me that he got precisely what he deserved. There is a parallel to this—more than one, I should imagine—but the one I'm thinking of I used in that speech of mine you heard the other day at Mont Saint-Michel."

Hart thought a moment and then remembered.

"You don't mean about what happened after the King of France, Philip the Fair, destroyed the Templars to get their money?"

"Very good, Mr. Hart! Your memory is quite excellent. Yes, exactly. Consider the questions it raises. Did God punish Pope Clement and King Philip the way Jacque de Molay, the Grand Master, swore He would? Or did the Grand Master simply foresee what the two of them, the pope and the king, had unleashed upon themselves, with their ruthless disregard for their own honor and all that they had sworn to protect: the Throne and the Church?" Jean Valette's gaze deepened, became more profound. "Or did he, in those last few moments of an agonizing death, see the future with a clairvoyance that we, the living, cannot understand, see with utter certainty that someone listening, or someone who only later heard, what they would take as a promise from God, and, determined to be God's own messenger, would arrange to hasten the deaths of two men who had been cursed? Or that it might be done by someone who did not care what God intended, but for whom the deaths of one or the other would advance their own worldly ambition? And, finally, what did he have to lose, the Grand Master, if nothing happened as he said it would, when there was always the chance that just enough would happen that someone would remember, and remembering, interpret things as if they had?"

"Those are interesting questions," agreed Hart. "But how do they apply here?"

"Because however you choose to answer the questions, they all point to a lesson no one seems to understand: the one who seems the victim is often the one in charge. The Grand Master seemed to have lost everything: his Order, the Order's money, and, finally, his life. But the future—that, as it turned out, he still controlled."

"You mean, could still foresee."

"Control the future, foresee the future: it all comes to the same thing, if you think it through."

Jean Valette hesitated as if he was not sure whether he should stop there or try to explain. It was easier to let the matter rest, easier to let his visitor try to figure out what he meant. That is what he would have done with nearly anyone else. There was too much danger that he would be misunderstood: most men only learned what they thought they already knew.

"Rousseau, the French philosopher, the one who is famous for talking about the rights of man, foresaw the future. Thirty years before it happened in France, he wrote that the world was entering the age of revolution. The problem was that Rousseau was a genius while the people who read him were not. They distorted his teachings and through those distortions helped bring about the revolution he said would happen. The same thing happened later, at the end of the nineteenth century, with that other genius, Nietzsche. He foresaw a future of terrible wars and the need to rescue humanity from the leveling effects of mediocrity. He spoke of the need for a higher order of humanity; the Nazis read into that their own delusions of themselves as a master race and everyone else a slave.

"Rousseau, Nietzsche: both saw what was coming and became the text on which stupid, evil people could write their own interpretation. They bear some responsibility for what happened; they were too intelligent not to have seen the danger in how they would be misunderstood. And yet, on a deeper level, they offer to anyone willing to spend the time, willing to learn how to read carefully, that is to say slowly and with an open mind, the only real understanding of the world in which, for better or worse, we live. Rousseau wrote about the coming age of democratic revolution; Nietzsche about the reaction to that, that other kind of mass movement in which one man, the leader, imposes his will on everyone else. Now someone needs to write about what is going to happen in the next hundred years and what can be done about it. I tried."

Hart, who had followed as closely as he could, was not slow to see the implications.

"Yes, you're right, Mr. Hart," said Jean Valette before Hart had opened his mouth. "If I tried—if I'm still trying—to write about the future, and if to foresee it is in some sense to control it, then...? Come with me. If we're going to have a serious conversation, there is a better place to have it."

They started down a long hallway that ran parallel to the one Hart had taken earlier to the Hall of the Four Sisters and his meeting with the American reporter. This one, like the other, was paved in polished white tile, the walls hung with rich tapestries and countless paintings by old masters. The chateau was ancient, but far from a crumbling wreck. A makeshift project of never finished restoration, it was to all outward appearances perfect in every detail, as good, or better than, that day it was finished, nearly a thousand years ago. More than once in the short time he had been here, Hart had found himself pretending, and pretending, for a few moments, believing, that he had gone back in time, perhaps not so far back as the beginning, but hundreds of years, when the old masters were the new masters and the French Revolution was still far off in the distant future. He had wondered, he wondered now, what it must have been like to have been born here, raised here, and lived here all his life, remote from other people and everything they believed. It might not be the whole explanation, but it was surely a part of what had made Jean Valette what he had become: an exile from the very world that through the power of the very thing he seemed to hold in contempt, money and an endless supply of it, he had come to influence, if not dominate. Passing a vaulted window, Hart glanced into the moonlit darkness and in the stillness of the night felt a little of the aching loneliness of someone who had himself become a stranger far from where he wanted to be.

"I need to leave tomorrow," he said as they walked together toward an open set of doors.

"That's not possible," replied Jean Valette. He said this decisively, as if the matter were entirely up to him. Hart was stunned. He stopped and looked straight at him.

"Are you telling me that I'm a prisoner here?"

"Not to me, to necessity. Where would you go? What chance would you have?" he asked with an impatience which, when he realized how it must sound, changed into a look of sympathy.

"I can't stay here forever," protested Hart. "I have to do something to clear my name."

"We've taken a major step in that direction," Jean Valette assured him. "You just need to give it a few days. Carlyle will be back in New York tomorrow. He'll write his story. With the proof I supplied, Russell will have to leave office and Hillary Constable's political career will be over. But as to your other point," he continued with a smile that seemed to carry a challenge, a dare he was fairly certain his guest would never take, "you could stay here forever, or as long as you like. I would enjoy the company: someone interested in serious things, someone with whom I could actually carry on a conversation without having to hide the meaning of everything I say. And of course you would not be alone. It would not be difficult to make arrangements to have your beautiful wife come to join you." With an expansive gesture, he invited Hart to consider the possibility of life in the chateau. "I've lived here all my life and I'm not sure I've seen every part of it. The two of you can use however much of it you wish."

Beneath the haughty exterior, the studied condescension of his manner, the attempt to make an extraordinary offer seem a matter of no importance, Hart thought he could detect a strange hope that he would take him up on it. It was a hope Jean Valette would never express. He had too much pride to admit he had any need he could not satisfy without the help of others.

"Carlyle's story will help clear me, but if I don't go back and find out who was behind the assassination—whether it was Russell or Constable's wife—a lot of people will still think that what they're saying is true: that I murdered him because he was sleeping with my wife."

"What does it matter what others think?" asked Jean Valette with a sharp turn of his head. "You know the truth. You're not responsible for the ignorance of people who believe you capable of murder." As he lifted his chin, his eyes became cold, distant, and defiant. "I learned contempt at an early age. It was a gift, if you will, from my father, when he played the part of a collaborator for the French resistance. I was with him, a young boy, one day in the street when there were no Germans around, no one the crowd had to be afraid of. These people, none of whom, you understand, had the courage to be in the resistance themselves, surrounded my father, pushed him, kicked him, spat in his face, called him a traitor, a coward, a rich bastard who had sold out his country for money. And the whole time they were doing that, trying to humiliate him, he was looking at me, his only son, only four years old, trying to tell me with his eyes that none of it was true, that he was not what that mob said he was. But I was a boy, a child, and all I heard were the words, and the look of hatred in their eyes. Later, my father told me that it was not true, that he was not any of the things they had called him. But of course he could not tell me the real truth, that he was in the resistance, and so I thought— and you can see how awful this is to admit—that my father had lied to me, that he was the collaborator all those mindless people thought and said he was. So, no, Mr. Hart, I'm not much persuaded by what the crowd might think, and, frankly, after what you have now learned about how easily the crowd can turn, neither should you."

He paused, and with a confidence so complete as to leave no room for disagreement, made a remark that caused Hart to wonder whether Jean

Valette's claim to see the broad outlines of the future was less the result of study and intelligence than the madness of a completely disordered mind.

"That will be especially important for you to understand when the same people who are now condemning you give you their support, when Russell is gone and Hillary Constable can't become president, when both of them are facing criminal charges and the country turns to you. You're going to be the next president, Mr. Hart. There really isn't any doubt about it." He seemed to laugh in silence at some private joke. "I don't imagine you would believe me if I told you that I saw that this would happen the day I discovered that Robert Constable believed in nothing but his own importance. But enough of this," he said, turning on his heel. "We have more serious matters to discuss."

The long silk robes worn by Jean Valette swept across the floor as he led Hart through the entrance into an enormous square room with a ceiling at least three stories tall and bookshelves covering all four walls. A double landing, connected to each other by staircases in two different places, gave access to the higher regions of a library that could easily have held twenty, or even thirty, thousand volumes. The shelves, however, were almost all of them empty; the only books, three or four dozen volumes, some of them tattered and torn, threadbare with frequent use, sat an ungainly medley on a few shelves directly behind a desk that not only caught Hart's eye, but held it there. Like so much else in the chateau, it was obviously hundreds of years old, an ancient, hand-carved piece of furniture, constructed by the finest craftsmen at no doubt prohibitive expense, but still looked new.

"A gift," explained Jean Valette. "From Louis XIV. He said it was in return for the hospitality of his trusted friend, Monsieur de la Valette, and it may have been, if you include in that description the willing eagerness of the young and ravishing Madame de la Valette to exchange the bed of her husband for that of their sovereign." Jean Valette scratched the side of his face, an idle gesture of wistful curiosity. "In those days, no one could be too sure of their fathers, and as someone—I think it was Tocqueville— pointed out, they enjoyed themselves in ways we can no longer imagine or appreciate. It isn't the kind of desk I would have chosen, but by some miracle the library and everything in it escaped the flames when the chateau was put to the torch in the early days of the Revolution, and so, like my father before me, I use it now whenever I am here, when I get away from work, and sit up all night reading, studying, what I should."

Hart could not stop looking at all the vacant shelves, hundreds of them, towering high above and circling all around, not a bit of dust on them, polished to a deep luster as if they had just been built and were waiting for the next morning when, one by one, each of them first catalogued, each priceless volume would be added until all the shelves were filled.

"Nothing in the library was burned, not the books?" he asked, puzzled by their absence.

Jean Valette dropped into a yellow upholstered chair and motioned for Hart to take the one on the other side of the desk. Throwing one leg over the other, he sat sideways on his hip and gestured toward the empty shelves.

"I read them all. I kept only the ones worth reading."

Hart was not sure he understood. His eyes wandered again to the vacant shelves that climbed three stories to the ceiling. It would have been impossible to read all the books they must have once contained.

"I read them all," repeated Jean Valette, amused at Hart's incredulity. "I didn't finish very many of them, and with some of them I read only the first few pages, enough to assure me that I was wasting my time, that the author was only repeating, and usually not very well, what someone else had said before. Most things written, whether the author knows it or not, are purely derivative."

"And these are all you kept?" asked Hart, nodding toward the few dozen on the shelves behind where Jean Valette was half-reclining in his chair.

"Yes, but as you can imagine, it took years to get to this point, years spent night after night in this library of diminishing volumes, before I finally got rid of everything that is not necessary."

Hart observed the glowing confidence in his eyes, the proud sense of accomplishment. He had seen something of that look before, mainly on the faces of winning candidates on the night of their election. He had seen it on full display the first time Robert Constable won the presidency. But that paled in comparison to what he now was witnessing. The look on the face of Jean Valette had nothing to do with ego, with triumph over someone else. It was the pride of his own achievement, one that owed nothing to what anyone else might think about it.

"The other books, the ones you didn't want to keep: some of them, I imagine, quite old; many of them, perhaps, first editions—you didn't...?"

"Burn them? I should have, burned them for all the error they contain; but no, I gave them to universities mainly, and other repositories of useless learning. Did you ever read Rousseau?" he asked suddenly. "You should. You'll learn more about the foundation of the modern world, the one in which we live, than all the other things written since. And then, after that, if you read Nietzsche, you will have the beginnings of an understanding of the crisis which for the most part we don't even know we're in."

Jean Valette's eye was drawn, almost reluctantly, as it seemed, to the only photograph, indeed the only object other than a reader's lamp, on the desk. It was a picture, a very old picture, of a young woman.

"My wife," he explained with a sad, distant look as he struggled with his emotions. Embarrassed, he sat up straight, took a deep breath, and emitted a gentle, almost shy, laugh.

"More than forty years now, and every time I look at her, the same thing. Worse, really, as I get older; worse with each year I know I've missed. I had a feeling—I hope you don't mind my saying this—that we had this in common, that you would know what this feeling is like. When I started following your career, I was struck by how beautiful your wife was. I was certain that you must have fallen in love with her the first time you saw her."

The look in Jean Valette's eyes, the deep sympathy in his voice: Hart felt a bond, an attachment that he had seldom felt with anyone. He remembered, as if it were yesterday, the moment he first saw Laura, and the utter certainty, the strange, miraculous certainty, that if he never saw her again he would never forget her face, that if they never exchanged a word, she would always be a part of him.

"Yes, that's exactly what happened," he confessed. "The very moment."

"There are things we know instantly, or never know at all. I was young, and very rich, and from one of the oldest families in France. If I was not the most handsome of men, there were those who thought that, even leaving the money aside, I was not without charm. I was, in other words, quite full of myself. And then I saw her, and I forgot about my own existence. I did not exist without her. I saw her. That was all it took: one look, a smile, a slight, shy hesitation in her eyes, and then the certainty, that feeling you can never know again. I was in love, and so was she. It was perfect; more than perfect: enchanting. We were married, and we had two years, two years that passed like two days, and then we were to have a child, and just like that, she was gone, died in childbirth along with the child."

Jean Valette tightened his left hand into a fist as a shudder passed through him, and then stared straight ahead until he had himself under control. His gaze softened, became, as it were, more forgiving of what he thought a failure in himself.

"My life was over and I was only twenty-four. For two years, I did nothing, nothing at all, except stare at her picture and wonder how long I would have to wait to die. It took a long time, but I kept hearing her voice—there are times I still hear it now—telling me she wanted me to live, to do something of importance with whatever life I had left. I knew that whatever I did, it would never again by interrupted by happiness. That's when I went back and resumed my study of serious things. That's when I decided I would try to write something—not right away, but when I was ready, which I knew would not be for many years—that might be worth reading."

More than what Jean Valette said, the manner in which he said it, the smooth cadence, the deep resonance of his voice, gave Hart the feeling that what he was going to hear this evening he would never hear from anyone again. Among the other strange eccentricities of Jean Valette, there was nothing conventional in the way he saw the world. That was what more than anything else held Hart's attention, what he could not get over: the way that Jean Valette seemed to see everything from a distance, a stranger in his own time.

"And I finally did, just a few years ago, after endless years of study, after years of dealing with all these supposedly important people in the world of politics and finance. I wrote the book I wanted to write, the one in which something of what will happen—must happen—in the future is foretold."

He reached inside one of the three drawers just below the top of the desk, that gift for infidelity in all the joy of life, and pulled out a thick, four-hundred-page manuscript.

"Of course no one would publish it." A wry grin cut a jagged line across his mouth. "One publisher told me that probably only ten people in the world would understand it. If he included himself, the number should be nine. It was my fault, really. I had not yet learned how to lie, to tell the truth in a way that everyone who would be offended by it would not be able to discover it." He tapped two fingers on the manuscript. "And now, after I don't know how many revisions, it is finally finished."

"Will you take it back to that same publisher?"

"Last I heard, he was in an asylum. Driven mad, they say, by his fear about the future. That's my fault as well, I suppose," he said with what, if it was not satisfaction, was at the very least cruel indifference.

"Your fault? I don't understand."

"He turned down the manuscript, rejected what I had written."

"Yes, but that still doesn't explain why he went mad. Publishers reject things all the time."

"He did not know that The Four Sisters owned the company that owned his company. I did not think it fair to tell him that when I asked if he would like to publish what I had written. I did not want to do anything that would affect his unbiased judgment. He made his decision," he said with a shrug, "and I made mine. I could have had him fired, but instead I just made sure he knew that from that point forward his future was in my hands. The strain of worrying whether each day might be his last seems to have been more than he could handle." A thin smile floated over his mouth. "You look shocked. Do you think he would have felt in any way responsible if I had suffered a breakdown because of his rejection of what I had done? I know the man. He would not have given it a second thought. Why should I? Remember, I did not do anything except acquaint him with the reality of his situation. In a way, it's no different than what happened with Robert Constable, or for that matter, what is about to happen to his wife and to Irwin Russell. They were all the prisoners of their own ambitions, and their own fears."

His eyes darted first one way then the other, moving in short, explosive bursts. He seemed nervous, full of energy, anxious to get to what he wanted to say, and yet still not quite certain how to begin. He had turned his head to the side, casting a long glance at the empty shelves, seeing in his mind the exact titled sequence of each volume they had once contained. Suddenly he jerked backward and studied Hart with what seemed a new interest.

"How old are you?—Never mind! In your forties; you still have the excuse of your youth." He pushed the manuscript across to Hart. "I don't know if you will understand it; I don't care if you believe it. But take it, read it, study it, think about it, let it settle in your mind, then work your way through it again."

Jean Valette sat as if frozen to the spot, and then, an instant later, laughed out loud. He jumped out of the chair and threw up his hands.

"No one understands, no one has any idea what I'm talking about! No one has seen the things I've seen, things that have not happened yet, but that I know as well as anything I know about the past!"

He began to talk faster and faster, trying to explain, and then, without so much as a moment's pause, lapsing into a long flight of French, and he was not talking to Hart anymore, he was talking to himself, taunting himself with knowing things he could not explain, not if he had a hundred years to try. The world was mad, or he was—there was no middle ground. His eyes grew wide—whether with wonder at what he saw, or rage at what he could not make anyone see—and then, as his eyes rolled higher in his head, his jaw tightened and began to tremble, and he pounded both fists so hard on the desk that the lamp would have fallen over if Hart had not caught it and put it back.

"Read it!" he implored. "Whenever you can, whenever you want," he went on, quickly coming back to himself. "You might be—no, I'm certain of it: You'll understand enough of it, the broad outline, to grasp the main intention."

Wrapping his arms around himself, he began to pace back and forth. There was a slightly puzzled expression on his face and a kind of laughing awareness of it in his eyes. From a sideways angle, he glimpsed Hart, who wore a puzzled expression of a different kind.

"I need to be careful. It's a curious change of phrase, don't you think, to say on the one hand that someone is out of his mind, and to say on the other that someone has lost his mind. Lost it, out of it—the real danger is to live too much inside it." He stopped pacing and as if he had just remembered something of great importance, faced Hart directly. "I need to be careful that I don't end up like him."

Hart had no idea whom he was talking about.

"There is a marvelous description that when I first read it thought might one day, if I worked hard enough, be written about me. I do not, you understand, put myself in the same category, but precisely for that reason the danger is perhaps even greater.

"'Nietzsche sought, by a new beginning, to retrieve antiquity from the emptiness of modernity and, with this experiment, vanished in the darkness of insanity.'

"He saw what would happen in the twentieth century and it drove him mad. I see what is going to happen in the twenty-first century, and perhaps with the same result. Read what I have written. You may think I've already gone mad. But I don't think so. Not yet, anyway."

Jean Valette sat down, took a deep breath, and, as it seemed, caught his balance.

"'God is dead.' You've heard that phrase. Do you know what it means? It isn't simply a denial of the existence of the Christian God: it is the greatest event in the life of man, the ultimate crisis in human history. The death of God means the death of belief in anything worth looking up to. It means the 'last man,' the man who has ceased to aspire, the man who no longer knows anything heroic, any dedication, any reverence. The last man: everyone wills the same thing, everyone is the same, everyone is equal, the perfect conformity of perfect mediocrity in which everyone is satisfied; worse because no one knows, no one remembers that there is anything else, that there is a difference between better and worse. It is the world in which we live now, the only acceptable, the only legitimate objective, comfortable self-preservation in which all anxieties are removed, or at least treated, by pharmaceuticals and therapy."

"You paint a fairly bleak picture. Most people aren't quite that pessimistic," replied Hart. Even as he said it, he felt a tinge of embarrassment, a sense that he was repeating something that he did not quite believe.

"The people in the picture never see themselves, do they? Only someone outside it knows what they are really like, and how much better they could be. That's what I'm trying to tell you—what I tried to write: the West is in a crisis and it doesn't know it. The West has forgotten what it stands for, has forgotten what it believes, or used to believe, because of course now it does not believe in anything, except its own superiority to everything that preceded it, every age that believed in something worth dying for. The situation is very simple: The West does not believe in anything and Islam, like Christianity and even modern science, believes in something that is not true: that the world came into being and must therefore have an end. Isn't that what both Christianity and evolution teach: that, whether it happened in six days or millions of years, human beings were created by something that was not human, and that nothing we do here on earth has any great importance?

"This isn't what we used to think, before Christianity and the other revealed religions taught us to despise the notion that the work of humanity was to achieve, try to achieve, the perfection, the excellence, intended by nature. Read Plato, read Aristotle, read more than a thousand years later Maimonides; discover the ancient guarded secret that everything that comes into being, including all human individuals, pass out of being, but that the world itself is eternal. But start with Aristotle, read in the *Metaphysics* the passage where at the conclusion of several hundred tightly reasoned pages he concludes that change has 'always been. And so with time…. Accordingly, change is as continuous as time; for time is either the same as change or is in the same way bound up with it. But there is no continuous change except locomotion, and no continuous locomotion except cyclical.' I think I remember that right.

"It is the only hope we have: to go all the way back to the beginning if we are going to see our way clearly ahead. That's why I wrote what I did, what I hope you will read; that's why I started the school, the academy, so that sometime in the next generation there might be a few men and women who understand the fallacies of the modern age, and the need for a new religion. That's why I did what I did with Constable and the others, so there might be someone in a position of authority and power who could at least start to change directions. That's why I chose you, Mr. Hart: because there is more to you than ambition."

CHAPTER 24

DAVID ALLEN HAD barely slept in three days. He tried to relax, he tried to tell himself that every crisis had an end, he even tried sleeping pills, but nothing worked; nothing could stop the frenzied, thousand thoughts a minute movement of his mind, the compulsion to try to find answers to questions he did not know how to ask. His blood pressure, always high, was off the charts; the thumping in his chest was loud enough to hear. He began to have a nervous tic at the corner of his mouth. Without warning, a quick incessant blinking would suddenly take possession of his tired eyes. Like the world around him, everything was going to extremes.

For three days, Bobby Hart's administrative assistant had been forced to answer accusations, each one more damaging than the last, about the senator's part in the conspiracy to murder the president. Allen had started with an angry denial, outraged that anyone would suggest such a thing was even possible, but then, as more and more evidence was produced, when documents were discovered proving Hart had paid the assassin, he found himself on the defensive, arguing that despite what all this seemed to prove, it was not true. Then, when Hart escaped arrest at the embassy and disappeared somewhere in France, even that became impossible and he was reduced to mumbling the obligatory "no comment" each time he had to pass through a phalanx of shouting reporters in the hallway outside the Senate office.

By this time, there were not more than a dozen people in Washington who did not believe what everyone else believed, that Bobby Hart was behind the murder of Robert Constable, and probably less than half that number who were still willing to say so. David Allen was one of them; Charlie Finnegan was another. Both of them knew Hart too well, knew too much about what he had gone through with his wife, to think that the case against him was anything other than a deliberate fabrication, part of a conspiracy that had started with the murder of the president and had perhaps always been intended to end with the blame fixed on someone else. In the hours after Hart had gone missing in Paris, Charlie Finnegan met secretly with David Allen to decide what they should do.

An unmarked door just off one of the main corridors in the Capitol opened on to a narrow hallway in which certain members of the Senate had private rooms where they could spend time alone, or sometimes not alone, away from the prying eyes of reporters and the constant demands of staff, a place where they could, if they wanted, actually think.

"Atwood is lying through his teeth!" exclaimed Finnegan, shaking his head in angry disbelief.

He gestured toward a brown sofa which, along with a matching leather chair and a coffee table, made up the furnishings of the room. Allen sat down, but Finnegan was too agitated even to stand still. He kept moving, a few slow, hesitant steps in one direction, a few steps back, an awkward, sliding motion in which he would suddenly dip his shoulder and turn to the side, stop, stare down at the carpet, and then, shaking his head again at the enormity of what had happened, start off on another short, distracted journey.

"It's that goddamn Atwood! He's at the center of this. He's lied about everything. When Bobby went to see him—did he tell you this? He said that he had told the FBI, that they had started an investigation, and that the CIA was aware of it as well. Then we have the director of the CIA in front of the committee and Bobby asks him and he doesn't know anything about it! And now this—announces that Constable was murdered and that the Secret Service—the Secret Service, for Christ sake!—was investigating, and they find the assassin, the woman who was in the room with him that night, and she died trying to escape, but they found all the evidence they needed in her apartment. In her apartment, for Christ sake!"

Finnegan took one more step and wheeled around.

"Her apartment! This professional killer, so good at what she does she gets Constable to take her to bed so she can put a needle in him; so good at what she does that she gets that poor bastard, the agent who was supposed to be guarding Constable, to help her get away; so good at what she does that no one seems to know who the hell she is—keeps records in her apartment like she was some tax accountant afraid of losing even one receipt? Notice, by the way, that the only records they found were about this one job; not a shred of evidence about any of the other murders she must have done! It's Atwood. He's in the middle of this. The only question is who he is working for. He wouldn't have had any reason to do this, go to these lengths, get rid of this many people and then frame Bobby for it, on his own."

While he listened, Allen thought back to the last time he talked to Hart, when Hart was in New York meeting with Austin Pearce. He remembered the reason why he had tried to reach him.

"Quentin Burdick came to see Bobby the same day he died, that afternoon. Bobby was in New York. He had gone up to see Austin Pearce. I'm not sure why Burdick was here, but he must have come to see someone. He said he had to talk to Bobby. It seemed quite urgent. He said Bobby would know what it was about, but then he said that he wouldn't, that he would think he did, but he wouldn't. It was all very mysterious. He said to tell Bobby that it was what they talked about before—The Four Sisters—only that there was a lot more to it than what he had thought then."

"Bobby told me about that—Burdick had asked me about it once—The Four Sisters."

"He didn't tell me."

"He couldn't. He only told me because he thought I might be able to help. Did Burdick say anything else?"

"Not really. He had a package with him. I don't know what was in it, but it must have been important the way he held onto it."

"He didn't talk about anything else? Nothing?"

"We just talked about the rumors going around. What Russell was going to do: whether he would try for the nomination, and whether he would have any chance against Hillary Constable if he did." Allen narrowed his eyes and tried to remember. "There was something. It was odd. Burdick wanted to talk about the reasons why Russell had gone on the ticket with Constable, why he didn't stay chairman of Senate Finance instead. He went through all the things that had been said at the time, but then he said that the real reason was because Russell did not have a choice."

"Didn't have a choice?"

"I don't know what he meant. I asked, but all he would say was that he couldn't tell me yet. Whatever it was, he seemed pretty damn certain of what he knew."

"Didn't have a choice," repeated Finnegan in a pensive voice. "Constable would have done that, used something he had, something he knew about Russell, to force him to do what he wanted, run for vice president. If that's true, you could see why Russell might decide that.... And now Constable is dead, and Russell does not have to worry about whatever Constable had on him and he becomes president in the bargain."

Almost immediately, Finnegan changed his mind. He made a dismissive gesture with his hand.

"But if Russell wanted Constable dead, why wait until now when he has only a few months to establish himself in the office, and when the public's sympathy is all for Constable's wife? He knew from the day he agreed to run for vice president that she was only waiting for the end of her husband's second term to run for her first."

"Unless something happened," said Allen, "something that made him think he was going to be in real trouble if Constable lived."

Finnegan put his hand on the back of his neck and twisted his head from side to side. He remembered things now in a different way than he had remembered them before. Everything had a new importance.

"The story Burdick was working on, the connection between Constable and The Four Sisters. Bobby was convinced that was what got Constable killed. The story would have destroyed Constable and any chance Hillary had to become president. Maybe they were all in on it, Constable, Frank Morris, and Russell, too. Maybe. I don't know. I still think it had to be Hillary. Russell doesn't strike me as ruthless enough to do something like this. And Atwood—where do you think his loyalties are? Who would he trust enough to do something like this: organize an assassination and then arrange the murders of everyone who started to get close to the truth? It had to be Hillary Constable."

Allen bit his lip and thought hard. He had never trusted Robert Constable and had never liked his wife, but facts were facts and all of them seemed to suggest that Finnegan was wrong.

"She would have to be a fool. She had to know that as soon as Constable was dead all the power would be in Russell's hands and that everything would change. It's one thing to have a weak vice president, someone who can't win the presidency on his own, someone who could not mount a serious challenge to a woman as popular as she is. It's something else again to defeat an incumbent president of your own party, a man the whole country wants to succeed after he has taken over for the victim of an assassination. I don't know if Russell is behind this, maybe it was Hillary—it has to be one of them—but if Russell wanted it done, Atwood would have done it."

Instead of a reply, Finnegan sat down on the edge of the chair and lapsed into a long silence. Finally, he stood up and with his hands behind his back started shuffling back and forth. A moment later, he stopped abruptly and looked straight at Allen.

"What if it were both of them? What if Russell and Hillary Constable were in it together? What if they decided Constable had to die—because it was the only way to stop the story about The Four Sisters coming out— and they made a deal. You've heard the rumor; you know what is going to happen: she's going to take his place as vice president. What if this was part of the deal?"

There was a certain clear logic in the murderous precision of the scheme. It was political calculation carried to a Machiavellian extreme: the removal of an obstacle to ambition, and done in a way that by blaming it on someone else makes you the object of universal sympathy and good will. Allen saw at once how each part fit.

"Russell serves out the remainder of Constable's term and then has a term of his own. Hillary is vice president and then has the chance to run for two terms on her own. A devil's bargain that gives them both what they want and that gets rid of the only threat they face, Bobby Hart, by blaming it all on him. And they won't have to worry about him defending himself, because—"

"Because he'll be dead, killed while he was trying to get away!"

"What can we do?" asked Allen. But for the moment, Finnegan had no answers.

If Allen had barely been able to sleep before, now he could not sleep at all. He lay awake all night, wondering what was going to happen, not just to his friend of twenty years, but to the country. It had been bad enough, the nearly eight years of Robert Constable's lying, ineffectiveness, and treachery, but four, eight, twelve years of government by a band of assassins? The killing would not stop once the two of them, Constable's wife and vice president, had what they wanted. If history proved anything, it proved that no one was more suspicious than the man or woman who had come to power through an act of violence. Anyone thought to be a threat, whether a political rival or someone who might discover what they had done, would have to be dealt with, eliminated, made to disappear; and every time it happened, every time they were forced to commit another murder, another violent act, there would be another cover-up, and another set of secrets that would have to be protected. The circle would keep widening, spreading death and destruction, until, finally, the circle, as always happened, would be driven back on itself, and the ones who had started everything in motion would themselves become the victims of some new aspirant to power.

Allen did not know what to do. There was no use telling anyone that Bobby Hart was innocent. There were some on the senator's own staff who did not believe that. Several of them had resigned immediately, afraid of the damage that might be done to their own careers; others, Allen knew, would follow shortly. If even people on Hart's own staff thought he had done what everyone said he did, no one was going to believe that Russell and Hillary Constable were guilty instead. Whatever the charges, whatever the risk, Bobby had to come back. Allen knew that he would try, that he would never leave his wife here alone, but why had he not at least tried to call, to somehow get a message to him that he was all right; let him know something—anything—that might help put his mind at ease? Hart had not even called Laura, though strangely enough, she did not seem much worried about it.

Allen, who lived for politics, had never felt entirely comfortable around Laura Hart. She was not quite like anyone he knew; she certainly was not like most of the other wives of successful politicians. She was in love with her husband, which in Washington was rare enough, but she was in love with him not because, but in spite, of who he was. Allen had for a long time resented her, convinced that Hart would have run for president if he had been married to a woman who, like most political wives, dreamed of being first lady instead of living alone, just the two of them, somewhere in the seclusion of the Santa Barbara hills. He did not change his mind about that, but he did change his mind about her. He realized that the reason he felt such a distance in her presence was because her world was made up of only two people, she and Bobby, and that while she could be a good and trusted friend to others, all her thoughts were about him. Beneath the surface, that fragile exterior that had nearly shattered, down deep in her soul there was a kind of strength that in the days of changeable attachments and replaceable relationships was not seen so much anymore. She believed in her husband, but more than that, she believed in them, the two of them together. David Allen envied them a little for that.

"You look awful, David," she said when she opened the door.

Allen stood in the doorway of the small apartment the Harts had taken in northwest Washington. He was breathing hard, worn out from all the restless days and sleepless nights. Laura led him into the living room and insisted he take off his jacket.

"Really, David, you can't take all this on yourself. You're not going to do

Bobby any good if you kill yourself from worry and overwork."

Allen sank into an easy chair and wrapped his hands around a cool glass of lemonade. Laura sat on the edge of the sofa just a few feet away. Her eyes were clear and a faint smile played on her lips.

"Yours is the first friendly face I've seen in days. Except for Charlie, of course. He came by as soon as I got back."

"Why did you come back? Wouldn't Bobby have wanted you to stay at home, in Santa Barbara, while all this is going on?"

"Yes, you're right, he would have. But as soon as I heard—I had just gotten home—I knew I had to come back. I wasn't going to hide, try to run away. I wanted these people to know that I wasn't afraid of what they were saying, that all these accusations were false."

Without makeup, her hair pulled back in a ponytail, dressed in a black turtleneck, she had the clean, well-scrubbed look of a woman who never lived too far from the drifting white sand of an ocean beach. Allen felt a desire to offer her what assurances he could, a need to tell her that things were not as bad as they seemed.

"No one who knows you, no one who knows both of you, believes any of it. You have to know that."

Her smile seemed to forgive the lie, and, more than that, thank him for what she knew he was trying to do.

"You know us, and Charlie knows us. There aren't many others, though, are there—people who know us well enough to believe that we aren't what other people say we are? But that only makes what you and Charlie have done more honorable." She got up, walked over to the window, and looked down at the street. "The reporters got all they needed. They seemed surprised by what I told them."

Allen rubbed his chin. His eyes began to blink.

"Surprised? Yes, I suppose you could say that."

Laura folded her arms and leaned back against the window sill. There was a strange, wistful look in her eyes.

"Shocked, I suppose. I'm not sure why. They accuse me of infidelity and adultery, of having an affair with Robert Constable, but think I'm too fragile—a woman who may or may not have had a breakdown—to respond the way I did? I told them the truth, and did it in a way I hoped they might understand."

"Oh, I think they understood," said Allen, shaking his head at the effect it had. "I think everyone understood."

"And who knows, there might even have been a few of them who believed me when I said it." She looked down at the empty street again, remembering the crowd and the stunned reaction when she finished telling them exactly what she thought. She hoped that when he heard about it, Bobby would understand why she had thought she had to do it.

"All I said was that I'd never slept with anyone except my husband," she explained, turning away from the window. "And that even if I had been single, I never would have slept with anyone who had slept with as many women as Robert Constable. Then I told them that if they were going to run a picture of me and Robert Constable, taken at some event I don't remember, to suggest that we had an affair, they might want to run a picture of Robert Constable and Bobby Hart to show that I would have had to have been not only a fool, but blind, to have done what they said I did. And then I told them that if they were going to accuse someone of murder because the president was screwing his wife, they better include in their list of suspects half the married men in Washington, to say nothing of the married women in all the other places he had been."

Tilting her head to the side, Laura fixed Allen with a look that seemed to defy him or anyone else to tell her that she should not have done what she did. But almost immediately, she relented, drew back as if none of it mattered. There were more important things to think about.

"Bobby left a message on the telephone in Santa Barbara. He told me—he didn't need to, but he told me—that none of it was true, that he was going to prove it, and that he was going to be okay. I haven't heard anything since. But don't worry, David. Bobby will be fine. I'd know it if he wasn't."

Allen was almost willing to believe it. It was said that twins could feel what each other felt; why could not she have that same telepathic gift when her whole life was bound so closely with his?

"It's only been a few days," said Allen. "We'll hear something. He'll be back soon."

Instead of being comforted, Laura seemed alarmed. She shook her head emphatically.

"No, he can't come back, not while this is going on, not while everyone thinks he hired someone to kill the president. They'll arrest him, if they don't kill him first," she said darkly. "That's the reason I asked you to come by. I need your help."

"Anything. What do you need?"

"Quite a lot, I'm afraid. As soon as I know where Bobby is, I'm going. I'm leaving the country and I may need some help to do it. I don't imagine they can stop me from leaving, but I don't want anyone to follow me, to use me to find him. The other thing," she said hesitantly, "if we can't come back—"

"Bobby will come back. He isn't going to spend the rest of his life hiding. He won't do that, he'll—"

"What other choice will he have? They'll kill him—whoever did this thing. They'll kill him before they'd ever let him go to trial. You know it as well as I do. You know what people are capable of, how easily they can turn on you when they think you're in trouble."

"He'll come back," said Allen in a firm, resolute voice. "Bobby never ran away from a fight in his life, and we both know it, don't we?"

All the bravery vanished from her face. She seemed to grow visibly smaller, shrinking back inside herself, as she contemplated the end of the one last thing that had given her hope: the chance that, whatever happened here, she and Bobby could find refuge in another place, safe from all the insanity that now threatened everything.

"Don't...," she begged. "Don't say that. It's all different now. This isn't just another fight; this is survival. There are no more rules. Don't you see that? They're going to kill him. They won't stop trying until they do it."

There was nothing more Allen could say. He told her, as he got up to leave, that whatever happened, she could count on him; that only she and Bobby could decide what they had to do, and that he would help in any way he could. She kissed him on the forehead, something she had never done before, and thanked him for being such a loyal friend. She was just reaching for the door when the telephone began to ring.

"It's Bobby," she said, and went quickly across the room to answer it.

Allen stood mesmerized, convinced against all reason and logic that she was right, that there was something uncanny and inexplicable about the things she knew. He watched her lift the receiver, watched her eyes come alive before it was even close enough to hear, watched a broad triumphant smile streak across her face at the voice she somehow knew would be there, and heard the whispered shout as she spoke out loud the name that meant more to her than life itself. He watched as the joy turned serious and she began to make another effort to be brave.

"He's coming home," she said when she hung up. "He called from the plane. He lands in two hours."

CHAPTER 25

THE MESSAGE, DELIVERED that morning by courier, could not have been more explicit. Jean Valette would call that night at eleven-thirty, that it was a matter of some urgency, and that she should be there. Hillary Constable knew she had to take the call, knew that she could not afford to get on the wrong side of Jean Valette, but the timing was all wrong. There was too much at stake, too many things that had to be done just right, to start worrying about the past. The president had been dead only a few weeks, and now the country had been informed that he had been murdered by a senator, the husband of a woman with whom he had been sleeping. She was not just walking a fine line; she was walking two of them at once. She was both the widow grieving for her dead husband and the victim of his infidelity; a woman who loved her husband and hated what he had done; a woman who while dealing with all of that was about to become the vice president of the United States. She had to convey an inner strength, the courage to confront death and betrayal and rise above them, forgive the injury and honor the memory of a man who, with all his faults, both she and the country had chosen. She practiced in the mirror a smile best suited to express both sadness and gratitude.

She could not say that she was excited that she was about to be named vice president, to take the post vacated by the man who had now taken her husband's place; she could not say that she looked forward to next summer's convention when she and Irwin Russell would be nominated to run in their own right for those two offices. She said instead that no one was better equipped than Irwin Russell to continue the work her husband had started and that she was glad to now have a chance to make some small contribution of her own.

They stood together in the Rose Garden on a sultry, sun-drenched afternoon, the new president and the woman whose name he was sending to the Hill for confirmation as the new vice president. Hundreds of reporters sat on folding chairs while the television cameras captured the event for the evening news. It was a formal announcement, a matter of public importance, done with dignity and respect. The president read his statement and the soon-to-be vice president made a brief reply. There was time for a few questions.

The questions were polite and mainly about process: How long would it take the House to act? Would there be hearings or, given the circumstances, would the House proceed directly to a vote? There was a tacit understanding that this was not the occasion to ask anything about the murder of Robert Constable or the sensational accusations made against the senator now on the run somewhere in Europe. One reporter did ask whether Russell had considered anyone else for the vice presidency, or whether "Mrs. Constable" had been his only choice.

During his long years in the Congress, Russell had been known as diligent, hard-working, and dull, but also, unlike many of his colleagues, modest and self-effacing. There was none of that now. He was confident, decisive, without any apparent doubts about anything.

"There was no one else. The choice was obvious. Hillary Constable changed the definition of first lady. No one knows more about the way government works. No one is more dedicated to public service. And let me add: No one cares more about others and less about herself. I think the record proves that," he said in a way that by its very ambiguity reminded everyone of what she had gone through with her husband.

"I have a question for Mrs. Constable!" shouted a young reporter at the end of the first row. "Philip Carlyle of the *New York Times*. Do you intend to report the money that you and your husband received over the years from a financial institution in France, tens of millions of dollars from The Four Sisters?"

Hillary Constable stiffened, but only for an instant, and then she had the look of a woman used to being treated badly.

"I think you're referring to certain charitable contributions made to one of the foundations established by my husband to provide assistance to people who need it," she replied with a weary, and much put upon expression. "That has been reported every year, so far as I know, by the people responsible. I was not involved in any of that, so I could not say with complete certainty, but I believe that to be true."

She turned away, but Carlyle was not finished.

"No, I'm talking about tens of millions of dollars paid into various accounts, money that benefited you directly. Do you have any comment?"

"You've obviously been misinformed." She looked at him as if she had suddenly realized what he was saying. "You think my husband, who, whatever human faults he may have had, dedicated his life to this country, would have done something like that—taken money from someone? What kind of people do you think we are? You really ought to know what you're talking about before you ask a question like that!"

"You deny it then?"

"Of course I deny it! I've never done anything like that in my life!"

Careful to get it down exactly the way she said it, Carlyle did not fail to notice that she had shifted ground and was now talking only about what she had done. Not that it mattered, given what he had learned.

"President Russell!" he shouted as he scribbled the last few words in his notebook. "Do you have any comment, anything you would like to say about The Four Sisters?"

If Russell heard the question, he ignored it. With a quick smile and a brief wave he thanked everyone and with Hillary Constable beside him walked toward the West Wing as if everything had gone just as planned. Privately, the president was furious.

"I thought this story died with your husband," he said with a withering glance.

Hillary Constable ignored him. She looked around the Oval Office, noticing the changes. The photographs on the credenza were now pictures of Russell and his dowdy middle-aged wife, pictures of their children and their grandchildren, traditional family pictures instead of the endless gallery of famous and important people that Robert Constable had kept there to remind himself how far he had come from his hardscrabble beginnings in America's heartland. Russell had not yet replaced the desk, the one that had been used by Theodore Roosevelt, the one that Constable had chosen to paint himself as less partisan than some of his immediate predecessors, the desk that seemed to give him tangible proof that he was as good, or could be as good, as the great ones had been.

"This 'story,' as you put it," she replied finally, "is the only reason you're sitting in that chair. I wouldn't think you could have forgotten that."

No one sat down in the Oval Office until they were first invited to do so, but Hillary did not think she needed anyone's permission. She took a chair in front of the desk and began to remove her gloves.

"How much do you think he knows?" asked Russell. The lines in his forehead deepened with worry. "It seemed like he knew a lot. This wasn't supposed to happen. Everything was supposed to be taken care of. Atwood said—"

"Atwood said!" cried Hillary angrily. "You're really quite pathetic! You decide you want something, but you're afraid to go get it. You spent too much of your life making deals. You should have stayed in Congress! You can't compromise your way out of this! You knew what you were doing when you got involved, when you blackmailed your way onto the ticket four years ago."

Russell's face turned red. The veins in his temples throbbed.

"I did no such thing! If anything, it was the other way round. It was your idea—his idea—not mine!"

A dismissive smile spread across her face and stayed there, taunting him with her indifference to how he chose to remember things. He could rewrite the past any way he wished; what was important was what they had to do now.

"No one can prove anything, not if we keep our story straight. That reporter—Carlyle—maybe he learned something from Quentin Burdick, but all he has are questions. He doesn't know anything."

Russell was not so sure.

"Burdick may not have known anything either," he said with a caustic glance. "And look what happened to Robert."

They stared at each other, reluctant to say anything more about the murder that had led to this, a forced marriage of ambition that neither of them had wanted.

"None of this would have happened if it had not been for The Four Sisters. I tried to warn him. Even after it started, I tried to get him to stop. I told him there was too much to lose, that sooner or later someone would find out, but nothing was ever enough for him. He thought that nothing could touch him, that he was indestructible. And then, when the whole thing started to come undone, when that damn Burdick started asking questions, he was like some scared kid caught trying to steal something. He could have lied his way through it, but he was too much a coward for that. He would have told Burdick everything, and tried to blame it all on other people." She looked straight at Russell. "But you won't have a problem doing what you have to do, will you?"

Russell picked up the telephone.

"Will you send in Mr. Atwood."

He turned back to Hillary.

"I think you're right. No one is going to be much interested in something that may have happened between President Constable and some investment firm overseas. The only thing the public wants to know is when we're going to catch the man responsible for his murder."

A moment later, the door opened and Clarence Atwood stepped inside.

"Sit down," said Russell, gesturing impatiently toward the chair next to the one Hillary was occupying. "What's happened since I talked to you this morning?"

Atwood seemed nervous, ill at ease. His shoulders slouched forward; his jaw began to tighten. He looked from Russell to Hillary and then back to the president.

"Nothing."

"Nothing, nothing at all? You don't know anything about where he has disappeared?"

"He's not in Paris…at least we don't think he is."

Russell glared at him. He had expected more than this.

"The FBI, the CIA, the Secret Service—all the resources of this government, and the help of other governments as well—and the best you can do is tell us that you don't think he's still in Paris?"

Atwood bent his lanky frame closer to the president.

"We have run into some problems with the French."

"What kind of problems?" demanded Hillary. "There aren't supposed to be any problems—remember? You knew how to take care of everything!"

Atwood's head snapped around. There was open defiance in his eyes, challenging her to say what she meant. She stared right back, daring him to try to force her hand.

"What kind of problems?" asked Russell in a firm voice. "What do the French want?"

"They want to know what two men from our embassy were doing, whose authority they were acting on, when they broke into the apartment of our political attaché and killed him along with Austin Pearce."

Russell and Hillary exchanged a worried glance and then looked at Atwood. Russell could barely speak.

"They're convinced that Hart was not involved?"

"They know Hart was not involved. There was a witness. She was talking to Hart when the shooting started."

"What have the French been told?" asked Hillary, her own voice suddenly weak and hollow.

"That they must have been acting on their own, but that we're conducting an investigation to make sure."

"Do they believe that?"

"No, Mrs. Constable, they don't. They not only know that Hart was not involved, they know he tried to save Austin Pearce. They've started asking questions. They think that there must have been a reason why two men from the embassy—they know the functions they performed—killed Pearce and the other guy. They think it was because of what they had learned from Hart.

They think that someone in the government—this government—arranged the murder of the president and is now trying to blame it on the senator."

"The French can believe whatever the hell they want!" cried Hillary in a rage. "There's nothing to link any of us to that! Who's going to pay any attention to some vague suspicion of the French police?"

A bitter smile cut hard across Atwood's crooked mouth.

"For one, that same reporter—Philip Carlyle—who was asking questions about The Four Sisters. He just got back from Paris, where he was spending time with the detective investigating Pearce's murder."

The president stood up, a sign that the meeting was over. There was only one thing he wanted to know.

"Can you control this?"

Atwood thought about it for a moment, and then nodded slowly.

"I'll take care of it."

Hillary and the president were left alone. For a long time, neither of them said anything.

"You didn't know anything about your husband's financial dealings," Russell said presently. "You have no reason to think he ever did anything with this investment firm, The Four Sisters, or anyone else, that was not what it should have been. There were a number of contributors to the various foundations that the president established to do good works. Other people took care of that. You had your own work inside the White House, trying to help the people of this country."

There was a hint of disapproval, regret that he could not be free of all this, in the way Russell looked at her as he summarized what would have to be her public position. His resentment, however, was nothing in comparison to hers.

"You don't have to tell me how to handle this. I don't recall that we ever asked you for your advice when you were my husband's vice president."

"It might have saved you some embarrassment if you had!" he shot back. Her eyes went wild with anger.

"The only reason you're sitting in that chair is because—!"

"But I am sitting in it, and there is nothing you can do about it now." A smile full of malice twisted slowly across his mouth. "There never was anything you could do about it. Did you really think that once I took over, you could run against me for the nomination?"

"I could have beaten you, and we both know it!" she cried, jutting out her chin.

The smile on Russell's face deepened and took on another meaning, one they both understood.

"Yes, but you didn't run, did you? The world would have found out the truth about you and The Four Sisters, and a few other things besides. And what could you do?—Tell about me? I didn't take anything like as much as you and Robert did; my involvement was minor compared to yours. Don't look so upset. You're going to be sitting here one day, or at least you'll have your chance, just not as quickly as you had hoped. You're about to become vice president, next in line of succession."

A strange look of cruelty and contempt gleamed in his eyes as he looked past her for a moment. He laughed silently as at some private joke.

"That means you get to go home every night and hope that when you wake up the first news you'll have is that the president is dead. I should warn you, however, that with none of the careless habits of your reckless husband, I won't be an easy victim should someone decide they can't wait for the accidents of mortality. Now, if you'll excuse me, I have to study the speech I'm scheduled to give this evening when I introduce you as the next vice president and tell how we propose to build on the foundation of our beloved predecessor."

The president had his speech, and so did she. In front of a vast audience in the Kennedy Center she struck just the right chord: somber, serious, and, despite the tragedy of her husband's death, still hopeful that the country could move forward, building on what Robert Constable had done. There was a moment when it all seemed too much for her. She had just finished telling them, all these people who had supported her husband in the past, how the night at the last convention, when Irwin Russell's name had been placed in nomination for vice president, he had said to her that Russell was the one man who could take over and continue his legacy if anything ever happened to him. There was a catch in her voice; her lips trembled, a tear came to her eye. The audience rose as one and began to applaud, a long, somber tribute to the memory of her husband and to what she had been forced to endure. She flashed a brave smile and managed somehow to go on. Whatever else anyone might remember about those two speeches, they would remember that. Hillary was sure of it.

She knew then that what she had said earlier in the Oval Office was true: that Irwin Russell would have had no chance had she chosen to run against him, that the nomination, and the election, would have been hers for the asking. If it had not been for that damnable secret she would have been here tonight launching her campaign for the presidency instead of being forced into the second place part that, except for the title, she had been playing for the last seven years. Everyone was there to see her, not the accidental president no one had seriously thought would ever hold the office. They lined up, nearly all of them, almost three thousand men and women, waiting to tell her how much they loved her and how much they admired her courage.

She began to realize that it was not too late. She could become vice president, wait a few months, and then break with Russell over some made-up issue, announce that she did not have any choice, that she had promised her dead husband to complete his unfinished agenda, but that the president wanted to take the country in a different direction, one she could not in conscience follow. The country would have to decide. She would run for the presidency herself.

Why had not she thought of it before? Russell could not threaten her with exposure, not after he had vouched for her honesty and integrity by choosing her to become his own vice president. Some of his people might start rumors, but that was a game two could play.

Careful to maintain an air of reserve, she kept shaking hands, thanking each one for the kind and thoughtful things they had to say, promising to do everything in her power not to let them down. The line passed from her to the president, but she knew they had all come to see her, and he knew it, too. She could see it in his eyes, this sense that he was an afterthought, a necessary obligation, a price the crowd was willing to pay for the chance to first have a few moments with her.

"They all love you, Hillary," said the president when it was finally over and they stood outside.

"They loved Robert," she replied.

Russell's smile suggested that they both knew the truth, knew that the crowd had loved Robert Constable only because they had not really known him. It also suggested something deeper, something that Hillary understood immediately: the crowd loved her for the same reason.

"I better go," she remarked coldly. "I have a very long day tomorrow."

"I'm sure they'll all be busy now," said the president as he turned and got into the limousine.

She watched the motorcade speed away and then, full of thoughts of her future, stepped into her own waiting car, and headed home. It was ten minutes past eleven. Her mood began to darken as she remembered the call she had to take in twenty minutes. Why was Jean Valette calling her, and why now, the night before the last piece would be in place for what she had been waiting for all her life?

Maybe it was nothing. Perhaps he just wanted to offer his own congratulations. Probably he wanted to remind her that he had always been their friend, her and Robert's, and that he hoped he could in some manner be helpful in the future. That was it. Everyone wanted to remind you of their friendship once you had a position in which you could do something for them. Perhaps she ought to tell him that it might be best if they put things on hold for a while, that things were a little too delicate to do anything that might cause someone to start looking at what their relationship had been like before. Jean Valette would understand. He was too intelligent not to realize the consequences of making a mistake at this point.

The house was cloaked in darkness. Two Secret Service agents escorted Hillary inside while several others took up their positions on the grounds. Though she was not yet vice president, as the former first lady, and the widow of a slain president, she had never stopped being under their protection. Leaving the two agents downstairs, she went up to the privacy of the second floor. She did not like coming back to an empty house. She was used to having people around, people who worked for her and shared her ambitions, people who were always full of ideas, eager, all of them, to be the first with the latest rumors or the latest news. She needed that, the constant noise, the constant attention, the sense of being in the center of things, but tonight she was all alone. Everyone who worked for her had been at the Kennedy Center, listening to her speech.

The study was pitch-black. She turned on the desk lamp and sat down. It was almost eleven-thirty; the call would come any minute. She glanced at the photographs that covered the desk, a chronicle of what now seemed ancient history, the times beyond remembering when she had last had the chance for what might have been a normal life. She wondered why she still kept them. She supposed it was to remind her of the price she had paid, and how that price had been so much greater than what she had originally imagined.

She remembered what it had been like, when she was young and attractive and every man she met eager to have her, and how she had known even then that any one of them would be a better husband than Robert Constable. Knowing it, she had done it anyway, because Robert Constable was going to be president, and no one was going to be able to stop him. It seemed odd now, looking back, that she had never once doubted that extraordinary, improbable fact. She had known he was going to be president, and she had known that there was every chance he would make her life a living hell. She had hoped she might be wrong about that.

The clock struck eleven-thirty. She moistened her lips and began to rehearse in her mind what she was going to say. It was so quiet she could hear her own breath. A minute passed, and then another. She tapped her fingers softly on the desk's leather top. Five minutes passed, then ten.

"Damn," she muttered in frustration. "Five more minutes, that's all I'm giving him."

Suddenly, she felt a strange sensation, one she could not account for, a kind of warning, a premonition, that something was different, not quite right.

"I'm afraid Jean Valette won't be calling tonight. I've come instead."

She jumped to her feet, pointing into the darkness at the other side of the room, where from the chair in which he had been sitting Bobby Hart rose to greet her.

CHAPTER 26

HILLARY CONSTABLE STARED at Bobby Hart in wild-eyed disbelief.

"Where did you come from you? How did you get here?"

"What's the matter, Hillary? I thought you would be glad to see me. Didn't I do everything you asked, try to find out who killed your husband before—what was it? Yes, I remember: before all the rumors started and the country tore itself apart? Didn't I find out everything you wanted to know about how much of Robert Constable's involvement with The Four Sisters could be traced back to you?"

In the dim light of the desk lamp each movement cast a shadow on the wall, creating the illusion that they were on a stage playing to an audience they could not see.

"When I asked you to do that, I didn't know you were the one who had had him killed!"

Hart had been sitting in that darkened room for a long time, waiting for her to come in, waiting to confront her with what he knew. He had been thinking about what he was going to say to her, what she was going to say to him, from the moment he had gotten on the private plane from France. He thought he was ready for anything, but when he heard this he could barely restrain himself.

"I was the one who had him killed! You miserable…. Who the hell do you think you are? Your husband was a liar and a cheat, and the biggest thief who ever held the office, but you—you're worse. I know all about you; I know all about you both. The Four Sisters didn't come to your husband, he went to them. He started it, he demanded money, tens of millions, and you knew all about it, didn't you? You knew what would happen if someone got hold of that story; you knew what would happen if he talked to Quentin Burdick. That's why you did it—why you had your husband killed—to protect yourself!"

"That's a damn lie!" she screamed back. "I'm going to put an end to this right now." She picked up the phone, but Hart caught her by the wrist and forced the receiver back.

"You're not going to do anything."

"And just how are you going to stop me?"

"With this, if I have to."

He pulled his jacket to the side, revealing a pistol tucked into his belt. He saw the smirk start onto her lips, the arrogant dismissal of what, despite the gun, she thought an empty threat.

"You think I won't—after what you've done to me? You think I don't know how? I remembered well enough when I had to shoot the son-of-a-bitch who murdered Austin Pearce. Trust me, I'll use it if I have to."

The smirk vanished, replaced with uncertainty if not yet fear.

"Why are you here? What do you want? What do you hope to prove? Everyone knows what happened, why you had Robert killed. You think that because you somehow got back into the country, all you have to do is hold a press conference and announce that you're innocent?"

"You've already done that for me today, in the Rose Garden, you and Russell, when you denied knowing anything about The Four Sisters. Weren't you a little worried when you did that? Didn't you wonder how much Philip Carlyle really knew?"

"You weren't there. How do you know the name of the reporter?"

Hart smiled at her in a way that made her mouth go dry.

"We were for a while both guests at the home of Jean Valette."

Darkness swept across her eyes and for a moment she thought she was about to faint. She took a deep breath and dropped into the chair.

"At the home of Jean Valette," she repeated in a lifeless monotone. "I didn't... What you said I did—I didn't have anything to do with Robert's murder. I really thought—when I saw the evidence, the records of payment—I thought what they said about you was true. But, Jean Valette—why would you, why would that reporter...?"

Hart had seen too many of the different faces of Hillary Constable, too many masks put on for effect, to believe any of them authentic, especially one as convenient as this, the practiced look of a woman misunderstood.

"You really believed, when you saw the evidence...? Of course you did. There were only two people who had something to gain by the president's death: Irwin Russell and you. The Four Sisters story would have forced the president to resign. And you—what chance would you have had to run for anything after a scandal like that? But instead, Robert Constable dies, Russell becomes president, and you become—what?—president-in-waiting? You told me you were going to run against Russell. Why didn't you? Nothing could stop you. That's what you said. But there was something, wasn't there? Russell knew about The Four Sisters, because he had done the same thing as Frank Morris. Except that Russell didn't have a conscience, he wasn't any danger to the great Robert Constable. Unlike Frank Morris, he didn't have to be killed."

"You're guessing. You could never prove anything like that."

"You didn't have your husband killed?"

"No, I swear. I—"

"Then Russell did."

"I can't believe that he would—"

"More likely, you were both in it together. Atwood arranged everything, didn't he? And, as you told me yourself, Atwood always did what you asked him to do. He tried to frame me for it. He tried to have me killed. He had Austin Pearce murdered. Which one of you asked him to do that?"

She did not answer, and Hart became more agitated and impatient. His eyes were cold, determined, and lethal.

"When did you decide to do this? When did you decide to set me up?"

"I didn't!" she protested.

His hand moved toward the gun.

"All right, it's true: I wanted you to find out how much of what Robert had done with The Four Sisters could be traced back, how much I might have to explain. And there is something else. I was afraid. I thought Robert was killed to stop him from talking to Burdick. I thought someone connected with The Four Sisters must have done it." With a plaintive glance she asked, "Isn't that what you thought: that The Four Sisters was behind everything?"

"It's what you wanted me to believe, part of the way you used me. And it almost worked. I was going to kill Jean Valette if I had to. But you made a mistake when you had Atwood try to implicate me. Atwood works for you."

"Atwood works for Russell!" she shot back. "Russell is now the president, or have you forgotten that little fact?"

"He won't be for too much longer," said Hart, subjecting her to a scrutiny so close she felt a shudder run up her spine. "And you won't be taking his place."

"Why do you say that? What is it you think you know?"

He just looked at her, a grim smile on his face.

"You were staying at Jean Valette's?" she asked, trying to draw him out. "When everyone was looking for you, when you were supposedly on the run somewhere in Paris, that's where you were, at the chateau?"

"He said you both had visited. Yes, I was there for a while, and so was the chief of detectives of the Surete. We were joined by that New York reporter, Philip Carlyle, and things got quite interesting. You should have been there. I would have liked to have seen your reaction when Jean Valette began to tell him about how the president of the United States extorted tens of millions of dollars from companies he owned, and how both you and Irwin Russell knew all about it. But that was just the beginning. Before Carlyle left, Jean Valette gave him all the documentation needed to prove every charge: bank records, wire transfers, numbered accounts—every penny The Four Sisters was forced to give you and your husband. That's why Carlyle asked you what he did this afternoon: so that when his story runs on the front page of this morning's paper he can print your categorical denial, or rather, given all the evidence he has, your categorical lie! You're not going to be confirmed as vice president and you're not going to run for president. You're going to be indicted as a co-conspirator for fraud and, unless I miss my guess, for murder."

There was a sharp knock on the door.

"Are you all right, Mrs. Constable?" asked a Secret Service agent. "We thought we heard voices."

Hart warned her with his eyes. She went to the door and opened it just a crack.

"No, I'm fine. I had the radio on."

She turned around, but Hart was gone. Breathing hard, she braced herself against the desk. Then she picked up the telephone and called the White House.

"I need to speak to the president!"

The voice at the other end told her that the president had retired for the night and left instructions not to be disturbed. She slammed her hand hard on the desk and shouted:

"I don't care about his instructions! Wake him up, goddamn it! Tell him it's urgent!"

While Hillary Constable waited impatiently for Irwin Russell to come to the phone, Bobby Hart made his way through the shadows of the leafy back yard and out to the end of the street where Charlie Finnegan was waiting in his car.

"What did she say?" asked Finnegan as they drove down the block.

"Just what you'd expect: that she didn't do it, that she thought I did, that she had thought at first that The Four Sisters was behind it. She did admit that she knew something about what Constable had been doing and that she was worried about how much she might have to explain. That's why she asked me to look into it. What she can't explain is Atwood. She tried to blame it on Russell, said Atwood works for him."

Folding his arms, Hart leaned against the passenger side door and shook his head, discouraged, as it seemed, by what had happened.

"I'm such a fool sometimes. I thought that the shock of seeing me would be enough, that she'd just confess, that she'd tell me everything. She's probably never told the truth about anything in her life, and I thought she'd tell the truth to me!"

"You didn't really think that," protested Finnegan with a cynical laugh. "You might have hoped she would, but you knew better than that. If she went to trial and got convicted, she'd insist with her dying breath that she was innocent. Her life means nothing if she ever admitted to what they really were. And as long as she doesn't admit it, or even if she admits some of it and explains the rest away, there will always be people who believe in her, who believe in them. So long as there is a mystery about who really had her husband killed, she'll always be remembered, she'll always be important. Isn't that the reason everyone wants to become famous, so they'll never be forgotten?"

Hart was not listening. He was too caught up in what he knew he had to do.

"She did it, she and Russell both. I'm certain of it. The only problem is I can't prove it."

"You may not have to. Atwood may prove it for us. In just a few hours, all the pressure is going to be on him." He nodded toward the lights of the White House looming in the distance. "You know she had to be on the phone the moment you were gone, telling Russell what you told her, trying to figure out what they can do to save themselves. I don't imagine either one of them is going to be getting any sleep tonight."

They drove to Finnegan's apartment just off Dupont Circle. A pre-war building in which most of the tenants worked for various foreign missions, it gave Finnegan a place to get away from people who worked on the Hill, a place where he could pass almost unnoticed among the others who lived there. He had insisted Hart stay with him until it was safe for him to go home.

"Laura okay?" he asked. He tossed his jacket on a chair in the kitchen, opened the refrigerator, and looked over his shoulder. "Beer?"

"Sure. Thanks. And yes, Laura is okay, though a little angry with me right now."

Finnegan snapped the caps off both bottles and put one on the table in front of Hart.

"She wanted to stay, didn't she?" Finnegan plopped down on the chair opposite. "Good thing she didn't. God knows what's going to happen now. She's home in Santa Barbara? Good. You'll see her in a few days."

A bright, fearless smile cut across Finnegan's mouth.

"The Senate is full of guys married to women more qualified than they are to hold the office. But you and I, my friend, are the only two ready to admit it." He laughed quietly and took a drink. "Now, tell me something more about what happened over there. I know about Austin; I know about the rest of it. Tell me about Jean Valette."

Hart leaned his elbow on the table and bent his head forward. He was not sure where to begin, or whether there was anything he could say to describe what Jean Valette was like. He was not even sure he could describe the effect Jean Valette had had on him.

"He's either the most intelligent, the most profoundly intelligent, man I've ever met or the craziest. When you're with him, everything he says makes sense. He held me, for hours at a time, mesmerized by the astonishing things he said. He seemed to have all of history in his mind. Not just dates and places, battles, wars, things like that, but how they were all connected to each other and what they meant. When we look at history, we look back; he starts at some point in the past and looks forward. That's the difference, I think: he seems to put himself back in time, to see things the way they were seen at the time. It was not like anything I've ever heard. but then, later, when I was alone and thought about what he had said, when I was not under the force of the magnetism he has—eyes that I swear could make you believe anything—then I was not so certain that it was not all lunacy, a madman's description of the world."

Finnegan pushed back until the front legs of the chair were off the floor. With his tousled reddish hair, he looked more like a graduate student having a beer late at night at some Ann Arbor tavern than a member of the United States Senate. But for all his youthful appearance, there was a serious dedication, an intense earnestness, a power of concentration that few others in the Senate, whatever their age, could duplicate. Others could talk endlessly on the Senate floor, their colleagues half asleep; Finnegan, with an instinct for the heart of the matter, never spoke to anything but the point.

"He said he knew all this would happen? Not that Constable would be murdered, but that Constable, and the others, would one way or the other all be destroyed?"

With so many other things on his mind Hart had forgotten that he had mentioned this.

"You told me yesterday, on the ride from the airport. But there's a question, isn't there?" The two front legs of the chair hit the linoleum floor with a clatter as he bounced forward. "If he knew that, if he was so certain that once Constable, and poor Frank Morris, and that fool Russell, became involved, grabbed millions for themselves, they would end up killing one another, why did he do it? It's no answer to say because it was the only way some of the companies he controls—that The Four Sisters controls—could do business here. He knows this will destroy them. He doesn't really need more business, does he? He's one of the world's richest men." Finnegan's eyebrows shot up. "And from the way you describe him...well, would you say he was someone driven by the need for money, this strange recluse with that diminishing library of his? There's only one conclusion you can draw from this, isn't there? For whatever reason, Jean Valette wanted them to destroy themselves. Listen, if someone tells you they're suicidal and then asks if they can borrow your gun...well, you get the idea."

Hart remembered the remarkable expression on the face of Jean Valette as they sat together, surrounded by towering banks of empty shelves, and the sense of something electric in the air as he began to tell him about the book he had written, and how, if he was not careful, what he had learned about the future might truly drive him mad.

"Jean Valette isn't much interested in what happens to individuals. He thinks there is too much at stake for that. And there is something else," said Hart with a deeply troubled expression. "The fact that no one else seems to think there is any crisis only makes him more certain that there is."

Finnegan glanced at his watch.

"It's late. Better try to get a few hours sleep. We've got a lot to do in the morning."

Nodding in agreement, Hart started to get up, but then stopped and shot a quizzical glance at Finnegan.

"What about the Secret Service agent, the one who was there the night Constable was murdered, the one I met when I had that meeting with Atwood at the Watergate? Richard Bauman—what were you able to find out?"

Finnegan pushed his chair close against the table and emptied what was left of his beer into the sink.

"All anyone knows is that he quit, and then disappeared. No one has seen him; no one knows where he went. No one knows for sure if he is still alive."

"I thought he might know something," said Hart. "When I met him that night he seemed genuinely distraught, kept blaming himself for what happened, for helping the killer get away."

"Get some sleep," said Finnegan as he walked him to the door of the second bedroom. "In a couple of hours the papers hit the streets and this whole town is going to blow up."

It was a figure of speech, of course, not meant to be taken literally, but in places like the White House and the various offices on Capitol Hill it was a fair description of the reaction to the story Philip Carlyle had written under the kind of banner headline used only for a domestic crisis or war. Carlyle had everything: dates and places where meetings had taken place, records of each transaction by which the Constables, along with Irwin Russell and the late Frank Morris, had enriched themselves and violated the public trust. It was all there, every seedy detail in an epic tawdry tale of narrow-minded greed and corruption. But that was only half the story. Bribery and extortion had been the prelude to murder.

Instead of starting with the murder of Robert Constable in a New York hotel room, Carlyle started with the two murders in France. Why were Austin Pearce, the former secretary of the treasury, and Aaron Wolfe, head of the political section at the embassy in Paris, killed by two American intelligence agents stationed at that same embassy? Carlyle reported that the chief of detectives of the Surete was convinced that it was to stop them from revealing what they had learned from Bobby Hart about who was really responsible for the assassination of Robert Constable.

"'It clearly was not Senator Hart,' insists Inspector Dumont. 'He came here looking for the connection with The Four Sisters. The two killers were not working for him. He was downstairs talking to the landlady when the shooting started. He ran upstairs, tried to save Mr. Pearce, and was almost killed himself. He shot the assailant, wounded him in the shoulder, and forced him to flee. Hart did not kill anyone, but someone in your government is trying to kill him.'"

By nine o'clock those who had not yet read the story were rushing out to buy a paper so they could. It was all anyone could talk about. Nothing got done. Everyone was on the phone, trying to find out what others thought, or huddled together in small groups in the corridors trying to figure out what was going to happen next, whether Russell would resign or be impeached. That was the only choice he seemed to have. The White House went silent. There was no comment from the president and no indication when there might be one. At Hillary Constable's house, no one would answer the door. At eleven o'clock it was announced that Senator Finnegan of Michigan would hold a press conference at noon. He had new evidence about the murder of Robert Constable.

The hallway outside Finnegan's office became impassable, cameras, television lights, and, as it seemed, every reporter in Washington, crowded together, waiting for Charlie Finnegan to step through the door and tell them what he knew. The air was thick with anxiety, suspense, and something close to panic. The country was at a crossroads and no one could know which direction it would take. One president had been murdered; his successor was about to be forced from office. The woman who was about to become vice president, the woman who would have succeeded Russell, was guilty of the same crimes as her husband. Charlie Finnegan took it all in stride. His opening remark was a bombshell.

"The murder of President Robert Constable was organized and arranged by the head of the Secret Service, Clarence Atwood. Mr. Atwood did not act alone. He was taking orders from either Irwin Russell or Hillary Constable or more probably both. As you know from today's report, Robert Constable and his wife, along with Irwin Russell and former congressman Frank Morris, all took part in a scheme of bribery and corruption. Quentin Burdick, a reporter you all knew and respected, discovered this. He had an interview scheduled with the president. That interview never took place; the president was killed the night before. He was killed out of fear that he might talk, that he might try to blame everything on the others. That would have ruined everything, not just the president's own reputation, but the political ambitions of his wife as well as the vice president's career. They would all have gone to jail."

As soon as Finnegan finished, the questions started, one on top of the other. Finnegan held up both hands, quieting the crowd, and then slowly, methodically, called on each reporter who raised a hand.

"How do you know? What evidence do you have that Clarence Atwood arranged the murder? What—?"

"Murders," corrected Finnegan. "Robert Constable was not the only person he had killed. There was Frank Morris, then Quentin Burdick, and then the two in France: Aaron Wolfe and Austin Pearce."

"But what evidence do you have?"

"First, he lied when he told Senator Hart that an investigation had started into the death of the president, and that both the FBI and the CIA were involved. Second, he knew that Senator Hart had started an investigation of his own, trying to find out who was behind the murder of Robert Constable. He knew it because Hillary Constable told him what Hart was doing, and because Atwood met with Hart to discuss it. Atwood framed Hart for the murder, fabricated evidence, because he had to discredit anything Hart might say about what he found." Finnegan leaned closer toward the battery of microphones. "He framed Hart because then they could have him killed, shut him up forever, and claim, like they did with that paid assassin of theirs in New York, that he was trying to get away."

"But Hart was trying to get away," protested another reporter. "If he's innocent, if Atwood did it, why is Bobby Hart still running?"

A cheerful grin broke unexpectedly across Charlie Finnegan's slightly freckled mouth.

"That's a damn good question. Why don't we ask him?"

And with that, he reached behind him, opened the door to his office, and Bobby Hart stepped out in front of the cameras and an audience of reporters that for half a second was rendered speechless.

When it was over, after he had recounted most of what had happened and what he had learned, after he had patiently answered their questions, Hart went to his own office, where he found an exuberant and exhausted David Allen.

"We had a few defections," said Allen in a wry, understated way. "But it's always good to find out who you can trust."

"A few?" asked Hart, as his eyebrows danced higher. He dropped into a chair on the other side of Allen's perpetually cluttered desk. "There's hardly anyone here."

Allen's look mimicked Hart's own.

"Any minute now the calls will start coming in, all of them telling me how sorry they are, how stupid they were, that they never really believed you did anything like everyone else seemed to think you did. What do you want me to do?"

"Let them come back. There was a point I almost thought I must be guilty."

Hart's secretary, one of the few members of the staff who had not doubted his innocence, came rushing in, her hand trembling as she handed him a slip of paper.

"It's Mr. Atwood. He says you need to call him right away. That's his number. He sounded strange, unbalanced; desperate, I think."

Hart took the number and went alone into his own office. He could feel the anger rising up inside him, rage at what Atwood had done, not just to him, but to Laura too. Why was he calling now? To ask forgiveness, to offer explanations, to try to make some kind of deal?

The voice at the other end answered on the second ring. The one-word greeting, that single "hello," had the weak, lifeless quality of a man in mourning. "Oh, it's you," he added when Hart identified himself. Then there was nothing, a dead silence.

"You called me," said Hart finally. "What is it you want?"

At first Hart thought that Atwood had started to cough, but then he realized that it was laughter, the bitter laughter of an angry, broken man.

"You think you have it all figured out, don't you? You think you know what happened and why. Let me tell you something, Senator: you don't have the first clue!"

Hart was not impressed.

"I'm really not worried, Atwood. It will all come out at your trial."

"Trial? Is that what you think is going to happen?" There was another long silence, and then he added: "You want to know what is going to happen? Listen to this."

There was a sudden, violent roar, an obscene, mind-numbing noise, and then there was no sound at all. Hart jumped out of his chair and ran to Allen's office.

"Call the police. Clarence Atwood has just shot himself."

CHAPTER 27

BOBBY PUSHED OPEN the iron gate at the head of the drive and then stood there, taking in the view, the endless horizon of the blue Pacific gleaming in the late day sun, remembering how much Laura liked it here, how much he liked it here, away from all the glamour and glitter, the half-truths and lies, of politics and Washington. It was paradise, the Garden of Eden, and in what now seemed a singular act of stupidity, he had left it of his own accord, tempted by ambition. He was home, a place they both loved, but instead of telling Laura that they could stay here forever, that after everything that had happened, all the treachery and murder, all the hurtful false accusations, they could finally live a quiet, private life, he had to tell her something else. As he saw Laura open the door and start running up the drive, laughing and crying at the same time, he wished more than anything that he could tell her that, that things were now going to be the way they were at the beginning when every day was perfect and they knew nothing would ever change.

Laura threw herself into his arms and for a long time they just held each other and did not say a thing. With his arm around her shoulder they walked in silence to the house, lost in the simple irreplaceable comfort of being together again.

"I should have met you at the airport."

"All I've wanted to do is see you here, alone, no one else around; no crowds, no reporters—just us."

They went inside and Bobby laughed a little, surprised that everything was just the way he remembered it. He felt as if he had been gone for years, half a lifetime, nothing that could be calculated by the normal measurements of time. Things had moved at too quick a pace for that.

"You must be exhausted," said Laura as she made him sit down. They were in a sitting room just off the living room, where they often spent their evenings watching the sun slip out of the sky and set the sea on fire. "I'll get us something to drink."

Content to breathe the familiar air of home, Bobby watched her walk away, and, watching, could feel what it felt like at night when she was lying next to him and there was nothing else he wanted to do and nowhere else he wanted to be. He was grateful that he had found her, grateful that he had never lost her.

"I watched it all on television," said Laura after she gave him a cool drink in an ice-filled glass. "It was very dramatic, the way Charlie did that, opening the door and you stepped out. I started to cry, and then, when I saw the stunned looks on the faces of those reporters, I started to laugh."

She had started talking, and now she could not stop. Her excitement grew with every word, as she recounted what she had seen.

"And the coverage has been non-stop, everyone with an opinion about what is going to happen and, as usual, no one knows what they're talking about. Except of course that Russell has to go, that Hillary Constable is finished, and that one or both of them may have had her husband killed. Everyone knows now that Atwood had it done; everyone knows—" Suddenly, she stopped. "I'm sorry; I forgot. He really killed himself while he was talking to you on the phone? How awful! Why did he do that, though? Why did he want you to know that he was doing that? Was it his way of getting back at you for finding out what he had done?"

Bobby tapped the edge of his glass.

"He wanted to let me know that I wasn't even close to the truth. That's what he said, but I'm still not sure what he meant. He didn't kill himself because he was innocent. Unless he was just angry and deranged, lashing out at the world the way people about to kill themselves sometimes do, unless he just wanted to make me wonder if I had made some kind of tragic mistake, it has to have something to do with Hillary and Russell, something about why they did what they did. I don't know. But Atwood's dead and his secret, whatever it was, died with him. And so has any chance of proving that Hillary and Russell are responsible for Robert Constable's death and the deaths of all the others."

"But they'll still face charges, won't they, for what they did with The Four Sisters?"

"Maybe not."

"But why? They have all the evidence."

"Hillary can claim that she did not know anything about what her husband was doing. And as for Russell, he's trying to make a deal."

There was a look in Bobby's eyes that told her that this had something to do with them, that whatever deal the president was trying to make might have serious consequences for how they lived their lives.

"A delegation from the House and Senate, led by Charlie Finnegan, met last night with Russell in the White House. They were there until almost three in the morning. They told him that his only choice was resignation or impeachment, that if he chose to fight, if they had to impeach, they would gather all the evidence from every source they could find and that not only would the vote for impeachment be unanimous but he would then certainly face criminal charges in a court of law."

Laura summed it up neatly.

"If he is impeached, he goes to prison, but if he resigns…?"

"That's the question. Russell wants a promise of immunity, or the promise of a pardon from his successor. Charlie was furious. He told Russell that no one was going to promise him anything, certainly not a pardon for crimes that—and Charlie said this to his face—might include conspiracy to murder. Russell looked like he had been hit by a truck. Charlie told him that the best he could hope for was that the fact he chose to resign instead of putting the country through the ordeal of a trial of impeachment would be taken into account in whatever deal he made with prosecutors. It might be enough to keep him out of prison."

Laura caught the omission, the thing that had not been said. She felt a catch in her throat at what she had begun to foresee.

"There is no vice president. If Russell resigns, who…?"

Bobby got up and, forcing a smile, held out his hand, beckoning her to come outside. He led her through the rose-covered yard, out to the far side of the pool. The air was sweet with the scent of the bougainvillea and the distant, salt-water sea.

"Remember when we came here, remember how we said that whatever happened we would always have this place? I know how difficult I've made things for you, how hard you've tried to make things easier for me. But something has happened—"

"Just tell me, Bobby. Whatever it is, it's all right. Whatever you think you need to do, that's what I want you to do. It's something about Charlie and that meeting with the president last night and the fact that there isn't a vice president and—"

"Russell had to promise to nominate a new vice president, someone they would name, someone who would be confirmed immediately and would take over the moment Russell left."

"It's you, isn't it?" she asked with a smile that surprised him with its eager confidence. "It should be you. It had to be you. You're the one who saved the country from that band of murderers and thieves. Who else could it be?"

"But what about you?" he asked. "I know how much you hate that life, all the nonsense that is involved. Everything we do, everything we say—the only privacy we'll ever have is late at night. It wasn't a week ago that nearly everyone in Washington thought I was a murderer and that you were...."

"A whore?" she laughed. A sly, knowing grin tripped across her fine, lovely mouth. "There are worse things than being married to a man other people think would kill the man who took advantage of her. No, Bobby, I'm stronger than I was. Don't worry about me; think only about what you have to do. When it's all over, when you're finished, we'll come back here. Think about all the things we'll have to talk about."

They went inside and Bobby noticed a package on the table in the entryway.

"It just came this morning," explained Laura. "I was so excited to see you, I forgot all about it. It's from some place in France."

She waited while he opened it. There was a thick manuscript inside with a few lines scribbled on the cover.

"It's Jean Valette, the book he has been working on, a book he wanted me to read."

Bobby thumbed through the pages. He looked again at the cover. Jean Valette had written in a flamboyant hand: "Read it, study it; do it slowly, take your time. That is all I ask."

"I looked at it briefly while I was there: four hundred tightly reasoned pages, full of historical and philosophical analysis. The crisis of the West," said Bobby, shaking his head at the enormity of the task. "It took him twenty years to write it; it will probably take me that long to work my way through it."

Laura noticed the time.

"It's almost six. He said he would come back. He does every day."

Bobby was confused.

"Who is coming back? Every day?"

Starting four or five days ago, six o'clock. He's very polite. He calls from the gate, asks if you're here and when I tell him you're not, he thanks me and says he'll try again tomorrow."

"Maybe you should have called the police," said Bobby, a little worried.

"No, he's fine. The second time he came, I went out and spoke to him through the gate. He told me he had met you once and—"

"Met me once? That could be anyone, some crank; or worse, some—"

"No, I told you, it isn't like that at all. He said he had met you once and that Quentin Burdick told him he could trust you."

"What did he look like?" asked Bobby with a sudden sense of urgency. "Middle-aged, medium height, medium weight, someone you wouldn't notice in a crowd?"

A sad smile crossed her mouth as she nodded.

"I think that you might not notice him if you passed him on an empty street. He's very nice, painfully polite."

"And he's coming at six, five minutes from now?" asked Bobby, just to be sure. "I better go meet him."

Bobby walked up the long driveway to the iron gate that stretched between the vine-covered white stucco walls that kept the house, and the two people who lived in it, safe from the prying eyes of the world. At six o'clock an aging beige automobile that no one would ever notice much less want to buy pulled up and the driver got out. Hart pushed the button that opened the gate and Richard Bauman quickly slipped inside.

Bobby had not seen the former Secret Service agent since the night he met with Clarence Atwood at the Watergate. Bauman had not changed in any obvious way, but there was still a difference: He seemed more certain of himself; all the guilt he had felt that night was gone.

"Come inside," said Hart as they shook hands.

"No, I don't want to be a bother."

"What can I do for you then? My wife told me that you had been here every day."

"She's been very nice about it. Yes, every day. I knew you would come back here. I could not stay in Washington. I would have been dead by now."

"Come in," said Bobby. "We can talk."

"Can you come with me?" asked Bauman politely, but with insistence. "There's something I have to show you. It's what I gave Quentin Burdick, what probably got him killed. It's in my room, at the motel where I'm staying. I didn't want to carry it around with me, in case I was being followed."

"Sure, all right. Tell me where it is. I'll just grab my keys and tell Laura where I'm going."

The motel was one of the cheaper places, where tourists on a budget liked to stay, rooms with a view of the parking lot and a long walk, a mile or more, to the beach. Bobby sat on one of the two plastic chairs, Bauman sat in the other. A tattered leather briefcase lay on a wooden table next to them. Bauman removed a large manila envelope and handed it to Bobby.

"It's all here, everything I got from Atwood's office. I made copies and put the originals back. I gave one to Burdick—decent man, told me there might not be anyone else around to trust, but that I could trust you. They were all involved, you know; one way or the other, all of them: Constable, his wife, Russell, the others. Whether they knew what was going to happen, whether they had any part in the decisions that got made—doesn't matter, they were all responsible."

Bobby bent toward him. Bauman was a completely honest man. He knew that, but he still was not sure what Bauman was trying to tell him. He tapped his finger on the envelope.

"You got this from Atwood's office, and you gave it—a copy of it—to Quentin Burdick?"

"Yeah, that's right," said Bauman with a slight, embarrassed smile. He would try to be clearer. "Atwood hired the girl. All the records of payment are in there. But the girl wasn't just some paid assassin; she was one of ours, someone who did things that no one is supposed to know. Atwood knew everything about all of them, what they had done, the money they had taken—all of it. That was the leverage he had, that and the fact that he didn't have any reservations about doing whatever seemed to be necessary."

"But he wouldn't have had any reason to have Constable killed," objected Bobby. "Russell and Hillary Constable had a lot to lose if Constable lived, and a lot to gain if he died. Atwood had to be working for them, didn't he?"

"That's right. Atwood didn't do this on his own—have the president murdered, I mean. Because the rest of what happened: Burdick, what happened to those two in Paris, the attempt to make it seem like you were the one responsible—I'm pretty sure Atwood did that on his own; did it, as far as I can tell, with the consent of both Russell and Mrs. Constable. Once the president was killed, all they cared about was protecting themselves and getting what they wanted. They depended on Atwood for that. Do what's necessary, that's what they would have told him, and no one needed to tell him what that meant."

Bobby was on the edge of his chair.

"But then, if it wasn't Atwood on his own, and if it wasn't Russell or Constable's wife, who told Atwood to kill the president?"

Richard Bauman nodded toward the heavy envelope.

"There, on the last page, I think you'll find the answer. It's how the whole thing started, isn't it?" he asked as Bobby dug through the documents.

Bobby pulled out the last page, read it through quickly, and then, scarcely believing what he had seen, read it through again.

Bauman nodded.

"Atwood wasn't working for the president, or the president's wife. He wasn't working for Irwin Russell. He was always working for The Four Sisters. He was working for Jean Valette."

"Jean Valette, who helped save my life, helped restore my reputation, provided the evidence to destroy both Hillary Constable and Irwin Russell - Jean Valette ordered the murder of Robert Constable?" asked Hart, as angry as he had ever been.

"There is no proof," said Bauman, with a helpless shrug. "Nothing that would ever get a conviction. Atwood was paid a lot of money - millions - by The Four Sisters; but there is nothing to link Jean Valette directly to murder. Atwood could have done it on his own, done it for the same reason the others had: to keep Constable from talking about what he knew."

When he got home, an hour later, and told Laura what had happened, what Roger Bauman had discovered, he could only marvel at how easily he had let himself be deceived.

"I should have known," he said, shaking his head. "It was right there in front of me. Everything with Jean Valette - everything! - has a double meaning. He told me I was going to be president. What he meant was that it had already been arranged. He set everything in motion, moved everyone around like pieces on a chess board. He put them - all of them! - in situations where they thought they had only one choice - the choice that led to their own destruction. It was in that speech of his: the call to recapture former greatness; it was there, right in front of me, when he showed me the portrait gallery of his ancestors, the line that goes back a thousand years. He thinks himself the last Grand Master, destined, like his namesake five hundred years ago, to save Europe and the West, save western civilization, from a danger no one else knows exists." Hart's eyes lit up as he remembered something more. "Ten men, acting together, disciplined, devoted to a cause, can change the world. That is what he said, and that is what he believes: Ten men, willing to follow where he wants to lead them; ten men everyone else will follow."

"But you're not one of them, Bobby," insisted Laura, reaching out to touch him on the sleeve. "He may have controlled everything that happened, manipulated everyone the way you say he did, and he may have wanted it to end like this, with you as president, but he doesn't control you. He never could, he never will. You're not like the Constables: there is nothing you want that he can give you."

Hart shook his head and with a rueful smile got up from the kitchen table where they were sitting and walked over to the window. He watched the sun slide down from heaven and set the sea on fire, watched as the stars came out to watch what the day had made them miss.

"What is it, Bobby? What are you thinking?"

"I told Charlie Finnegan that Jean Valette was either the most intelligent or the craziest man I had ever met," he said, as he turned to face her. "Everything he said - about the meaning of the past, what has to happen in the future - made perfect sense when I was there, listening. And now he has sent me that," he said, nodding toward Jean Valette's thick manuscript with its brief, but urgent, plea that he read it, and read it slowly. "Doesn't control me? Not by force, not by buying me with money, but what other effect his use of words? He held me captive when he spoke. What happens now, if I read what he has written?"

THE END

About the Author

D.W. Buffa studied under Leo Strauss at the University of Chicago, served as special assistant to U.S. Senator Philip A. Hart, and for nearly ten years practiced law as a criminal defense attorney. He is the bestselling author of fourteen novels and three works of non-fiction, and his book *The Judgment* was nominated for the Edgar Award for Best Novel. His novels have been published in fifteen languages. Visit him online at www.dwbuffa.com.